EXTRA
ORDINARY

DANIELLE K GIRL

CHAPTER 1

RYDER CARLSSON STANDS PERFECTLY still in the shadowed hallway of Clarendon House's upper east wing. Until a moment ago she was alone in the gloom, her only company the taffeta-clad women and top-hatted men in the heavy-framed portraits hanging along the walls. Goosebumps prickle down her arms. She lifts the thermal camera. Aims the lens towards the figure standing at the far end of the hall. Breathe. Focus. Keep it together. It's a fight to hold the device steady. The house is an ice-box without its hearth fires burning, but the heat would screw up the equipment readings. Taint the evidence. Ryder tightens her hold. Evidence like this. Don't mess it up. Get it recorded. Prove it's not all in her head. But there is nothing on the screen. She jiggles the camera, glaring at it.

"Seriously? Come on. It's right there."

The thermal image shows a hallway emanating mostly blues and greens, no trace of the fiery reds or burnt oranges that would indicate body heat. A muted yellow surrounds a potted palm in a thigh-high vase, but a heat signature there is to be expected, the plant is a living thing. The same can't be said though for the obscure blob beside it; vaguely man-shaped, short and squat, with broad shoulders, and a rounded bald head. Ryder squints. The silhouette wasn't there a few minutes ago, was it? Nope. Maybe? She's been stalking the hallways of this turn-of-the-century freezer for a few hours now. Between the chill, the late hour and her own desperation, it's possible her imagination is messing with her. Ryder lowers the camera, letting it rest against her jeans. She presses her lips tight. The figure is still there. A darker pitch of black among the shadows. This is insane. Or she is. It's one or the other, always has been, and the well-worn thought never fails to churn her stomach like a bad egg.

All at once a rustling sound reaches Ryder. Something moving the fronds of the potted palm. A chill finds its way beneath her ponytail. She glances at the camera but it indicates no change, and the EMF meter in her pocket is silent as a tomb. Ryder clenches her jaw to stop her teeth from chattering, a familiar panic coiling itself around her insides. Her eyes sting, beginning to water, but she refuses to blink.

Stop freaking out. This is not in your head, don't go there. You're not delusional. Think straight.

But if she was thinking straight, she'd be doing what most other fifteen year olds are doing this long weekend; shopping, video game marathons, or lying on the couch eating junk food and binge watching TV. Definitely not hunting ghosts. Ryder swallows hard. Seeing the things she does makes keeping a clear head near impossible.

Dry eyes won't stay open a second longer. Ryder closes them. This has to be real. They *all* have to be real. Not hallucinations. The medical journals have a list of clinical terms for people who imagine things that aren't there. Chances are the doctors wrote down a few of them on her mum's file. Ryder's dad won't say much about the woman who walked out on them, but once, years ago, she overheard him describe her mother as delusional and completely lost.

Ryder opens her eyes and blinks against the darkness. The gloom at the end of the hallway is just that, gloom. Empty space. The apparition is gone. If it was there at all. For a moment, she doesn't move. Doesn't breathe. A blooming heat fills her cheeks. Frustration loosens her jaw.

"No. No, you don't. I saw you. You were there." Ryder shakes the camera, taps it against her hand; blues and greens, and a flash of fire engine red as the focus hits her skin. "I saw it. It was there. Damn it."

She breaks into a jog, pulling a flashlight from the depths of her jacket pocket. Her ponytail beats out the rhythm of her steps against her back, and her purple Dr Martens thump against the thick, lavishly embroidered carpet. She strides past the watchful portraits. The paintings are probably priceless, or at least ridiculously expensive, but right now they're just plain creepy. Elegant ladies in corsets and reams of flowing silk, and steely-faced men in elaborate lace collars, their eyes following Ryder's every step. Another shiver darts across her shoulders and she shrugs against it. Her faded denim jacket is one of the better gifts from her dad, but it's not exactly designed for the midnight chill.

The walkie-talkie at her waist clinks against the metal studs on her belt, the sound oddly comforting. The device reminds her she's not entirely alone. She's dragged two others into her search-and-find mission. Right now Sophie and Christian wander the rooms and halls of Clarendon too. Sophie is a willing accomplice, but Christian not so much. Ryder runs her fingers over the top of the walkie-talkie but stops short of using it. What would she say? Hey guys, seeing things again. Take my word for it. She shakes her head, and her long brown hair caresses the back of her jacket. Raising the flashlight all she sees now is the palm, in a vase so intricately painted it would be at home in a Chinese emperor's throne room. Ryder jabs her booted toe against the base. The vase tips, sending a sprinkle of chocolate brown soil and white stones onto the carpet. "Oh crap." Ryder lunges, grabbing the rim, fingers digging into the soil as she pulls it upright. It's heavier than it appears. The coarse leaves scrape down the side of her neck. "Great, sure Ryder, break the antiques. Make the night perfect," she sighs.

Her grandad, Jack, is a good friend of the owners, a fact he kept unusually quiet about until recently. Maybe this is why. When he invited them up for the long weekend, Ryder thought Christmas had arrived half a year early, but now she's almost repaid the favour by breaking stuff. Ryder dusts off her hands. The walkie-talkie at her waist sputters and hisses with a connection. Christian's voice booms the length of the hall. "So, Carlsson. Does this town have a Burger King or something? Seriously craving a double cheese right about now."

Ryder winces, turning down the volume. "No. I told you on the way up here, the town barely has a bakery, let alone fast food. Seriously Chris, you ate like a fiend on the train, how can you be hungry?"

The train ride from Hobart to Evandale is just over three hours, and for two hours and fifty minutes of it, Christian ate.

"Just how I roll, my friend. This belly needs constant filling." He lets out a satisfied sigh, but his mouth is too close to the mic, and it sounds like the venting of a steam train. "Seriously though, I'm so bored. Have you had enough fun looking for imaginary things that don't exist yet?"

Ryder considers her reply, her fingers hovering just above the receiver button.

"This is Sophie, do you read me. Over." The youngest member of the trio by three months and two days.

Stifling a groan, Ryder pushes down on the receiver. "Considering it's only the three of us here, Soph, you don't need to say your name and over every time you radio in." She's lost count of how many times she's told Sophie that since they arrived three hours ago.

"Roger that, Captain." Sophie's voice echoes through the cheap walkie. "Having any luck? Sad to say, the ghosts aren't biting over in the west wing. The EMF meter is pretty quiet and no drastic temperature changes. How about you, Ry? Picking up anything with that sixth sense thingy of yours?" There is a pause, then the walkie crackles. "Over."

Ryder hesitates. Not because of the 'over,' and not because Sophie wouldn't believe her. Sophie believes every little speck of dust they catch on camera is an entity of some kind. Ryder could tell her she just had tea and sandwiches with the Queen of England's ghost, and Sophie would squeal with delight. Which doesn't help anyone's sanity. "No, nothing tonight." Ryder clears her throat. Until she has something tangible recorded, she will say nothing. "I can barely see my own shadow, let alone anyone else's. I'm going to head downstairs. Maybe it's time for a biscuit break."

"Roger that, over." Sophie signs off, and Christian mumbles something about burgers, but Ryder clips the walkie-talkie back to her belt and doesn't bother to reply. She surveys the empty space in front of her, chewing on her bitten-to-the-quick thumbnail. Goosebumps erupt along the length of her arms, but that's been happening all night. Aside from the lack of heating, insulation in the old house isn't great; there are gaps everywhere, beneath doors and in between window panes, letting in a draft. And there's every chance she's letting Clarendon House's haunted reputation get to her. If she can't find evidence in a place supposedly riddled with paranormal activity, then she's back to scrolling through medical websites. Ryder shakes herself, trying to ease the stiffness in her shoulders. She paces back up the hallway. The untied laces on her left boot flick against the carpet.

As she passes by the open rooms, moonlight filters into the hall in elongated patches. Strange, she didn't notice the pearly highlights earlier. Peering into one of the rooms, she glimpses the tusk-like moon hanging in a clear sky. It was so dark in the hallway earlier she expected at least a bit of cloud cover. Her flashlight sweeps across the room, passing over the brass bedhead, and onto the bed itself where a sheet of clear plastic covers the double mattress and burgundy satin bedspread. A cluster of white pillows nestle around a wide-eyed porcelain doll dressed in a turn-of-the-century gown which matches the bed covers.

"That's not creepy, at all." Ryder turns to walk away. All at once, the world tilts and spins. She clutches at the door frame.

Spots fill her vision. No stranger to fainting spells, Ryder forces herself to take a deep breath. When she was younger and having blood tests what felt like every second day, it happened most times. Keep breathing, deep breaths, the nurses would tell her. Just like then, it works now. The wave of dizziness sweeps by as quickly as it arrived. Gingerly, she straightens, still hanging tight to the frame. "Okay, maybe I need a burger too." She laughs, uneasily.

The hallway has grown dim. She glances towards the window. The moon is there, with not so much as a mist drifting past it. Squeezing her eyes open and shut a couple of times doesn't shift the gloom. Ryder lifts one hand, not certain she's steady enough to let go entirely, and brushes her fingers over her face. Her skin is icy cold.

"Very funny, Ryder." Christian's voice, very close and very loud, rocks Ryder back on her heels. Her flashlight's beam darts through the air like a maddened firefly, and much to her own horror, she screams.

CHAPTER 2

I T'S A SHORT-LIVED SOUND. RYDER bites down on her bottom lip, cursing her jittery nerves. Christian waves his hands at her. "Not in the eyes, man. Are you trying to blind me?" With his bleached hair and white hoodie it's a good thing Christian inherited his Portuguese mum's olive skin, otherwise he'd blend in with the ghosts. "We've been calling you, Ry. What gives?"

What gives? He somehow managed to get right up close, without Ryder noticing. And he made her scream, something she despises doing.

"Calling me? What are you on about?" Ryder still holds fast to the bed frame. Her gaze slides around the room. The strange dimness is gone. The other pieces of furniture in the room, the high red-wood dresser over by the door, the oval mirror on the wall, are all discernible now.

"Seriously? You're going to be that lame?" Christian pushes up the sleeves on his hoodie. The Astana Cycling Team's small aquamarine and yellow logo is emblazoned on the front. "If you think going radio silent then slamming a couple of doors is going to freak me out, you are sadly mistaken my friend."

Ryder bites her lip, catching sight of her reflection in the mirror; a startled deer in headlights. When had she gotten so pale? Ryder glances over at Christian and catches sight of the door. He had to open it when he arrived. A prickling sensation washes down the back of Ryder's neck. She didn't touch the door when she came into the room. It was wide open. He's regarding her with an expression somewhere between bemused and pitiful.

"Stop being a jerk, Chris," she says. "I'm too tired for this rubbish."

Christian frowns, the piercing on his right eyebrow like an odd-placed mole. "Soph and I have both been trying to radio you for about ten minutes. Figured you were just trying to freak me out."

Ten minutes. Not possible, but then Christian has no sense of time, he's always late. Ryder runs her hand over the walkie-talkie attached to her belt. It hasn't made a sound since she stepped into the room. The prickly feeling trails down her back. With some reluctance, she lets go of the bed.

"Maybe I just tuned you guys out." She rubs her thumb against the dial. The volume is definitely not muted. Maybe a wire has come loose. She tugs the walkie off her belt just as static hisses through the device. Sophie's voice comes through loud and clear.

"Chris, did you find her? Come on, this isn't funny." Her voice is slightly out of sync on the two walkies. And she's skipped her 'over.' Sophie is worried.

"I'm here, Soph." Ryder forces a smile into her voice. "Don't know what happened with the radios but I'm all good."

Not entirely true. But she's going to act like it is. She needs to leave this room. Outside, the air may be cold, but it's crisp, refreshing, not stuffy and stale—like in here. Fresh air will fix this. "You'll be relieved to know, Chris, I'm calling it early." Ryder balls up her fist, gives him a gentle punch in the shoulder. He's head and shoulders taller than her so she needs to stretch. "We're done for tonight. Soph, meet us down in the foyer, okay? I'll call Jack to come get us."

Christian whoops and tries to high-five Ryder. She ignores his raised hand, her own palms too damp and clammy for contact. It would only raise questions, and Ryder learned a long time ago to keep quiet when she's not feeling well. Sophie's reply brims with her usual chirpiness. "Okey dokey, roger that Captain. Over."

Ryder's eyes flutter open. Someone is tapping on the feather-down quilt she has cocooned herself in. No guesses who it is. She snuggles deeper under her pillow. It can't possibly be time to get up, she barely shut her eyes. There wasn't even time to dream, which is kind of blissful.

"Come on Miss Carlsson, up and at them, as they say." Sophie sing-songs the words, something she knows very well Ryder can't stand, especially first thing in the morning. On the Grade Nine camp last year it took a carefully flung shoe to put an end to the morning ritual.

Under the layers, Ryder's voice is muffled. "Soph, if it's before ten, I can't be held responsible for my actions." The memories of last night are tapping at her brain, but Ryder refuses to let them in. Way too early for that.

"Charming, it's barely nine and you are making threats already." The mattress jiggles as Sophie sits down. "I need to talk to you. Did you sleep okay, or are you going to be super grumpy all day?"

The pillow still covers Ryder's head, she's not ready for daylight yet. "Define, sleep okay." She presses the heels of her hands to her eyes, wiping away sleep caught in her eyelashes.

"Cacophonic dreams again?" Sophie says.

"Yup, that would be them."

That's what Sophie's taken to calling Ryder's dreams. Most nights they are filled with the clamour and din of a hundred different voices, all speaking over the top of one another. Ryder often wakes drained, head ringing. This morning though, there is none of that. Ryder breathes deep. Her little nest of pillow and blanket is lavender scented. Jack has used the same washing powder for as long as she can remember. Sophie tries to tug the pillow off Ryder's head. "I keep telling you Ry, chamomile tea will help."

Ryder holds fast. "And I keep telling you it does absolutely nothing, but thanks anyway, Doctor Kynton."

The tug of war ends, and Sophie sighs. "You really are such a joy in the mornings. Seriously, I need you to wake up and focus. You have to look at this."

Ryder stretches her bare arms out of her quilted haven. It's cool in the room. Her grandad never got around to putting in central heating in the upstairs rooms. For the first six years of her life, this was where she and her dad lived, sharing the house with Jack; her dad trying to learn the ropes as a single father, her grandad leaving him to it, working long hours doing whatever it was he did at The Harlow Institute.

"See what?" Ryder yawns, pulls the covers up a little higher. Going to the bathroom would be a great idea. Maybe she can keep the quilt wrapped around her and make a run for it down the hall. At least her head isn't spinning. Ryder frowns at the memory of her weird fainting spell.

"Hey, earth to Ryder." Sophie clears her throat. "You told me you didn't see anything worth seeing last night. Are you sure that's true?"

Ryder pushes the pillow away, and the smack of daylight hits her square in the face. The burgundy curtains around the bay window are wide open. It's overcast outside but after being buried in the dark, the light stings like saltwater in her eyes. "Well I can't see a thing anymore." Before she can grab the quilt and drag it back over her head, Sophie is there in a blinding blur of superhero red hair and screamingly loud floral pyjamas. Ryder relinquishes the covers with an irritated huff. "Soph, seriously, an inquisition before coffee is not going to happen."

Like she's magicked it into being, Sophie brandishes a generously proportioned canary yellow mug. Rich coffee aromas waft against Ryder's nostrils and she takes a long breath, sucking all the goodness in. Mixed in with the divine scent is the less appealing chemical tang from Sophie's barely-a-week-old hair colour.

"Miss Carlsson, do you really think after nine years of friendship I don't know this already?" Sophie says.

"I didn't drink coffee till I was twelve." Ryder shrugs. "So technically it's only three coffee friendship years."

Sophie never rises to Ryder's jabs and now is no exception. She reaches to pick up something off the floor between the two beds. They are sharing this room, and Christian is in a room further down the hall, in a bed about a foot shorter than he is.

Ryder glances out the bay window. A smattering of light rain marks the glass. From up here on the second storey the tops of the trees in the bushland surrounding Jack's property are visible; eucalypts, pines and other bushy Australian greens. When she was little she used to scare herself stupid at night, imagining what ghoulish things watched her from the woods. Sipping on the scalding coffee, Ryder winces. Her sense of being watched goes such a long way back. If she is losing it, then surely she'd be a complete delusional mess by now?

"Righto." Sophie settles on her knees beside the bed and props a laptop on the covers alongside Ryder. "You need to see this." Her words are garbled. She's got a piece of toast sticking out of her mouth and a smudge of Vegemite on her upper lip. Her mum's family, back in South Korea, are dumbfounded that she can eat the stuff.

"Where's mine?" Ryder's stomach rumbles, despite the fact she agrees with Sophie's relatives. Vegemite is disgusting, but dinner on the train early yesterday evening was a very long time ago.

Sophie jerks her head towards the bedside table. Nestled among the framed photos Jack has displayed there, is a plate with a single bread crust. Sophie has never eaten a crust of bread in her entire life.

"Wow, best friend ever." But Ryder munches down on the morsel anyway, too hungry to care she's getting Sophie's leftovers.

"You need to take a look at this footage from last night."

Sophie frowns, studying the screen in front of her. "Something weird happened."

Ryder takes another bite, not bothering to look just yet. No point getting riled up. It doesn't take much for Sophie to classify something as weird. Every dust fleck they catch on camera is a paranormal orb to her. Her enthusiasm is well intentioned of course. She wants Ryder to find what she's searching for; a reason to believe she's not a little messed up in the head. It's very sweet but ultimately unhelpful.

"Something weird huh," Ryder says. "Did you get footage of Christian looking remotely interested?"

"No, there's no such footage I'm afraid." Sophie taps at the keyboard, almond-shaped eyes narrowed. "Almost got it, hang on one tick."

Ryder plucks at a minute tear near the hem of her emerald green pyjama shirt. Where did her dad get this again? Singapore? Beijing? One by one she starts rattling off his list of work sites in her head. Anything to distract her from tearing the laptop out of Sophie's grasp and taking a look. It will only bring disappointment. Like every other time. A little audience stares out at her from the photos on the bedside table. She doesn't recognise the raven-haired woman in one of them. She's standing beside Jack, and judging by the way they gaze at one another he sure recognises her. And likes her. Ryder screws up her face. Her grandad dating is kind of weird, though to be fair she never knew her grandmother. He's been on his own a very long time.

"Okey dokey, here we go." Sophie hits the space bar and spins the screen so Ryder can see it. The footage begins to play. "You know how we said we lost contact with you? Our radios were playing up, lots of static and not much else. Then, I checked all the cameras at round the same time. That's when it gets interesting."

They have three DV cameras to work with when they go hunting, two of them courtesy of Sophie's brother, Kye, who works for a local TV station in Hobart, the third one Jack sent

Ryder for her birthday last year after she mentioned in a phone call she'd been watching one of those 'ridiculous ghost-hunting shows.' That's what her dad calls them. Apparently Jack doesn't agree. Father and son don't agree on much. Ryder leans in, hands cupped around the warm mug. Sophie has footage from each camera playing on screen. A stream from the downstairs dining room where a chandelier, like a ghostly octopus, stretches over the twenty-seat dining table, another stream is of a hallway similar to the one Ryder was in but there's no sign of the potted palm. The third stream comes from one of the house's two kitchens; a room brimming with hanging pots and pans, and fake fruit and veges in baskets to help wandering tourists imagine life at the turn of the century, when the place was owned by a wealthy sheep farmer. Sophie taps a zebra-print painted fingernail against each box, "See the time stamp, it's the same time in each of these rooms, okey dokey? Now watch."

The images wobble and then shiver completely out of focus. They do this several times, in unison, before all of the pictures contract in on themselves, like a scene fading to black in an old movie. The footage shrinks all the way down till each are just pinholes of black.

Clutching the mug harder, Ryder says, "The batteries died?" The toast sits uneasily in her belly.

Sophie makes a dismissive click with her tongue. "All at the exact same time?" She shakes her head, brilliant red bob sweeping back and forth like the head of a mop.

A moment later every screen fills with a whitewash of static. Ryder puts down her mug. She can hear Jack whistling somewhere downstairs, along with the clank of dishes being stacked. On screen, the static ripples, like the rings that form in a pond when a stone is dropped into the water. The circles of static shimmer. Then the live feed returns. Each room is exactly as it was before, nothing out of place. All empty. Ryder keeps her eyes on the laptop, conscious that Sophie is watching her.

"Kind of weird I guess, but camera glitches happen." Ryder

shrugs. Her stomach knots.

"Sure," Sophie nods. "Glitches happen. But on multiple pieces of equipment, at the same time?"

She holds up her favourite piece. The EVP recorder. A small device, not much bigger than a mobile phone. It records electronic voice phenomena, voices unheard by the naked ear at the time they are recorded. Ryder learned fast not to spend nights home alone listening to *YouTube* uploads of recordings. Every sound in the house became a marauding spirit out to get her. In a year of hunting though, she and Sophie had only captured an EVP themselves, once. At a derelict hospital outside of Hobart. Sophie had been ecstatic, and Ryder nearly cried with relief at the first shred of proof they'd found, even though the voice was indecipherable.

"You got an EVP?" Ryder tucks her feet into her waiting Ugg boots, needing to move. Her body is tingling with energy. The coffee most likely. Nothing to do with what Sophie is showing her. Nope.

"Not exactly. But I'd been doing a recording just before I ran into Christian. I forgot to turn off the recorder." Sophie hits the play button.

It's just Sophie and Christian talking at first, or rather, arguing about the paranormal. Then Sophie directs a question at Ryder. There's no response. Sophie tries again. But her sentence is swallowed up by a great burst of crackling, screeching static. It's a terrible, loud jumble of electronic beeps and whines. Ryder winces at the playback. "What is that?"

Sophie doesn't answer, pointing to the EVP recorder. The playback continues and something less mechanical pushes its way through the chaos. Murmuring. It might be voices, it could just be a whir of interference, but it's making Ryder's ears ring. She's about to tell Sophie to switch it off when it vanishes. Complete and sudden silence.

It's got to be the caffeine making Ryder's heart thump hard and fast. Sophie is scrutinising her like an ant under a microscope.

"You saw something didn't you, Ry. Come on, sweetie, don't hold out on me now. The look on your face says it all."

Turning away, Ryder stands up. It's hard to breathe. "Can you play that again?"

Sophie takes her hand. "Of course."

CHAPTER 3

A HEAVENLY AROMA OF GARLIC AND fresh bread fills the kitchen. Sophie is chowing down on her second plate of eggs, exclaiming over the bulky white stove top and oven that could feature on *Antiques Roadshow*. It's probably worth a small fortune; definitely way older than Jack is, and the gleaming enamel and various multi-coloured dials are all in perfect working order.

Ryder watched the DV cam footage three times before Jack called them down for breakfast.

"It would be nice to get the kitchen redone." Her grandad's broad frame takes up a generous portion of the compact kitchen. He's a solid, bulky guy, but not in a too-many-pizzas kind of way. Christian asked Ryder once after seeing a photo if Jack ever played rugby. But she couldn't recall her grandad playing golf, let alone a contact sport. "Always had some ideas for a new layout, but I didn't exactly retire a millionaire from the Institute."

That's about all Ryder knows about her grandad's work at the Harlow Institute. It's some kind of private research facility, and the pay was awful and his retirement package very average.

"Eat up Ryder, my love." Jack spoons more eggs onto her plate, despite her protests. The fluffy golden morsels tumble next to the homemade croissant, dripping with butter from the farm next door.

"I seriously can't eat all this." Ryder puffs out her cheeks.

"Save it for Chris, he'll be hungry again in about ten minutes."

Christian's wearing the same hoodie and jeans as yesterday. Chances are he's slept in them and has just brought a single change of undies for the whole weekend. He rubs his belly and holds up three fingers. "Three plates. I'm done. Delicious, thank you, Jack. Mind if I switch on the TV?"

"Of course, no problem. Glad you enjoyed breakfast." Jack laughs, before turning his attention back to Ryder. He nods at the jumper she is wearing. "That the latest from your dad?"

"Yep. Turns out he does have time for sight-seeing on work trips sometimes. Who knew?"

The navy blue jumper has the *NASA* logo on its front, a nice souvenir but she would have preferred an actual visit to the Kennedy Space Centre with her dad. Whatever automation engineers do, never involves your kid apparently. Jack's smile plumps up his cheeks, ruby red from the heat of the stove top. Raising his wiry silver eyebrows, he says, "Well at least you got something, I haven't even had a phone call in a while." He pauses and his smile fades. "Sophie tells me you were sick a few weeks back. You looking after yourself, young lady? I know your dad isn't around as much as he should be."

Ryder throws Sophie a daggered glare. "I'm fine. Thank you for asking. It was just a cold—half the school had it. I took a couple of days off, all good." Ryder stabs her fork into her croissant. Sophie means well but this is exactly why she didn't mention the near-fainting spell from last night. People stress. Jack can't stress right now. She needs him to take them back to Clarendon House.

Jack wipes his thick hands on a cherry print tea towel, regarding her. He's let his speckled gray beard grow a little longer since she saw him six months ago. He usually keeps it trimmed with military style precision. "Nothing to do with the glandular fever?" he says.

Ryder stifles a groan. Her dad and her grandad are paranoid if she so much as sneezes. Any sniffle or fever and they lose it. Convinced that she's relapsing. That somehow the weird virus that put her in intensive care when she was six years old is flaring again. Two years ago, she got glandular fever and it was as though the sky was falling. Her dad basically quarantined her, no visitors for nearly two weeks. Jack called daily, sometimes it felt like hourly. Over-reaction central.

"Just a cold. Plain and simple," she says. "And trust me, Petra keeps me well fed when Dad's away. Actually, when he's home too. Cooking's not his thing."

Sophie gasps through her mouthful of croissant. "Oh my god, Petra's lasagna is to die for. You should see how many slices Lucas can scoff down."

Ryder isn't sure what her Dad's *thing* is at all, aside from being a workaholic. As a result, her neighbours, Petra and her son Lucas, have become a second family over the years. They moved in next door about a year after Ryder and her dad relocated to Hobart. Ryder coughs, the scrambled eggs sticking to the back of her throat. Lucas. He's got a major cycling race this weekend. One that's being televised, and one she swore they'd all watch. Well, Christian swore they'd watch. It was one of his conditions for coming along.

"Damn it." She tilts her head towards the TV room. Christian lies with his long, lanky legs draped over the arm of the blue-checkered couch. "Chris, is Lucas's race today or tomorrow?"

"Today," Christian says. "Midday. He tried your mobile about an hour ago, and I told him you were still comatose upstairs. He wasn't surprised."

Ryder ducks her head so the others won't see her frown. The race is in an hour. She'd been about to ask Jack if he could take them to Clarendon after brunch, but now they'll have to wait. There is zero chance Christian will leave the couch till the race is done, and next to no chance he won't tell Lucas Ryder skipped it to go back to her 'spook hunting', as Chris so eloquently calls it. He saunters into the kitchen, typing something into his phone as he walks, brown eyes narrowed in concentration.

"He's really psyched about this one." Christian shoves his phone into his pocket. "I reckon he's got a chance too."

Jack glances up from the sink, the pink gloves he's wearing covered in suds. "Lucas still into the bikes then?" They've met only once or twice over the years, back when Jack still came to visit in Hobart. But though he doesn't know Lucas well, he knows he and his mum Petra are a huge part of Ryder's life. And that Lucas is a brother to Ryder in all but blood. Big, annoying brother. She only sort of misses him at school. He graduated last year and headed to university to study veterinary science.

Christian swipes a piece of croissant off Sophie's plate and dodges her retaliating fork jab. "Oh he's well into cycling, yeah. He's doing the Devon 80 road race, over in Launceston. Wish I could be there too." His olive skin deepens with a blush. "Sorry…Jack, no offence."

Jack's blue eyes dance as he waves a hand, flicking suds onto the floor. "No offence taken at all, my boy. I know how ah, determined Ryder can be when she sets her mind to something. I suspect you had no say in this weekend away."

Sophie giggles into her coffee. Christian's features soften, a shy smile appearing. "That's pretty much it, yeah. But Lucas is going to swing by on his way home Monday, we'll head out for a ride, and then he'll drive us all back to Hobart."

Though he's got one hand shoved into his pocket, all nonchalant, his free hand toys with the piercing in his eyebrow. The onyx coloured stud is only about two weeks old, a meagre act of rebellion in the face of his parents badly negotiated divorce. He's taken to twisting the little stud instead of twisting knots into his shock of snow white hair when he's nervous or excited.

"Putting up with a whole weekend of ghost hunting for one ride?" Sophie grins. "Hope it's worth it."

He flicks at her ear but says nothing, heading back into the TV room. He'll be blushing, like he always does when Lucas is mentioned. Ryder didn't see it to begin with, the change in Chris every time Lucas is around. Once Sophie pointed it out though,

Ryder wondered how she could be so blind. Christian is quiet and introspective, even around her and Sophie. But when Lucas talks to him, Chris gets *brighter* somehow. He smiles a lot, has a lot to say, and appears comfortable in his skin, for once. But forget trying to talk to him about it. Ryder let that chat slide a long time ago.

Sophie pats her hand. "It's okay sweetie, the race isn't long," she says. "I'm sure Jack can take us to Clarendon straight after. We've got plenty of time."

She's right, they have the whole long weekend and it's only Saturday. But still, Ryder is impatient to get going. Jack takes her plate and cutlery, dumping them into the steaming water. "You want to head there during the day? Must have been a good night, or was it not so good? Didn't find anything?"

Jack's never flinched at her interest in the paranormal, but if her dad knew he'd invited them to check out a haunted house he'd flip. Which is exactly why she's told him nothing about this trip. Ryder shrugs before sucking down the last of her coffee. "If we can, yeah." She's not quite ready to tell Jack anything either. Not till they have something recorded.

A short time later Christian calls Lucas on *Skype*. He leans on the table beside Ryder so she can see the screen while Sophie stretches up on tip-toes behind them. Lucas's face fills the small screen.

"Guys!" He waves with a gloved hand. "Oh Ry, you made it out of bed before noon. Good to see."

"Whatever. Didn't have time to shave this month, Lucas?" She brushes her fingers against her chin, referring to the dusting of sandy coloured stubble across his chin and jaw.

"Oh wow, so harsh. You must have just woken up." Green eyes sparkle beneath a thin red pressure line marking his forehead. The perils of helmet wearing. His auburn hair, already cropped short, is pancake flat against his skull. Not a great look. Chances are even the Lucas appreciation society at her school might deduct some drool points today.

"Hey, Lucas. Good luck." Sophie calls out. "Knock em dead, or whatever it is you do in cycling."

"Thanks Soph, will give it my best shot." Lucas's smile dimples his right cheek. "Hiya, Chris. Thanks for your text earlier."

"Yeah, no problem," Chris can't seem to decide what to do with his hands, flexing them, cracking his knuckles.

"That piercing new, buddy?"

Christian touches his finger to the new stud. "Oh, yeah. Couple of weeks old."

"Looks awesome, mate."

"Thanks." Christian's blush creeps down his neck, and his smile stretches from cheek to cheek.

Another rider taps Lucas on the shoulder, muttering something about registration. Sophie calls out with more overly exuberant good luck wishes, and Ryder encourages him to break a leg, which earns her a glare from Christian. Lucas laughs it all off and ends the call. Ryder glances at the clock and sighs before heading upstairs to study the footage again.

Without doubt, it's the slowest couple of hours in history. But they are finally in the car. Jack and Christian are discussing the race, with most of the commentary coming from Christian who is bubbling with details of how awesome Lucas did. Admittedly, Lucas is insanely fit. Ryder would have been out after half the first lap. And no doubt the posse of hair-flicking seniors who still ask after Lucas at school were watching too, sighing over his, allegedly, great legs and butt. Gross. Good race or not, Ryder almost wore a hole in the carpet from tapping her feet against it, impatient to get going.

"He lost, that doesn't seem so awesome." Ryder's annoyance sharpens her words. She sits in the front passenger seat, arms folded, watching the rain thump down on the windscreen while the wipers scrape their way back and forth across the glass. The rain hasn't let up for hours.

"Third, Ryder. He came third," Christian says. "That is really good against that group."

"Uh-huh." It's over. That's all Ryder considers good about it.

"Well, for all it's worth I thought it was interesting to watch." Jack doesn't bother to flick on the indicator when he turns off the deserted main road and heads up Clarendon House's long sweeping driveway.

"It was interesting watching Ryder try to stay awake." There's a smile in Sophie's voice, but Ryder doesn't respond. The house is tantalisingly close. The moment Jack steers the car round the circular drive in front of the entrance, a weight drags at her belly. The gearbox protests as Jack crunches the old rusty once-red station wagon down a gear, and then shudders when he turns off the ignition.

"So you'll just give me a call when you're done here?" Jack says.

"Yeah." Ryder stares up at the raised veranda that lines the front of the majestic old mansion.

"So pretty." The squeak of the car door as Sophie opens it, nearly drowns out her words. "I'd love to live in a place like this."

Sophie isn't exactly dressed to move in. She's wearing a brilliant jumble of mismatched colour; a flowy Hawaiian print green skirt teamed with a bright yellow cardigan and zebra print sneakers. Clarendon House is a bit more elegant. It's a three-storey Georgian home, built back in the 1830's by a wealthy English sheep merchant, according to *Google*. Its brickwork is painted a soft lemon yellow. Four imposing pillars reach up to a flat roof that juts out over the main entrance area. White framed windows, each with their own stone carved overhangs, surround the stark white double-panelled front door. There are five windows along the top floor and four downstairs. Ryder stares up at the second level, trying to work out which room she'd been in. The heaviness in her belly deepens and is joined by a pressure at the back of her eyes. A weighty discomfort she gets sometimes in places like this.

"You'd live here even with the uninvited house guests, Sophie?" Jack opens his door and stands beside it, one foot still in the car.

Sophie smiles. "Absolutely. They're the best part. Have you ever seen anything here, Jack?"

"Seen anything?" Jack scratches at his chin. "No. No, I haven't been as lucky as you seemed to be last night. Sophie told me you got some interference on the videos?"

Ryder grinds her teeth, casting a glare at her friend. But Sophie is too busy nodding at Jack to notice.

"Nothing to get too excited about." Ryder moves to the boot, grabbing the equipment case there. The urge to press at her temple, try to ease some of the pressure, is nearly overwhelming but a hint of anything wrong and Jack'd have her back home in no time. She slams the boot closed and heads to the front steps, her thick-soled boots crunching on the gravel.

"I can vouch for there being nothing to get excited about," Christian says.

Jack's laughter rumbles in time with some distant thunder. "Well, at least they have someone to keep their feet on the ground with you here, Christian."

Ryder raises her eyebrows. "Says the man who gave me my first book on the paranormal. And invited us to a haunted mansion."

Jack shrugs. "You said you had no plans for the holiday weekend. What's the harm, eh?"

"Well, if you ask my dad," Ryder says, "he'll give you all the harmy details."

The jovial expression on Jack's face softens into something more melancholy. "He means well. We just have different ways of dealing with these things. That's his choice."

These things? A potentially unstable daughter, or hunting for Casper the Friendly Ghost? Before Ryder can ask what he means, Jack waves goodbye. "Righto, everyone enjoy. Let me know when you're ready to come home. I'm a phone call away."

CHAPTER 4

RYDER CLOSES THE FRONT DOOR, cutting off the breeze that makes the rain dance wildly. Sophie and Christian have disappeared into one of the rooms down the hall, Christian showing little interest in Sophie's set-up instructions. She wants everything and everyone pretty much exactly where they were last night, hoping that replicating the conditions will replicate the results. Whatever they were. Interference, Christian insists, and Ryder can't totally disagree. Someone calls out to her, her name echoing down the hall.

"What was that?" She squints, trying to work out which room it came from, and who it was. Too deep a tone to be Sophie, but not sounding quite like Christian either. Sophie pokes her head out of a doorway further down and Ryder jumps.

"Did you call me?" Ryder hopes her voice sounds steadier than her nerves feel.

"No, I thought you were calling me."

"Didn't say a word."

With the heavy cloud cover outside, the unlit rooms in the house are dim and the corners full of shadows. From another room comes the sound of rushing water. A few moments later Christian heads up the hallway towards them, long legs making short work of the distance. "Okay," he says, "let's get this over with huh? What are we doing?"

Ryder frowns and the pressure behind her eyes builds into

something with a sharper edge. "Chris, did you call out to us a second ago?" She toys with the zipper on her puffer jacket, running it up and down the silver join.

"While I was in the bathroom?" Christian screws up his nose. "No. I didn't."

"Okey dokey," Sophie says. "Now that is kind of weird right? Are you feeling anything else we should know about, Ry? Getting any vibes?"

Digging her fingertips into the side of her head, Ryder tries to get at the dull ache there. "I'm not sure-"

Something heavy hits the floor above them. She and Sophie jump, knocking into one another. Christian points to the ceiling, like they might have missed the thud somehow. "Don't even think of calling that a ghost. Is there someone else in here?" he says.

If it is a ghost it's the most lead-footed one Ryder's ever heard. A couple more thumps, like someone is hopping across the floor above them, reverberate down into the foyer. Sophie plants her hands on her hips, staring up at the ceiling.

"As much as I hate agreeing with you, Chris, you could be right." In a determined whirlwind of colour, Sophie marches towards the staircase. "I'm going to check."

"Sophie wait," Ryder says. "What if someone's broken in?"

From above comes a drawn out scrapping sound, like someone is hauling a piece of furniture across the room. A chill tickles the back of Ryder's neck. Christian is frozen in place, lips pressed tight.

Sophie is the first to move, again. "Jack said some renovations are going on, right?" she whispers. "Maybe someone is doing overtime."

"There's no cars outside, Sophie." Ryder shakes her head. "And Jack specifically said they don't work over the weekend."

"Well, we need to see who is up there." Gathering her skirt, Sophie trudges up the stairs.

"Not a great idea, Soph." Christian doesn't move from his place near the front door.

To catch up with her friend, Ryder takes two stairs at a time. Sophie is small in stature and nimble as a bunny. She stops at the landing. When Ryder reaches her, it's not hard to see why she hesitated. The upper level is cloaked in darkness. Most of the doors down the hallway are closed, and with no windows into the corridor itself there is no natural light. Sophie peers into the blackness. "Lights aren't working," she mutters, flicking the switch beside her. "Power is on downstairs though."

"Do you have a flashlight?" Ryder tries to catch her breath, one eye on the nearest door. None of these were closed when they left last night, she's certain of it.

"No. I probably didn't think this idea through very well."

"Don't let common sense stop you now. Did you close these doors before we left last night?" Ryder coughs. She really needs to work on her cardio. Her heart thumps like she's just run a marathon, not a flight of stairs. The stirring of a headache anchors in deeper behind her eyes.

"You okay, sweetie?"

"Fine. Never better." Ryder straightens, and the hallway tilts. Whispers echo down from the hall to their left. The same direction the heavy sounds came from. She presses her hand against the banister, only just stifling a gasp.

"Ryder? What is it?"

Sophie touches her hand to Ryder's arm. The contact sends another wave of goosebumps over Ryder's skin. "Can you hear that? Voices. Like there's a radio on somewhere or something." Her brain throws out a raft of possibilities. Maybe Sophie's right; there is a tradesman here somewhere, working on some part of the house.

The whites of Sophie's eyes almost glow in the dim light. Behind her the hallway is dark as pitch, not a hint of light coming from beneath the doors. "I can't hear a thing," she says. "It's so unfair, why do I never hear anything?"

"Believe me, I really, really wish you did."

A great crash of thunder pummels the sky, shaking the floor beneath them.

Sophie shoves up against her. "Oh I hear that. I definitely hear that."

Christian pounds up the stairs. His snow-white hair even wilder than normal. "All right, I'm just about over this. What's going on?"

His voice trembles, and he huddles in close to Ryder's other side, but she's too preoccupied with the strange whispers to give him any grief about being scared. The hushed voices float out of the darkness, low and indecipherable. She stares hard into the inkiness of the long hallway, hoping her eyes might adjust. Then takes a step forward.

Christian grabs her arm. "Hey, where exactly are you going?"

"Down there. I need to go down there." She blinks rapidly, confused at her own choice of words. The gloom presses in on her.

"You do not need to go into the creepy dark hallway." Christian tugs her back. "Look, let's at least go get a flashlight, or something."

He's never been so right about something. They need to leave here. So why can't she bring herself to turn away?

"Let's go." Sophie turns, already putting Chris's idea into action. "It's like a black hole down there."

But Ryder doesn't have time to go hunt for a light. She has to go down there. Now. She pulls out of Christian's grasp and walks forward. Three steps later and pain, sharp as a knife tip, runs across her forehead. She buckles forward, flailing to find the wall, feeling the bumps of the wallpaper beneath her fingers. Sophie calls out to her, her voice muffled but distinct among all the others that float in the air. Ryder tries to turn around, to head back to her friends, but the darkness swamps everything. She can't even make out the carpet beneath her feet. The ache in her head intensifies, filling every bone in her face. Ryder fights to take a deep breath, but the syrup-thick air won't move into her lungs. Panic flutters through her body, making it tremble. She opens her mouth, calls out for help. Only a fragile gasp escapes.

The whispers grow louder, moving closer before morphing into a dull roar. Ryder lifts her hands and covers her ears. The cacophony of sound is frighteningly familiar; as though a hundred people are speaking to her all at once. Just like in her dreams. Ryder curls forward letting go of the wall. The weight of the air presses down like a blanket on her shoulders. She calls out, but again the sound is little more than a husky whisper. Ryder sinks to her knees. The carpet is soft beneath her fingers but she can't see it, can't make out a single feature around her. Ryder clamps her hands harder against her ears but the voices are relentless. And getting louder. She squeezes her eyes closed, curling into a little ball on the ground. The darkness bears down on her. Crushing her.

Someone touches her forehead. A gentle press of fingertips against her skin that erases the terrible ache in her skull. Ryder blinks her eyes open. A girl with luminous white skin and sharp features crouches beside her.

"Get up, Ryder."

The girl presses her hand to Ryder's cheek, then steps away. In a flurry of limbs, Ryder pushes herself to her feet, adrenaline making her feet fly down the hallway. Sophie and Christian are still near the top of the stairs. The hallway is dim, everything is shadowy, but Ryder can make out the carpet, the banister.

Sophie let's out a cry and runs towards Ryder. "What just happened? Where did you go?"

"Turn around," Ryder shouts, waving her friend back. "Get downstairs, go."

Thunderous vibrations rattle the mansion, and the chandelier above the stairs tinkles. Christian glances at it before following orders and sprinting down.

"What the hell is happening?" He shouts over his shoulder. "What did you see down there?"

"I don't know." Ryder ushers Sophie ahead of her. She takes a bit more convincing than Christian who is almost all the way down.

"Why are we running?" Sophie says. "Was it something bad?"

Ryder doesn't answer her. Her mouth is sandpaper dry. She steals a glance over her shoulder. Whoever or whatever it was, isn't following. No one stands at the top of the stairs. There's no sound of pursuing footsteps. No sign of the girl at all. Girl or ghost? Do apparitions even get that real or solid? Maybe delusions do. Perhaps that's what the headache was, her brain finally snapping. Ryder shakes off the cold clutch of panic. Sophie asked her where she went. And everyone ran when Ryder told them to. Something happened.

They clatter into the entry foyer, bunching up together.

"Outside?" Christian hesitates, pointing towards the door. The pounding rain is visible through the glass panes in the door, a strong wind whipping the downpour into a wild frenzy, buffeting it around like confetti. Ryder stares at it, mind racing through options.

"The most comfortable option would be to remain indoors, I suspect."

They spin round, searching for the source of the soft feminine voice. The girl sits on the balustrade at the top of the stairs, dangling booted feet over the railing. She eyes them the way a bird might regard three little petrified worms. No one moves. Ryder doesn't even breathe. Then the girl pushes off, her black coat flying out behind her. She drops like a stone towards the tiles.

CHAPTER 5

SOPHIE SQUEALS. RYDER AND CHRISTIAN don't make a sound. Right before the girl hits the ground, surely about to break both ankles, she suddenly stops. She hovers there, before setting down with a gentle touch of her toes to the floor. Rain hits the outside of the house, rattling window panes and echoing through the foyer like shudders of gunfire.

They stare at the girl, and she stares right back. She's young, not much older than they are, perhaps even a few years younger. Her features are sharp to the point of being gaunt, and her short, severe pixie cut only accentuates the fact. Her hair is jet black. Like her clothes. The knee length coat shimmers satin-like beneath the elaborate chandelier hanging from the high ceiling. The girl bunches her shoulders like she's trying to ease a muscle ache, and the light glints against the row of silver buckles down the front of her coat. Ryder always assumed she was the palest person in the world, but not anymore. The girl's alabaster skin is ghostly against the dark material.

"Hello, Ryder." She holds herself rigid, chin tilted and shoulders pulled back.

It is the second time she's addressed Ryder, and for the second time Ryder can't reply. Her throat is rough and dry, her heart beating like a frightened bird in her chest. But the headache has eased, and, best of all, the others are seeing what she is seeing. This is no delusion. The distant rumble of thunder fills the silence, and Christian shuffles beside her. She should say something but her jumbled thoughts make it impossible. Ryder just stares. Something very strange just happened, but it's like waking from a dream. The memory of it slips away the more she tries to grab hold of it.

Sophie takes a tentative step, and Christian hisses at her. There is only the slightest hesitation before she continues.

"Hello there," Sophie says. "You shouldn't actually be in here. Unless you know the owners?"

Ryder glances at her friend. Only Sophie could manage to sound so chirpy at a time like this. Compared to the visitor, Sophie is a carnival of colour with her bright hair and clothes. The only splash of brightness on the stranger is her eyes. Purple, really vibrant purple.

"Owners of what?" The curve of the girl's heavy dark eyebrows suggests she is frowning, but the rest of her expression is marble smooth.

"Oh, this place." Sophie gestures to the foyer, like a game show model presenting the grand prize.

The girl's gaze moves between Sophie and Ryder and then falls on Christian who huddles in behind them. It lingers on him for what seems way too long, before sliding back to Sophie. Contact lenses, Ryder decides, still fixated on the girl's eyes.

"I do not know the owners, no." The girl says with a hint of an accent Ryder can't yet pin point. "Do you?"

Sophie pauses. "Well, technically, no."

"But we have permission to be here." Christian remains in close behind Ryder, his hands gripping the back of her jacket.

"Well, that's very good for you then, I presume?" She doesn't smile, but Ryder can hear the bemusement in the girl's voice. There is definitely an accent of some kind. If Ryder had to guess, maybe Scandinavian. One of the girl's from Lucas's senior year was a Danish exchange student.

"It is good to have permission, absolutely." Sophie nods before throwing Ryder a questioning glance. The conversation isn't exactly firing.

You appear to be unwell, Ryder.

The girl's voice is impossibly close, and Ryder stumbles back. She treads on Christian's foot and he hisses, but steadies her. "Ryder? What's wrong?"

Confusion overwhelms her, and the words won't come.

"Oh, my apologies." The girl rests her fingertips against her lips. "A little too loud?"

"What did you just do?" Ryder's dry throat scratches out the words.

I spoke to you like this. I'm speaking to you all like this, but only you are hearing me. Which is very interesting, yet so disappointing at the same time.

Ryder cries out, clamping her hands over her ears. But the girl's voice is somewhere deep inside Ryder's skull, resonating there.

Sophie grabs her wrists, hazel eyes wide with concern. "Speak to me sweetie, what's going on?"

"Can't you hear it?"

"Do you mean the rain?" Twisting her lips, Sophie glances towards the door.

Not the rain, Ryder wants to shout back. She bites her tongue.

They cannot hear me. Thankfully, the girl lowers her voice this time. *Though I am trying. How quaint, a world with so little telepathy.*

Telepathy. Ryder stares at the stranger. Madly trying to work out if she's actually passed out, finally lost her mind, or this is real.

"Ryder? Speak to me, you doing okay?" Sophie is on tip-toe, right up close, trying to peer into Ryder's eyes.

Doing okay might be a bit of a stretch, but at least her heartbeat has slowed a beat or two. Ryder nods, edging her friend to one side. "Who are you?" she says.

The stranger sniffs, or laughs, the sound comes and goes before Ryder can decide which it is.

"We can talk of much more interesting things, I assure you," the girl declares.

"It seems like a pretty interesting topic to me," Ryder returns. The sound, no, the *feel* of the girl's voice lingers inside her head.

The girl's shoulders lift and she exhales in a lengthy sigh. "My name is Olessia. I am a visitor. I'm here for nothing, and no one, in particular. I just want to be here. There is your answer." A smile pulls at her lips, but it's not altogether friendly.

She gave them an answer, sure. Just not a very detailed one. Ryder stares down, giving herself a second to work out where to go next. Christian steps out from behind her. The girl's gaze snaps to him, like a frog spotting a fly. He pushes his hands through his hair, making more of a knotted mess. "I don't understand what's happening."

But Ryder has no chance to reply.

"That's because nothing whatsoever is happening," The girl says, still watching him. "Which is becoming quite dull. I had higher hopes for this place after what I've heard."

Christian barely raised his voice above a whisper. The girl, Olessia, can not only get inside a person's head, she has fantastic hearing as well. Ryder's belly roils, Jack's breakfast sitting heavy. "So, what exactly have you heard about…this place?" she says.

The stranger flicks Ryder's question away with a wave. "Aresh always made it sound so interesting. So charming." She steps closer to the nearest doorway, off to the right of the stairs. It leads into a dining room with tall, narrow windows that give a sweeping view of the properties carefully maintained gardens. "So far, it all just seems rather damp."

With that, she strides into the room and disappears from view. No one moves. Christian and Sophie might not have experienced the nails-on-chalkboard feel of telepathy, but their apprehension shows in the flutter of Sophie's hands, and the way Christian twists a strand of stark white hair round his finger, over and over. Sophie is first to speak. "To be fair, she's right. There has been quite a lot of rain today." She shrugs at Ryder's raised eyebrows. "What? It's true."

"The inclement weather is being exacerbated by the slipstream," Olessia calls from the adjoining room. "I'm surprised the reaction isn't a little more extreme in a world like this."

Ryder considers asking what a slipstream is, when Olessia suddenly reappears. Her coat is unfastened and it makes a metallic clink as it brushes against her legs. The three friends shrink back. Christian reaches for the door handle, but Ryder grabs his hand. It seems a better idea to stay put, they can't exactly out-run her. The girl stops, regarding them. The moment stretches on. A breeze weaves around them, a draft coming from beneath the front door perhaps. Ryder barely dares to blink. Sophie's breathing comes in quick little intakes. It must have dropped ten degrees since they rushed into the foyer, and it's difficult to stop teeth from chattering.

Strapped around Olessia's narrow waist is a dull gray utility belt. The type police or a soldier might wear, but of the six or so devices strapped to it, Ryder doesn't recognise a single item. The plus side is that nothing resembles remotely a gun or a knife. Most of the pieces are no bigger than a mobile phone. One near her left hip could sit alongside the quartz crystals they sell in new-age hippy stores.

Without so much as a bend of her knees, the girl lifts off the floor and sweeps towards them. Sophie makes a funny squeaking sound, like she's not sure whether to gasp or scream. She presses against Ryder, who in turn shoves against Christian. The momentum pushes all three of them up against the front door. Olessia's trajectory comes to an abrupt halt. She jerks back, as though she's hit an invisible wall, but her violet eyes don't leave their faces.

"Already afraid." She whispers, her voice so soft Ryder strains to make it out.

Olessia's shoulders slump, reminding Ryder of a deflating balloon. Though Olessia's expression remains cold and smooth, an energy has left her. Her boots touch down on the tiles. The material of her coat jingles, like a fine chain mail. Sophie has dragged Ryder to too many Renaissance faires not to recognise the sound. But one thing the amateur costumes at the local Hobart Faire never had was the soft blue glow emanating from beneath the cuffs of Olessia's coat. Sophie takes a small breath. "Your eyes," she whispers.

Olessia's eyes, with their purple hue, were odd to begin with. But they are something else entirely now; a shimmering, luminescent shade of violet come to life. Shifting and swirling like miniature storm clouds. Olessia's gaze drifts from Sophie and then to Ryder. Her whirling irises have morphed from luminous violet to deep plum. Olessia's attention slides to Christian. He reels back under the scrutiny, but with the solid door behind him, there's nowhere to go. The thump of his body against the wood is the first sound in what feels like an eternity. Ryder moves her fingers, brushing them against his hand. Hoping he gets the message. Don't move. Olessia's eyes dart to where Ryder's fingers hook around Christian's thumb, before she glances away again. Ryder swallows hard. Christian's finger trembles beneath her touch. No one makes a sound. Olessia holds herself so still it's hard to tell if she's breathing at all. Her jaw is set, a muscle working there. She blinks, lifting her head. Her eyes, changed again, are now pastel lavender but the churning at least has stopped. No more storm clouds. "I will take my leave," she says. "There is no welcome here, I see."

It isn't what Ryder expects to hear. Though, truthfully, she isn't entirely sure what she expected. "Wait, what - "

The front door thrusts against them, knocking the three of them back into the foyer and very nearly off their feet. Ryder stops Sophie from landing on her knees on the tiles and they stumble together, only just managing to stay upright. A blustering wind sweeps into the foyer, rattling the palms in their expensive pots. Sprays of fine mist speckle Ryder's face.

"Where did she go?" Sophie stands in the open doorway. Rain pounds down from the sky, like it's trying to bore its way deep into the earth. A torrent of water cascades over the guttering off to the right. But there is no sign of the girl.

"I didn't even see her go out." Christian tugs the hood of his jacket over his head, holding it in place against the wind.

Racing out onto the wide landing between the doorway and the steps to the drive, Ryder scans the grounds. The concrete canopy above her is too high to stop the wind-slanted rain from reaching her. Droplets run down her cheeks and dampen her hair. She shields her eyes, peering down into the misty gardens. Even if someone was out there, amongst the topiary and hedges, it wouldn't take much to hide. Sophie joins her, shoulders hunched against the onslaught.

"She can't be gone." Ryder presses her hands to her temple. But the headache is long gone. Disappearing the moment the girl materialised. Just like the voices did. The very same voices that drove her crazy most nights in her dreams. Ryder stares back at the house. Christian is huddled by the door-frame, watching them. No doubt wondering when they'll get soaked enough to come back in.

"She can't be gone." Ryder wipes a droplet from the tip of her nose. "This isn't happening."

"What could we have done, Ry?" Sophie's teeth chatter. "I mean, she was very sweet and all, but she didn't seem like the type we could stop leaving." She gestures towards the garden. "Case in point. She just vaporised."

It takes effort not to snap out a snarky reply. But this isn't Sophie's fault. It's not anyone's *fault* that the girl is gone.

"I don't think she vaporised. She was real, Soph." The rain is icy and her clothes are near drenched, but Ryder doesn't want to move. "Wasn't she? I mean, we've been hunting for ghosts but what did we actually just find?"

Sophie's lips glisten as water streams down her face. "I don't know, sweetie. I really don't. Whoever she was, she wasn't from around here, I know that much. But I saw her." She glances over at her friend. "This time we all saw her, Ryder."

We all saw her. Four words to be framed and hung up on a wall somewhere. Four beautiful, welcome words, now laced with something bitter. "Yeah, but we all lost her."

CHAPTER 6

ALIEN. SOPHIE WHISPERED THE WORD on the drive back, and Ryder can't get it out of her head. She flips it back and forth in her mind, moving it from the 'no way' part of her brain, to the 'why not' section, so many times she's lost count. One thing Olessia wasn't, was a ghost. Jack slices up the vegetable lasagna, fresh out of the oven, and slides a generous portion onto her plate. On any normal day, the waft of garlic and oregano and baked cheese would send Ryder's senses into overdrive. But tonight isn't a normal night. Any night you think you might have just crossed paths with an extraterrestrial being, is destined to be abnormal. She jabs her fork into the steaming layers of pasta. Getting any food past the lump in her throat will be a huge task.

Whatever Olessia might be, she isn't coming back. They waited another couple of hours, and at Ryder's insistence, set up some of the cameras and sensors. But their soaked clothes and the unheated house became an unbearable, bone shaking combination and Ryder finally agreed it was a waste of time. Jack collected them just after five, a little surprised they were calling it a night so early. By the time he checked over the property and made sure it was all locked up and secure, it was dark outside. Was Olessia still out there somewhere? Or had she jumped on some express shuttle back to wherever she came from?

The clang of pots jerks Ryder out of her thoughts. Jack wipes his hands on a tea towel before heading over to the coat stand near the kitchen door. "Righto, enjoy that everyone. I'm sorry to have to run off in the middle of dinner." Jack tugs on his *Driza-bone* coat. "Floodwaters wait for no one, I suppose. Don't know how long I'll be, to be honest."

Ryder forces herself to take a mouthful. Jack's been darting pained glances at her since she got in the car. And she knows he's trying super hard not to ask her if she feels sick.

"No, we understand," Sophie says. She's having no trouble on the eating front, using another piece of garlic bread to soak up every bit of sauce on her plate. "Are you sure we can't come and help though? I haven't done any sandbagging before, but I'd be happy to give it a go."

"Yeah, I'm up for it." Christian nods, a small dollop of tomato sauce stains the corner of his mouth.

The heavy rain wasn't just at Clarendon House. It's been torrential for hours, all around the area. The river on the east side of Evandale is threatening to break its banks. An old buddy of Jack's, an ex-workmate from the Harlow Institute, lives out that way, and the guy's farm is a little too close to the river for comfort. The idea of getting soaked again isn't exactly appealing, so Ryder's glad to see her grandad shake his head.

"No, no, no," Jack says. "The river is running pretty strong, it's too dangerous. And I don't want you out in this weather. You were all drowned rats when I picked you up. Ryder, you should be more careful if you've just gotten over the flu."

Ryder scoops another forkful of lasagna and plasters on a smile. "I had a cold. The most pathetic cold ever. Not the flu."

"Well, my answer still remains," Jack says. "You all stay nice and dry, and I'll be back when I can. I've got my mobile but I've left the number for Dillon's farm. I'll see what I can find out about the rail lines too. I'm hearing some murmurs about the line up north being in danger of going under if this keeps up overnight."

Sophie stops with a pasta laden fork halfway to her mouth. Her gaze darts to Ryder. She mouths a word. Slipstream. Olessia said something about slipstreams being responsible for the bad weather. Whatever they are. Whoever she was. Ryder bites into the squishy pasta. Even if this is the world's best lasagna, and chances are it is 'cause Jack cooked it, she hasn't noticed. The only thing she can focus on is that they have lost her. Alien, or elf (Sophie's favourite theory), supernatural being, or trespassing Gothic runaway (Christian's favourite theory), whatever Olessia is, she is gone.

"All righty, bye for now. Be good." Jack pulls up the collar of his jacket and steps out into the weather.

A rush of damp, frigid air sweeps into the room and plays with the wildlife-print tablecloth. Ryder pushes her plate at Christian and he takes it without a word, making light work of the leftovers.

Twenty minutes later the table is cleared, dishes done, and Christian and Ryder move into the lounge room. No one says much, each occupied with their own thoughts. Sophie hums a tune as she heads upstairs to change. A fire crackles in the hearth, making shadows dance around the room. Ryder settles into a deep-seated wingback armchair, draping her legs over the armrest. Jack's favourite chair. The fabric is faded now, but it's a patchwork of different red patterned materials. She remembers sitting in the chair when she was small, a box of Legos on her lap, building a little fleet of whatever she was into that week: boats, planes or cars. Spaceships.

Shaking the thought away, Ryder flips open the laptop. They set up a couple of the cameras in Clarendon House, after Olessia disappeared. It was Ryder's idea. Clinging to the possibility that maybe Olessia just hid from them inside somewhere.

Sophie saunters back into the lounge room. She's slipped into her favourite fluoro-pink track pants, which have barely lost a hint of glare in the years she's owned them. Her lilac sweater is emblazoned with a disconcertingly large picture of a fluffy white cat. She plonks down next to Christian on the brown leather sofa, spilling a drop of the tea she's nursing.

"So anything?" She tucks her feet up beneath her, spilling another few drops onto her track pants.

Christian pulls out the earplugs he's using to listen to the EVP recordings. "What are you on about?"

She nods to the recorder in his hand. "Did we catch any disembodied voices on tape? That's what I'm on about."

"I've only listened to about five minutes, so no. The only weird thing I've heard so far is you and Ryder talking to empty rooms."

He laughs, dodging Sophie's half-hearted slap with ease. Ryder rests her head against the seat, watching them. Christian was rattled by Olessia, utterly silent the whole way home. His strained laughter now says he's still dealing with it, but he's insisting Olessia is some kind of elaborate prank and they'll see themselves on one of those shows where audiences laugh at stupid people being made fools of.

Ryder twists the end of her long ponytail around her fingers. Her still-damp hair smells faintly of Sophie's strawberry shampoo. "So what's your take then?"

"My take?" Christian tugs at the neck of his black jumper. Turns out he had more than one in his backpack.

"Yes," Sophie says. "Do you think your girlfriend is an alien or an elf?"

Christian gives her his best surly look, dark eyebrows knitting together. "The only one from another planet here is you, Sophie."

Ryder gives him a wry grin. He might be right, but Sophie has a point. Olessia focused in on Christian, her whole demeanour changed after he recoiled from her.

"God knows why," Ryder says, "but Olessia seemed to find you very interesting, Chris."

"Very interesting." Sophie nods.

With a scowl, Christian replies. "Don't be ridiculous."

Probably a good thing Olessia left, the little love affair was going nowhere fast. And a broken-hearted extraterrestrial can't be a good thing. Ryder frowns at a thread hanging off the sleeve of her black and gray flannelet shirt.

"Well, either she fancied you," Sophie says, "or Olessia was planning to eat you at some point. I've seen those TV shows. Maybe you just escaped certain death."

When Christian shoves her off the couch, Sophie moves over to Ryder. "Okey dokey, I get the hint. Ry, can I braid your hair. I need to do something to distract me. Here, sit on this." She pats the footstool in front of the armchair. "I'll sit in the chair."

It's not the best deal ever made, but Ryder could do with a distraction too. She closes the laptop and heaves a sigh, shifting down onto the low stool. Sophie perches herself on the much more comfortable armchair. Grabbing the TV remote, Ryder flicks through channels. Sophie slides her fingers into the damp threads of Ryder's long hair with well-practised ease, parting the strands into sections.

"Maybe we could watch a movie?" Sophie says.

"Yeah, maybe." Ryder winces. "Can you keep the hair attached to my scalp?"

"Doing my best, grumbles."

"Sorry, Soph. I'm just trying to process all this."

Sophie pauses, kisses the top of Ryder's head, then continues with her work. The volume on the TV is muted but Ryder doesn't bother to turn it up, something about the crackle and snap of the fire is soothing. The weather is big news, with footage of dirty churning flood waters spilling over bridges and sweeping away everything from rubbish to an empty dog kennel. A pat on Ryder's head signals the braiding work is done. A relaxed French braid that captured every last strand of Ryder's long hair. Sophie's is fast, usually a good thing considering how much Ryder hates being her guinea pig. Tonight though, she could have done with a longer distraction.

Sophie hops off the armchair and throws herself onto the pile of cushions at the end of the couch. Christian wraps the headphones around the recorder, placing it on the coffee table in front of him. "Zero, zilch, nothing." Disappointment clips his words.

"I feel like we should watch *ET* or something." Sophie sighs. "Mourn our loss."

"Or Independence Day," Christian grins.

Ryder doesn't join in on the banter. She shrugs when Sophie picks out a DVD for them to watch. Sophie at least is still in the mood for the supernatural, choosing an old 80's movie, *Poltergeist*. It takes Ryder an effort to muster up half a smile and nod at the selection. She curls herself into a tight ball in the depths of the armchair. Though she's seen the movie a dozen times, it's still a better option than chatting. The others seem to share the sentiment, settling into silence the moment Sophie hits play.

Ryder stares at the screen but her head is full of Olessia; the way she emerged from the shadows and turned those incredible, preternatural eyes on them. When Ryder's phone buzzes in the depths of her faded black tracksuit pants she jerks upright. A text message from Lucas.

How's the ghoul hunting going?

No ghouls at Clarendon House. She replies.

It isn't exactly a lie. They chat back and forth for a few minutes, and then Ryder tells him she's heading to bed, which is a lie. But Lucas is too good at working out when something is bothering her, so she has to cut the conversation short. She tosses the phone onto the footstool.

Sophie pauses the movie. "What did you tell him?"

Ryder runs her tongue over her bottom lip. "Nothing…I didn't tell him anything."

Which, all things considered, is a little odd. She frowns, tugging at the loose thread on her sleeve. Lucas knows about all the paranormal research stuff. He doesn't say much about it, but definitely doesn't laugh at her. He would have listened if she told him about the girl with the storm eyes. Probably would have gone with the same prank theory as Christian, but he would have listened. He's the one who listened to her blubber one Mother's

Day a couple of years back because she didn't know what it was to have a mum. Ryder's cried on his shoulder about three times more than she'll ever admit.

"You didn't tell Jack anything either." Sophie's almond eyes are thoughtful.

"I figured when he picked us up and you said nothing, that we were keeping this a secret, for some reason." Christian sits with one of the cushions pressed to his chest, chin resting on it. He's not scared he insists, just comfortable.

Sophie's jet black, carefully shaped eyebrows disappear beneath her fringe. "Want to tell us the reason?"

"I don't know why." Ryder shrugs. "I have no idea why I didn't tell Lucas either. It just didn't seem…it didn't seem right to say anything."

Right or safe? The loose thread snaps free.

"I don't get why you wouldn't tell your grandad, Ry." Christian stretches his arms over his head. "He invited you here to creep around a haunted house. The guy worked at Harlow Institute for a thousand years, that place is all about fringe science right?'

"That's all urban legend rubbish." Ryder stares into the glowing embers. They'll have to grab some more wood soon, the fire has burned right down and already a chill is settling on the room. "It's bio-engineering mostly, some robotics. But Jack was in administration, a paper pusher, so far as I can gather. Not exactly groundbreaking stuff."

None of which answers Christian's question about why she isn't telling Jack. Ryder taps a finger against the worn fabric on the seat of the chair, conscious that Sophie is still watching her. Her friend is terrible at hiding how she feels, something Ryder has always loved about Sophie. But seeing the concern crease the corners of her eyes now is too much. Question time is over. At least till Ryder can work out an answer. She pushes herself to her feet and heads towards the kitchen.

"I'm going to get some more firewood. It's getting cold in here."

CHAPTER 7

WHISPERS SWARM OUT OF THE pitch black, surrounding her. Ryder tries to lift her arms but her bones are concrete blocks, dragging her further into the nothingness. The mutterings grow louder, the voices hollering and screeching, reaching a crescendo that threatens to crack her skull. Ryder screams but nothing escapes her mouth. She's the only silent thing in the maelstrom.

Ryder's eyelids fly open. Someone is stifling her, covering her face. It takes a few panicked breaths to realise the attacker is her own mattress. She flips onto her back, sucking in the cool air. The digital clock on the side table gleams crimson numbers - *0330.*

"Damn it."

Ryder sits up, brushing at her damp cheeks. It's been a strange couple of days, but dream-crying? Swinging her legs over the side of the bed, Ryder miscalculates the space and her knee hits the bedside table. A picture frame topples over, making a sharp sound against the glass top. Ryder freezes. A thin blade of moonlight pushes through a crack in the curtains, but it only reaches the bottom ends of the twin beds. Sophie is a dark blob beneath her covers. She rolls over, muttering, before her breathing regulates again into the steady rhythm of sleep. Pulling on a pair of thick blue house socks, Ryder pads out into the hallway, leaving the bedroom door ajar. Her parched mouth cries out for water. Perhaps it will clear her head too, the echo of the dream-screams still ring in her ears.

Three skylight panels allow moonlight down into the hallway. At some point after they all went to bed, the rain stopped and the storm clouds parted. The moon is a fingernail-like sliver amongst a smattering of stars. Jack text them around ten to say it was going to be a long night. The knot in Ryder's belly eased the moment he told them he'd likely stay at his mate's place overnight. More time to sort out the muddle of her thoughts.

Ryder passes Christian's room, two doors down from the one she shares with Sophie. The door is closed. Ryder folds her arms against the night chill, walking gingerly down the corridor, taking care to avoid the places she knows the wood creaks. Her feet are toasty warm in the socks, but her flimsy night-shirt and matching shorts aren't much protection against the cold. She reaches the window at the end of the hall. Outside, the unsealed driveway meanders along the side of the house, down to the paint-deprived garage at the back. No sign of Jack's car. Relief washes through her, so strong she can't help but feel a bit guilty.

Thirst and a full bladder lead her into the bathroom. The room has an unusual feature, garish orange carpet. It's soft beneath her feet, and she can at least pretend it's a little warmer than the wood. A night light, plugged in above the sink, throws stark bluish LED light over the small room. The flush of the toilet is a lion's roar in the quiet room. Washing her hands beneath a flow of icy water, Ryder turns to reach for the towel when a flicker of movement outside stops her. She edges closer to the bath which sits beneath the only window in the room, a wide rectangular pane facing onto the backyard. Water taps out a beat, dripping from her fingers onto the enamel. The backyard isn't the house's best feature. Jack is a great cook but a lazy gardener, and the yard is in desperate need of a once-over. In some places, the grass is almost as high as the brown corn stalks in the vegetable patch beside the garage. Ryder squints. Shadows move within the bushland beyond the yard, seeming to dart amongst the snow white trunks of the ghost gums. A breeze toys with the branches, and a chill crawls up the back of her neck.

"Just the wind, Ryder." She grabs a hand towel and rubs at her hands. "Get a grip."

The chill isn't done though. It slides down her arms, raising goosebumps the lengths of her arms. Her head tells her to get back into her warm bed, but her feet don't get the message. A shadow sweeps by the window. It's large enough to momentarily block the light from the sliver moon. Ryder drops the towel and clambers into the bath, getting right up close to the window above it. Her socks slide on the enamel surface, and she clings to the low windowsill to keep upright, her eyes fixed on the shadow as it moves around the yard. Olessia is back.

And she is flying around Jack's backyard. Ryder breathes hard, fogging up the glass. She wipes it away with frantic hands. Olessia has her arms wide, soaring through the air like a fragile Peter Pan, moving at a pace that makes the overgrown grass shiver beneath her. She's not wearing her coat, just long dark pants and a vest, cut high around her thin neck, leaving her luminously white arms bare. Almost bare. Pressing her nose up against the glass, Ryder tries to make out what's around Olessia's lower arms. There is a covering there, fingerless gloves perhaps. Glowing, fingerless gloves. The faintest trace of blue light shimmers around Olessia's wrists.

"What are you doing out there?" Ryder whispers to the empty room. If she presses any harder against the glass, chances are the old panes will crack.

Olessia shifts into an upright position and touches her feet down on a birdbath at the centre of the yard. The moss laden structure is barely visible beneath a rogue climbing rose. Tapping her bare feet against it, Olessia launches upwards and as she does, the blue light around her hands flares, like a flame igniting paper. It fades a moment later. Ryder watches her rise higher and higher. She cranes her neck, following Olessia until she drifts out of sight, above the house.

"No, don't go. Don't be gone." Ryder curses at the sticky window latch, heaving against it. With a quiet hiss the window gives and the momentum jerks her sideways. Her leg scrapes against the faucet and she winces, glancing down.

"You've finished your sleep then?"

Ryder's head jerks up. Olessia hovers just beyond the second-storey window. Ryder lunges backwards. She lands hard on the edge of the bath, lips pressed tight to stifle a cry. Olessia draws in closer to the window, drifting up and down like she's standing on a boat. Clambering out of the bath, Ryder back peddles towards the bathroom door, but stops short of running from the room. Leaving would involve turning around to see where she's going, but she can't take her eyes off Olessia.

"You can fly." Ryder cringes at the high pitch of her voice.

"How very observant of you." Olessia hunches over, making herself small enough to get in through the window. She doesn't have to do much, it's a generous window, oversized for a bathroom really, and Olessia is petite. Scrawny, actually. But the way she moves reminds Ryder of the astronauts on the space station, and the slow deliberation of zero-gravity movement. Even brushing their teeth looked graceful.

"And...you came back." Stating the obvious, again. Ryder would bite her tongue but she doesn't want to risk moving. She's not entirely sure what made Olessia run last time. And it's clear she's not exactly brimming with happiness to be here right now. Her smile is lopsided and doesn't reach her violet eyes. She tilts her chin, somehow managing to peer down her nose at Ryder, despite the fact she is the shorter of the two of them. The scrutiny is short-lived. Olessia picks up a hairbrush that sits on a shelf above the sink. She tilts it this way and that, eyes narrowed, a frown creasing the marble smoothness of her face. Maybe aliens don't brush their hair. Ryder should probably explain what it is, but she's distracted by the gloves Olessia wears. They appear to be made of a tight-fitted, satin-like material, a gunmetal gray that catches the light as she moves. Ryder can just make out a faint pattern across the surface.

The material starts just below Olessia's elbows, running down over her hands and ending at the knuckles of her fingers. Olessia taps the hairbrush against her right arm and Ryder raises her eyebrows at the unexpected sound. A metallic clang. The hairbrush is plastic, so the sound has to be coming from the gloves. Well, not gloves, exactly. Gauntlets? Sophie the Renaissance faire addict, is going to flip. Ryder takes a deep breath to steady herself. Keep things simple, she decides, don't bombard Olessia with questions just yet. Don't give her a reason to run, or fly, again.

"That's a hairbrush." Ryder's voice cracks. "To…brush your hair…with."

"Your talent for explanation is quite remarkable." The lop-sided smile becomes a sneer, sharpening Olessia's already razor features.

Ryder's cheeks flush with heat. Her first attempt at small talk with an alien isn't going well. Alien. The label doesn't seem so wild now. Olessia's paleness and sharp features give her an ethereal quality but she's no apparition. She is solid, real. She is standing, barefoot, in Jack's upstairs bathroom. Ryder can see her shadow, and a couple of dirty footprints on the carpet. Whatever Olessia's been doing, it's involved walking in mud.

Olessia drops the brush into the sink, the way you might drop a piece of fruit with a worm in it. Ryder has a sudden, irrational urge to tell Olessia to pick it up. But instead she says, "I just thought maybe you didn't have hairbrushes…wherever it is…you come from."

There is no trace of a smile on Olessia's elven face, no expression at all that Ryder can read. Violet eyes regard her, unblinking. Ryder may well have just blown intergalactic relations over a hairbrush. She doesn't dare take a breath. The stare-fest goes on a for a few seconds, Olessia's gaze boring into Ryder like she's trying to get inside her skull, which, maybe she is. Considering the telepathy thing and all. Just when Ryder decides it's a good idea to turn away, Olessia throws her head back and laughs. A high girlish, tinkling sound.

"I knew it," she says. "I knew you wouldn't disappoint me."
The laughter ignites the colour in her eyes, a vibrant amethyst.

Ryder nearly chokes on her relief. "Disappoint you? What
do you mean?"

"Oh, you are interesting. So very interesting." Olessia raps
her finger against one of the chunky buckles that line the front
of her vest. The top itself is tight against her slim frame. The
clothing has a uniform vibe to it. Military precision in the sharp
cut and starkness of it.

"I'm interesting?" Ryder searches for a reply. "Well, thank
you?"

"Is he your paired one?" Olessia says suddenly. "The boy
who is with you."

"Christian?"

Olessia nods. "Are you a pairing? Partners? Mates?"

Ryder bites at the inside of her mouth, conscious that all
trace of amusement has left Olessia's face again. "No, no it's not
like that. Christian doesn't-" She lets the sentence fade away. If
he wants to tell an extraterrestrial his business, well, that's *his*
business.

"All right, I understand. He does not wish to pair with you."
Not exactly what Ryder said, but it seems to satisfy Olessia. She
adjusts her utility belt, the objects there clinking together softly.
One resembles a little silver boomerang. It sits just off centre
glinting in the night light. "I must say I'm intrigued by your
explanatory prowess. You will make an excellent guide to the
Iondar Realm."

Wherever she is from, they're not oblivious to sarcasm. But
Ryder isn't about to start a competition.

"Iondar Realm?" She frowns.

Olessia gestures towards the window, a haughty movement,
like a queen waving from her balcony. "Your Earth is a part of
the Iondar Realm. And I want you to show me more of it. I can
see that Aresh didn't exaggerate its beauty."

"Oh, okay." Ryder digs her fingers into her braid, Sophie's

handwork tight suddenly. "I understood about one percent of what you just said."

"Well, I would hardly expect full understanding from a species such as yours," Olessia says.

Queen of sarcasm or Empress of bitchiness? Ryder folds her arms, undecided. "Excuse me?"

Getting all insulted is totally nonsensical, but Ryder is covered in goosebumps, her belly and chest hurt from the knots in them, and her eyes ache from lack of sleep. There is a limit to what one person can take in a day.

Olessia continues, the smirk holding. "Your indignation is unnecessary, and unflattering. I state only fact. The realm of Bax Un Tey is thousands of times the size of the Iondar Realm, with lifeforms and technologies that your kind are far from understanding." Her gaze shifts to the window, her voice softening. "Perhaps that is what she loved so much about this place. The simplicity."

"Who loved this place? I'm sorry, but who or what is a Bax Un Tey?" Just two questions to add to a rapidly growing list. Actually, three. "Wait, how do you know English so well?"

Olessia flicks her fingers, batting away Ryder's query. "Unimportant details. Let us go. You must show me what is out there, I'm sure your descriptions will be most informative." All at once, she strides towards Ryder. The sudden movement takes her by surprise and Ryder lurches backwards, her heel clipping the bathroom door, swinging it shut with a resounding clunk. She presses up against the wood, turning her head and clenching her eyes shut. "Don't hurt me."

There is silence. Nothing else. Ryder opens one eye.

Olessia leans against the sink, one hand tight around its edge. "Why would you say that?" The steel in her gaze wavers. Something pained tugs at the corners of her eyes. "I see now it was a mistake to think you might differ to the others. I should not have returned."

Ryder swallows, her cheeks flushed. Why did she say that?

Olessia is acting like an aristocrat, all tight shoulders and upheld chin, it's irritating, but hardly threatening. Everyone is fast asleep in their beds. If she wanted to hurt them she could have done it long before now. Olessia steps into the bath, the gleam of blue light returning to the gauntlets. In one fluid motion she rises up, hunching forward to make her way out the window.

"No, don't go," Ryder cries, loud enough to wake Christian next door— if he didn't sleep like the dead. Definitely loud enough to stop Olessia in her tracks. She pulls back from the window and lowers herself to the floor.

"It is not necessary to shout. I am right here."

Ryder scrunches her toes into the carpet. "I just...don't go. Please. We haven't met anyone like you before, and I don't know how to handle this. Just...give me a second to stop freaking out, okay? I've got so many questions..."

And Olessia has answers. Not just about her world, her life, but maybe Ryder's. Those whispers in the hallway yesterday, they are all too familiar. Ryder balls her hands into fists. The thought of Olessia leaving digs a hole in her chest, and she can't take a breath deep enough to fill it. Ryder relaxes her toes, and steps away from the door.

Olessia regards her, eyes shadowed. "Believe me, your reaction is among the least disturbing I've experienced. And quite intriguing. I believe you might not run if a creature from the Arlion pursued you. You may not have met someone like me Ryder, but I certainly didn't expect someone like you."

This time when Olessia approaches her, Ryder holds her ground though her heart pumps like a wheel on an out-of-control steam train. Is fifteen too young to have a heart attack? And what the heck is a creature from the Arlion? Whatever it is, Ryder's certain Olessia is wrong. She would run. But at least the tension has left the air. Olessia actually has a smile on her narrow, gaunt face.

"Now, as you so astutely pointed out when you saw me, I was flying. Give me your hands, if you would like to do the same. The time I have to explore this place may be very limited. I cannot afford to spend it standing in this confined space." Olessia lifts her hands, palms up, waiting. Ryder chews at her lip, absorbing everything the purple-eyed girl just said.

"It will be perfectly safe," Olessia continues. "I don't intend to lose my guide." The metal on her arms gleams powder blue, and it's easier now to make out the pattern that covers the surface of the gauntlets. It's actually the same symbol repeated. With its long sweeping strokes, it's a style reminiscent of Kanji. Ryder tried and failed Japanese class last semester. The symbol on Olessia's arm is a sweeping P shape, with an embellished square surrounding it.

"A signature of sorts." Olessia nods down at the design, bending her wrists back and forth. The metal moves as easily as the satin Ryder mistook it for. "Now, I can't stand here forever like this. I'll offer only once. Do you want to fly?"

Inside the bathroom, the idea doesn't sound so dangerous. Ryder nods and places her shaking hands over the top of Olessia's. Any second now her heart is going to race itself into oblivion. Olessia interlinks their fingers. The metal is heat-pack warm. Ryder stares down at their hands. Both pairs are pale, though Olessia's skin takes it to another level of translucence. Then the metal begins to move.

"Holy sweet craziness," Ryder whispers under her breath.

The gauntlets are melting. Thin rivulets run from Olessia's forearms and flow, thick and warm as candle wax, onto Ryder's hands. The streams of liquid move slowly, shaping themselves around each curve and bump, over her wrists and gliding up her arms. The strange metal hardens, cupping itself against Ryder's body with a gentle press. In no more than a minute, Ryder wears two perfectly moulded gauntlets. Mirror images of the ones Olessia still wears.

CHAPTER 8

RYDER'S GAZE SHIFTS FROM THE gauntlets to Olessia three times before she says a word. "What is this stuff?"

"Elthar." Olessia drifts up and over the edge of the bath, hovering just above the hot and cold taps. The blue glow emanates from the gauntlets again. The elthar, whatever that is. Ryder runs her fingertips over the metal encasing her arms. It's still warm to the touch. The symbols imprinted on Olessia's gauntlets are visible on Ryder's too. She taps her fingers against the material. The undeniable ting of metal rings out, but the feel of it against her skin is much more like the smoothness of silken gloves.

"How did it do that?" Ryder holds her hands up in front of her face, mesmerised. "Some kind of self-generation?"

"Self-replication, yes. You are a clever girl, aren't you?"

Ryder glances at her, not sure if it is a compliment or a jibe. Olessia's expression is a work of marble-like indifference. Deciding to take it as a compliment, Ryder opens her mouth to ask another question when all at once the metal brightens. It's subtle at first, just the barest aura of light around the edges, the softest sky blue. And with it comes a rush of heat. The warmth of the metal seems to soak down into her bones and trails its way along her skeleton, spreading across her shoulders and down into her ribcage.

"What's happening." Ryder clenches her fists. "It's getting really warm, take it off." Her body jerks, and then lifts an inch off the floor. Ryder sucks in her breath, arms rigid with panic.

"Relax, you are barely off the ground," Olessia says. "It's not exactly dangerous."

"I didn't put myself up here. I'm not exactly in control. That's dangerous enough."

"I am controlling the elthar, you are safe." Olessia drifts towards her. "Just relax. The heat is completely normal."

The ugly orange carpet draws further away, and Ryder rises higher into the air. The warmth, like honey oozing through her bones, branches out through every rib, down the length of her spine and into her legs. She's a metre off the ground now, the ceiling drawing uncomfortably close, but her movement is slow and controlled. She finally takes a breath. "Oh my god, I'm flying." She laughs, a maniacal edge to the sound.

"Not really. You're floating. But you are doing well." Olessia drifts around her in a slow movement. "Do relax though; you look like you're tied to a pole. I assure you, you are in no danger." She's not smiling but there is clear amusement in her voice. The blue sheen from Olessia's gauntlets mixes with the violet in her eyes, transforming them into a rich plum shade. She is watching Ryder closely but not in that haughty way, it's more like Lucas after Ryder beats him on the rare occasion at chess; surprised approval.

"Try moving your arms, there really is no need to just hang there," Olessia says.

"I'm not just hanging here," Ryder says, indignant. But Olessia is right. She hasn't dared make any move, aside from blinking. Her upward rise stops. She hangs midway between floor and ceiling, her body as warm as if she were sitting in a steam room. Minus the steam. "How are you doing this?"

"Would you understand if I told you? I don't think so." There it is again, the aristocrat with the attitude.

"Try me." Ryder says.

"Not until you stop acting like I have frozen you in place. Move your limbs. I'm controlling your buoyancy, but you can move at will."

Ryder flexes one hand, then the other. Nothing much happens, aside from it being far easier than she expects. Ryder points and flexes her toes, then bends her leg. She can't stop a smile. "So there you go, I'm moving. Now tell me how you're doing this." The altitude is making her cocky.

Olessia drifts in behind Ryder. "A kinesis connection with the elthar."

"With a metal? Kinesis is normally with living organisms isn't it? This is metal." Ryder shifts her shoulders, trying to rotate around. Her body moves as directed, drifting in the same fluid way Olessia does. No shift in height, no wobble or hint of instability. "Oh, wow. That was easier than I thought."

"It is not a difficult procedure." Olessia sniffs. "Nor is it a metal, as you define it."

Ryder splays out her arms, moving them through the air. A thrill of excitement shivers through her. Growing bolder each moment, Ryder tilts back and forth in little half-bows. It's no different to doing it when you are standing on solid ground.

"May I?" Olessia gestures towards Ryder. "This will be faster if I assist."

Ryder straightens and nods. Olessia places her hands on Ryder's shoulders and presses down with enough force to tilt Ryder forward again. But this time it's all the way forward. Ryder tries to counter the force of Olessia's touch. She jerks her head up, battling to right herself, but Olessia may as well be a bodybuilder.

"Hey, wait," Ryder cries.

"Put your legs out behind you, don't just bend forward." Olessia's frustration clips her words. "Lean forward, and lay yourself out horizontal. You're barely off the ground, what do you think is going to happen?"

It takes three attempts, and several more dismissive clicks of

Olessia's tongue before Ryder lays flat out in the air. It's another fifteen minutes, and what Ryder assumes are many extraterrestrial curses, before she is gliding about in the confined space of the bathroom. It doesn't make for much of a flight, from the window to the door and back again. But the buzz of adrenaline wouldn't be different if she just climbed Mount Everest. There is a line of sweat on her brow and an ache in her cheeks from smiling so much. She contemplates a full roll, but there's a chance she'll end up smashing a mirror, or with a foot stuck in the toilet. It could get messy.

"Is this how everyone gets around where you're from? That Bax...place." Ryder's forgotten the name; it sounded like something out of a fantasy novel. There is a noticeable pause before Olessia replies.

"No. They certainly do not."

"Why not? I would if I had the choice." Ryder tingles with the thrill of being airborne. She lets her fingertips brush against the carpet as her body rotates in a slow, sweeping circle.

"You would not have that choice." Olessia stands over by the window, gazing out into the yard. Ryder lets a moment pass before she asks another question.

"What do you do on Bax-"

"Bax Un Tey is the realm. My world is the largest in that realm. It is called Siros." There's an edge to Olessia's voice, but Ryder pushes on.

"Sorry, Siros, then. What is it you do there?" Ryder's bet is on the army. Olessia certainly has the stiffness for it, and she could pass for a drill sergeant the way she ordered Ryder about earlier. Olessia stands by the window, silhouetted by the illuminated gauntlets. Her answer is slow in arriving. Outside, the trees sway back and forth. Shadowy masses move across the sky, the clouds returning to blot out the stars.

"I did as I was told." Olessia's melancholy radiates off her, almost as tangible as the elthar's glow. All at once, Olessia curls herself into a ball, and glides through the open window. A moment later the heat beneath Ryder's gauntlets builds and she sweeps towards the window. She flails her arms, dragging them through the air like a swimmer trying to paddle backwards.

"Olessia, what's happening? I don't want to go outside."

Olessia hovers just beyond the window. "Then what is the point of being able to fly? Come now, Ryder. Trust me."

"Trust in this case might be a bit of an issue." Ryder's breath comes in short, panicked bursts.

"Lie flat, just as you did earlier." Olessia directs. "If you don't, you are going to have a nasty collision with the window."

"Not if you let me down." Her upper body edges back, but Ryder's legs skid forward; an inelegant ice-skater on unforgiving ice. Maybe she can jam herself against the window. A few bruises are worth it if means not falling two storeys.

"I am not going to let you fall." Disdain colours Olessia's words. The pace of Ryder's movement kicks up a notch and the window rushes up to meet her. In the end it's instinct that decides her course of action. Shoving aside the plan to face plant against the window frame, Ryder tucks her legs up beneath her, hunching forward. "Oh my god." Her toes brush the windowsill, and something catches against her sock, threatening to yank it off her foot. Then she's clear, high above the ground, arms slapping at the air like a maddened scarecrow. Clad in a flimsy pair of pyjamas and thick woollen socks, it must be quite the sight. Ryder twists round, trying to reach the window and hold on before she's dragged out of reach. "Olessia, stop. Let me down." Ryder doesn't care if she wakes the neighbour one kilometre over, she wants solid ground. The window frame slips out of reach.

"Relax." Olessia draws near and attempts to take Ryder's hand. "It's perfectly fine."

But Ryder snatches it away. "Put me down, right now." Panic crackles through her words. Her legs are peddling away like she's sitting on an aerial bike. Ryder isn't dropping like a stone, so that's a good thing, but it's hard to breathe through the tightness clenching her throat. "You cannot just throw people out a window. Put me down. Now."

One thing to be said for unadulterated terror, you don't care what you do or say to get away from it. Ryder glares at Olessia, sheer panic giving her the strength to keep eye contact when Olessia stares right back.

"Fine." Olessia tosses her head.

Their descent is a well-controlled, steady thing, right till the very end. The elthar's blue glow extinguishes a second before touchdown and Ryder rolls her ankle when she hits the ground hard. Olessia doesn't have the same landing issues, alighting with dancer-like grace.

"You did that on purpose," Ryder cries, but Olessia's expression gives nothing away.

The porch light blazes on, bathing the yard, and the door squeals in protest as it's flung open. Sophie dashes outside, her long floral nightgown swirling around her legs. She runs straight at Olessia.

"Sophie?" She ignores Ryder's call, coming to an abrupt stop in front of Olessia, who regards her with a baleful gaze.

"Whatever you're doing, you should stop. Right now." Sophie holds her arms like she is about to karate chop the girl in front of her. "I know martial arts. It's super great that you've come back. But play nice. Leave my friend alone."

Ryder hurries in between them, still shaky on her legs but grateful the ankle roll didn't do any lasting damage. "Soph, what are you doing? You've watched *The Karate Kid* seven times; it doesn't mean you know martial arts."

Olessia says and does nothing; a statue of haughty poise.

"I heard you shout at her, Ry." Sophie holds her defensive pose. "And I saw you...I don't know...were you falling?"

"Flying." Despite herself, Ryder smiles. "And I'm okay. So thank you for coming to my rescue, but I've got this."

Sophie stares down at Ryder's arms, catching sight of the gauntlets. The glow around the metal is gone, the gauntlets are a dull gunmetal gray once again but they're still a beautiful sight. "Oh my god. What are these?" She grabs Ryder's hands, turning them this way and that.

"I'm curious Sophie." Olessia watches them from a distance. "What plan of attack did you have for me?"

Not taking her eyes from the gauntlets, Sophie answers. "Well I...I was going to...actually I had no plan whatsoever. I heard Ryder yelling, and when I couldn't find her, I came looking."

Olessia presses fingertips to her chin, her eyes deepened again into a plum shade. Her eyes seem to morph with her mood, which is kind of freaky, but mostly beautiful.

"Your bravery is quite astonishing," Olessia says. "If not utterly foolish."

Sophie lifts her head, finally releasing Ryder's hands. "She's my friend."

"Your friend," Olessia repeats, a faint frown appearing.

"You don't have them where you're from?" Sophie smiles, rubbing her arms against the cold. Her grandma nightie is long sleeved flannelet and warm, but her feet are bare on the wet grass.

Olessia shakes her head. "No."

Crickets chirrup somewhere in the grass around them. In the distance an owl sends out a soft call. Ryder can't help but wonder if Olessia's lack of friendships has anything to do with pulling people out windows. She glances up at the bathroom window, measuring the distance she could have fallen. Could have, but didn't, an inner voice reminds her.

"Do you want to talk about it?" Sophie presses.

"No, I do not." Olessia frowns. "What I wanted was to learn more about this place. Ryder made it very difficult-"

"You threw me out a window-"

"I did not throw you out-"

Ryder's temper flares. "How many times did I say no? You just completely ignored me. I'm not sure how it works on

Siros, but here when someone says they don't want to jump out a window, they mean it." The breeze caresses the back of her neck and she shivers. The warmth from the ignited elthar was, admittedly, very pleasant.

Olessia lifts her slight shoulders. "But without encouragement they would never know what they were missing."

"Encouragement?"

Whoever or whatever Olessia is, infuriating runs in the genes.

"Okey dokey." Sophie hops up and down, waving her arms in their faces. "Time out. Please tell me you have a set of those gauntlets that will fit me, Olessia. Because I would love to know what I'm missing. And I would like to know where Siros is and probably a million other things."

The sky chooses then to open up, drenching any further conversation with icy, sharp raindrops. Sophie shrieks. "My hair." She grabs Olessia's hand, pulling her towards the house. The wide-eyed shock on Olessia's face brings a bemused smile to Ryder's. No friends, and apparently no hand-holding for this alien either.

CHAPTER 9

S OPHIE RACES UP THE STAIRS, taking two at a time. "Get up Chris." Her bellow is impressive, considering her petite size. "Get up Chris. She's back, and we were right. Alien."

Ryder cringes, glancing at Olessia, but she's more interested in the photos around the TV. Grabbing hold of the poker, Ryder jabs at the fire, trying to stir it back to life. The steel rubs against the elthar still clasped around her arms. Olessia hasn't asked for it back, and Ryder hasn't offered. Though it's no longer spreading toasty warmth through her body, there's something comfortable about the way it clings to her.

"Christian will join us." Olessia seats herself in the patchwork chair, perched on the edge like she's sitting on a faded throne. Her elthar has contracted down into slim cuffs on her wrists.

"Yeah. If Sophie can wake him."

"I could wake him."

"No. It's fine." Ryder spins around, half expecting to see Olessia running for the stairs. She's sitting on the chair, seeming a little lost, the ever-shifting shade of her eyes a soft lilac. What is it with this girl and Christian? Well, seeing him after he's just woken up might be just what she needs. He's not the greatest morning person, let alone middle-of-the-night person. "Can you pass me that box of matches?"

She points to the box on the coffee table. Olessia picks it up and hands it to her. It's a totally benign thing to ask, but Ryder's oddly tongue-tied at the thought of anything deeper. Everything she's tried to ask so far seems to rile Olessia, like each question is a fly landing in her soup; immensely annoying.

"You are not feeling discomfort," Olessia says. It takes a second for Ryder to work out she's talking about the elthar.

"Discomfort? No." The opposite really, the gauntlets are as comfortable as her wool socks. Well, at least before the sodden ground ruined them. "Should I be?"

Olessia rises from the chair, and kneels down beside her. "I should take them back." Another question not answered. Ryder holds up her hands. The process works the same in reverse. The elthar liquefies and slithers off Ryder's arms, melting into the cuffs on Olessia's arms and leaving no trace that the replicate ever existed.

"Man, tell me I'm not still sleeping," Christian says.

Ryder and Olessia turn in unison. He and Sophie stand in the doorway, mouths open. Christian's hair is doing a spectacular bird's nest impression and he's in his long-sleeved pyjamas; brown with white dots, a favoured set he's worn for about two years and one his mum has sewn up holes in several times. But Olessia doesn't seem to have a problem with his dishevelled appearance.

"Christian, would you like to try the elthar?" she says, fussing with her hair, though her pixie-cut is too short to get remotely mussed up.

"You…you're back?" He stutters.

Sophie steps in between them and hands Olessia a pile of clothes: a pale pink t-shirt with a smiling pug dog on the front, and an orange cable-knit cardigan. Bright, loud and not necessarily matching. Very Sophie. "I thought you might want to change. Not sure if you packed clothes for your trip from… where is it that you are from exactly?"

Olessia ignores the question but takes the pug shirt and slips it over her vest. She sniffs at the cardigan, before pulling it on too. It's quite the contrast, the vibrancy of the clothes against the starkness of Olessia's own.

"A place called Siros, in a place called Bax Un Tey," Ryder answers for her. The place where she has no friends, and does as she's told. A neat, sparse summary of what Ryder knows about Olessia.

"And that?" Christian points to the elthar but doesn't approach, keeping the sofa between him and Olessia.

"Let me show you," she says.

About an hour and a half later, Christian is no closer to knowing exactly *what* elthar is, but he knows what it can do. So does Sophie. The rain eases long enough for Olessia, still wearing the bright orange cardigan and pink pug shirt, to take each of them on flights around the house. Because Ryder was the human guinea pig and didn't plummet to her death, neither of her friends take much convincing when Olessia offers.

"What were you so scared about?" Christian asks Ryder, as Olessia guides a giggling Sophie around the back yard.

"She's about a metre off the ground," Ryder replies, folding her arms with a huff of annoyance. "I was two storeys up."

Christian isn't so brave when his turn comes. He tries his best to act calm and collected as his feet lift off the ground. Olessia stays a lot closer to him than she'd done with Sophie. A brush of the shoulder here, a touch of their hands there. Next lap round, he is holding Olessia's hand. Prickles of unease wash over Ryder. Olessia has telepathic skills, what if this is some part of that? Brainwashing to get what she wants? When they touch down a short time later, Ryder buries the thought. Olessia and Christian are both red-cheeked and smiling. If it wasn't for the too-vibrant mauve of her eyes, Olessia could be any teenager crushing madly on some guy she'd just met. Whatever her intention, Ryder decides there are more important things to find out.

The sun pushes a few weak morning rays through the cloud cover, brightening the dim room. The fire burned down a couple of times over the last few hours and each time Ryder got it burning again, chasing the chill out of the room. She stares into the flames, her eyelids heavy. Olessia can eat a serious amount of pancakes and loves maple syrup with a passion, but that's about all they've found out. Everyone asks her questions but she keeps redirecting the conversation, asking about their lives, making them sound so much more interesting than her. Ryder knows for a fact that can't possibly be true. It's nearly six in the morning before Olessia gives them some information.

"The realms are like...bubbles." She raises her glass of chocolate milk, the third she's drunk so far.

"Bubbles?" Ryder frowns.

"Yes, someone told me once that it was the best way to describe things to people like you."

Someone. Like that Aresh person she'd mentioned, the one who told her how amazing Earth was. Ryder chews on a fingernail, deciding not to throw another question into the mix. It's taken this long to get Olessia to reveal anything more at all. She and Christian sit side by side on the sofa. They both have their bare feet up on the coffee table, legs almost touching. Olessia's legs are about half the length of Christian's gangly limbs. At least she washed her feet before putting them up on the furniture, but it took some convincing.

"What do you mean, people like us?" Christian bites into the last pancake. Stone cold by now, no doubt.

"Less...enlightened." Olessia smiles, no trace of the indignation she levelled at Ryder when answering a similar question.

"So does that mean people from your world...Siros, is it?" Sophie sits on the floor in a kitten-print dressing gown, focused on Olessia and waiting till she nods before moving on. "They've been here before?"

"Well, of course," Olessia says. "The Bax Un Tey Realm was the first to perfect inter-realm travel. It's a big part of the reason why Siros and Zentai are at war. There is disagreement over who controls the technology."

Though it's not any huge surprise that all worlds have conflict, it's still strange to think that two places they don't even know exist, are fighting over something humans know nothing about. Ryder tucks her feet up beneath her on the patchwork chair.

"Is that why you're here?" Sophie says softly. "To get away from a war?"

Olessia's violet gaze turns icy. The way she stares at Sophie sends a tingle of unease through Ryder.

"It's just, I thought maybe the clothes you were wearing," Sophie says, flustered. "I just thought maybe it was kind of a uniform, military maybe. I'm sorry, I didn't mean to offend you."

Olessia's gaze grows distant, some of the ice melting. "I am not part of that war. I want nothing to do with it."

An awkward silence fills the room until Ryder takes a deep breath and redirects the conversation back to basics. "So, bubbles would help us understand where you are from?"

Olessia closes her eyes. When she opens them again her attention is centred on Ryder, and there is no trace of a chill at all. "Yes, yes. Let me show you."

Lifting her glass to her lips, Olessia blows into the liquid. Little flecks of brown milk pepper the end of her nose. Christian and Ryder exchange an amused glance but Olessia doesn't seem to notice. She is too busy blowing noisy bubbles into her milk. A moment later she stops and holds the glass towards Ryder. Sophie rocks onto her knees, moving in to take a peek.

"Lots of very nice bubbles," Sophie declares.

"All different shapes and sizes, all interconnected." Olessia sets the glass down on the coffee table. She points to a bubble that is several times larger than any other. "Bax Un Tey is this large orb, Siros is within it. As is Zentai." Then she indicates a bubble the size of a grain of rice. It's wedged in between Bax Un Tey's considerable balloon and two other pearl sized orbs of chocolate goodness. "This one here is the Iondar Realm, your realm, with your Earth."

Christian scratches the side of his head. "So we're talking dimensions or parallel universes or something?"

"Inter-dimensional travel." Sophie's eyes widen. "Do you have a spaceship?"

Olessia yawns and Ryder wonders how long it's been since she slept. Over-tiredness might explain the mood swings anyway, the sudden unpredictable surly turns. The alien is just plain old tired and grumpy.

"There's no need for a craft in the space I travelled, though you do require one for the Rivers, which are much larger passageways through the Arlion." Olessia isn't heading for bed just yet. In fact, marble smooth expression aside, Ryder gets the vibe that Olessia is enjoying her reveal.

"Oooh, Arlion sounds fancy." Sophie pursues her lips, nodding like she totally gets it. Which she totally doesn't. Neither does Ryder. But it's okay. This whole crazy night isn't in her head, and neither is Olessia. Ryder might be bamboozled, but she isn't hallucinating. Probably never was. The thought helps keep her hands from shaking too hard.

Touching a finger to the bubbles, Olessia pops a couple. "That film that makes up the bubble itself, is called the Arlion. It's what connects all the realms, essentially a realm unto itself. It is not fancy, as you say Sophie, on the contrary. But it enables those with the necessary advanced technology to move between realms. I used a slipstream I knew of, and it brought me to that house. And you."

She darts a glance at Ryder, but like most of Olessia's expressions, this one isn't decipherable. What Ryder does understand is Clarendon House has some kind of portal leading into it. Perhaps a pitch black portal with a choir of whispering voices? She takes a sip of what's left of her soda, choosing her words. "So, this portal in Clarendon House. Could we be...I don't know...susceptible to it? I mean, could a human sense it somehow, maybe even...like...hear it?"

Part of her expects Olessia to laugh, turn up her little button nose and launch into a lecture about how such a primitive species has no hope of doing any such thing. There's no laughter. No snide comment. Olessia sweeps her spoon through the remains of her bubbled milk.

"There would be nothing to hear." She keeps her eyes fixed on her glass. "So in that regard, the answer is no. Could they sense it? I would have thought that extremely unlikely. But even I do not know all things about all worlds, and the people in them."

It's a notable change from her earlier smug comments about how inferior Earth and its people are. Sophie gives Ryder a thumbs up. But Olessia's reply isn't exactly a yes. It's a huge maybe. A huge, unlikely maybe. Rubbing her eyes, Ryder tries to gather her thoughts. The telepathy thing has been bugging her, among many other things.

"So what could-"

Her mobile phone buzzes its way across the coffee table with a text message. Blinking to focus, Ryder reads the message. Jack thinks they are all curled up in bed at this hour, so he messaged instead of called. The news isn't good.

"We've got a problem." A watery hurdle actually. Ryder sighs, rubbing at her neck. "The flood waters are rising. He wants us on a train home. Today."

CHAPTER 10

OLESSIA SITS UP, HOLDING HERSELF in that stiff, controlled way she has. "He will be returning here soon?"

Ryder nods. "That's what he said, yeah. Just having some breakfast and heading home. He figures we're all still asleep I think."

"Oh man, we have to leave today?" It would be mildly amusing any other time, hearing Christian whine about the fact they had to leave the very place he describes as 'boring as hell'.

"They're going to close down the rail line if the rain keeps up even an hour or so more." Ryder flicks the phone from one hand to the other, not sure how to reply.

Jumping from her spot on the floor, Sophie claps her hands. "Olessia you have to come with us."

No one, including Olessia, protests. Everyone is silent, looking to the others for some indication of where they are going with the crazy, but not-so-crazy idea. Olessia is first to move, shifting her feet off the table and standing up. "You have elders though, do you not? Like the man who is returning here now? Elders do not, in my experience, react to things they don't understand with the same generosity of the young."

Not for the first time, Ryder has to wonder how old this girl is. Sometimes she talks like a wise old sage. Other times she's fawning over the Earth boy.

"My parents would freak." Christian nods, like he deals with extraterrestrial secrets every day. Up till about twelve hours ago he was one of those people who made Ryder doubt her own sanity. According to Christian, there was no chance whatsoever anyone like Olessia could possibly exist. Paranormal or alien, he believed in none of it.

"I think my mum would love you." Olessia fixes Sophie with a withering stare. "But I'm not going to tell her anything, I swear. Oh my god, Olessia I have a brilliant plan. Ryder's dad is away. You could stay there, no one will know." Sophie claps herself again. "Does no adults mean almost-adults as well though? Ryder's neighbour, Lucas, is practically her brother, but they don't have the same parents. Anyway, it could get tricky to keep you hidden from him, but he's only twenty, and in all honesty not very adult."

"Are you done?" Ryder raises her eyebrows.

"It's perfect Ry, come on." Sophie turns back to Olessia. "You said you wanted to explore. I can put some makeup on you, maybe get some contact lenses. Say yes. You'll love Hobart. We can take you to *Mona*. It's an art gallery, the stuff there will blow your mind. Do you like hiking? I mean you seem to like nature, playing in the mud and stuff. Amazing hikes around Hobart-" She stops, this time getting the stink-eye from Ryder. Olessia on the other hand, appears to be mulling over the idea; if the barest trace of a frown on her forehead is anything to go by.

"Your place could kind of work, Ry," Christian says.

"Maybe, yeah." He's not the one who'll have a telepathic alien in his house though. One that didn't think twice about dragging Ryder out a window. It's all starting to make her head ache and the pancakes aren't sitting so well. Ryder gathers up the plates and empty glasses, stopping Sophie when she goes to help.

"It's okay, Soph. I just need a minute."

Ryder leaves them all chatting about how they are going to handle this, beginning with where Olessia can hide when Jack comes home. No one took much convincing not to tell the adults, and Ryder has no objection. Listening to all the things Olessia told them, about other worlds and other wars, she can't shift a gut instinct not to tell Jack.

Ryder stares at the water flowing into the sink, watching the suds gather atop the hot water. Bubbles interlinking with bubbles. Worlds connecting with worlds, passageways linking them all. Slipstreams and rivers. The whole thing really is making her head hurt. Ryder squeezes her eyes shut. Where do the whispers fit into all this? Only just last night they invaded her dreams so loudly it woke her. And then she found Olessia. Coincidence, right? Olessia said the portals were silent.

Ryder shuts off the taps. Somewhere in the wall the water pipes clunk and thud. She's not so sure she believes in coincidence anymore. Gloves on, Ryder dips the first syrupy plate into the water and stares out over the row of potted herbs that sit on the window ledge above the sink. The coriander is doing great, but the parsley is a dead brown mess. Beyond the veranda, the morning sun paints everything a soft ember orange. Her head is really thumping now. Probably should grab some painkillers. A wayward strand of hair falls across her face. Ryder lifts her head to try and shift it, then stops dead.

A woman stands in the backyard. Over by the red iron shed next to the carport, half hidden in the shadows. Ryder doesn't dare move, head still at an angle. Darts of pain jab at her temples. The woman gazes around the yard, like she's admiring the view. Her hair is silver-gray, about the same length as Ryder's, hanging low on her back. The pastel green dress she wears is flowy and light, with long split sleeves and cinched tight at the waist. Way too overdressed to be traipsing around Jack's backyard. And nowhere near warm enough. A friend of Jack's maybe? It seems kind of early for visits. The woman steps out of the shadow. Her dress shifts and billows like a breeze has caught it, but the trees in the yard are completely still. There's something else as well. Something that locks Ryder's breath in her chest.

The woman is translucent. The faintest hint of the trees and shed behind her are visible through the folds of her skirt.

"Guys." It's meant to be a shout, but Ryder only manages a whisper.

A plate slips from her fingers into the suds and splashes hot water back onto her hands. Despite the sting, Ryder doesn't move. The woman drifts closer to the house. She takes steps like a person would, but each takes her further than any human stride could. Watching the ghostly stranger glide closer, Ryder holds her breath. For a second the woman appears almost solid, completely real. Her features draw into focus. The contours of her face are fine and sharp like Olessia's, but without the hollow cheeks. An older lady, at a guess Ryder would say old enough to be Olessia's mother. She has some major scars down the side of her face, burns maybe, running all the way from edge of her eye down her neck. The focus blurs, and the details are lost. The woman is only a few metres from the veranda when she casts her gaze up and stares straight at Ryder. Even with her face a blurry blob, it's not hard to tell she's taken by surprise. Her gliding progress comes to a sudden halt. One slender, translucent arm reaches to cover her mouth.

You see me. You see the Rising.

The voice is low in Ryder's head, but the shock of it is like a punch to the jaw. Her bare foot slips on wet tiles and her legs go out from under her. She hits the floor butt first, just as someone rushes into the room. Someone with petite bare feet, elongated toes, and desperately pale skin. Olessia.

"No. Aresh?" she whispers, then all at once lets loose with a stream of words, strange words that Ryder doesn't understand. The room fills with light, and a gush of whistling air rattles the plates gathered by the sink. Wrapping her arms around her legs, Ryder buries her face into her knees.

CHAPTER 11

PORCELAIN SMASHES AGAINST THE TILES. Ryder parts her fingers. Broken shards, the remains of one of the plates, dot the floor beside her. One piece has come to rest up against Olessia's right foot. Ryder squints, thinking maybe she hit her head when she fell. Nope. Olessia is definitely glowing. Ryder pulls her hands away from her face. Olessia still focuses on the yard, so intent it seems she's trying to bore a hole through the glass with amethyst bullets. The chanting has stopped, and her hands are by her side, fingers flexed and rigid. It's definitely there, a faint glow around her body, white as a snowfield. Not the blue glow of elthar, this is something very different.

And then it is gone. Switched off like a light. Olessia clenches her fingers into balled fists, bracing herself against the sink, before she crouches beside Ryder.

"Are you all right? Are you hurt?" Brilliant amethyst swirls around her pupils, miniature storm clouds. She takes Ryder's hand, holding it too tight.

"No, no I'm not hurt." Confused and ruffled, but not hurt. And the headache is gone, evaporating in the chaos.

"You're certain?"

"Yes."

Relief mingles with something steely in Olessia's expression, which does nothing to steady Ryder's nerves. What exactly had the woman intended to do? There's no chance to ask. Sophie arrives in a blaze of red hair and concern and Olessia backs out of the way.

"Did you hit your head, Ry? Can you get up? You really shouldn't get up till we see if you're okay," Sophie peppers her with questions and tries to keep Ryder from getting to her feet.

"I'm okay, Soph. I'm okay." She takes Christian's offered hand and he pulls her to her feet. Apart from a damp patch on her backside, she really is fine.

"What just happened?" Christian darts a glance between them, but Olessia avoids his gaze.

"There was someone here," Ryder says. "There was a woman out -"

The woman is gone. But it's what Ryder spies on the window ledge that causes her words to die on her tongue. The potted herbs are all brittle and brown. Not just the parsley. The coriander and whatever else the others are. All of them. Dead.

"I must leave." Olessia has moved to the far side of the kitchen. Not even a hair out of place to show for whatever just happened. "Sophie would you collect my clothes please. I need to change."

"Go?" Sophie shakes her head. "But who was that? Are you in some kind of trouble?"

"Are we?" Ryder watches Olessia carefully. From the corner of her eye she can still see the herbs. The ones that were alive about five minutes ago.

"No," Olessia says. "Aresh is here only for me. She has no interest in any of you. You are not a concern."

But the expression on Aresh's face when she spotted Ryder, the tremor in the words she whispered into Ryder's head, didn't seem so disinterested. Ryder lifts the red plastic tub containing the well-dead coriander. "Did she do this, or did you? I mean, it kind of felt like being caught in some kind of crossfire there, that's kind of a concern."

As was the super-glow version of Olessia, but Ryder would

start with the basics first. It's a simple enough question but Olessia doesn't answer. Just stares at the plants. It hardly seems possible, but her face grows paler.

"What just happened, Olessia?" Ryder blurts it out, harsher than intended. Something about Olessia's gaze rattles her. There's been an aura of resolve about the girl since the moment she arrived, but there's a chink in the armour now.

"Ry." Christian puts his hand on her shoulder. "Let's just take this slowly."

"You don't look so good," Sophie steps towards Olessia. "Can I get you something?"

Olessia raises a hand to ward her back. "No. I'm fine. Where are my boots? I wish to leave." The elthar is still in its simplest cuff form around her wrists, not even a hint of light emanating from them. They weren't the source of light Ryder saw a few moments ago.

"They're upstairs," Sophie says. "Are you sure…"

There's no doubt Olessia is sure about leaving. She's already doing it. She pauses in the doorway. No sign of the sage old wise woman now. It's a very young, very guarded girl who opens her mouth to speak, but then lowers her eyes and leaves without uttering a word. Sophie follows after her, asking her to reconsider. And if not, whether she wants a lunch packed.

"Seriously, Soph." Ryder sighs, pulling the small pan and brush from beneath the cupboard.

"You're just going to start cleaning?" Christian says. "Ryder, what the hell just happened in here? Can't you say something to make her stay?"

"When did I become her best buddy?" The broken pieces of crockery tinkle as she sweeps them into the pan. Her hands are shaking but she makes sure to keep them out of Christian's line of sight. If he can't tell by the dead plants and smashed plates that they are in way over their heads, then she's not going to spell it out to him. This wasn't how this was supposed to go. Finding evidence of the paranormal, the extra-terrestrial, whatever the hell this is, should be taking her away from nervous break-down town, not towards it.

Sophie shouts from the top of the stairs. "Guys, is Olessia with you?"

"No." Christian nearly knocks the pan flying from Ryder's hand in his haste to get out of the kitchen. They meet Sophie at the bottom of the stairs. Her eyes searching the hall behind them.

"She was gone by the time I got up there," Sophie says. "What do we do? Should we go look for her?"

"No." Ryder's butt aches where it slammed against the kitchen floor. "If she wants to be gone, there's not much we can do to stop her."

It's better that way. Safer. Sophie's hazel eyes shimmer with tears, Ryder should hug her, but contact would only give away the fact she can't stop shaking. Back there in the kitchen, seeing that woman, Ryder had the faintest sense of familiarity. Not that she knew her, nothing as strong as that, more a sense of having seen her somewhere before. Probably just the fact she looked so like Olessia. Or the telepathy is short circuiting Ryder's weak human brain and she really is losing it.

Sophie wipes away a tear. "She just seemed so...I don't know...so lonely? She could have stayed here, we could help her."

It's selfish, completely, but Ryder breathes a relieved sigh when the sputter of Jack's beat up station wagon fills the air. In a few minutes he'll come through the kitchen door, all smiles and full of tales about the flooded night. And they won't be able to talk about Olessia, about any of the things that make it impossible to stop trembling.

"Do we say anything?" Christian fiddles with the piercing in his brow.

"Maybe he'll help us look for her?" Sophie's face brightens.

For the second time in just a few minutes Ryder shuts down Sophie's idea. "No. We can't say anything, promise? Olessia didn't want him to know anything -"

"And she might still come back, right?" Christian says. "I mean, maybe it will be like last time?"

Christian seems to be waiting for her to agree, so Ryder nods. "Maybe, yeah."

A gust of cool air signals Jack's arrival. "That you, Ryder?" he calls. "Didn't think you lot would be up." He joins them in the hallway, cheeks pink from the morning air. "Everything all right?"

He pulls off a red beanie, strands of his peppery hair stick out at wayward angles. Dark circles rim his lower eyelids.

"Yeah all good," Ryder says. Probably too enthusiastically, judging by the bemused frown Jack gives her. "How was your night?"

He takes off his *Driza-bone* coat, draping it over his arm. "Long and tiring. But the farm is safe, for now. Did you happen to get my message about the trains?"

"We just got up so I hadn't had a chance to answer yet." The lie rolls off her tongue more smoothly than she would like. Christian and Sophie shuffle their feet, concentrating on everything but Jack. Not the world's greatest secret-keepers.

"Yeah, it's frustrating, but I'm afraid we're going to have to get you on the midday train back to Hobart if you don't want to be stuck here for days."

Hobart. Her own bed. Somewhere far from those dead plants in the kitchen. Ryder works to keep disappointment plastered on her face.

"I wouldn't mind. I'd love to be stuck here." Sophie's voice wavers. Jack's an observant guy, a trait Ryder hopes fails him now.

For now, it seems to. He smiles at Sophie. "And you know you'd be more than welcome. It's great to have you all here. But I don't think your parents would be impressed if you missed any school next week. I'm going to have a shower and catch an hours sleep before we start thinking about getting you into town, okay?"

Before he heads down the hall to his room, he gives Ryder a hug. His solid, broad frame offers a makeshift barrier between her and the kitchen. And what just happened in there.

"Sorry it all has to end so quickly like this," he says. "I don't feel like we've even had a chance to chat about what you found at Clarendon. I want to hear all the details."

Ryder presses her face into the curve and warmth of his shoulder. "Well, we can talk on the phone, once we're back in Hobart. It's been amazing fun but we don't have much to report."

Lying to him so easily, the one person who never questioned her need to know what *else* might be out there, cuts at her. One day she'll tell Jack what's happened. He walks down the hall, the exhaustion from a night spent sandbagging evident in the droop of his shoulders. If he had noticed the plants in the kitchen, or the broken plate, Ryder isn't sure she wouldn't have blurted the whole story out to him. But those things also steel her resolve to keep him out of this. Now she's seen how broken things can get.

CHAPTER 12

JACK WAVES AND TAKES A step back from the train carriage. He's smiling but it doesn't quite reach his eyes. The door slides shut, and Ryder lets out a sigh of relief. She walks slowly back down the aisle, using the seats to steady herself as the train gathers momentum. The carriage is nearly full, unusual for midday on Sunday of a long weekend, but the threat of cancellations has a lot of people worried. Ryder lifts the collar of her faded denim jacket, trying to block the cool air blasting in from the vents. She edges in between Christian and Sophie, who sit across from each other, to get to her window seat. The seat opposite Ryder is empty so she kicks off her purple Dr Martens, another *sorry-I'm-not-home-for-your-birthday-again* present from her dad. She has a wardrobe full of apologies. Ryder props her feet up on the chair, her left big toe sticks through a hole in her favourite skull print socks.

"Ryder?" Sophie nudges her. "You okay?"

"All good." Dry and unconvincing, but it's the best she can do.

Christian shifts in his seat, extending one long leg out into the walkway. His red sneakers have seen better days, the fabric scuffed with intertwining black and white laces that would snap with a good pull. He's gazing out at the passing scenery. No one's said anything much all morning. Maybe, like Ryder, they don't know where to start.

"We could play eye-spy…or something." Sophie tucks her feet up beneath her, cocooning her legs in the folds of her hibiscus print skirt.

"No." Christian pulls his wallet from his pocket, glancing at the money inside. "I'm going to get something to drink, anyone want anything?"

Ryder shakes her head, but Sophie holds up her glass water bottle.

"A refill thanks."

Christian leaves, and Sophie and Ryder sit in silence. She should probably say something to her friend, Sophie's not usually so pensive, but where to start? Across the aisle, a well-coiffed elderly lady sits with her Sudoku. She doesn't know anything about chocolate bubbles. Doesn't know that a girl with hurricane eyes could make her fly. A ribbon of unease threads its way through Ryder's chest. The wrinkled but elegant woman will step into her normal, comfortable life when the train arrives in Hobart. She won't feel scared or hollow or strangely lost when she opens her front door, won't realise she never stopped to think about how it would feel to actually *find* a ghost on a ghost hunt.

Ryder catches sight of a TV above the interconnecting doors. The news is on. She can't hear what's being said, but a headline banner runs across the bottom of the screen.

Freak electrical storm hits Tranmere area in Hobart.

"Check that out." Ryder points to the screen. "Lightning storm hit the phone tower across the river from school."

Tranmere, in Hobart, is just across the Derwent River from their school, Taroona High. The aerial footage shows the new phone tower up on Blackrhine Hill, constructed less than a year ago to give the eastern shore better reception. The thin antenna at the top of the tower has snapped and hangs precariously, like a slender broken branch. The view pans out across the wide river, sweeping back towards the western shore. For a second Ryder gets a glimpse of the white buildings of Taroona High nestled on the riverbank.

Tuesday they are supposed to be back at school, carrying on like nothing out of this world happened at all.

"When?" Sophie leans into the aisle, trying to catch a glimpse.

"Last night I guess," Ryder says.

"Well, hopefully the storm hit the school too." Sophie yawns. "Cause I'm not sure I can just go back and act like everything is the same as when we left on Friday. We flew, Ry. We flew. And we had pancakes with an ET, a very pretty if not slightly underfed ET. How does Economics compete with that?"

Her laughter jerks, fragile and short-lived. Even Miss Positive herself, Sophie Kynton, is struggling with this weekend.

"Do you really think she'll come back?" Sophie says finally. "Or is this just going to feel like a bizarre dream in a week or so?"

The hairs on the back of Ryder's neck bristle. "I haven't had time to think about it yet really."

The lie is so obvious, and so badly told, Sophie just rolls her eyes and lets it go. She gets up, her skirt falling in folds around her, and heads to the bathroom. Ryder stares out the window. It's only midday but the heavy layer of cloud makes it feel more like early evening. Farmland and bushland intermingle on either side of the tracks. One moment, black and white milking cows graze in rolling green paddocks, the next it's towering eucalypts and paperbarks.

Ryder's pocket buzzes with a text. It's from Jack. She races to read the message, her stomach leaps at the idea that maybe the flooding has been downgraded. That they can go back. But no.

Just when I thought I could get an afternoon snooze in, alarms are going mad over at Clarendon House. On my way there now. Maybe you did upset the ghosts after all.

He added three little smiley faces. But Ryder doesn't smile. Sophie and Christian return together a few minutes later. Ryder holds up the tiny screen for them to read, gripping hard so it doesn't shake.

"Oh my god, do you think Olessia's gone back there?" Sophie clutches the water Christian brought her.

"Before we jump to conclusions, not everything is going to be supernatural or alien or whatever, right?" Christian says, mouth half-full of donut. "Maybe someone actually tried to break in, or we didn't reset the alarms properly when we left last. I dunno."

"You dunno?" Ryder blinks. "That's it, just dunno? Come on, you can drop the sceptic act now. You do get what she is, don't you Chris? She's not human. Neither is that woman, Aresh, whoever she is. We know nothing about them, who they are, why they are here. But we do know there is a portal at Clarendon House. The place Jack's driving to now."

Christian leans forward, bracing his elbows against his knees. "Ryder, what happened in the kitchen? I mean you were freaked, completely spooked, kind of the way you're looking right now. Did that woman hurt you? Did...did Olessia?"

In a slow back and forth, Ryder shakes her head. "No. It wasn't like that. I believe Olessia when she says that Aresh is here for her. But...it wouldn't be safe to get in the way of that. Not at all." She blinks, trying to dislodge the picture in her mind; the shrivelled herbs beneath the window, the glare surrounding Olessia as she raged at Aresh. Ryder had been so focused on keeping Jack in the dark about Olessia, she hadn't thought about Clarendon House.

Sophie cups her hand over Ryder's balled fist. "Call him. Right now. Chances are it's a faulty alarm, or a terrible thief. Clarendon's been there for over a hundred years and I think we'd remember reports about alien arrivals. But this is Jack, and we need to warn him if there's the slightest possibility he's in danger. He'll believe you. He'll listen."

When Ryder doesn't immediately move to dial, Sophie jumps to her feet and reaches for her embroidered suitcase in the racks above them. "I'll do it."

"I'm calling, I'm calling. Give me a second." Ryder punches

in his contact. It connects and begins to ring. Of course she has to tell him, that she hesitated at all gives her a guilty pang. It's not like Olessia is ever coming back, whether they tell elders or not. The phone keeps ringing, bleating into the stratosphere, unanswered. The train jiggles as it slows, pulling into Bridgewater station. A tiny unmanned station, in an area that's mostly industrial and unfinished housing estates, about forty-five minutes from Hobart central. The train shudders to a stop.

Jack's number clicks over to an automated voice. Please try again later. Later is straight away. Redial. Ryder taps her foot against the floor, knocking out an uneven rhythm. One passenger alights at Bridgewater, a Lycra-clad guy wheels his bike off the carriage, and Christian makes some comment about how expensive the bike is. Neither Sophie or Ryder respond.

"Lucas would be impressed." He shrugs.

The cyclist coasts down the ramp towards the carpark, passing a broad-shouldered man who is making his way towards the train with heavy-footed strides. He's wearing military fatigues, sand-coloured with splotches of gray, orange and green. His blond hair is cut in a severe crew cut and he wears wraparound sunglasses. Probably from the Army Cadet training facility at Bridgewater; Sophie's brother did a survival course there a few months back. This guy is definitely not one of the young cadets though. With the way he charges towards the train, gaze fixed on it like he's going to push it off the tracks, he has to be one of the sergeants. Or whatever those army types are called.

"Check out this guy." Ryder dials Jack's number for the third time, trying to ignore the tightness in her chest. "Is he going to get on the train or just ram into it?"

Sophie leans over her. "That is one angry looking man."

"Looks like a boot-camp instructor I had once," Christian says. "Hated that guy so much."

The man stops in front of the lead carriage, the one ahead of theirs. He stands motionless, hands behind his back. A sudden jab of pain sears through her right temple and Ryder grimaces, clutching at the side of her head. At the same time, the rumbling of the train's electric motor sputters and dies. The lights in the cabin blink off and the dull light of the autumn afternoon fills the carriage.

The driver's voice hisses over the speakers. "Bear with us folks, just seem to have lost power. We should have it sorted in a minute."

"Ry, you okay?" Sophie tries to pull Ryder's hand away from her head. "You've gone really pale."

You are not safe. Do you hear me?

Olessia's voice pinpricks against Ryder's skull. She clutches both hands to her head, dropping the phone and rocking forward with the pain.

"Ryder, sweetie. What's wrong?" Concern laces Sophie's words. "Talk to me."

"Is she going to hurl?"

"Shut up, Chris," Sophie says.

Their voices are distant, muffled, like they're talking to her through the glass window.

Do you hear me, Ryder? Olessia's voice booms in her skull, like a miniature orchestra is playing symphonies in there, and using the back of her eyes as bass drums. .

"Yes," Ryder hisses. "But it hurts, really hurts."

Don't speak out loud, it weakens the clarity.

Already Olessia is using the 'I'm-so-much-grander-than-you' tone. If she could stop grimacing, Ryder might smile.

How else do I speak, can you hear me? It seems impossible anyone could hear that, her own voice in her head.

I do. My apologies for the connection issues. I wasn't sure I'd reach you. Is this better?

Even before Olessia finishes asking the question the sharpness fades, the percussion section grows silent. There is still a pressure filling Ryder's skull, the kind you get going underwater in a swimming pool. It's not great but bearable. She wipes at her nose, half expecting to see blood on her hands. Nothing.

I felt it, and yes, much better. Exhaling, Ryder straightens. Christian and Sophie stare at her like her head just spun round. But explanations can wait till later. *What's happening?*

How does Olessia hear her? Ryder's voice seems so teeny inside her own head.

You must move from where you are. There is nefarious energy surrounding you. See the danger. Open your instinct and see the danger.

The door at the far end of the carriage is flung back against its hinges. The heavy-set soldier steps through, haloed by the emergency exit sign, the only source of light in the carriage. His reflective sunglasses are pitch black in the dull light, giving nothing away. See the danger. The guy has the bearing of someone who likes to eat small children for breakfast and pick his teeth with the bones. Even with ten rows of people between them, he's making the back of Ryder's throat clench. Danger.

"We need to get off." Ryder shoves her feet into her boots, no time to tie laces. "Now."

Without hesitation, Sophie is on her feet, pulling down the bags from the overhead racks. She shoves Chris's backpack into his lap. "Chris, let's go."

"But why are we-"

Ryder grabs his hoodie, dragging him to his feet. "That guy is bad. Olessia said to run." Again, details can wait. "Go." She pushes her friends ahead of her, grabbing the equipment case off Sophie who's loaded herself up with everything. Ryder swings the strap of her candy-red duffel bag over her shoulder and they race down the aisle. Not exactly an understated exit. Muttered, angry words follow them down the aisle, their bags thumping against the seats.

Olessia, you there? I think he's here, right now. Where do we go?

Away, just get away.

Ryder glances over her shoulder. The man strides down the aisle, giving reassuring nods to the other passengers. "Nothing to worry about folks." His voice is a low surly growl. Likely none of the other passengers would dare question him. "Come on now kids, your parents paid good money for this course. Best you come on back now."

Several of the passengers laugh, making comments about the youth of today, cheering on the Sumo-sized soldier as he herds his runaways.

"Go faster, get off the train, go." Ryder presses her hands against Christian's back, pushing him faster down the aisle.

Sophie is first to the exit. She presses the button that should release the door.

"Power is out." Christian grabs the handle, pulls against it. "It will open manually."

As soon as the gap is wide enough, Sophie jumps off the train, one hand bunching up her long skirt, her arm cradled around her embroidered suitcase. Christian follows. The train rumbles with a surge of power, and the driver announces, with far too much enthusiasm, that all is well again.

"Apologies for the inconvenience, we will get underway immediately."

A series of warning beeps announce the door is about to close. Ryder leaps out onto the platform. She runs towards the others, her duffel bag bouncing against her hip, the equipment case clutched against her chest. Sophie and Christian are already halfway down the platform. Behind her comes the sound of the carriage door thumping closed. Nothing after. No footsteps. She dares a glance back. He's off the train. Again, just standing there. A Terminator waiting for the go signal. The train begins to move, engines straining to pick up speed. Trying to run forward and glance backwards is no easy task, but Ryder keeps the man in sight as she bolts for the ramp down to the carpark.

Olessia, what now? Where are you?

Maybe Ryder's doing the telepathy all wrong in her panic, but there's no answer.

All at once, statue soldier becomes terrifying walking man.

His long, purposeful strides manage to sound like a hammer blow each time his feet hit the concrete.

"Keep going." Ryder's duffel bag hits the railing. Staggering, she struggles to catch her breath and the others move further ahead. Christian and Sophie race out into the parking lot, empty save for two cars. The entire station is surrounded by bushland, thick scrub that offers no hint of any houses nearby.

"Go where?" Sophie cries.

Racing down the ramp to join her friends, Ryder's too busy freaking out to notice the potholed surface. She narrowly avoids twisting her ankle, but isn't co-ordinated enough to keep hold of the hardcase. It jolts out of her arms, and skids across the gravel. She should let it go, get her balance and get the hell out of here, but Ryder finds herself reaching for it.

Sophie screams, and Christian shouts her name. There's no chance to even lift her head before something slams into her back. She cries out, falling hard onto her knees, loose gravel biting through her jeans, pain searing through her thighs. A terrible smell permeates the air, putrid as rotting fish. Gagging, Ryder tries to get to her feet. She's barely made it into a crouch when she is hit again. A solid punch to her shoulder that flips her onto her back. Her cry sticks in her throat. The thing trying to pummel her into pieces is not the soldier. It's not even human.

CHAPTER 13

EACH NERVE ENDING, EVERY MUSCLE jolts into flight mode. Get up. Run. Run fast. Exactly what the others are shouting at her to do. But Ryder can barely blink, let alone bolt. Terror makes it impossible. The soldier is gone, but shreds of his clothing hang from the skeletal frame of the horror standing over her. Its eyes are protruding orbs of pure white bearing down on her. Ryder's chest burns. Between the stench and the horror, she can't breathe. Christian and Sophie are a screeching chorus, 'run.' Her legs won't hold her though, two trembling lengths of jelly. The creature moves in, leans down towards her. An angular head tilting back and forth as it studies her, so close its rancid breath moves the hairs on Ryder's head. Her guts roil, and her brain is scrambled mush, trying to comprehend what she's seeing.

"Ryder!"

White-eyes jerks its lanky body towards Sophie's pitched cry. The movement so violent Ryder expects its membranous gray skin to tear. It only gives Sophie the barest glance before returning to Ryder. Thin cracked lips part, twitching like twin threadworms stuck to its face. There's no trace of a nose or nostrils, just a jagged, fleshy hole where it might have been. And it's the only trace of flesh on the creature. The limbs on its skeletal frame are far too long for the short torso, like it's been stretched on a rack. White-eyes raises a bony three-clawed hand to her face. Long black claws, like diseased fingernails, reach for her. Head spinning and her heart punching its way out of her chest, Ryder strains to drag herself out of reach. Her body betrays her, her knees locking. She sits there, resting back on her hands, like a sunbather on the most horrific of beaches. The creature traces a razor sharp tip across the soft skin of her cheek. It has to be a dream. She hit her head when she fell, knocked herself out. A man can't become a nightmare.

She has the vague sense of movement nearby. Someone else is close. Familiar voices, strained with desperation. Sophie and Christian. The thud and clatter of things falling reaches her paralysed senses; sticks, stones, a tin can. They're throwing things at the creature. The talon moves downward, tracing a path over the curve of her jawbone. Those bulbous eyes never leaving her face.

It lets out a hiss of breath and mucous splatters onto Ryder's neck. Bile burns her throat. Till now the drag of the talon was painless, disconcerting and gut-wrenching, but painless. All that changes the moment it reaches her collar bone. The talon pierces her skin, a too-thick needle sinking its way into her body. A strangled scream bursts from Ryder's clenched jaw. If she doesn't pull herself together, this thing is going to kill her. It's a slap to her senses. She lashes out, pounding her fists against the monster's protruding rib cage. Not much of a hit, but still it seems to catch White-eyes off-guard. It rears back, lifting its elongated arms away from her, and a fresh wave of stench smacks her nostrils. Adrenaline pushes Ryder onto her hands and knees, the bitumen is coarse against her skin, but she'd walk on hot coals right now to get away.

"Ryder, over here." Christian races towards her, brandishing a pathetic-sized stick.

"Get back." Ryder tries to stand but her legs don't hold her. Christian is waving the stick about, shouting at the creature, trying to get its attention off Ryder. The wretched smell is getting stronger. White-eyes is moving closer. Ryder catches sight of a broken bottle on the ground. A shattered beer bottle. She reaches for it, grasping it as the creature takes her by her injured shoulder and hauls her to her feet. White-eyes is freakishly tall, lifting her till only her tip-toes scrape the ground. Panic fuels the wild swing of her arm. The broken glass tears through the mould-gray skin of the creature's upper arm. A thick black ooze streams from the wound. But the monster doesn't let her go. White-eye's grip is firm. Warmth runs down Ryder's chest, beneath the layers of her clothes. Ryder clutches at the bony arm that dangles her above the ground. Someone is screaming but she's not sure if it is her. Tiny spots of light appear in her vision.

White-eyes pulls her in closer, its hot rotten breath flooding her nostrils. Over and over she lashes out, landing solid kicks to its body. A body not as frail as it appears. Unflinching, it dangles her like a rag doll. Christian slams the stick against the back of the creature's legs, limbs as gangly and narrow as a giraffe's. The stick shatters like calcified bone.

"Get away from her." His voice is hoarse and cracked with panic. Sophie is there too, but spots of white light are blooming in Ryder's vision. The world fades to a pin-point, then it's all gone. Now there is nothing but white light. And silence. Total silence. In fact, no senses at all. No pain. No disgusting smell.

Images take shape in the light. Familiar images. Jack working on his station wagon, Sophie and Christian finishing a level on the Playstation. The images are random, but Ryder recognises them. Her memories. They flick by gathering so much speed they're nothing but blurs of colour. Then they begin to slow. Another time in her life fills her senses. A hospital bed, a nurse watching a monitor. Her dad. Tired and unshaven, running his fingers across her forehead, trying to smile, the worry burrowed deep across his face. There's a reason his honey coloured eyes are so dull. He's not sure his six year old is going to live. Even in her weird dream state the memory scrapes at Ryder's insides. There's relief when it fades.

Another arrives.

Olessia, drifting down the stairs at Clarendon House. The vision is so crystal clear, Ryder feels she could reach up and take Olessia's hand.

All at once the light whips away, like curtains opening back onto the real world. The carpark. The silence breaks and the agony in her shoulder returns. She's still hanging in mid air, the smell of rot still invading her nostrils and churning her gut. White-eyes lets out a screech and releases her. Ryder's legs buckle and she hits the ground hard. With a groan she rolls onto her back and finds herself staring up at the dull afternoon sky. Someone leans in close and Ryder aims a weak slap their way.

"Ryder, it's me. It's Christian. Quick, get up.' Christian drapes her uninjured arm over his shoulder, lifting her to her feet.

Ryder gasps against the pain. She slides her hand beneath her jacket, and her palm comes away bloodied; red and black liquid blotching her skin. Any moment now she's not going to be able to hold back the bile burning a hole in her gut.

"Quickly, Chris." Sophie's whisper is heavy with panic. "Oh my god, Ry, are you okay?"

"Where did it go, Soph?" Christian hisses.

"Still somewhere in the bush. I can hear it but I can't see it."

Christian moves at a pace Ryder's legs can barely keep up with. She stumbles, head foggy, body aching.

"What happened?" Her words slur, and her head is a bowling ball atop her shoulders.

"It let you go." Sophie jogs alongside them, trying in vain to hold a handkerchief against the wound on Ryder's shoulder. "Just kind of threw you to the ground and ran off."

"Ran off?" Ryder stumbles on the uneven surface and the jolt is sheer agony for her shoulder. Splotches of white fill her vision again, her friend's words all muffled. Breathe, she reminds herself, keep breathing. There's no way even both of them could carry her if she is an unconscious lump. Ryder needs to stay on her feet.

"It ran into the bush. Sniffing the air and stuff, like it caught a scent or something." Through the fogginess, she hears the waver in Christian's voice. "God, what was that? I don't even know what I just saw. Let's get to the road, wave someone down."

"Oh Ry, what did it do to you." Sophie lifts the handkerchief gingerly, peering at Ryder's shoulder. "We need to stop that bleeding. Chris, did you try your phone? We need to get her to a doctor."

"Of course I tried my phone. There's no signal. Let's just get to the main road. We need to get to the main road."

He's clinging to the idea as tightly as he is clinging to Ryder, and his whole body trembles. The carpark is near the size of two tennis courts, but it might as well be ten football fields for the likelihood Ryder has of crossing it. She blinks against a prickling heat behind her eyes.

"I can't do this." She drags her feet, leaning hard against Christian.

He struggles to keep them both upright. "Whoa, hang in there Ry, nearly there."

"Hang on, guys." Excitement pitches Sophie's words. "Can you hear that? Someone's coming."

Ryder struggles to focus. There it is. Low and throaty. A motorbike. Moving at speed. A few heartbeats later the bike, sleek and red, thunders in through the main entrance. The rider is headed straight for them, showing no sign of slowing. Christian inhales sharply. "Is he even going to stop?"

The rider swerves around them and Ryder catches a glimpse of dark hair and pale features. A guy, young, probably not much older than Lucas. She clutches Christian's arm, shifting to follow the bike. The rider picks up speed again and drives for the bushland at the far end of the carpark.

Sophie's hand jerks up, pointing to something at the far side of the carpark. "It's back."

The creature steps out from the cover of the bush, the sight of it sending Ryder's stomach heaving again. The rider slams on the brakes and jumps clear of the bike. He leaps upwards, like he's being propelled off a trampoline. His dark clothing catches the light with flashes of silver. The bike thuds onto its side and slides with a grinding screech across the bitumen. The dark haired man lands, black coat splaying around him where he crouches. When he flicks it back to stand, there is a glimpse of something beneath. A smooth panel of body armour on his chest. Pewter coloured, it reflects the light dully. The metal is flexible, moving with the contours of his slender body, and hazed with a soft cornflower blue. A flutter of recognition moves through Ryder's woozy brain. "Elthar. He's wearing elthar."

There are gauntlets too, more complex than the ones Olessia wore.

"But who is he?" Sophie raises her voice over the growl of the bike.

Whoever he is, he's at least as tall as Christian. Though White-Eyes stretches a head and shoulders above him, he is not dwarfed by the creature like Ryder was. The nails-on-chalkboard sound that escapes the monster suddenly tails off into a single, discernible word. "Guardian."

White-eyes seems hesitant about moving any closer, swaying side to side, long arms hanging limp beside its gaunt body. The man remains silent. Standing perfectly still in a haze of blue. His hair is knotted in a bun at the base of his neck, the strands pulled back in a tight, severe style. It matches the rigid way he holds himself.

Lightheaded all at once, Ryder leans hard against Christian and he has to brace himself to keep her upright. Her shoulder burns with pain, but she can't tear her eyes away from the crackling tension of the stand-off. That the two aren't friends is evident in the guarded way the creature regards the man.

"Let's get out of here." Christian shifts his hold, trying to get a better grip.

Ryder bites her lip to stop from crying out. If someone held a lighter against her skin, she guesses it would feel just like this.

The puncture wound smolders with sharp heat. "I can't."

The words have barely left her when the creature lunges. The elthar-clad man is within reach, but White-eyes is a sloth compared to his adversary. With whiplash speed the man rises into the air. The creature quickly rights itself, throwing one long arm up over its head, reaching for the man's boots. But he just curls himself into a tight ball and somersaults over White-eyes. As the rotation brings him level with the monster's back, the light catches on something in his hands. He strikes out and White-eyes roars with a husky cry, spinning in wild circles and clawing at its own back, trying to reach something there. The sound of its cry reverberates through Ryder's skull.

"Are you seeing this?" Sophie takes Ryder's free hand, her palm sweaty and warm. Of course she's seeing it. Either side of the creature's crooked, protruding spine are slash marks that gleam with a white-hot light. The creature roars again, a deep and guttural sound filled with fury and pain. Ryder blinks, wonders if she is hallucinating from blood loss. The monster is crumbling away. Flakes of its papery skin peel off its body. It's right arm dissolves into minuscule pieces that drop to the ground like confetti.

"Oh god." Christian whispers. Sophie makes a choked, gagging sound but doesn't let go of Ryder's hand.

Within seconds a pile of ash-like material is all that remains of the nightmare. The man holds his hand over the remnants. Despite the stillness of the afternoon, the particles lift up into the air and drift away. Vanishing. He turns then, and regards the small huddled group for a moment, before walking towards them. Marching, really. Steps sure and measured. His dark hair has loosened from the tie that held it at the nape of his neck. Long strands shadow his face. He is definitely tall, would probably challenge Christian's six foot four inches. His dark coat flutters around his calves, and its silver buckles glint in the dying light. Ryder takes note of the straps looped around the thighs of his cargo-style pants, the type meant to hold a weapon.

"What do we do?" Christian says. "Someone, tell me what we do here."

Even if this guy were to aim a gun or a laser, or whatever it is the aliens use, Ryder couldn't run. Her legs threaten to buckle any moment, and the fire raging in her shoulder is creeping down into her chest. Christian's embrace is the only thing keeping her upright. Sophie doesn't say a word but her grip on Ryder's hand tightens, her breathing short and shallow. The man draws closer. There is no mistaking the elthar now. But where Olessia's gauntlets were sleek and glove-like, the coverings on his hands are something more brutal. Crescent-shaped blades run the length of his middle and index finger, from knuckle to base of his nails. But with each step he takes, the weapons devolve, melting like heated wax into the darker material beneath them.

Sophie presses in against Ryder's side. "He just saved us, he's one of the good ones, right?"

"Saved us or killed White-eyes?" Talking is getting complicated, Ryder's lips don't quite form around the words. She focuses on the guy to fight off a rush of dizziness. Now he's closer she's not sure how old he is. Maybe it's the scowl on his face ageing him and the military air of his clothing. What is it with aliens and militaristic clothing? Well, there is Aresh. An exception to the rule. Ryder's thoughts scatter like a packet of dropped skittles.

CHAPTER 14

I T TAKES A SECOND TO register she is falling. Christian, distracted by the approach of the stranger, isn't holding her tight, and though Sophie holds her hand in a vice grip, she's not strong enough to stop Ryder slumping onto her knees. For the second time she hits the bitumen, and stones dig into already bruised skin. She takes a deep breath, and discovers it's a terrible idea. The rise of her ribcage tugs at the muscles around her collarbone, which shifts the skin around the puncture wound. She rocks back onto her haunches and into Sophie's arms. She cradles Ryder, telling her to breathe. Ryder grunts, wants to tell her it's a bad idea, but she's not certain her lips form any coherent words.

Someone kneels in front of them, and Ryder finds herself gazing up at the stranger. He's definitely no older than Lucas. But the two guys couldn't be more different. The one staring down at her right now has dark, heavy eyebrows curving over sea-water gray eyes, a flat nose flared at the nostrils, high sharp cheekbones and a square chin beneath pale skin. If he were human, she might guess Japanese or Korean. But he is not human. What he just did is giveaway enough, but the swirling gray in his irises leaves no doubt.

"Is the wound from the Placer?" he says. A deep voice, a little rough. Replying takes more effort than Ryder can muster, so she just stares. There are dark line markings beneath his lower eye lids, like smudges of war paint. The man leans in closer and Sophie edges them back.

"Wait, just-" Christian flutters his arms in a lack-lustre attempt to ward the guy away. Ryder doesn't begrudge him when he steps aside. There is something about this guy who stands over them, something other than the fact he isn't human, something other than the fact his mouth forms a heart shape when he closes it. She blinks, unsure where that random thought just came from. Ryder barely checks out guys when Sophie gives her no choice in the matter, let alone when she's half-conscious.

"She's hurt." Sophie hesitates. "She's bleeding."

"And I asked you if the Placer is responsible for the injury." From where Ryder slumps on the ground he seems like a giant. Or a Gothic angel, she can't decide. Skittle brain is getting worse. "The longer you take to confirm it, the more opportunity the toxins have to kill her."

"Kill her?" Sophie gasps. "What are you talking about?"

"Placers have venom in their claws. She has been poisoned." He delivers the message in a flat, disinterested way but there is an energy about him, a coiled tension. Ryder swallows, her throat tight. She wants to ask him to help her. Wants to tell him she doesn't feel good, at all. But when she opens her mouth, it's a cross between a hiss and a sigh that escapes her. The stranger waves Christian aside and this time he doesn't protest. The guy kneels in front of her, takes something from a narrow pocket at his right hip. "Jarran stones should neutralise the toxin."

"Should?" Christian says.

"I don't believe they have been used on your kind before."

The man holds two oval stones, each no bigger than ten cent pieces, both smooth with pearly lusters. Ryder watches his fingers move towards her, feels them brush against the side of her neck. He slips her jacket off her shoulder, and then eases down the sodden material of her t-shirt before pressing a stone into the curve between her neck and shoulder.

The relief is instant. Heaven. Ryder sighs, her eyes flicker closed, and she slumps forward.

"Ryder?"

Ryder squeezes Sophie's hand. "Fine." One word, but it's a big improvement on hissing.

And she's more than fine. She's warm and gooey, like that moment after a massage when you're half-asleep and every muscle is loosened. No pain, not even a trance of discomfort, just a perfect little cloud of dreamy contentment. Someone takes her hand, their fingers soft against her wrist. She opens her eyes, and he is there. Right there. If she could remember how to lift her hand she would touch his face. That hard but beautiful face with its strange markings. Those storm-cloud gray eyes. Her gaze drifts down to the where the v-line of his shirt exposes the skin at the base of his slender neck. If she could work out how to lift her arms it would take no effort to touch him. His skin is marble smooth, and near translucent pale, just like Olessia, but he's definitely no relative. Not unless her family adopted a K-Pop band member recently. He leans closer, and she breathes in the faintest hint of a spice she can't put her finger on. She's considering cardamom or sage when all at once he scoops her up in his arms. He gets to his feet with barely a waver, like she's a bag of candy floss. At that moment, she might as well be.

"You have pretty eyes." Ryder rests her head against his shoulder. His shirt is rough and cold against her cheek, some kind of thin layered metal overlays the fabric beneath. The elthar sits in two thick cuffs around his wrists.

"Where are you taking her?" Sophie's voice is faint and distant. And he doesn't answer. Ryder presses her ear against his chest, listening to his breathing. And the uneven rhythm of his heart; fast, fast, fast, slow, slow, fast, slow.

"That's a nice sound, you could dance to it." Her words come out slippery and impossible to hold onto, and she has no clue why she is saying them at all. Her chin is damp, she's pretty sure she's drooling. But Ryder doesn't care, one little bit. He carries her to one of the two cars in the parking lot; a shiny royal blue Mercedes. He sits her up against the front wheel. Ryder reaches out to touch the polished door. "So shiney."

"What's wrong with her? What have you done?" Sophie puts her hand on the guy's shoulder. If looks could kill, she'd be in trouble right now. He's eyeing her the way Christian's dad did when he first saw his son's eyebrow piercing. Ryder wants to clap Sophie's bravado, but she has no idea how to make her arms move. She giggles instead. Ryder never giggles. Laughs, even snorts, but giggling? Nope. Still here it is, high and childish. Okay, the floaty cloud is taking her way too high now. She wants to get down. Her calf muscles seize with a cramp, a deep ache that travels up her legs and spills through her torso. She groans through clenched teeth.

"Stay calm. You are fine." The stranger is back, close and real and certain. "The Jarran stones are breaking down the toxin, but it may be uncomfortable. Keep breathing. Focus on something."

He is the closest something. And his eyes make for the perfect distraction from the sharp twinges moving through her body. The colour in his irises swirls faster, moving through all the hues of the grayscale; stormcloud, gunmetal, a deeper charcoal. Ryder's thoughts are clearing, her puffy cloud of oblivion fading. The ground is solid beneath her again. Her teeth chatter with the shivers rushing through her, but the spasms ease. She lets out a long sigh.

"No more pain?" he asks.

Ryder shakes her head. The achiness is still there, but her nerves endings don't burn like hot coals anymore. "No more pain."

His eyes settle into a smoke-ash gray. She may be reading it wrong, chances are she's not seeing straight right now, but it seems to Ryder that a tension left his face, as though he wasn't convinced the stones would work. Her belly churns with the thought, and the gurgle is embarrassingly loud.

"Ryder, can you hear us? How are you feeling?" Christian stands behind the guy, his face twisted with concern. She's never seen him so afraid.

"Doing okay." She smiles at her friend, before focusing on

the stranger. "Did Olessia send you? She knew that thing was here, she warned me."

He leans back, an unreadable expression crossing his face. "Olessia did not send me no, I was directed by another. What do you mean she warned you?"

Ryder taps her temple with her index finger, her movements still laboured. "I heard her-"

"You? You heard her?" A lift of his dark eyebrows and a hint of a smirk weave a knot of warm indignation in Ryder's chest.

"Yes. I heard her. Who are you exactly?"

"That is no concern of yours."

"I'd say it's a pretty huge conce-" Ryder shifts onto her knees, hesitating as the world spins. She reaches for the side-view mirror. The pain might be gone, but she's not sure how steady she'll be on her feet. He watches her, with a cool, blank expression, stepping aside when Sophie moves in to help.

"Okey dokey. Everyone's a little stressed out." Sophie makes sure Ryder isn't about to topple over before she continues. "Back to basics. My name is Sophie." She holds out her hand. "What is yours?"

He stares at her hand like she offered him a piece of rotten fruit. The knot in Ryder's chest twists hard. The guy who probably just saved her life has an ugly attitude.

"I'm not going to bite," Sophie says, hand still extended.

Perhaps he doesn't like the insinuation he's afraid, because he takes Sophie's hand, gives it one strong shake and lets go. All the while his lips are pressed, eyes guarded.

"I am Sebastien."

"Hello, Sebastien." Sophie smiles, but he doesn't return the favour. "This is Christian and the girl you just saved is Ryder."

Ryder lifts her hand to touch the stone at the curve of her neck. She has no clue what this thing is or does, only that it's working. And it doesn't appear that Sebastien is going to explain any time soon. He doesn't so much as glance at either Ryder or Christian after Sophie's introduction. He turns his attention to the car, pulling a device from one of his deep pockets. It resembles a bottle-opener, but apparently it's great for opening doors. He brushes the device over the handle of the passenger door and it swings open. The car alarm trills out a high pitched warning, and everyone shrinks back, covering their ears against the onslaught of sound.

"Turn it off," Sebastien shouts at Christian. Evidently the device isn't so great at stopping tripped alarms.

"It's not my car." Christian shouts back, palms pressed to his ears.

Still uneasy on her feet, Ryder's not keen to leave the support of the car but the noise is deafening. Sebastien presses at the device, jabbing it towards the car with each selection. The piercing ring continues. She's considering trying to move away when a voice reaches through the din.

"Leave them be, Sebastien."

Ryder cranes her neck to follow the sound. Olessia rushes towards them, cobalt light shimmering around her hands. She touches down, an impact hard enough to make her rock on her feet before she rights herself. The movement shifts her coat back. She's still wearing the ridiculous pug shirt Sophie gave her at Jack's place. Olessia strides into the space between Sebastien and Ryder's huddled group, points a wand-like device at the car and the alarm falls silent.

"I knew she'd come back," Sophie whispers.

Ryder presses her fingertips to the Jarran stone, it's warm against her skin but a faint ache is building in her shoulder around the wound. Olessia knew that monster, the Placer, was following them but she didn't make it in time. He did. So, if she didn't send this guy, then who did?

"What have you done, Sebastien?" Olessia speaks in a low, dangerous way. She is barely chest-high to his lean form, but there is a steeliness about her that renders her the more imposing of the two. Ryder can't see her face, but she suspects it mirrors Sebastien's. Hard as nails.

"I've done what Aresh directed me to do," he says. "Saved these humans from the mess you've made."

"Saved them? From the attack you and Aresh arranged?" Olessia's anger chokes her. "They could have been killed."

The ghost woman arranged to try and kill them? Ryder rests her weight against the now-quiet car, frowning. Sebastien folds his arms across his chest and regards Olessia with eyes like gray daggers.

"Even if Aresh thought for one moment she might be able to use these people to bring you in, you know full well she would never allow any harm to befall them in the process. Don't insult the Laudine, any further than you have already." Sebastien's tone matches her venom. "No, this is what comes of your foolishness, Olessia. Did you truly think someone like you could just move through the Arlion with no repercussions?"

"How dare-"

"Spare me the tirade, I know it word for word. At what point did you delude yourself into thinking that running away was ever an option? Your refusal to acknowledge what you are capable of brings harm to others. Your stubbornness endangers people. Do you understand?"

"Be quiet." Olessia raises her palms towards him, like she's trying to fend off his words. "Say nothing more."

Watching the two of them trade angry words, Ryder brushes at her forehead. Sweat beads there and her cheeks are flushed and warm. A little disconcerting, but she's not about to interrupt the conversation. Ryder tries to peel the Jarran stone off her skin, but it's stuck firm.

"I'll speak until you finally listen." Sebastien folds his arms.

With a defiant tilt of her chin, Olessia laughs, short and bitter. "And you'll lie to me as all the others do. If I find that the Claven or my father had anything to do with this attack, if they have tried to hurt these people to get to me and you knew of this, I will-"

"You'll do what, Olessia?" Sebastien steps close to her. If

she is trying to intimidate him it's not working. "What will the Laudess of Bax Un Tey do to her anointed guardian, tell me?"

There is a pause before she answers. The carpark seems impossibly quiet, not even a breeze to rustle the leaves. Ryder doesn't dare swallow, let alone make a sound. Beside her, Christian and Sophie stand perfectly still.

Olessia's shoulders slump before she gathers herself again. "Watch your tongue, Sebastien, you're going too far. I will not return."

An unhappy smile pulls at his lips. "Laudess, you have no choice. The Presider will never stop looking for you, and you've already endangered these people. Don't add any more casualties to your list. Don't do that to yourself." He breathes out and closes his eyes for a moment. Perhaps it's just the black markings beneath his eyes exaggerating the effect, but Sebastien seems exhausted. Bone deep tired. Ryder can't shake the sense this is an old and embittered argument. One he appears ready to give up on.

"Let me go, Sebastien." Low and menacing, Olessia's words are a fraction above a whisper.

He doesn't hesitate. "That is impossible. You know that as well as I do."

"You saw what happened at Vale Leven, you of all people should not demand this of me."

"Olessia, you are losing your focus, gather yourself." The sharpness drops from Sebastien's voice. "Focus on me."

There is a plea lacing his words, but Olessia wants none of it. She steps back when he reaches for her and lifts a hand to the base of her neck, circling it with her fingers. "Leave me alone, Sebastien. Just leave me-" Olessia snaps her mouth closed. For a moment it seems she might throw up. "Get them away, Sebastien. Now." Olessia's voice cracks with strain.

All at once she dodges around them with a speed that seems to take even Sebastien by surprise, a twist of confusion marring his smooth features. After a moment of hesitation he takes off after her, long legs eating up the distance between them. "Olessia." He calls. "Wait, this is senseless. Let me help you. Breathe. Control the Beckoning, it does not control you."

"Okay." Christian watches them, eyes wide. "What the hell is happening?"

Ryder lifts her shoulders in a shrug, and a rush of heat swamps her. Blood rushes up her neck, into her face, heating her cheeks and making her head spin again. She clutches at the Jarran stone. Either the stone is messing with her, or the toxin is. Something is gripping her body hard as a fever, weighing her down. When Sophie takes her hand, it's enough to make Ryder wince, her skin hyper-sensitive to the touch.

"Sit down, Ry." Sophie tries to lift her into the car's passenger seat, but Ryder shakes her head.

"Get it off me." She claws at the Jarran stone. "Sophie, I need to get this thing off me."

She barely notices when Christian guides her more forcefully into the car. Sophie's insistent questions go unanswered. Ryder has no clue what's wrong, only that the interior of the car is no better than a sauna. Strands of her hair stick to the sides of her face.

Ryder...take...here...

The message from Olessia is so faint Ryder barely registers the words. She waves back her friends and pushes herself to her feet.

Olessia? Are you okay?

She must be pulling a weird face, because Christian and Sophie both frown at her.

Take...them..,

Ryder catches sight of Sebastien and Olessia. They are on the far side of the carpark, right up near the tree line. Olessia is on her knees at the base of a soaring, reddish-brown paperbark tree, both arms wrapped around her midriff, her back to where Ryder stands. Sebastien crouches, not beside her, but a few paces back. But it's not the strange distance between them that catches Ryder's attention. It's what's happening to the trees behind them.

CHAPTER 15

"DO YOU SEE THAT? THOSE lights?" Ryder says.
Christian shakes his head. "Light? What do you mean?"
Ryder's eyes are wide open, and a rush of an old, familiar
unease mingles with the heat coursing through her body. She needs
them to see this. The colours drifting through the bush like wayward
mists are vibrant. Impossible to miss. Halos of light, most soft and
peachy, like the dying flare of a sunset. They flow around the trees,
silhouetting the trunks and the branches, radiating from each and
every leaf, pulsing like ethereal blood through veins.

"It's...I think it's...some kind of...aura." Ryder runs her
tongue over her top lip, and the tang of sweat hits her taste buds.

"You're seeing auras?" Sophie shades her eyes, like that will
help. "I can't see it. What does it look like?"

"It's kind of beautiful." Ryder whispers. Her skin aches with
the weight of the air around her, and her tongue sticks to the roof
of her dry mouth.

"I'm not seeing anything but that jerk freaking Olessia out,"
Christian says. "Man, you look like you're burning up, Ry. We
need to get you to a real doctor."

The way Christian and Sophie fall into the familiar pattern notches
up Ryder's unease; Sophie humours her every word, Christian makes
her doubt her own senses. They may not be seeing this, but she is.
Ryder squares her shoulders. This isn't a delusion, or a toxin-induced
hallucination. This is real. She's never been more certain.

"He's not freaking her out." Ryder shakes her head. "He's trying to help her…" The hairs on the back of her neck stand at attention when her gaze drifts to Sebastien. Encasing his lithe, long body is a thin edging of white light. His aura is faint, and if she didn't squint she might miss it amongst the dynamic glow coming from the trees. There it's as though the Aurora Borealis lights are trapped within the bush. Varying shades of sunset oranges and peaches, and licks of yellow flow around the leaves, circling the limbs and curling around the trunks. All at once the scene freezes. The flow just stops, the colours hang there, completely still. "Wait, hang on. Something's…"

The word dies on her dry lips. Changing, something is changing. The auras stream away from the trees, cascading like liquid rainbows towards the ground. They flow straight towards Olessia. She has her hands clamped either side of her head, rocking back and forth, seemingly oblivious to the maelstrom of colour swamping her. Sebastien reaches for her, something clutched in his outstretched hands, a circlet of gleaming gold. He is straining to reach her, but he doesn't do the simplest thing. He doesn't step any closer.

"Ryder, look." Sophie clutches her arm. "Look at the trees, the smaller ones. I think I see something."

There's no question what she's pointing to. The shrubs nearest to Olessia are wilting. The leaves were vibrant greens a moment ago, now they are mostly brittle and brown. The sunset glow still bleeds from them, but there is much less of it now. A branch snaps free from one of the larger eucalypts and tumbles to the ground in a whirl of dry leaves.

"Coriander," Ryder breathes. A droplet of sweat trails down her forehead.

Sebastien lunges forward, circlet raised in both hands. Olessia cries out and the sound is filled with pain. She throws one hand towards him. His body lifts off the ground and he is hurled through the air. The circlet slips from his grasp, hitting the bitumen with a metallic clang.

"Get behind the car." Christian drags Sophie and Ryder along with him, racing to the other side of the blue Mercedes.

Ryder kneels beside the front wheel, and leans forward, ignoring Christian's call to stay out of sight. The thin circlet has rolled halfway between Sebastien and the car. He lies on his side, his back to them, his outline trimmed with the mist-white aura Ryder saw earlier. Knocked out cold.

"No, Sebastien. No." Olessia's cry is a wretched sound, ripped from somewhere deep and painful. She tries and fails to get to her feet, managing only one faltering step before she is back on her knees. Behind her almost all trace of the sunburnt light is gone, just a few ribbons of it slide through the base of the trees, snaking their way towards her. The trees nearest to where she sits have lost all but a few of their leaves, the rest lie crisp and brown on the ground around her.

"Do we help them? Ry, what do we do?" Sophie's fingernails dig into Ryder's wrist, threatening to pierce the skin. A glance down and Ryder stops dead at the sight of the dust-rose sheen emanating from Sophie's skin. Her aura. Ryder's frightened gaze darts to Christian. His face is flushed with panic, waiting for her to answer Sophie's question, but Ryder can't force a word past her lips. The same dusty-rose sheen silhouettes Christian. Ryder fights to keep the fear from her face.

First the herbs on Jack's windowsill, now the scrub-land. Whatever this is, whatever Olessia is doing, it's killing things. What did Sebastien call it? The Beckoning? Ryder wipes a distracted hand across her cheeks. The heat and humidity in the air presses in on her. *Take them*, Olessia said. The thought was distorted and unfinished, but Ryder has no doubt about it now. Take them away. Far away. Sebastien lies still on the ground. She's so distracted by her own thoughts it takes a second to process what she's seeing. Sebastien's faint white aura is lifting, drawing out from his body and crawling over the bitumen like an early morning mist. Streaming as all the others did, towards Olessia.

"Oh my god." Ryder cries, her voice hoarse with horror. "Everyone, move."

"And just leave them?" Sophie says. "But he's hurt-"

More than hurt, he's dying. Ryder can barely breathe with the thought. The guy who just saved her life is losing his. And there is nothing she can do. She presses at her chest, trying to get some air in.

Christian is wide-eyed. "I don't understand what's-"

"Just get up." Ryder snaps. She grabs a handful of Sophie's jumper and hauls her friend to her feet, rough and unapologetic. Sophie can complain about pulled threads and ruined stitching later. Then, Ryder sees it. The dusty-rose sheen straining away from Sophie's hands. Pulling away like steam rising into an exhaust fan. The shock of it sways Ryder on her feet, and she steps away from her friends.

"Ryder?" Christian still crouches on the ground, confusion and fear wrinkling his face.

A whip-like crack pierces the air, and one of the thicker branches of the eucalyptus snaps free, taking out a few finer branches on its way. Dust and debris plume into the air when the cluster of dead branches hit the ground. Olessia rocks forward, doubled over, her head nearly buried in her lap. She's cocooned in luminescent, writhing colour. A flash of light draws Ryder's attention. The circlet lies in a no-man's land between Sebastien's prone body and the car they shelter behind. Its surface glints, reflecting the illuminated air.

"Go, get out of here." She throws the order at Sophie and Christian like a drill sergeant, and it's enough to make Sophie jump. Ryder doesn't have time to see if they follow instructions. She whirls around and races for the circlet. Her boots thump out an uneven rhythm as she leans down and grabs it and then drops down beside Sebastien, wincing at the impact on her already bruised knees. Her hair sticks to her damp face like it's glued there.

"Sebastien." She grabs his shoulders and rolls him onto his back. "Tell me what to do. Hey, come on."

Sebastien's eyes are closed. His face is a dull gray, lips blue, bare arms cold against her hands. She forces the image of Sophie and Christian this way, out of her head. Think straight now, freak out later. The ghostly haze of his aura pools around her legs. She needs to do something, or she is going to lose him. Ryder loops her arms in beneath his armpits, trying to get some kind of grip so she can lift him and drag him away. But her energy is so sapped by the humidity, the attempt leaves her breathless. She grits her teeth, tries again. His body shifts a bare inch or so before her shoulder screams. Hell of a time for the alien painkiller to wear off.

"Please, you need to wake up. You need to help me." Ryder coughs with the effort of speaking, her own breathing shallow. Her skin is clear, no sign of an aura at all, but the weight of the humid air is growing, crushing her. She is considering slapping Sebastien's face, like they do in movies, when he stirs. His eyes open a fraction, revealing dish-water gray irises. "The senlier will contain it," he whispers.

"Senlier?" Ryder holds up the circlet. "Do you mean this?"

His eyes roll back in his head, and he goes limp in her arms. Ryder coughs again, trying to get a lungful of air. She needs to do something right now, or she isn't sure she'll be able to get to her feet again. Lowering Sebastien's head gently to the ground, Ryder pushes herself to her feet. No easy task when the air itself is a lead blanket. At least his aura has stopped flowing towards Olessia. That has to be a good sign. Her legs take a moment to get into rhythm and threaten to buckle. A wave of dizziness tips her forward and the ground rushes up. She squeezes her eyes closed, bracing for impact. Instead, her body jerks backwards, a pressure hard against her torso forcing her back on her feet. Breathing hard, Ryder glances around her, expecting to see someone there. She's alone. The only one standing.

Rushing to Olessia's side, Ryder thrusts the circlet towards her. "Here, take this." The swirl of brightly coloured auras around Olessia sweeps outward under the force of Ryder's arrival. Olessia's gaze lifts. The violet of her irises is bleeding out into the white of her eyes, and it takes Ryder some effort not to flinch. Pain etches lines into Olessia's marble skin, and the faint trace of veins is visible beneath her skin. Olessia reaches for the circlet in a slow, agonised movement that forces a groan past her lips. Her fingertips touch the tiny crown, the senlier, and a blinding white light fills the air. A blast of heat slams against Ryder, throwing her backwards. For the second time that day she is flat on her back in the middle of Bridgewater station's carpark. There is movement, and voices, around her, but her eyelids flutter against a sea of snow-storm white. Some of the voices are familiar, Sophie and Christian. And another. Ryder tries to blink through the splotches filling her vision. She can't be hearing right.

"Ryder? Ryder can you hear me?"

This must be concussion; she felt the smack of her head against the bitumen when Olessia sent her flying. Because that can't be Lucas she's hearing. Distant, like he's on the other side of a vast canyon, calling to her. She wants to answer him but he's getting further away. Everything is. Fading. Darkening.

CHAPTER 16

Wake now, little one. You must wake now.

THE WHISPERS DART AROUND HER, tickling the side of Ryder's neck, soft as butterfly wings. She smiles. Darkness cloaks her, warm and inviting. But not too warm, the oppressive heat is gone, she is light and comfortable. Like she stepped out of a soothing bath that's wiped away all the pain and every ache. Best of all, the fear's evaporated. Chased away by the ones protecting her. Watching over her. She rocks her head from side to side, and it sends gentle, minuscule waves rippling through the darkness around her. Shapes of the purest, deepest black shift in and out of focus around her. Kaleidescope patterns, ever changing.

Wake now.

The whispers are more urgent. Ryder sighs. "Just a little longer."

"Ryder? Are you awake?"

The question spills into her midnight world, loud and obtrusive. A low growl accompanies it. Ryder opens her eyes. The light rushes back in, and so do the memories. Olessia. The senlier. The dusty-rose auras. Sebastien dying in her arms.

Ryder jerks upright and immediately regrets it. Something presses on the wound at her shoulder, sending a rush of pain across her chest. A seatbelt. She's in a car. The low growl is the sound of the engine; an engine being pushed hard. The car travels at speed down a double-lane road in an area she doesn't recognise. But she recognises the driver. The street lights outside flash against his face.

Ryder stares at him, wondering if she's still unconscious. And this is all still a crazy dream. The ache in her shoulder is kind of ruining the theory. "Lucas." Unable to think of anything else to say, she says it again. "Lucas."

"That's my name." He glances at her and grins, a familiar dimple forming in his cheek. "How's the head? How many fingers am I holding up?" He takes one hand off the wheel, holding up three fingers.

"Three." She frowns, rubbing at the bump on the back of her head. "Lucas what are you doing here? Where are the others?"

The car swings hard around a right-hand turn, and Ryder clutches at her armrest, her fingers digging into the padded leather. This is definitely not Lucas's car; with cracked vinyl, and food wrappers on the floor. Here it is all cream coloured leather, polished trims and the strong scent of expensive.

"They're safe. Sebastien has taken the others with him."

There's a moment of relief, hearing that he's alive, before Ryder's thoughts gallop ahead. "How do you know his name?"

"He told me."

She stops scanning the streets, trying to work out where they are, and pulls the seatbelt clear of her body so she can twist to face him. He really needs a shave, his auburn stubble even more noticeable now.

"You've just let Chris and Sophie go off with...Lucas, they aren't human."

"That's not a nice way to talk about your friends, Ry." He laughs, seemingly amused by his own joke.

"Shut up." Ryder shakes her head. "Listen to me. Olessia is....well I don't know exactly, but something bad happened back there. She's got some kind of power I think. She lost control though, nearly killed that guy. She wiped out a forest, Lucas."

She waits for the lop-sided, slightly-condescending grin.

Maybe even a pat on the head. He'll never believe her. Ryder braces. But neither comes. Lucas keeps his eyes on the road and his lips are a tight line of concentration. "The Beckoning, that thing she can do, it's called the Beckoning, apparently."

Ryder wishes his smile would appear, make this all go away. "So, I'm telling you that those people aren't human and you're not batting an eyelid?"

But Lucas's attention is elsewhere. There's a device lying on the dashboard, one her barely-focused eyes missed until now, some kind of fancy GPS. Ryder does a double-take, realising the device isn't *lying* on the dash at all. It just floats there, suspended above the leather. Projecting up from the horizontal surface is a 3-D road map, with incredible detail. It's taken from an aerial view, like the news helicopters doing the morning reports and it clearly shows a royal blue Mercedes travelling through the streets. When the miniaturised car on the dash turns right at the exact same time Lucas does, Ryder gasps.

"I can't believe you stole a car." Lucas is the guy who made her tell a shopkeeper she ate a plum in-store, when she was eight. She had to use her tooth-fairy money to pay for it. "Seriously, stop this car and tell me what the hell is going on."

But he doesn't slow, not even when the light ahead turns orange and they are too far away to have a hope of crossing the intersection before it hits red. Running the red light, Lucas's thoughtful expression doesn't change, and she wonders if he noticed at all. "We can't stop yet," he says when the thankfully-empty intersection is behind them. "When things calm down a little, we need to chat."

"Chat? Chat? About what? The fact you've never mentioned you know someone like Olessia?" Her palms are damp, the sweating she thought had stopped, has returned.

"I don't *know* Olessia, but I know of her."

Ryder clings to her seatbelt, holding so tight her stubby fingernails bite into her palm. "She's not exactly from around here. I know for sure you didn't run into her at a cycling meet."

"I know she's not from around her, Ry." His focus shifts between the road, the rear-vision mirror and the device on the dash, in quick succession.

"She's an alien. So is the guy you just sent Chris and Sophie off with. And you're telling me you *know* that."

"I know that," he says.

Ryder stares at her friend. Her brother. She knows every freckle on this guy's face, knows the story behind the scar on his left hand. Knows how much he hates pineapple and loves anchovies. He can't *know* about aliens. Ryder flinches against the thoughts crowding in on her. She turns from him and stares outside. The low purr of the car fills the cabin. Her shoulder aches, her whole body aches. Even her scalp aches. Sophie's braid feels way too tight. Lucas, the guy who'd taught her to ride a bike, the guy whose mum took Ryder to buy her first bra, is sitting there telling her the whole extra-terrestrial, extra dimensional, whatever extra-thing it is, isn't news to him.

She presses her forehead up against the window, the coolness of the glass soothing.

"Ryder?" He tries to reach for her, and she slaps his hand away. "Hey look, it's all going to be okay. Chris and Soph are safe, I promise you. There's no way I would have let them go if I thought they weren't safe. Come on, you know I wouldn't. I want to get you to a doctor. You might have concussion or something and that gash on your shoulder looks nasty. A friend of mine from Uni, his brother is final year medicine. We've hung out a few times, good guy. He'll take a look at you, not ask too many questions."

"Not ask too many questions?" Ryder glares at his reflection in the window, in no mood to look straight at him. "If you think I'm going to do the same thing Lucas, you've got another thing coming."

He laughs, in that lilting, pitchy way he does. "Oh believe me, I would assume you had bleeding on the brain if you didn't ask me a tonne of questions."

"It's not funny. None of this is funny."

Not even remotely. She's discovering it's possible to feel like you're falling, even when you're sitting down. The moment Lucas didn't look her in the eye and answer her question, her stomach lurched like she was headed down a dip on a rollercoaster. It hasn't let up.

"Sorry Ry, I know it's not. This is my dumb way of trying to lighten the mood. When I got there and saw you lying on the ground like that…it just…it freaked me out. I'm just glad you are all okay."

Ryder rests her head against the seat. Okay? Depends on the definition. Her eyes are dry and sore. Parts of her body she never knew existed are aching, like she's run some obstacle course for a week. It's tempting to let the hum of the engine and the contoured comfort of the seat lull her off to sleep. Maybe then she could go back to that inky shadow world, where whispers flitted around her like watchful guardians. Thing seemed so much simpler there. Ryder rubs at her eyes with the heels of her palms. No more dreaming. She calls herself a ghost hunter, but when the spooks aren't in any of her books she wants to run and hide in her dreams? It's pathetic. Ryder shifts in her seat, adjusting her jacket, pushing back the loose strands of hair around her face, pulling herself together.

"Where is he taking them?" she says. "That Sebastien guy, where is he taking Sophie and Chris?"

Up ahead a set of lights turn red. It seems like Lucas is going to ignore that fact. Again. He doesn't brake till he's right on the white lines of the intersection.

"Well, that part I'm not sure of, and that's the honest truth." Lucas taps his fingers on the wheel.

"Are you kidding me? You don't know where a couple of aliens have just taken my best friends?" She's just assuming Olessia is there too. Sebastien seemed pretty intent on keeping her in sight.

"Not yet." Lucas throws the car into gear and the wheels

squeal with the thrust of the car. "They will let me know when they've found somewhere safe to base, and work out what the heck to do. This isn't exactly part of any plan. The whole thing with the Laudess-"

Ryder stiffens at the familiar word. "Sebastien called her that too. He called Olessia the Laudess." She tugs the seatbelt away from where it presses too hard against her shoulder. "It's a title or something, right? Is she like a royal or something?"

"Not quite."

"I swear Lucas, if you don't tell me something solid right now I'm going to lose it completely." All this time he'd watched her playing around with the paranormal and he hadn't said a word. It boiled her blood just thinking about it.

"Hey, hey calm down. You need to take it easy, please, Ryder." Lucas glances at her, green eyes narrow with concern. "Look she's not going to turn up in a ballgown any time soon. But she is next in line to the throne, if you want to think of it that way. The Beckoning, that thing you saw her do, it's some kind of genetic mutation, from what I understand. It's incredibly strong in her family bloodline, they've ruled the place for ages, and her dad took it to another level. From what I can gather, it's manifested even more powerfully in Olessia. Which makes her the next to rule. But we're talking more like sergeants and generals, than prince and princesses."

"Her dad is the Presider." The one Sebastien said would never stop searching for her, the one Olessia blamed for the Placer attack. Olessia has run away from home. From a father who's sending monsters to hunt her down.

"I'm surprised you have any questions left," he says. "You seem to know a lot already."

Lucas rubs his knuckles hard against the top of her head. Ryder jerks away, and her head smacks against the closed window. "Ouch. Whoever you are, you're definitely still annoying." She runs her fingers over the bumps and divots of her braid. Despite everything that's happened, Sophie's handiwork has barely loosened. "And apparently you're all grand theft auto pro now too. Petra would be so proud."

"I didn't steal it." But he does sound guilty about it. "I'm borrowing it. It was better that Sebastien used my car, less chance of getting pulled over."

"He knows how to drive?" She raises her eyebrows. "Sebastien?"

"A car? No, Sebastien has no clue. But he was pretty insistent he could handle it. The guy's got a chip on those wide shoulders, that's for sure. But I said no. Christian has his learners, and he agreed to drive."

"Oh my god. Chris has driven maybe a handful of times. Learners are supposed to have adults in the car-" It's completely lame to be spouting road rules, but at least those rules make sense. Unlike the rest of this day. And possibly most of Ryder's life.

"Sebastien's an adult." Lucas shrugs.

"A human adult, Lucas. Pretty sure the government means a *human* adult needs to be in the car."

Lucas bites on his lip and says nothing, eyes fixed on the road. They pass a road sign that declares they're eight kilometres from Claremont, a suburb in towards the Hobart CBD. Ryder doesn't know the area all that well, her house is over the other side of town, but she's discovering Claremont has a lot of industrial parks. They've already passed a couple of timber yards and some other warehouses. Now they fly past a row of take-away food shops, the type that do burgers to-die-for, and fish coated in ridiculous layers of batter. The shops are all closed up on a Sunday though, and there's barely any cars on the road, which is a handy thing considering the speed Lucas is driving. She glances at the device on the dashboard. Little symbols pop up randomly and hover over various points on the map. The symbols are familiar, vaguely Japanese in appearance, but with extra dashes and curves that set them apart. Just like the symbol on Olessia's elthar.

"Please tell me you haven't always had this." Ryder jabs a finger towards the device.

"Sebastien gave it to me. It's called a Tyius, I think he said. So no, I haven't always had it."

It occurs to her that she's never had to wonder if Lucas is a good liar or not. A little knot forms in her chest, and tightens. Ryder watches an elderly couple walk along the sidewalk with their white fur-ball of a dog. The first people she's seen out and about. Dog walking would be nice. Nice and normal. "But you know how to read what it's saying, in some language that is clearly not English."

Lucas slips away from her with every long second it takes him to reply. The trace of a smile leaves his face. He shifts in his seat, running his hands up and down the curve of the steering wheel.

"Lucas, what…are you…who are you?" Ryder's tongue can barely form the words. What is she even thinking? He's nothing like Sebastien or Olessia. The colour in his eyes doesn't swirl like mini-whirlpools.

He grimaces and a muscle in his jaw flexes. He is supposed to laugh at her, tell her she's overtired. He could tell her she's lost the plot right now and she'd take it. It wouldn't be as isolating as his silence.

"Ryder, I'm going to-"

Whatever he is going to do, or say, or promise, is interrupted by a jingle of bell-like sounds coming from the GPS. The Tyius isn't happy. A mechanical but vaguely feminine voice utters a couple of words in a language as unrecognisable as the letters that stream alongside the right of the image. The aerial view from the Tyius tilts hard right, crossing over to the next block and a sprawling roundabout there. A car is hurtling down one of the roads towards it. The Tyius zooms in on the vehicle. The silver sedan appears harmless enough. The Tyius blurts out a string of nonsensical words and Lucas's expression hardens.

"What's happening?" Ryder is on the edge of her seat, as close as the seat belt will let her get to the display.

"We might have some company."

Lucas veers off the road, heading down a narrow roadway behind a cluster of shops. The road is full of potholes and bumps, and though Lucas is trying to steer clear of them, every now and then he fails. Each thump sends a stab of pain through Ryder's injured shoulder. She grits her teeth so hard she is pretty sure they'll crack if he doesn't let up soon. They reach the end of the alley, and he swings a hard right. The Tyius mutters more incoherent things and Lucas responds by accelerating. Up ahead a street sign reads 'Patterson Industrial Estate, 2 Kms'.

"Can you elaborate on the company?" Ryder slides back into her seat, watching the speedometer climb. "Lucas, do you think maybe we should slow down?"

Up ahead, warehouses and factories loom on either side of the road. Most of their gates are all locked up tight for the long holiday weekend. Security lighting, brighter than bright, illuminates some of the yards. Further ahead off to the right, there is a flicker of movement in one of the yards. Ricchon Boat Builders, according to the signage. And the gates are open. Ryder leans forward, trying to work out what she's seeing.

"Lucas, stop!" He slams on the brakes, and Ryder braces her hands on the dashboard. "There."

A silver sedan pulls out from behind the half-built hull of a catamaran, and shoots out onto the main road. Lucas curses. In plain old English.

"Hold on, Ry." He throws the car into reverse and hits the accelerator.

CHAPTER 17

L UCAS PUSHES THE CAR INTO a tight turn. The back right wheel nudges the curb and he struggles for a moment to keep them from spinning a full three-sixty. Lucas doesn't utter a sound as he brings the Mercedes back under control.

"Who are they?" Ryder twists to peer out the narrow back window, but the sedan has its high-beams on and she has to turn away.

"It's not anyone we want to stop and chat with." He frowns, wrestling the car around a bend. The Tyius is oddly silent. "This doesn't make sense. The Tyius should have been all over them. They can't have worked out how to block it. Hold on, this will get a little rough."

"They?" Ryder pushes into the snug hold of the contoured seat. "They who? The police?"

Lucas hurtles them into a sharp right, the tyres squealing in protest at the sudden change in direction. Ryder catches a brief glimpse of a second car, a white SUV, pulling out of a side-street. Lucas sees it too, and judging by the swear words that leave him, he isn't happy about it. Lucas isn't big on cursing. Nor does he usually drive like a deranged rally car driver. Whatever is happening, it's not anything good. But there are no sirens, no sign of any police lights or markings on the cars pursuing them.

"Where did you learn to drive like this?"

He doesn't answer, steering them into a laneway barely wide enough for the vehicle. Ryder squeezes her eyes shut. When there is no sound of metal grating on brick, she opens one eye. The car is desperately close to the looming walls of the warehouses either side of the laneway. If Lucas moves the steering wheel just fractionally, they'll be losing expensive blue paint and side mirrors against the metal and brickwork. But he doesn't stray an inch too far. They shoot clear of the laneway and out onto a wider road.

"Do you have any idea where you are going?" Ryder's voice is high and tight.

"Yup, I know this area. Did work experience at a vet hospital not far from here." Lucas fights with the wheel. The engine is like an impatient lion beneath the hood. "Okay, we're going to have to scrap that doctor's visit. Sorry Ryder. You doing all right?"

She's managed not to throw up, that counts for something. "Peachy."

The roads are in poor shape. The Mercedes speeds along a stretch of undulated bitumen and the vibrations try to shake Ryder's teeth loose from her gums. But they are almost clear of the estate. A sign up ahead advises the distance to the nearest entry onto the Brooker Highway. That's a stretch of road she does recognise. It's the main thoroughfare from the bottom of Tasmania to the very top of the island.

"Man." Lucas slams his hand against the steering wheel, his gaze darting to the rear vision mirror. "Give us a break."

"They're still on us?"

They are not words she expected to be saying today. Or ever, really.

"Yup. We'll lose them on the freeway. This little baby is made for the open road. So long as they don't call in the cops, we should be good."

Ryder's fingers ache from clenching the armrest. She leans forward, using the side-mirror to check out the road behind them. The cars are still following, a good way back, but there is no traffic to lose them in. They leave the estate and the road widens into double lanes each way. Car chases seem a lot more fun in the movies. She can taste something acidic at the back of her throat. It might have been a bit preemptive, congratulating herself for not throwing up.

"Okay." She focuses on something else. "So they aren't the police following us? You really need to tell me who they are. Tell me something, Lucas, or I'm going to hurl all over this perfectly lovely stolen car."

Maybe he hears the note of panic in her voice, because his answer comes quickly. "I'm pretty sure it is C-21."

"Right. Aside from the C being for crazy, what does that tell me?"

Lucas laughs. Amid the chaos the sound is oddly comforting. He steers them past a semi-trailer. It is lit up like a Christmas tree with orange and red lights.

"You've heard of Area 51 in America?"

Ryder nods. Of course. She'd come across it a few times when searching Google for 'unexplained phenomena'. Area 51: top secret military base in the middle of the Nevada desert that supposedly holds the bodies of aliens and their ship. All sorts of weird experiments happen there. It's a major UFO hot spot. She used to ask Jack if the Harlow Institute had any good stories like that. He'd laugh and say the American's love a good conspiracy story. That it was silly nonsense. Yeah, right.

"Well, the USA doesn't have a monopoly on those kinds of places," Lucas says, touching the air above the Tyius. A blue icon appears, like a bullseye but with more circles. "We've got one here too and it's called C-21. You'll never get anyone to admit it exists, of course. The government doesn't want anyone to know they are spending millions of tax dollars trying to keep track of all things not quite human. But I know it's headed by a guy called Benjamin Cooper. And he takes his job very seriously."

Up ahead the entrance to the Brooker Highway curves off

to the right. The interior of the car is bright with the lights of the semi-trailer behind them. The truck driver flicks on their indicator, headed for the freeway as well.

"Hang on." Lucas gives Ryder no time to do any such thing. He slams down on the brakes and the fancy sports car does what it's supposed to do. It stops dead. Ryder braces her hands against the roof, eyes fixed on the side-mirrors, as the massive truck bears down on them. The driver hits the airbrakes in a squealing, wheezing burst of sound, and a horn blasts out. The rig is so close Ryder can make out the horrified expression on the driver's face, a middle-aged woman. The huge trailer she's towing swings out, its tail end scraping at the concrete barriers along the roadside. White smoke billows from the dragging tyres and the waft of burning rubber fills the car. Lucas floors it again, leaving the jack-knifed truck behind. The driver jumps out of the cabin, shouting and waving a fist with a none-too-pleased finger raised.

"That should slow them down for a bit." Lucas grins. "Impressive, huh?"

"I'm not sure that's what the truck driver is calling it." She swallows hard. But he's right, it will slow them down. The SUV and the sedan are stuck behind a truck-sized road-block. "Warn me next time."

The Brooker Highway opens up in front of them, four lanes of road stretching north, away from Hobart. There is a smattering of traffic here. Everyone heading off to whatever normal Sunday evening activity it is they're bound for; out for dinner, visiting friends, going to the movies, heading off to training. Definitely not breaking laws, and causing accidents in a stolen car, while being chased by super-secret government agents. Ryder presses her fingertips to her temples.

"How you feeling?" Lucas says. "You doing okay?"

"Stop asking me that."

"Okay... It's just-"

She lifts a hand, palm facing him. "Are you sure it's not the car? I mean this car is stolen, Lucas. And you're driving like a maniac. They were probably undercover police cars."

Lucas turns back to the road. "I hardly think I was driving like a maniac. Professional, maybe. Maniac, no."

"Lucas!"

"The police don't have the equipment to block the Tyius, Ry. Whoever it is managed to stay undetected -" He points to the floating device "-it's not the police. Trust me. But I don't get how C-21 locked onto us. I mean we're miles away from the car park, that's where the main energy signature would have come from." He peers over at her, green eyes narrowed.

"What?" Ryder shrinks back. "Why the weird look?"

"Dunno, seriously, I don't know why half of this is happening. But I'm thinking, maybe, with you guys and Olessia back there, maybe some of the residual energy from the Beckoning is stuck to you somehow?" He rubs at the crown of his head. "Maybe that's what they are following. I don't know."

"Stuck to me?" Ryder resists the urge to rub at her arms, to flick off whatever it is that might be clinging to her.

"Sebastien said you'd done something really stupid, that you got too close to Olessia, that she nearly killed you." Lucas runs his tongue over his lower lip. "I dunno, could that have been enough to mark you or something?"

Ryder sits in silence. The carpark makes her skin crawl to think about. Not just because she witnessed Olessia syphon the life out of everything around her, but because Sebastien is wrong. Olessia didn't even hurt her. The Beckoning wreaked havoc on every living thing. Except Ryder. The girl with no aura. Now she does rub at her arms, trying to wipe down the goosebumps there. It's too much to deal with right now. Lucas won't be getting anything but a dismissive shrug from her. He's still talking, oblivious to her train of thought. So, not a mind reader, good to know. But he's something. A liar. And definitely a part of this. Ryder takes a breath to steel herself.

"Hey you're the one with alien buddies, don't ask me," she says. "But even if I was, like, marked, how can these C-21 guys trace it?"

Lucas scratches at the stubble on his chin. "It's not exactly the first time people like Olessia and Sebastien have been here. It was a long time ago but some tech got left behind. C-21 got a hold of it and they've obviously been working on reverse engineering. But I don't think anyone realised how far along Cooper was with that." His voice trails off, his focus drifting somewhere Ryder can't follow.

The highway on both sides is practically empty, and night has fallen. The lights of a single car are visible up ahead, two lonely dots of red on the darkened road. Ryder presses her hand to her upper arm, trying to relieve the ache that fans across her shoulder.

"The Jarran stones are probably wearing off," Lucas says it so easily, like they're just aspirin. She ignores him, leaning against the window and watching the road behind them in the side-mirror. Despite everything, she just wants to close her eyes and sleep.

The Tyius emits three sharp beeps, and all thoughts of sleeping are swept away. "Oh god, what now?" Ryder says.

Lucas doesn't reply, his fingers brushing over the screen, symbols appearing and disappearing at his touch. The Tyius screen splits in two, one half follows the path of their car. The other shows a very different angle, much higher in the sky.

"Lucas," she snaps. "I'm going to scream till your ears bleed if you don't tell me what's going on."

"Helicopter, they've got helicopters out." The car drifts across the line markings, Lucas's focus on the Tyius. "Elden Quarry's not far away. That'll work." He mutters the last part, Ryder barely catches it. But she recognises the name.

The abandoned quarry has been in the local news for years, most recently when a couple of idiot kids nearly got themselves killed, wandering around the site after dark. The place is full of rusting equipment and dilapidated buildings, not to mention a massive hole in the earth that no one can agree what to do with. The speedometer rises over the speed limit, and keeps climbing.

The Mercedes engine roars. The Tyius alerts them, yet again. A third viewpoint appears with 3-D images of the outside world. This time it is very definitely police cars, red and blue lights flashing.

"Is that-"

"Yes, police," Lucas says. "About a kilometre back down the highway. Man, Cooper is just not letting this one go. I'm betting the cars from the estate aren't far away either."

He taps a manic beat on the steering wheel, and chews on his bottom lip. Very little fazes the guy; rock climbing, exams, racing bikes, hanging with aliens and lying to his friends all his life. But now he's ruffled, and it's not helping her own nerves one bit.

"Okay, so what do we do?" Ryder gestures to the wide open road ahead. "What's with the quarry?"

"You'll see. Now just give me a minute to sort things out. You'll need to keep quiet."

She frowns. How is her keeping quiet going to help them avoid a police chase? He shifts back in his seat, his eyes on the road ahead. They pass a green sign which lists the upcoming cities along the Brooker Highway. She spots Devonport. Two hundred and twelve kilometres north. Ryder's never been there but she knows it well, the home of the Harlow Institute, Jack's old workplace.

Her tired eyes sting at the thought of her grandad. Did he get her message about Clarendon House? Ryder shifts in her seat, patting at her pockets, searching for her mobile phone, wincing when the movement twists her shoulder. But there's no sign of the phone.

Lucas jerks, like a shiver has taken him by surprise. It catches Ryder off-guard and she jumps. "You okay?" It's her turn to ask that overused question.

He nods. "Yep, just coordinating. Sebastien is going to meet us at the quarry, take you from there. I need to lead these guys away, and it's just getting too dangerous to have you in the car.'

"Sebastien?" She says it a little more forcefully than she intends.

"The guy from the carpark."

"I know who he is…" It annoys her, the way her chest tightens when she hears his name.

"The exit shouldn't be far off. Keep your eyes peeled."

But Ryder continues to stare at him. "How does he know where we are?"

Lucas taps his temple. "Just had a little chat with him."

"You can do that too?" She was wrong, he can do the mind stuff. That knot in her chest twists again. Lucas can read an alien alphabet, he's on a first name basis with a guy running a clandestine agency, and it's clearly not the first time he's sent out a telepathic hello. The guy sitting across from her is fast becoming a total stranger.

"Stop staring at me and start staring out there," Lucas says. "It's not a major exit. I doubt it's really an official exit at all."

Having something else to do, to think about, is what Ryder needs. Ryder turns but the Tyius display catches her eye. Before, it was clearly split into three different sections, different live views of different locations. Now the image is one single view.

"They're catching up to us," Lucas says.

She cranes her neck, peering up at the sky, searching for the giveaway blink of lights. Still nothing.

"Come on, come on." Lucas hunches over the wheel, scanning the roadside. "Where is the damn exit?"

Ryder squints. Trying to make sense of the blur of shadows at the side of the road. Then she sees it. Up ahead, the dirt of an unsealed road pales against the darkness. "Up there, is that it?"

"That's it."

Lucas hits the brakes, shifting into a low gear. But they are still moving too fast to make the turn. They slide sideways past the driveway entrance, and Lucas grunts, wrestling with the wheel. A puff of smoke from the squealing tyres sweeps past the windscreen. With the sideways shift of the car, Ryder has a clear line of sight back down the highway. The lights of the police cars dance over the lanes, bouncing off the white SUV that follows behind. The Mercedes hits the dirt road with a gravelly crunch, slamming through the near-useless chain that blocks off the access road. Lucas steers the car over the loose surface, a determined scowl pulling his brow low over his eyes. Bushland surrounds them, thick tree trunks lining the sides of the road. It is a wide road, having had to accommodate massive trucks and other machinery for years, but the heavy traffic has left it badly rutted. Lucas avoids one pothole only to drive them straight into another. The car becomes airborne, and then slams down onto the dirt. Ryder yelps as the impact jolts through her shoulder. The Jarran stones are definitely losing their effect.

"Hang in there, Ry," Lucas says. "I promise you the ride back with Sebastien will be a lot more comfortable."

"How exactly will he outrun a helicopter?"

"By having a faster one."

A lopsided wire gate blocks their way, with warning signs positioned across the criss-crossed mesh. Pressing down on the accelerator Lucas speeds towards it, and then through it, shattering the gate wide open.

"Oh the owners of this car won't be happy," Lucas grimaces.

The bonnet is a mess of scratched paintwork, and one corner of the windscreen has a spiderweb-like crack. They drive deeper into the quarry, passing a couple of rusted sheds that were once offices.

Beyond the reach of the headlights it is dark, pitch dark. The road is swallowed by the denseness of it, but Lucas doesn't reduce speed. Instead, he switches the headlights off and drives them headlong into an obsidian abyss. Even the glow from the Tyius seems to dim.

Ryder presses her hands against the dashboard, like that will help steer them somehow. "Lucas, seriously? What are you doing?"

"It's okay, I can…I've got this. We're good."

"Good?" Ryder opens her eyes wide, searching for some hint of the road ahead. Nothing, she may as well be wearing a blindfold. "There is no way you can see a thing. Tell me you're not just using that thing to navigate?"

Granted, that *thing*, the Tyius, is an incredibly detailed guide. It's just that the gaping pit of darkness it's showing, left of the road up ahead, is getting way too close. Ryder's breath catches. Navigating their way around the hundred foot drop essentially blind is insane. Alien tech or not, she wants to be able to see where she's going.

"Of course I can't see." There's an odd catch in Lucas's laughter. An irritation, or frustration, Ryder can't decipher which. He brushes his fingertips over the display, and a triangular symbol appears alongside the 3-D map. Veins of emerald light radiate out from the symbol, hitting the windscreen and spreading out across the glass, smooth as oil across a watery surface. When the crawl of emerald reaches the glass in front of Ryder, the world beyond illuminates and draws into crystal clear focus, the blindfold whipped away.

"Oh my god, that's awesome." Ryder is back on the edge of her seat, jaw dropped and eyes wide. It's a stunning sight. Not just any night vision; every rock, every piece of abandoned machinery is visible, bathed in the light of a dawning sun. A bulldozer looms out of the darkness to their right. They loop around behind it, following the curve of the road. The dirt track slopes upwards. The main gate is visible from this angle. It's a blaze of blue and red light.

"Lucas, they're here." Ryder slides back into her seat.

"They won't come in here, not without the helicopter to guide them. It's too dangerous." Lucas guides the car up the steepening incline. The road meanders to the left in a wide, sweeping arc, and Ryder finds herself staring down into the gaping maw of the quarry pit. She leans up close to the glass, squinting. Stones flick out from under the tyres, tiny bright specks that propel into the blackness, vanishing without trace. When her stomach ties itself into another unhelpful knot, Ryder sits back, fixing her eyes on the road ahead. Lucas shifts into a lower gear.

"Okay, pay attention," He pulls back the sleeve of his ash-gray sweatshirt. The silver band of his sports watch blinks with reflected light. It was a present from his mum, Petra, when he turned sixteen, and Ryder's pretty sure it hasn't been off his arm in the years since. "I can't go into details right now. But this watch, well it's not exactly a watch. It's made of something called elthar and-"

He must hear her intake of breath because he stops, darting glances between her and the road. "Ry?"

Lucas has had elthar all this time. The lies are stacking up so high her neck hurts. "I know what it is. I know what it can do." Ryder clutches the seat hard, the imprint of her fingertips will probably never leave the leather. "We went flying, at Jack's."

"Olessia took you flying?" He emphasises her name, incredulity bouncing off his words.

"She might have."

Now it's Lucas's turn for silence. He bites down on his bottom lip, working his jaw. Not usually the type to drop into a sullen mood easily, Ryder isn't sure if it's her or Olessia he's irate with.

"Okay, fine," he says, voice tight. "I guess that makes this a hell of a lot easier. Here give me your hand."

His tone, clipped and demanding, suggests it's not a time to protest. Ryder raises her hand, and he wraps his fingers around her wrist, glancing only briefly at her before his eyes are back on the road, guiding the car up the slippery road one-handed. His watch is ice-cold against the side of her wrist, different to the heat-pack warmth of Olessia's elthar. It begins to liquefy, the features melting into one smooth piece of metal and then softening further, moving like wax from his wrist to hers. Now the warmth begins to build, flowing down into her bones and chasing away the chill that settled there.

"So, when we reach the top you're going to jump out." Lucas makes it sound like she's just stopping to grab some milk from the store.

"Do I look like I've had stunt training?" Ryder tries to pull away, but Lucas's grip is rock solid. "Even if I didn't kill myself jumping from a speeding car, that's the quarry down there. Way down there."

He's not hurting her, not quite, but it's hardly comfortable. Her lower arm is now covered in a thin layer of elthar. As the dull platinum surface hardens, it's sheen lifts to something resembling polished silver. Lucas lets go of her hand, glancing away from the road.

"Give me your other hand. You won't be alone, I'll be guiding you."

She stares at him.

"Ryder, now… please," he snaps.

Seeing him this way, so rigid with tension, might be even more unsettling than what he's asking her to do. Lucas releases her left hand. Now she wears two gauntlets, and her body is warm with the energy. The heat is going some way to easing the aches lurking in her body. He nods to the Tyius, but he's barely glanced at her since the process began.

"We have about two minutes before the chopper is on us. You have to be out of the car before then. I'll slow down but I won't stop, they can't know that anyone left the car. You're going to jump out, and I'll control your direction until Sebastien catches you. Then I'll lead C-21 away. Okay?"

Ryder locks her gaze ahead trying to ignore the gaping maw of the quarry alongside them. "Okay? No. It is not okay. It's ridiculous."

"Ry, I am not going to let anything else happen to you." The irritation is gone, replaced with a gentler concern. "Please, trust me. You always have, don't stop now. Not now."

The road begins to level out as they reach the top of the quarry. Lucas leans forward, his face tight with concentration. Trust him? Sure, she's always trusted him. But with things like indoor rock-climbing, and learning to ride her bike. Not jumping out of moving cars with alien goo plastered to her arms. Take a breath Ryder. Breathing is good. Olessia hauled her out of a second storey window with this stuff, and Ryder lived to tell the tale. This is Lucas. She closes her eyes and knocks her head against the seat a couple of times until the lump there reminds her it's a bad idea.

"Will you be all right?" Ryder opens her eyes. She is actually considering doing this. Jump out of a moving car. Maybe the toxin from that thing has gotten to her.

"Oh, you do care." He throws her a lop-sided grin. The car slows. "Are you ready?"

"No." Her empty stomach heaves but she undoes her seatbelt. This isn't exactly learning to ride a bike, but she is a big kid now. Things get more complicated when you're a big kid. She grabs the door handle.

"I've got this okay, Ry? I've got you." He gives her shoulder a rushed but gentle squeeze. "I will never let you fall."

Too dry-mouthed to answer, Ryder nods.

"On my mark you're going to jump," Lucas says. "Ready. One, two, three."

The car door swings open before she even pulls the handle, and the elthar flares to powder-blue life. Over the throaty growl of the car comes the steady thump of the approaching helicopter. Her whole body heaves sideways, like she is a solid lump of metal being attracted to a magnet somewhere out in the darkness. It happens so quickly she doesn't have time to cry out. Suddenly she is clear of the car, flying out into the night like a giant, flailing ragdoll. Guided by unseen hands over the edge of the quarry, and down into the nothingness.

CHAPTER 18

THE SPEED OF HER FALL pushes her belly into her throat. Ryder tries to scream but her horror strangles the sound and makes it something gurgled and weird. He promised her. Lucas promised her she wouldn't fall and yet here she is. Ryder claws at the air, ready to try and let loose with another scream when the gauntlets suddenly tighten against her arms. Heat pulses up into her shoulders and down into her chest. Her fall begins to slow, like she's in a lift reaching its destination.

Lucas has her. Laughter, high and frantic, bursts from her lips. Ryder tilts forward, onto her belly, hanging skydiver-like in the air. Her legs and arms move at will, but it's all slow and heavy, like wading through syrup. And that's fine by her. It is a long way down to the quarry floor. Ryder holds up her arms, using the soft blue glow of the elthar to try and find the wall. It's closer than she expects, the jagged gray stone just beyond her fingertips. She stretches out her arms, trying not to think about the emptiness beneath her, trying to calm her breathing into something less ragged and gulping. Ryder's fingers brush against the rock just as a deep, pounding hum reverberates through the air.

She curls her fingers into fists, clutching her hands to her chest. The slow monotonous thud can be only one thing. The helicopter. She curses, her words bouncing off the rock around her. Ryder flails her arms, trying to shift herself back upright.

The way she is now, horizontal in the air, she's a floating bullseye. But her body won't do what she wants it to. Lucas is controlling things a little too well, she is locked in position. The air around her brightens, the searchlight creeping ever closer. Ryder coughs, tasting the gritty dust churned up by the aircraft. This is definitely not part of the plan. Lucas is supposed to be luring C-21, or whoever it is, away, but it sounds as though they are about to land on the cliff edge above her. The beat of the blades echoes off the quarry walls, a hundred drum beats out of time. She blinks against the debris being flung about in the churning air. What feels like peas from a pellet gun are finding her with pin point accuracy.

"Come on, come on," Ryder shouts into the chaos. If she can just edge closer to the rock face then maybe they'll miss her. She attempts to blot out her own rebellious thoughts, those telling her that if these guys are government, she has no hope. They have access to technology that would make her thermal imaging camera no more than a pathetic museum piece. She can't hide from them, they know how to find her.

They *are* finding her.

The searchlight crawls along the edge of the quarry above her, moving with steady purpose towards her none-too-hidden hiding spot. The bright light dips up and down the internal wall, crawling closer. She has nowhere to go. Ryder wriggles against her invisible bindings but her body barely responds. It's great that Lucas isn't letting her fall but she may as well be a mummy in bandages.

The light blazes down on her, bright as a miniature sun. It will be impossible for them not to see her. Except, it is impossible. She isn't in plain sight. There is a halo of dust around her. It clouds the air, a thick cocoon of tiny particles. Ryder should be choking, gagging on the heaviness of it but the air against her nostrils remains clear and breathable. Overhead, the sound of the helicopter is deafening. Its blades should be scattering the dust in all directions but the cloud doesn't move. Not a scrap of debris finds her. Her dust shield protects her, bouncing away the minute projectiles flung her way. The helicopter drifts higher into the sky and then moves beyond the edge of the quarry. The pounding beat fades. They didn't see her.

"You are safe."

Ryder starts at the sound of the voice. Voices. More than one person spoke the words. But they aren't in her head. Not this time. It comes from out there, in the darkness.

"Who's there?"

The blue glow suddenly flickers, like a flame straining to stay alight in a breeze. The pressure of the elthar around her arms eases. She kicks out and this time her legs respond. Now, when it doesn't matter anymore, she can tilt herself into an upright position. A smile brushes her lips just as her body begins to drop. Slow, painfully slow, but undeniable. The ground is moving up to meet her.

"Oh no,no,no-"

Ryder grabs for the rock, scraping the skin on her fingertips. The elthar is losing its hold on her. There is a tiny second to wonder what that means for Lucas before panic swamps her. Slow as the fall might be now, that could change any second. She must be at least six storeys high, it's a very long way to the quarry floor. Ryder claws at the wall, taking off more skin in the process, but ignoring the sting. Her fingers find a small jut in the rock and she clings to it, at the same time her left boot digs hard into a shallow crevice. A rush of air sweeps up from beneath her. Something is moving down there. And it's coming towards her. Ryder clings tight to the wall, bracing herself, before kicking into the shadows. Her foot strikes something solid.

A cry of pain rings out, followed by a string of words she can't understand, but is beginning to recognise.

"Will you stop it," a male voice says. "It's Sebastien."

"Sebastien?"

Ryder peers into the gloom. She can just make out a silhouette, drawing up towards her.

"Yes. But if you kick me again I will leave you to fend for yourself."

Now she can make out the very subtle gleam of his elthar. It shimmers over his chest and arms. Unlike Ryder's. The fading glow of her elthar sputters and then vanishes altogether. For a second she thinks maybe she can keep her precarious hold. She's never been more wrong. The elthar was supporting far more of her body weight than she realised. Now it's gone and she is a heavy mass of trembling body parts, one her fingers can't possibly support. She slips. But her scream barely hits the air before Sebastien grabs her. He wraps one arm around her waist and pulls her hard against his side.

"Be quiet," Sebastien hisses against her ear. "You will not fall."

Ryder wraps herself around him like a sloth clinging to a tree trunk, her head nestled against the hard plate of elthar that covers his chest. As too-personal as the hug might be, there is no way she's letting go. He tilts his head away from her like he's smelt something terrible.

"What's happening?" she says.

"Lucas is too far away, the connection has died." Sebastien speaks into the top of her head. "But so long as we maintain a connection, my elthar will support you as well." He still only holds her with one arm, the way Ryder saw Christian do once when his little niece, covered in paint after a disastrous finger painting session, decided she wanted a cuddle. "There is no need for you to have your legs around my waist. You can let go."

"Nope. I can't." From where she hangs, Ryder has a clear view down into the abyss. "Is Lucas going to be okay?"

Sebastien's armour is the least comfortable thing in the world to cling to, but Ryder holds on like her life depends on it. He is so solid, like his whole body is metal, not just the thin coating stretching over his torso.

"Are you trying to compress my lungs?" Sebastien makes a small indignant sound. "If you will calm yourself you'll find that you are floating. Not slipping."

Despite the fact he is the only thing stopping her from being a splattered mush on the ground below, she snaps at him. "I'll be calm when my feet are on solid ground, but thanks. What about Lucas? Will he be okay?"

"That is hardly a concern of mine." Sebastien draws them out further towards the centre of the quarry. The walls are frighteningly far from reach now. "Nor were you, but it seems I have no say in what concerns me at the moment."

She opens her mouth, ready to tell him just how much fun this is for her, when a familiar voice whispers into her ear.

Your friend is still free.

"Did you hear that?" Ryder shifts, tries to peer into the dark velvet depths. The quarter moon tries its best to shed some light into the belly of the quarry, but it's failing miserably.

"Stay still," Sebastien hisses.

"You didn't hear that?"

"No. I didn't."

"I've heard it a couple of times now."

"The Placer toxin can act as a hallucinogen. Those Jarran stones will be losing effect," he says. "I am returning you to Aresh. She will be able to remove any remaining toxin."

Taking her to Aresh? A slightly terrifying prospect any other time, but for now Ryder's too distracted to get so much as a goosebump. She is focused on the whisperer.

"There was all this dust." She lifts her head and feels him do the same to avoid his chin touching her hair. "I think it protected me, shielded me somehow…"

"Dust protected you?" he says, with clear bemusement.

Ryder's retort is interrupted by a loud hiss, like a semi-trailer suddenly applied its brakes somewhere down in the guts of the quarry pit. A great gust of wind sweeps up from below. The second time it's happened in the last five minutes.

"What is that?" Ryder's monkey grip tightens.

"The Aventar. You really need to let go."

A few feet beyond where they float, the darkness peels

away, revealing a rectangular outline of light. A clicking sound follows and the outline becomes a full panel of yellow light. It is a doorway, a small entranceway into an aircraft that hulks in the shadows right before them. The interior light spills out onto the craft's wing, illuminating a surface black and smooth as polished onyx.

"Where did that come from?" She is clinging to him way too tight and doesn't care.

"I flew it here."

Ryder can make out the rough shape of the craft. It has a snub nose that blends back into a helicopter style cabin. A wing juts out just below the open panel, stretching at least three metres out from the body, the wingtips curving back in a comma shape. The tail of the aircraft is lost in the darkness, but up on its roof, a single propeller blade spins lazily. It is like some kind of weird airplane and helicopter hybrid. How the searching helicopter didn't spot it, is just one more oddity in a weekend of weird.

"It's…it's beautiful." Ryder says.

"It serves its purpose," he says, but she thinks she hears some pride there. "Now sit still. I'm going to take us in."

They drift across the wing, their reflections rippling in the glass-like surface. Down below the aircraft, much further down, the quarry floor is now visible. The raven dark shadows have lifted. Sebastien's grip eases on her legs, getting ready to dislodge her before he's even gotten them through the doorway. He only has to crouch slightly to slip through the wide doorway, and then they are inside the craft. He lets her go before he touches down, and Ryder stumbles as her feet hit the floor. The surface inside is as black and smooth as the outside. But it's the other person who stands in the spacious, seat-less cabin that draws Ryder's attention.

"Oh my god, Sophie."

"Ryder."

They fling themselves at one another, Sophie squealing with delight. The elthar on Ryder's arms begins to retract, taking its warmth with it.

143

"Ryder, thank god you're okay." Sophie, shorter than Ryder, speaks into the folds of her friend's jacket. "Lucas? Is he…"

"I don't know. I think so." *Your friend is free*, the whisperer told her. It has to mean Lucas. She needs it to mean Lucas. "Are you guys okay? Where's Chris?"

"He's fine, he's with the others. We're both fine."

As Sophie fusses over her, Ryder stares at the interior of the craft. It's wide and long, six people could easily stand side by side, and a few more lengthwise. Most of the interior is empty, save for a bench seat up near the nose, the pilot's seat she assumes, though there are no visible control panels or joystick. The front window seems to be one single great pane of glass that curves all the way back to midway down the cabin. It is a flying goldfish bowl.

"Ryder, how is Lucas mixed up in all this?" Sophie hasn't let Ryder go. "I mean, did he tell you anything before now?"

Tell her he isn't who he says he is? That he'd lied to them all, for forever? Ryder runs her hands over the bands around her wrists. The elthar has reshaped itself into fine bracelets, back to its dull, cold self. Lucas let her hunt shadows for so long, knowing all along what lay beyond them. Ryder fights to smooth her expression, chase away the anger that comes with thinking about all the nights spent crying herself to sleep; convinced she was going to end up like her mum, certain she was losing her grip on reality. When all the while it was reality that was faulty, and he knew it.

"Ryder?" Sophie rubs Ryder's arm. And takes a guess at the answer. "I'm sure he had his reasons for not telling you."

"Yeah. I'm sure." Her gaze follows Sebastien as he walks up to the pilot's seat. The elthar armour is almost done contracting back into two cuffs around his wrists. The black vest and pants he wears appear to be simple cotton, like something you could buy from the local K-Mart. Ryder glimpses a patchwork of faded scars on his arms; some just tiny nicks, others long and raised. He catches her staring and a scowl crosses his face before he turns his back to them and sits down.

Sophie waves her hand in front of Ryder's face. "Why didn't Lucas come with you?"

Thinking about Lucas makes Ryder's head ache. She shrugs. "He had something he had to do…it's all kind of bizarre. There was some kind of, I don't know, secret agency tracking us." Sophie's eyes widen. Her brilliant red hair almost as messed up as Christian's on a bad day.

"Holy moly, secret agency? Are we in trouble?"

"I don't think they're interested in us. Lucas is keeping them distracted until they can get Olessia out of here." She shrugs. "This is all about her, really."

"Oh my god, Ry." Sophie splays her fingers, presses them to the folds of her skirt. "I think Olessia is like royalty or something, you should see how the others act around her."

"Others?"

But Sebastien speaks up before she can answer. "Take your seats," he says. "We're leaving."

Sophie loops her arm through Ryder's. "Let's go."

Ryder stares at the empty cabin. "Where exactly would he like us to sit?"

"Give it a second…there…look." Sophie points. "Careful, they come up pretty quick."

Towards the centre of the cabin, two panels slide back in the floor, allowing a pair of high-backed seats to rise up. They are contoured, and would be at home in a race car, except for the fact they seem to be made of metal.

"Oh don't worry, they're incredibly comfortable, trust me," Sophie says. "Check this out."

She sits down on the seat closest to the curved interior wall, and then touches a diamond shaped panel on the armrest. Twin ribbons of silver emerge from the top of the chair and slide down over Sophie's shoulders, crossing one another and buckling in down beside her hips.

"Leaving now, whether you're in or not." Sebastien settles into the pilot seat, lowering his arms onto the rests on either side.

"Quick, quick." Sophie waves Ryder into her seat.

Sebastien is true to his word. The craft, the Aventar, rises into the air. Ryder stumbles, hitting her knee hard against the seat. She bites down on her lip, refusing to make a sound and throws herself into the seat.

"Hit the diamond one." Sophie waves at the pattern on the armrest.

Ryder slaps the carved symbol. The silver ribbon launches itself down over her shoulders, pressing her tight against the seat, holding her steady. Sophie is right. The seat appears as though it will be cold and unyielding, but the metal moulds to her body in a snug embrace.

The Aventar shoots forward, the force knocking Ryder's head back against the chair. "Does he actually know how to drive this thing?" The cabin is completely silent. If the aircraft is making any noise at all Ryder can't hear it.

"He's not in the best mood," Sophie whispers. "You should have seen his face when Aresh said I should go with him. I thought he was going to pop a vein. I don't think those two are exactly best pals right now. They were arguing in some weird language, the only thing I could make out was Lucas's name. But from what I could gather, Sebastien and Aresh aren't seeing eye to eye at all."

Sophie is brimming with gossip, but Ryder only heard one thing. Aresh. She tries to lean towards Sophie but the armrests block her. "You've met her? Aresh?"

"Yeah, she's really lovely." Sophie claps her hands together, like this is some wild reality TV show and she is just happy to be part of it. "So regal, you know? I'm beginning to think we're hanging out with some serious royal blood. I mean Olessia has that air, right? And so does her aunt. I really hope they sort things out between them."

"Her aunt?"

"Yeah, Aresh is her aunt." Sophie nods. "Very friendly, lovely lady. Poor thing has some terrible scars on her face though. I wonder what happened."

"Scars?" Ryder hesitates. "And long white hair?"

Sophie nods. "And the most gorgeous roman style dress, you should see it."

But Ryder's already seen it. And she saw how desperate Olessia was to get away from her aunt. Ryder leans further forward, and the harness pinches the skin by her wound. She hisses.

"The Jarran stone requires replacement."

Sebastien's voice startles her. She hadn't even noticed him stand up from the pilot seat, yet here he is. Right beside her, hair untied now, its length brushing the tops of his shoulders. He strides away from them, towards the back of the craft. The Aventar continues to glide through the night sky with barely a shudder. Sebastien brushes his hand over the bare wall and a hidden door opens, parting like a curtain. He steps through the opening and the compartment seals closed behind him.

"I hope he's a better guardian then he is conversationalist," Sophie muses. "I think Olessia drew the short straw with that one. He's kind of cute I suppose, if you like frown lines and severe attitude problems."

Ryder can't help but grin at her friend's summary. Sophie has a talent for de-stressing a moment. A talent Ryder's grown more dependent on over the years. Sebastien returns, tossing an object towards her. Another Jarran stone. To her relief, Ryder catches the small stone. She's embarrassed enough by the memory of clinging to him like a frightened baby outside.

"You know what to do with it," he says. "I've decreased the dosage this time."

"Gee, thanks," she says. "You should have been a doctor."

But Sebastien pays no attention to her sarcasm. He waves his hand over the bare wall at the back of the cabin. Three screens light up the smooth surface. Each is showing footage of international news reports. One in Spanish, one in German, the final in English. But all three centre on severe weather events. Flash flooding in Barcelona, lightning storms in Cologne, and another report about the wild electrical storm that hit the Tranmere area of Hobart. A spokesman for the phone company is talking about the cost of repairs to the mobile phone tower as footage of the damaged structure plays out.

"It really took a beating didn't it?" Sophie kneels on her seat, the harness released, peering back at the screen.

Sebastien crosses his arms. "Ridiculous place to put it."

Ryder slides off her jacket, pulling back her t-shirt to pick at the worn Jarran stone, trying to work out how to remove it. She isn't about to ask for his help. "Ridiculous place to put the phone tower?"

"It's right at a River entrance," he replies.

Like a cat that's got the cream, Sophie practically dances in the chair. "Get this Ry, Blackrhine Hill is one of their portals, it's one of the Rivers, that's what they call the wider passageways. The narrower ones are Slipstreams, like the one at Clarendon House. But they can only handle foot traffic. Special foot traffic mind you, people like Olessia and Aresh can use them. But everyone else needs the Rivers, 'cause they need spaceships to survive the journey. Rivers are rare, can you believe there is one across the Derwent from our school? I mean, seriously, does it get any more incredibly awesome than that?" She shrugs one shoulder, smiling at the quizzical look Ryder directs at her. "Olessia and I chatted. We're like best friends now, sorry Ry."

Ryder glances at Sebastien. He keeps his eyes on the screens, but his frown deepens.

"Hang on." Ryder raises her eyebrows. "If you're saying Blackrhine is a River entrance, does that mean the damage to the tower was caused by someone flying a spaceship into it?"

"Bingo," Sophie says quietly, tilting her head towards Sebastien. He turns to face them, gray eyes narrowed into a glare that could melt wax.

"It is called an Aventar. And let me know when your realm even discovers the existence of these gateways," he says. "And then let me know when they can navigate into and out of one with one hundred percent accuracy, one hundred percent of the time."

The indignation actually manages to soften the sharpness of his face. Ryder busies herself with the new Jarran stone, pressing it onto an undamaged piece of skin near the wound. The flow of soothing heat spreads over her shoulder and the pain evaporates into the barest ache.

"It's impossible to make sharp turns at the point of exit." Sebastien's voice raises a notch. Their silence seems to annoy him even more than a snide comment. "The speed is too great."

"Okay, I'm sure it is." Ryder nods. Maybe it's the buzz of the Jarran stones, but she is enjoying the exasperated expression on his perfect face. "Just would have thought that being so advanced and all, it wouldn't have been an issue."

Sophie makes the time out signal with her hands. "Okay, let's be nice to the nice man who's in charge of the alien aircraft, Ryder."

"I'm just saying that -" Ryder pauses. "That thing that attacked us, the Placer, could it use a Slipstream?"

"Of course. They live within the Arlion itself, they can move freely." Sebastien says.

The Arlion, the space between worlds. Ryder recalls the way Olessia explained it to her, how all the worlds clung together like a cluster of bubbles and the walls of those bubbles were the Arlion.

"So maybe it followed Olessia?" The Jarran stones must be the perfect dosage this time, because Ryder's thoughts are clear. "Could more be coming? Jack said there was a problem at Clarendon House earlier today, the alarms and things going off." She sucks in her breath. "I haven't heard anything from him since he left to go there. I don't know where my phone is-"

She glances at Sophie who shakes her head. "I found it back at the carpark, it must have fallen out of your pocket when-" She wrinkles her nose at the memory. "Anyway, it doesn't matter. Sorry Ry, but our phones are all dead. Whatever happened at the carpark fried them all." Her face softens with a gentle smile. "I'm sure Jack is fine though. Right?" Her question goes to Sebastien.

Though his disinterested expression doesn't shift, the muscles in his jaw flex. He turns abruptly. "That is no concern of mine. My orders are to collect you and bring you to Aresh. I have neither asked, nor am I interested, in why. A Placer would hardly have an interest in an old human man. I believe your fears are unfounded." He brushes past her, gray eyes fixed on anything but her.

Ryder's chest tightens. Sebastien just said Jack was an old man. How did he know that? Breathing in through her nose, Ryder lets air fill her lungs entirely before she exhales.

"Ryder, we should sit down." Sophie waits for her beside their seats. It dawns on Ryder that Sophie probably talked about her grandad. She just said she and Olessia were practically joined at the hip. Ryder takes Sophie's outstretched hand. A flutter of nerves grip her. Aresh is waiting for them. For Ryder.

CHAPTER 19

T HE AVENTAR TOUCHES DOWN WITH a barely discernible thud. For the past fifteen minutes they've flown at a pace that blurred the ground beneath them, making it near impossible to work out what direction Sebastien has taken.

"How did they get here?" Ryder releases her harness, twisting in her seat to loosen up her tired muscles. The Jarran stones are doing wonders for the pain, but the exhaustion is sinking deeper. "And what is a Claven?"

"Don't know and not sure. Though I think a Claven is less a thing, more a group?" Sophie shrugs. She's been filling Ryder in on some new arrivals, two guys apparently even less cordial than Sebastien, who have joined Aresh and Olessia. What's becoming clear is that Olessia has really put a lot of noses out of joint by leaving.

"Let's go," Sebastien says.

He's halfway out the door before Ryder and Sophie are out of their chairs. They hurry after him, traipsing down the short ramp to the ground. It's cooler here than it was at Bridgewater. There are no visible lights around them, save for those from the Aventar. Overhead the sky is clear and the moon is just strong enough to cover everything with a silvery sheen. They've touched down in a scrap yard. Towers of flattened cars, and other piles of mis-shapen metal loom on all sides. The height of the weeds pushing up between the stacks of metal suggests the place hasn't been used in a while. Sebastien might be a lot of things, arrogant being one, but great pilot is on the list too. The Aventar is nestled in a space that barely accommodates it. Ryder's idea that the craft is a blend of airplane and helicopter is pretty accurate. Though, seeing it now, it's clearly more stealth fighter than commercial aircraft. The sleek black body has no visible joins or bolts in sight, as though it's crafted from a single piece of material. This close, Ryder can make out a subtle texture within the bodywork, a speckling not unlike granite. The craft has a three-pronged tail and a single overhead blade, all made of the same stone-like substance. Ryder squints. Either she's passing out in a very slow way, or the aircraft is fading.

Ryder searches out Sebastien. "Is it disappearing?"

"Camouflage," he says, not even glancing back at the craft. "The Aventar reflects what is around it."

Now she understands why the helicopter didn't spot the Aventar back at the quarry. It had literally become one of the shadows in the pit.

"Nifty." Sophie nods, hands on hips. "A chameleon flying machine. I didn't see that trick before we left."

"It's technology. Not a *trick.*"

Sebastien stalks away, and Sophie pokes out her tongue at his back. Ryder gives her a tired smile which quickly vanishes when Sebastien breaks into a jog. The thought of having to do anything more than stand on her feet is draining, let alone actually moving. But move they do. There's little choice if they don't want to get left in the middle of the scrap yard. They lose sight of Sebastien once or twice amongst the scattered piles of metal, and he doesn't even glance over his shoulder as he negotiates the grounds

"Told you he was fast." Sophie breathes hard.

He waits for them at a high wire fence that separates the yard from a flat grassy field. On the far side of the field, brightly lit under tall tower lights, is an electricity station. Four towers stand at each corner of the complex. The hum of the wires reaches them, pushed across the field by a faltering night breeze. The air is fresh, with the faintest hint of livestock. A safe bet they are some distance from the city.

There's a gap in the wiring, a hole that Sebastien crouches next to. He pulls the meshwork aside and steps through. Without pause he dashes across the open space.

"Seriously?" Ryder groans.

Sophie bunches the folds of her hibiscus-print skirt up over her knees, stepping through the gap like she's negotiating a minefield. When it's Ryder's turn she stands up too early and her jacket catches on a piece of wire. The rip of material splits the air.

"Damn it."

She runs a trembling finger over the torn denim. It's tough material but she's worn it to death since her dad bought it, years ago, on a trip. He found it in some random second-hand clothing store in Paris. Nothing fancy, the denim faded from royal blue to barely-there sky blue, long ago, and two of the navy-style buttons tore off at some point. But he picked it out himself. And, back when they talked about stuff like that, he told her her mum wanted to visit that city more than any other.

"I can fix it, don't worry," Sophie says.

Ryder nods, still thinking about her dad. He's never felt so far away. And it surprises her, how much it stings. Sebastien's not waiting for her to have a 'moment' though. They have to run hard across the field to keep him in sight. A fine white mist hangs over the surface of the field, and she discovers it's not as flat as she thought. Though there are no cows or horses in sight the ground's churned up, like it's seen a stampede recently, and the nose-wrinkling waft of manure grows heavy on the air. More than once Ryder loses her footing on the uneven ground. Where are they? Sophie has no clue, she spent most of the car trip tending Olessia and didn't take much notice of their direction. A hulking mountain range, just a series of bumps on the horizon off to the east, might be Mount Field National Park. But after Ryder nearly turns her ankle, twice, she gives up trying to figure it out.

Finally, lungs aching, they reach the outer gate of the power station. Sebastien is nowhere in sight, but the gate is open. The entire complex is surrounded by razor-wire topped fences, hung every few metres with warning signs about trespassing. There is a bright yellow one that declares '*Danger of Death*', just to make it clear. It shows an unfortunate silhouette man being electrocuted. Beyond the fence, in the midst of two huge gray transformers, and humming power lines, sits a flat-roofed, red brick building.

"This is where they're hiding out?" Ryder's breath is white against the cold air. The stitch in her side cramps hard, and her whole body is beginning to ache again. The second Jarran stone hasn't lasted like the first.

"Uh-huh." Sophie nods. "Apparently the electricity is a great shield against telepathy. Kind of an invisibility cloak."

"And who are they cloaking themselves from, exactly?" The sweat on her face takes no time to cool under the touch of the chilled night air. Behind them the mist is thickening, a carpet of white stretching out as far as she can see.

"Maybe more of those things that attacked you?" Sophie says. "Come on, it's freezing. Let's get inside."

They pass through the outer gate. The red brick building has only one visible door and as they walk towards it, it flies open, slamming back against the brickwork. Christian's long legs cover the short distance to where they stand in just a few strides.

"Ry!" He grabs her in a hug so tight it pushes the air out of her lungs.

Ryder gasps. "Shoulder."

"Oh, I'm so sorry." Christian eases his hold. Ryder clings to him as long as the pain will allow. Finally she lets go, but Christian keeps one arm around her waist. He leans in and kisses her on the check, which seems to surprise him as much as anybody. "I'm just so glad you're okay." Then he's gone, taking his blush with him. Sophie beams at him, raising her arms.

"Do I get a hug and a kiss too? Let's just make it quick, don't want Olessia to think I'm crowding her territory." She flutters her eyelids, a sickly sweet smile playing on her lips. But Christian leaves her hanging.

"What is up with you, Sophie?" He scowls, pulling up his hood against the cold. "You just left me here-"

"Left you under the very watchful gaze of Olessia. You're like the royal puppy or something-"

She giggles, but the deepening frown on Christian's face says he's not about to join her. "Just don't do that again okay? Don't disappear like that. We need to stick together, promise me guys." He glances between them, his scowl edged with apprehension.

Sophie crosses her heart. "Promise. Sorry, I wanted to come tell you but it's just...well Sebastien's not exactly the patient type."

Christian grunts and mutters something under his breath. But he seems happy with Sophie's promise because he turns to Ryder.

"Promise?"

"Hey, it's not like I had any choice in getting separated from you guys." Ryder wraps her arms around her midriff, the cold biting into her tired joints. "I was kind of unconscious, remember?"

Christian's face crumples. "Yeah, I remember. Lucas was freaking...how is he...is he coming here?" He glances behind her, like he expects to see Lucas saunter in across the field.

"No. Not yet. He's-" Ryder tries and fails to stifle a yawn. She is dead on her feet. If they don't get inside soon, one of them will be carrying her.

"He'll be okay though, right?" Christian digs his fingers through his hair, mussing up a spot that's flattened, like he'd been sleeping on it.

"It's Lucas. Of course." Ryder kicks at the ground, avoiding Christian's gaze.

The thought of being in her bed now, buried deep in the covers, head beneath her pillow, safe in the darkness, is so tantalising it chokes her up. When Christian wraps an arm around her and leads her inside, Ryder doesn't protest. The last time she lay in her own bed, the night before they headed up to Evandale, she had yet another restless night's sleep. This time it was because she was so excited about heading to Clarendon House. About finding her ghosts. She shudders and huddles in closer to Christian. Perhaps she should have been more careful what she wished for.

CHAPTER 20

T HE RED BRICK BUILDING IS basic inside, but at least it's warm. Ryder's cold fingertips tingle, adjusting to the temperature. The building's main room is no bigger than one of the classrooms at Taroona High, and it appears to be an odd mix of work station and living quarters. In the far back corner is a sink and a squat white oven, with a plastic table and chairs that have seen better days. Contrasting the homey feel there, on the opposite side of the room is a long green-gray control panel, with an array of buttons, dials and gauges. The glass in some of the panels is either smashed or missing altogether. On the wall above it are a couple of monitors which hang haphazardly, screens blank. It has the air of a space not used for a very long time. In the middle of the room a bulky brown couch is piled with blankets of all different colours and pattern. The room appears empty.

Christian helps her peel off her jacket. "Oh man, that shoulder looks nasty. Pretty crazy what happened back there, huh?"

He laughs, trying to sound flippant, but she's heard his laughter often enough. He's not finding any of this really funny.

"Pretty crazy." She squeezes his hand, hoping her smile is bright enough to cover how awful she feels. There's a band of pressure across her forehead that's growing more uncomfortable.

Sophie stands by one of the couches, and seems to be having a conversation with the blankets. Perhaps Ryder is more exhausted than she thought. She closes her eyes for a second, and then blinks. Neither she nor Sophie are delusional, not yet anyway. Someone is lying beneath the blankets. And that someone is watching Ryder.

Olessia.

Sophie adjusts a blue star-print blanket beneath Olessia's chin, tucking it in around her shoulders. Olessia gives Ryder a barely-there smile. Her face is even paler than Ryder remembers, and the skin beneath her eyes is dark with shadow.

"Ryder." She's hoarse, like she's been shouting at a football match all afternoon. "Are you okay? I'm so sorry-"

"Just rest, Ryder is going to be fine." Sophie fusses over her, tucking the blanket in tighter.

"I have much to thank your friend Lucas for too, it would seem." A smile brushes Olessia's lips, only to be lost in a grimace. She coughs - the sound coming from deep in her chest, dry and harsh.

Christian fills a chipped glass with water and takes it to her. "They said you need to keep drinking, time for some more." He places the glass gently against her lips and tilts it for her. Olessia takes one small sip then pushes the glass away, her attention squared on Ryder.

"I know you must be concerned for him," she says. 'But he will be fine. He is more than capable of dealing with C-21."

Ryder blinks, her eyes gritty with tiredness. "You know about them too?"

"Only what Aresh has told me." Olessia pauses to take another sip. "She had trouble with them on her last visit here. They are nothing if not persistent."

Her last visit? Lucas said C-21 had gotten hold of some tech because someone like Olessia had been here before. But Aresh is sister to the some big shot ruler, surely she wouldn't make a mistake like that? A mistake that means right now, Lucas is being hunted down like a fugitive. The weight behind her eyes spreads up into the crown of her head. This headache is coming whether she wants it or not.

"What will they do to him if they catch him?" Ryder says, furious and terrified for him at the same time. The fact is, the mess Lucas is in, is all his doing. If he'd said something before now Ryder would never have bought a stupid thermal camera. Never gone to Clarendon House.

"They won't catch him." Olessia's words dissolve into a coughing fit. Christian helps her sit up, rubbing her back as she tries to catch her breath. Sophie refills the glass. Water is a good idea. Ryder can't remember when she last had a drink. The headache could be plain old dehydration. She's about to ask if there is another glass somewhere when Olessia pulls free of the blanket cocoon, and presses her fingers to her nose. The tips come away marked with blood, brilliant candy apple red; not B-Grade sci-fi movie green, or oozy black. It's red. Brighter maybe than normal, but red. Ryder pushes her fingers to her forehead, massaging the tightness there. Olessia is bleeding, who cares what colour her blood is?

"Here, I've got a tissue." Sophie pulls a wad of snow white tissues from a hidden pocket in her cardigan. Of course she has tissues. Probably has lip balm, deodorant and wipes somewhere too. Olessia, head tilted back, takes one of the offered tissues and dabs it against her nose, very calm and deft. This isn't the first time she's had a bloody nose.

"Is this supposed to happen?" Christian hovers nearby. He hasn't walked away, impressive considering how woozy he gets when he has a papercut.

"This is what happens when she overexerts herself."

Ryder is so concentrated on Olessia, she doesn't notice Sebastien striding into the room till he's right up close. His hair is pulled back tight against his skull, not a lock out of place, and a tight fitted jacket covers his slender arms. He isn't alone. A woman follows him. The woman with the awful scar. Aresh. This time she is as real and solid as anyone else in the room. She wears the same flowing lime green gown Ryder saw her in, her white hair hanging in waves down the middle of her back. The scars on the left side of her face are pinker than Ryder remembers but just as extensive, running all the way from beneath her left eye down the curve of her slender neck. Her features aren't quite as sharp as Olessia's, but there is a similarity in the shape of their chins, and the curving upward line of their eyes. Aresh is clearly much older than Olessia, faint and delicate lines around the corners of her mouth and eyes. She doesn't even glance at Ryder when she walks into the room, her focus solely on Olessia. Which gives Ryder a chance to scrutinise her unreservedly, trying to pinpoint what it was that seemed familiar about her at Jack's.

"You must rest Laudess." Aresh brushes aside Olessia's fringe, damp with sweat.

More people enter the room. Two men, who march in with the air of a soldier's purposeful stride. The first is an older man, bald but for a thin trace of white beard around his jawline. Pale-skinned, with high cheekbones, sharp chin and long limbs, there is little doubt he too is from Siros. Both are dressed in plain long pants and buttonless long sleeved shirts, in material the colours of an autumn tree, speckled oranges and reds and yellows. Ryder stands in silence, a giant fish out of water. She throws a sidelong glance at Christian and Sophie, searching for some hint of what to do. They both step back from the couch when Aresh approaches. Sophie smiles at her, but Aresh is focused on Olessia and doesn't notice.

"Dashel, give me that Rai." Aresh addresses the bearded man.

"Yes, Laudine." He withdraws a small red bottle from a satchel strapped to his belt. He bobs his head again and doesn't make eye contact with Aresh as he hands it to her. He hasn't made eye contact with anyone since he entered the room. Aresh pours an oily substance onto Olessia's hand and massages it into her skin. She speaks to her as she applies the balm, whispering too quietly to hear. When she is done she kisses Olessia's hands, and then re-arranges the blankets around her, fussing like a mother might.

The tight band across Ryder's forehead is really pinching now. She would take a seat, but the second guy who entered the room is staring at her, dark eyes furrowed, and she doesn't dare move. Like the man called Dashel, this man's features are sharp, his skin pale and limbs just a fraction too long to be human, but he is far more heavy-set and imposing than Dashel. The colour of his skin is the only pale thing about him: his eyes, his hair, and his demeanour are much darker. An odd expression moves across his face, confusion and something else mixing there.

"I'm told you were a part of the Laudine's original Traverse crew to this realm, Verran." Sebastien's voice is an icy sliver. "You have spent time in the Iondar Realm before. Why then do you regard the human girl as though she has crawled out of the Arlion itself?"

Ryder's gaze drops to the tiled floor. Verran really is trying to stare a hole into her head. It wasn't her imagination.

"Concern yourself with the Laudess, as you should have done to begin with, boy." Verran's words seethe with disdain. "Perhaps then we would not be where we are right now."

She can't resist glancing up to see Sebastien's reaction. Ryder thought he'd given her some greasy looks so far, but they are nothing compared to the one he levels at the other man. This is a full on death stare. And Verran matches it with one of his own, tilting his head to keep eye contact with the much taller Sebastien. The tension between them weighs down the air in the room.

"Enough." Aresh rises to her feet, handing the bottle back to Dashel.

Her slight body contrasts Verran's bulk. He is considerably taller than her, but seems to wither under her radiant violet gaze.

Verran bows his head. "My apologies, Laudine."

Laudine. Lucas said Olessia is more like a General than a princess. So what does that make Aresh? Lieutenant? Aresh regards Verran for a few moments before turning to Ryder. The scarring on her face and neck are tight and raw, as though it's not fully healed. Ryder tries not to stare.

"We must clean that wound, Ryder, would you allow me?" Aresh beckons her forward with an elegant wave of her hand.

Though she has barely said more than a few words to Ryder, there is something compelling about the woman, something soothing and comfortable, and Ryder follows her towards the kitchenette. Christian shifts to sit on the armrest of the couch, and Olessia rests her head against his leg before closing her eyes, the palest shade of violet Ryder's seen her irises yet.

"So...is Olessia going to be okay?" Ryder's tongue sticks to the roof of her mouth. She really needs that glass of water.

"She will be." Aresh nods. "As will you. Here, please sit."

She gestures towards the small table and Ryder sits down on one of the chairs. The vinyl is split in the middle of the seat, and the sharp edge pokes into the back of her thigh. Oddly though, she doesn't want Aresh to know she's uncomfortable and says nothing. Aresh kneels beside her, the folds of her green dress blooming over the stained linoleum. She pulls Ryder's shirt away from the wound.

"This won't hurt but it will feel quite strange." Aresh takes the petite bottle Dashel offers her, this one splotched blue and silver, before giving Ryder a reassuring smile. The scarring at the side of her lip stops the smile from evening out, but Aresh's eyes are kind, and Ryder finds herself smiling back. Aresh holds the narrow bottle above the wound, shaking it like she is adding salt to a meal. Tiny silver flecks fall onto the puncture. A tingling sensation runs across Ryder's skin, and the pressure at her temples eases. Sophie joins them, leaning on the table and peering at Ryder's shoulder like she's observing a fascinating science experiment.

"Oh wow, that's amazing." Ryder is convinced Sophie's eyes can't physically widen any further. "How are you doing, Ry?"

Ryder gives her a thumbs up. Great, actually. Relaxed and comfortable. Like this is the most natural thing in the world to be here. To have Aresh fuss over her with the same gentle concern she'd bestowed on Olessia.

"The healing Rai will take a short while to fully neutralise any trace that remains of the toxin," Aresh says. "But be assured, it will do its job. You have been so very brave."

She clasps her hands around Ryder's, fingertips brushing the elthar bracelets still around Ryder's wrists. The thin bands seems so innocuous now, nothing more than rather plain pieces of costume jewellery. Aresh lets go and steps away in a rustle of material. Ryder watches her, still able to feel the press of her hands and the warmth from her touch. Aresh joins the others, who stand over by the control panels on the far side of the room. They speak in lowered voices, but it's a small room and Ryder catches every word.

"Laudine," Verran says. "I know of your affection for the people of this Realm, but I must insist we return our attention to what is important here. I ask you again to reconsider your plan. An attempt to travel through the Paldrian River unescorted, with such a precious cargo, seems utterly foolish. I strongly advise that we seek protective services from the Presider. Send for him now, don't leave us vulnerable."

"I'll ask that you do not refer to my brother's child as cargo, Verran." Aresh's smooth expression doesn't shift, but her tone is hard. "And we will not be advising the Presider of anything, as I have said from the beginning."

Ryder leans against the edge of the table, not caring that it digs into her side. The strange little flakes must be even stronger than the Jarran stones, because her whole body is jelly.

"Forgive me, Laudine," Verran says. "But I must voice my concern. If the Zentai learn she is here with such little protection they will be upon us. There is the chance they already know, the Placer that attacked these children may well have been a scout."

Sebastien crosses his arms tight across his chest. "Placers are scavengers, it would not be the first time they have randomly followed an energy trail through the slipstreams. The Zentai would surely send more than one simple beast if they hoped to take the Laudess of Bax Un Tey."

Dashel scratches at the fine line of his beard. "Agreed. Even if the Zentai managed to tether one of those mindless creatures to do their bidding, which is unlikely, they have no easy access into this Realm to claim her, Verran. They have only the Meeran River, and even the Zentai aren't that foolish. That River has been unstable for decades."

Zentai. Ryder's ears prick at the familiar word, but her tired mushed up brain can't process much right now.

"There are slipstreams they can use." Verran's lips curl in a snarl. The guy has a wolf-like quality. Not the sort of person you'd ever want to meet in a dark alley. "Granted they cannot send an army, but we are hardly one ourselves. Still, it's not this realm I'm concerned about. It's our return journey. Once we re-enter Bax Un Tey we will be vulnerable to attack without an escort. Had we known the nature of your summons, Laudine, Dashel and I would have brought another Aventar through the River when we responded-"

"Very true," Dashel says, rubbing at his chin and nodding. Something about the man's measured way of speaking and his contemplative frown, reminds Ryder of Jack. Ryder blinks hard, chasing back the prick of tears behind her eyes. Start crying now and she might not stop.

"Acquiring another Aventar would have brought undue attention to our mission." Aresh stands with her hands clasped in front of her, at ease despite the tension of the group. "It is my intention that our absence remain unnoticed."

Verran grunts. "Considering the attack from the Placer, it is safe to say that someone has noticed. My bet is on the Zentai. This is too great a risk, the Presider should be notified."

It hits her then, her sluggish thoughts finally narrowing in on where she's heard that word before. Zentai. Olessia's enemy, the other world her people are at war with. Ryder glances over to where Olessia lies, eyes closed, resting against Christian's thigh. So fragile, and half buried under the blankets. Fragile and young. Just a kid. The girl can pull the life out of everything around her, she's going to rule a world one day, and everyone seems to shudder when her dad's name is mentioned. Ryder's guessing it hasn't been the dream childhood. Sophie asked Olessia once if she was running away from the war and she got very prickly, said she wanted nothing to do with it. Sounds like the war has other ideas. A shiver traces its way across Ryder's shoulders.

I'm so sorry, Olessia. It's just a thought, not like Ryder was trying to send it out into the ether, but Olessia opens her eyes. Stares straight back at her.

Don't be afraid, Ryder. I will protect you. Olessia offers a smile, weak and unhappy, before closing her eyes again.

Protect her? Ryder's heart seems to miss a thump or two. Protect her from what? More of those walking skeletons? Or something else? Glancing over to the huddled group on the far side of the room, Ryder finds Aresh watching her. But the woman turns away quickly, returning to the argument continuing around her. Sebastien is levelling another death stare at Verran. "If you notify the Presider, he will bring an army to retrieve her. That kind of influx will have disastrous effects on the weather system here. This is not a vast world like Siros, it cannot handle-"

"Do not lecture me on facts I helped to establish. I understand this world far better than you, boy," Verran says. "It is no secret that you resent your post, Guardian. Perhaps you see an opportunity here to be rid of your commitments."

Sebastien steps towards Verran, his fists balled. "You go too far, Verran."

It doesn't seem to worry Verran. He squares up to Sebastien, raising his fist, pulling his arm back to strike the much taller and younger man. The punch never comes. In one swift movement both are lifted off their feet, and Sebastien is flung across the room. He hits the ground and slides along the floor, coming to an abrupt stop beside Ryder's chair.

CHAPTER 21

"**A**RE YOU ALL RIGHT?" RYDER lays her hand on his shoulder before she realises what she's doing.

"Of course." But Sebastien's storm gray eyes don't leave the floor as he clambers to his feet. She leans away, her cheeks warm.

"Is she doing that?" Sophie whispers, pointing to the other side of the room.

Verran is pressed up against the wall above the control panel, like a bug stuck to flypaper. His face is red with the effort of trying to move, but he doesn't seem to be able to do much more than wiggle his fingers. Aresh stands before him, hands clasped behind her back.

"Verran, you will hold your tongue." Something about her presence has changed, she seems *larger* somehow. She's not, not physically anyway, but there is a warrior-like fierceness about her that wasn't there before. "You are Claven, you provide counsel to the Presidership, you do not provide ultimatums. You do not accuse others of treasonous intent. I've made my decision. My brother will not be involved in the Laudess's extrication from this realm. And if you ever insult her guardian in that way again, I will-"

Dashel places a hand on her shoulder. "Laudine, for the sake of the Laudess, we must remain united. We must remain calm."

There is a pause, a moment when no one moves. Then the

tightness drops from Aresh's shoulders and she turns to smile at Dashel. All at once the warrior is a regal, composed princess again. "You are right, of course, my friend." Glancing back at Verran, she takes a deep breath. "Forgive me, Verran."

She releases whatever hold she had on him. Verran drifts down to the ground, the movement unhurried and steady. The surly expression doesn't leave his face, but there is no malice there as he regards Aresh. He steps up to her and they speak in hushed tones. Dashel suggests they move somewhere else for further discussion. Allow Olessia to rest. Both Verran and Aresh agree and head to the single door at the back of the room. Dashel invites Sebastien to join them, and though he mutters and scowls, he follows them out of the main area.

Olessia doesn't move, despite the chaos. Her eyes are closed and her cheeks glisten with silent tears. Sophie launches into stories about life in Hobart, trying to amuse her and distract her. It actually puts Olessia to sleep after about ten minutes. Sleep is a great idea, but before Ryder can even consider it she needs to change out of her disgustingly stained shirt. Following Sophie's instructions she heads through the same door the others used. She steps into the corridor, closing the door behind her. She can hear voices coming from the room off to her right; Aresh and the others deep in conversation in their own language. What would that be, Sirosian? Sirosonese? Sir? Ryder tilts her neck side to side, trying to get a crack out of the joints. The crush of the headache has died down to the barest pressure. Nothing bothersome. The pepper shaker worked miracles.

Second door on the left, Sophie told her. That's where Ryder will find their bags, and a fresh t-shirt. The thought of changing out of the torn, bloodstained shirt she's had on all day is akin to winning the lottery right now. She opens the door. It's not so much a room, as an oversized storage cupboard, with rows of shelving taking up most of the space. Ryder never thought she would be so happy to see that old duffel bag, a factory second with a misspelt logo she bought for a couple of dollars, years ago. It sits on a shelf towards the back of the tiny room, next to the equipment case. Ryder traces her fingers over the grooves of the hardcase, grateful for the peace and quiet. She's not usually a big fan of being alone. When her dad's away she practically lives at Lucas and Petra's place. Or Sophie's. In Ryder's experience quiet, empty houses didn't usually stay that way for long. At one point, she thought maybe the weird things she saw, the sounds she heard, were just her lonely imagination making friends for her.

She exhales, long and slow, until her lungs are empty. That theory is kind of out the window now. She tugs off the bloodied shirt. Since Aresh peppered her with the magic fairy dust, her shoulder is near back to normal. Balling up the bloodied shirt, Ryder clenches her fingers into the material. With everything that's happened, what has she learned? Okay, maybe she's not having a breakdown, but what does that leave? Ryder throws the shirt into her bag and rubs her hands across her face. Maybe this place has some beds somewhere; sleep would be heaven right now. She tugs a plain yellow shirt out of her bag and pulls it over her head.

"How is your shoulder?"

Ryder wheels around. Aresh stands in the doorway. She seems much more petite than before. All sign of the warrior is well and truly gone. She smooths the folds of her dress, despite the fact they're not out of place, then she wrings her hands. Her violet gaze flicking between Ryder's face and the ground. The woman who can apparently fling people around at will, is as uneasy as a job applicant at an interview.

"It's much better, thanks." Ryder clears her throat, but there's more awkwardness than apprehension in the sound. What's with that, why isn't she scared? The woman is a powerful extra-terrestrial being, there are reasons to be afraid. The silence stretches out. Sophie's laughter reaches them. The walls are evidently thin. There's another sound too, the clatter of dishes and water running into a sink. Aresh's restless hands move to her hair, patting at the already perfectly arranged white strands.

"I just needed to-" Ryder gestures to the duffel bag. "I just wanted to change my shirt."

"Of course." Aresh inclines her head. "I understand. I heard you in here and I just wanted to make sure everything was all right. You have had quite the experience."

So maybe super-hearing is one of Aresh's other talents. If she was in another room, mid-conversation with those guys, how did she hear Ryder sneaking down the hall? Aresh turns to leave, but stops at the door, one hand resting on the handle.

"Olessia tells me that you helped her gain control of the Beckoning." Aresh studies the metal door handle like it is a glistening diamond. "That in fact you were able to hand her the Senlier, and help her expel the Beckoning's power."

Expel the Beckoning? Okay, so that might explain the nuclear blast that knocked Ryder senseless. Aresh traces a fingertip over the door handle. There is a loud clatter from the main room, a plate dropping onto the floor but not smashing. And then Sophie, ordering Christian to get out of the kitchen and let her handle it. Handle what exactly, Ryder isn't sure. Cooking in that tired old space seems impossible. Never mind the lack of groceries. Ryder drags her focus back to the shoe-box room. "The senlier is that crown thing, right? Sebastien told me to give it to her so..." Ryder shrugs. "I did."

Aresh tilts her head, her face hidden from Ryder's view. "And you were unharmed."

It doesn't seem to be a question. Ryder runs nervous fingertips over the straps of her duffel bag, wondering what her chances are of getting past Aresh, and out of this too-small room.

"Is that a bad thing?" she says.

"No." Aresh turns in a hush of sweeping material. "No, no not at all. It is a wondrous thing. I would never want anything to harm you, Ryder. I have never wanted that."

She stops, her narrowed gaze darting to a space on the shelves to Ryder's right. There are some tins there, with no labels, a couple of boxes with fragile stickers. Nothing particularly interesting. She is about to ask if there is a problem when Aresh's attention returns to her.

"I must speak with you, Ryder. And this will be hard for you to hear." Aresh steps further into the room and the door closes behind her. The thunk of the latch makes Ryder shiver. There's no windows in the room, and the air tastes of old and forgotten things. It's way too quiet too. Like some giant cone of silence has fallen over them. Ryder strains to listen for the sounds of Sophie and Christian, out in the main area. Now there's nothing, not even the distant murmur of voices.

"What's going on?"

Aresh lifts a paint tin off one of the shelves and uses it as a makeshift seat. Her skirt flutters into an elegant, perfectly arranged layer around her. The single light bulb in the room casts a burnt orange glow on the room, and shadows the scars on Aresh's face. She touches the marks before speaking. "You must know by now that certain parts of your life are not as you expected." She pauses. "Perhaps you feel that Lucas is a stranger now. I want you to know that he is the person he has always been. He is your friend. None of this changes that. He loves you as you love him. Never doubt his loyalty to you."

The narrow rings of elthar around Ryder's wrists seem weightier suddenly, and the skin around them tingles. Everything is changed, but Ryder finds herself nodding.

Aresh continues. "Olessia has told you that I have been to your world before. Ryder, I need to show you what your part in that has been. It is too dangerous for you not to know now. He does not feel the same, and I hope he forgives me."

Who? Forgive her for what? And what the hell does any of this have to do with her? Ryder's thoughts slam against one another, tiny hailstones of confusion. It's hard to breathe the stuffy air. Her fingers search for the shelf behind her, something solid to hang on to. Fingertips met the smooth surface of the equipment case. That stupid, lame bag of childish toys. The ones she's wishing she'd never even thought about buying. Ghosts, huh? What was the big deal with hearing the odd whisper, seeing the odd shadow anyway? It didn't mean she was getting sick. Hell, her dad has never even admitted her mum was sick to begin with. Just unhappy, he said. Wanting a different life. Ryder bites at her bottom lip.

Aresh approaches her. There's nowhere for Ryder to go, her back is up against the shelves. But she's not afraid. She's still not afraid when Aresh cups her hands around her cheeks. Her touch is cool and soothing, eyes twin pools of lavender. Ryder stares at the thin line of Aresh's lips, willing them to stay closed. But it is too late.

"My little one, I cannot stay silent, not if I am to protect you."

Olessia promised to do that too, protect her. What's with all the protection? Ryder's a fifteen year old high school student, not a president. The blood rushes to her head and roars in her ears. Stop talking. She wants to shout at Olessia but she can barely breathe. Her heart punches out a crazy rhythm, but she stares squarely into Aresh's eyes. Neither one of them blink. Ryder's fingers dig hard into the equipment case behind her. The completely useless case. Her ghost is standing right in front of her.

"Will you allow me, Ryder?"

Ryder barely hesitates before nodding.

"Remain calm," Aresh whispers. "What you will see has already come to pass. You are in no danger. These are my memories."

She leans her head forward so that their foreheads touch, her hands still against Ryder's face. It is a quiet, serene moment and nothing else in the world exists. Just the two of them. Tears jab at Ryder's eyes and she lets them close.

It begins. And it's not so different to what the Placer did to her. Aresh's past flows through Ryder's mind, clear and full of life. And full of Ryder. As a child, barely five years old, playing in the backyard at Jack's place. Then, sitting beside Aresh who

171

laughs and claps along with her to the children's show they're watching. Next, Aresh's hand in hers as they cross the main street in Evandale, waving to Jack who waits in line at his favourite bakery. The confusing sense of familiarity she felt when she first saw Aresh is laid bare.

Ryder keeps her eyes clenched shut, but a tear escapes and threads a warm path down her cheek. Her childhood peels away. The life she thought she had, disappearing with each vision. First Lucas, now Jack. So many lies it's breathtaking. Aresh's memories reach the hospital, and what Ryder thought, till now, was the darkest time in her life. She stares down at herself, lying asleep in the hospital bed, hooked up to wires and tubes, and surrounded by beeping machines. Aresh is there alone, holding her hand, and brushing back her hair, murmuring gentle words of encouragement. Words that Ryder was oblivious to at the time. Aresh whispers to her to fight. She tells her she will find a way to save her.

In the real world, in the cramped storage room, Aresh's hands press tighter against Ryder's face. She makes a sound, a sharp intake of breath that might be a sob.

"I'm so sorry." Her breath is warm against Ryder's face. "Forgive me."

Ryder's eyes flutter open. She pulls away, lifting her face from Aresh's touch. "I don't...I don't understand. Forgive you?" For stealing chunks of her childhood, by hiding all those memories? Ryder winces under the weight of what she's just seen. Jack has kept an almighty secret for a very long time. The faintest hint of movement stirs in Aresh's eyes, and her jaw is set tight. But Ryder is the one who should be angry—who *is* angry.

Again Aresh busies herself with the folds of her gown, but this time she stares Ryder in the eyes when she speaks. "I had hoped it was done with, that you were safe. Forgive me for placing you in such jeopardy." She pauses, fingers clench tight around fabric. Aresh edges back with tentative steps, like she is afraid Ryder might bolt. It isn't far from the truth. "The illness you had as a child, your doctors thought they were dealing with a viral outbreak. But they were wrong. My brother Inel is a determined and brutal man. I underestimated the lengths he would go, as Presider, to gain advantage over the Zentai in this war."

The narrow edges of the shelving unit dig into the middle of Ryder's back, but they are the only solid, real thing right now and she doesn't move away. "You're not making any sense, what's the virus got to do with your...brother?"

This is what it must be like when the police turn up on your doorstep with bad news. The world gets teeny-tiny and boxes you in, your blood is ocean-wave loud in your ears. Ryder watches Aresh's lips as she continues.

"The virus was created on Siros, it was a weapon. Your people were test subjects." She lowers her eyes.

Twenty people died when the virus swept through northern Tasmania. And those who survived had immune systems that could barely handle the common cold. It's the reason why Jack and her Dad freak if she sniffs too many times. Aresh is still talking, she won't stop.

"We discovered...*I* discovered, a similarity in the genetic make-up between humans and the Zentai when I was here on a Traverse expedition. But Ryder, believe me, I had no idea how my brother would exploit that. My mission was exploratory only. It was never meant to aid a war machine, and I had no idea what was being done behind my back."

Ryder cradles her arms around her body, not sure how much longer she can stand here. "But I'm okay, I mean...I survived."

And she stopped follow up appointments over three years ago. The doctor didn't see the point in continuing them; she was healthy, with an immune system as resilient as any other average teenager. No apparent side effects from the super virus. Nothing, except for the small matter of hallucinations.

Aresh draws herself up, a trace of the warrior lighting her expression. "My brother used me, but he would not take you from me too. I found a way to save you, but I had hoped the repercussions of my choice might not be as they appear. Your strength is truly remarkable but for now we must work to ensure you remain unknown."

The air is unbreathable now. "I can't...I need to get out..." Ryder pulls at the collar of her shirt, stretching the already slack material.

"Ryder, no one must know of what you did for Olessia. Dashel and Verran especially must not know of it."

The roil of her stomach gives Ryder no choice but to run. She shoves her way past Aresh who begs her to wait, to calm herself. To be careful. But Ryder is done talking. She throws open the door and races into the hallway. Sound rushes back in and the first thing she hears is Sophie. She is calling out an excited but confused greeting. Jack has arrived. With all his secrets.

Ryder hesitates at the door to the main area, swallowing hard. Once she opens it, steps out and comes face to face with her grandad, it will all be irreversibly real. She steadies herself, takes a deep breath and opens the door. Jack is putting a bag of takeaway noodles on the table, and actually laughing at Sophie's exclamations over the prawn crackers. Seeing him freezes Ryder where she stands, the width of the room stretching into an impassable void.

"Look Ryder," Sophie waves her over. "Look who's here."

"Oh, my girl. It is so good to see you." Jack rushes over to her, crossing the void, arms raised. A beaming smile on his face. "Thank all the stars that you're okay."

It is the same delighted way he greeted her at the train station when they arrived in Evandale. As if nothing in the world is wrong. Jack's smile slips though, when she raises her arms, stopping him in his tracks. "No. Just....I can't do this...you need to leave me alone."

The colour drains from his cheeks. "Oh Ryder, what did she tell you? She promised me she would wait...." He tries to reach for her again, but with a twist of her shoulders Ryder slips past.

"Where are you going? There's Pad Thai," Sophie cries. "Your favourite."

"Ryder?" Christian steps in front of the main door. "Hey, what's-"

"Christian, please let her go." Olessia struggles to her feet, the blankets sliding from her shoulders. She gives Ryder a barely perceptible nod, and then collapses to the floor. Everyone rushes to her, and Ryder is left alone.

CHAPTER 22

RYDER'S BOOTS POUND ON THE packed earth, and she hurtles past the gray transformers lurking like sentries in the enclosed yard. She doesn't stop when she reaches the open gate, racing out into the field with it's sodden soil and cow-cropped grass. The area is drenched in fog now, far thicker than the mist from earlier. Ryder stops, hands on knees, chest heaving. She spits, trying to rid her throat of a burning sensation. At least she didn't throw up, not just yet anyway. And no one is following. She needed some space, and apparently Olessia gave it to her. The fainting display had an air of play-acting to it, a little too much drama. Ryder takes long, slow breaths that puff out clouds of chilled white. Leaving without her jacket wasn't her greatest idea, but then, she's hardly thinking straight. Doesn't matter, goosebumps or not, she's not going back in there. Not yet. She'll need some time before she's ready to sit round the dinner table, eating Thai and chatting about the weather.

Fog muffles the sound of her breathing, and quietens the world around her. The condensation isn't as insulating as whatever barrier Aresh created in the store room, but it is just as isolating. Ryder could be the only living thing for miles around, the stillness envelopes every inch of the landscape. She wraps her arms around her waist, but the solitude's not as comforting as before. If Sophie was here she'd say something fit for a greeting card, all positive and gooey and calming. Christian would know when not to say a thing at all. Ryder glances back towards the building. The door is closed, and swirls of fog creep toward the threshold.

The jangle of metal pulls her attention back towards the field. A solid figure emerges out of the gloom. The bearded man, Dashel, clad in a heavy brown coat that sweeps out behind him, cutting a swathe through the dense air. He catches sight of her. "What are you doing out here?" he says, peering at her like she's a bug under a microscope. Maybe that's what he's seeing. An oddity. He could well have been with Aresh on Earth, he may know what she did to save Ryder. The thought stirs her fragile stomach.

"I'm getting some air." She steps aside, allowing more than enough room for him to pass, and proud of how steady her voice sounds.

"You should be inside."

He shifts his weight, as though he's considering dragging her in there himself. So Ryder does the only thing she can think of. Something that's becoming a habit. She runs.

Ryder's haphazard jog over the uneven ground gets off to a slow start but builds momentum. And her fears are unfounded. A quick glance back tells her Dashel isn't following. He's walking back towards the building. The fog crawls in behind him, quickly covering all but the barest trace of his path. Don't say a word, Aresh told her. But don't tell them what? That Ryder handed Olessia a little crown and lived to tell the tale? Who's to say that Christian or Sophie wouldn't have been able to reach Olessia with the Senlier? Ryder's inner voice isn't playing fair though. It reminds her about the voices at the quarry, and the dust cloud that protected her. Reminds her that Sophie and Christian don't have an alien-dating grandad, nor were they ever poisoned by a power-mad ruler.

"It's all good. All good." She chants in time to her footsteps, pacing further out into the field. Distracted, she misses a depression in the ground, and falls in an inelegant heap. "Perfect."

The weekend is going from bad to worse. She rests back on her heels. The faintest hum comes from the massive powerlines somewhere above her in the dark. There are no traces of the lights from the station behind her or the scrap yard ahead of her. Weak moonlight illuminates the air but it's unable to penetrate too far into the fog. She grinds her hands into the ground; grass and damp soil squelching between her fingers. The fresh air is supposed to help her get it together, keep the roar of her thoughts down so she can think straight. But she is cold, and far too alone. Aresh's revelations keep playing over in her head. Little wonder Olessia ran away. Her father is a monster.

A flickering in the darkness catches her attention. Ryder squints, peering into the foggy curtain. Nothing. She squeezes her eyes closed. When she opens them again, the area around her appears brighter, as if the moon found an opening in the fog. Another dart of movement, this time to her right. A frosty breeze toys with the strands of her hair. She thrust her hands back into the damp soil, grabbing two heavy handfuls, tearing the grass free.

"Stop hiding." She pushes herself to her feet. "Show yourself now or just leave me alone."

She swings her arm back and throws the clumps of soil out into the fog. If it's Aresh, she hopes the dirt hits her square in the face.

"Whoa!" Sophie stumbles into view, her fox-eared beanie pulled down so low over her forehead her eyes are barely visible. She swapped her flowing skirt for a pair of bright red jeans and she clutches Ryder's jacket against her chest. "Hey if you don't want me to find you, don't call out to me. Rule one of hide and seek."

"I didn't."

"Didn't what?"

"Call out to you."

Sophie frowns. "Weird, could have sworn-"

Ryder doesn't wait to hear what she could have sworn. She

grabs her friend in a hug, burying her face into the cool polyester of Sophie's bright purple puffer jacket.

"There's a lot of weird going on, I'm sorry." She mumbles into the material.

Sophie's embrace tightens, and they stand like that for a few moments before Sophie speaks up. "Here, it's freezing out here, put this on." She hands Ryder her jacket, helping her to put it on, fussing over her, telling her the wound seems a lot better. Ryder steps away, wiping her nose on her sleeve edge. She'd almost forgotten about the puncture marks on her shoulder, since Aresh doused it with the little flakes.

"So, my friend," Sophie says. "Talk to me. Things are clearly not right in the world if you don't eat your Pad Thai. Now, aside from the obvious craziness that Jack and Lucas are mixed up in this, what did Aresh say to you? You were in there a while and Olessia didn't think it was a good idea I should interrupt...so spill."

She smiles, but Ryder doesn't smile back. Being vulnerable herself is one thing, but what does it mean for Sophie if Ryder tells her what Aresh said. She gives herself a moment, staring at Sophie's hands linked in hers. Sophie has zebra print, press-on nails on most fingers. Her left index finger, and right pinkie are bare.

"Oh yeah," Sophie says. "I forgot you said you'd redo my nails this weekend. Don't think any of this madness lets you out of that. Aliens don't get between manicures and friends."

And that's all it takes to decide. Dealing with this, without Sophie's slightly-nuts level of fortitude, isn't going to be an option. And besides, Sophie would nag the truth out of her eventually anyway. Resistance is useless.

"I know for a fact I didn't promise that." Ryder gives her friend a wry grin. "Chris is the expert at getting those things on, you know that." Her smile wavers as she considers what she's going to say next.

Sophie squeezes her hands. "Go on. Let's hear it."

It pours out of her, a torrent of info that makes Sophie's eyes bug. Ryder tells her about Aresh's memories, and her being in them. Tells her how the Presider made humans lab rats. How Aresh insisted she didn't know that the research team had nefarious ulterior motives. Tells her that somehow, Ryder got caught up in it all because of Jack, and that Lucas is a part of it too, though she has no clue how exactly. And finally, she tells Sophie that Aresh saved her life, somehow. And that has changed everything.

Sophie stays silent after Ryder is done. Lips pursed, shaking her head slowly side to side. Ryder is about ready to shake her when she finally replies. "Right, so let me get this straight," Sophie pauses. "What you're saying is, Jack made out with an alien?"

Ryder bursts out laughing, the sound echoing against the fog. "Oh my god, that's what you took from all that?"

"But, I mean where did they meet? Is there a dating app for this kind of thing?"

It's difficult to stop laughing, which makes a nice change. Ryder lifts her hands. "I didn't ask."

Sophie taps a finger to her chin. "Maybe the Harlow Institute is actually what the Internet thinks it is? I mean there have always been rumours about the place. That it's military or government or something, fringe science type stuff?" Then Sophie gasps. "Oh my god, she's the woman in the photos at Jack's place. That lady with the dark hair that's in so many of those shots."

"It doesn't look anything like her, and no scars either."

"Make up, change of hair colour, and take another look. It could totally be her. Scar might be from after she left here. She's an alien Ry, they have a spaceship, they can move between worlds like we take a stroll. I'm guessing she can alter photographs."

It sends an uncomfortable train of thought moving through Ryder's head. If it is Aresh in the photos, she's been with Jack for a long time. Ryder is barely a year old in one of them. How involved is her Dad in all of this? Sophie links her arm through

Ryder's and they stand in silence. The hum of the wires is the only sound around them. It is bitingly cold, despite the jacket, but she doesn't want to move. Definitely doesn't want to go back inside. She can breathe out here, even if her ribcage is icing up with each gulp.

Sophie breaks the silence. "I miss Lucas."

"He'll be okay," Ryder says, as much to herself as to her friend.

"Oh I have no doubt," Sophie replies. "I reckon they'll be kind of disappointed if they catch him. All that effort for a veterinary science major."

Long fingers of cold air brush the back of Ryder's neck. "Exactly." A vet science major who can read alien languages.

Sophie shivers too. "All right, it's freezing out here, we should go back inside. Find out what the plan is."

"How is Olessia?" Ryder peers around, trying to work out which way leads back to the power station.

"Better. When I left, Christian was trying to get her to eat something." Sophie turns in a full circle. "Do you have any idea which way we go?"

In the distance off to their left, a sound like the flutter of a flock of birds, echoes across the field.

"Did you hear that?" Ryder frowns.

"The wires?" Sophie says.

"No, no, not that."

It happens again, a chittering in the distance. It's clearer than before but this time, it's off to the right. Ryder shifts, straining to listen. It isn't birds. It's voices. A distant, gentle murmur of voices that is fast becoming all too familiar. This is the same sound from the quarry. She mouths a question to Sophie, *can you hear that*? Sophie shakes her head, her red hair swaying. Ryder stares out over the field. Something glints off to the right and a faint spot of light appears. It is a small orb, the size of an average light bulb, hovering just above the ground. She moves towards it, towing a reluctant Sophie along.

"Tell me you can see that?" Ryder points.

"See what, Ry?" Sophie grips her arm a little tighter.

Ryder doesn't reply. Something is happening to the light. It is stretching, contorting and growing. Morphing into something vaguely human. She can just make out a pair of legs, too lean and long to be truly human. A narrow torso stretches into a rounded blob that marks where a head might be. Curls of fog splay out from it, like snakes on a faceless Medusa. The murmur of voices grows louder, like whoever, whatever, it is has walked closer to where they stand.

"Sophie," Ryder whispers. "Please, are you sure you don't see it?"

This is what watched her. Not just in the shadows at Clarendon House, but from the corners of her own darkened lounge room. It skittered out of sight when she woke so many mornings, and scared the living hell out of her some nights when it stirred her from her dreams. Ryder presses her hands to her thighs.

"No," Sophie says. "And you're starting to freak me out now, Ry. What is it?"

The entire shape constantly moves, crumbling like sand one moment, only to reform the next. It repeats the pattern over and over, as though it struggles against some invisible force to hold its shape. Desperately fragile. Ryder holds her breath, willing it to hold on. The thought of it disappearing now makes the back of her eyes sting.

Leave here, you must go.

The voice rises up and over the whispers, but it has a strange echo to it, like a group of people speak the same words in near-unison, feminine and masculine at the same time. It's the voice from the quarry. Ryder stares at the apparition. Her hands are icy cold but calm and still. Her breathing is measured and eyes wide open. A sense of something falling away, a lightness, spreads across her body. The dank, suffocating weight of all those nights spent worrying, convincing herself that she was falling apart, ebbing away. Aresh wasn't her ghost at all.

Do not fear us, Ryder. We seek to help you.

"Who are you?" Ryder says. "What do you want?"

Sophie's grip is really starting to hurt but she stays silent.

To warn you. You must go from here, take the Laudess from here.

The apparition contorts, losing definition, and Ryder chokes back a cry. For so long this blurred, undefined darkness is all she's ever caught a glimpse of. It can't disappear again now.

"Who are you?" Ryder repeats, her voice overly loud in the stillness. The apparition draws into sudden, sharp focus, and Ryder lets out a relieved breath.

I am Padellah. One ethereal arm drifts towards her, like it's trying to shake hands. Ryder doesn't move. *We are the Cyne. You must leave here. Make the Laudess leave. It is unsafe here.*

The warning sends her blood rushing, making her lightheaded.

"Please tell me what's happening." Sophie dances up and down beside her.

"There's something here, I've seen it before. So many times before." Ryder can't take her eyes off the apparition. "It's incredible, Soph. I wish you could see it."

"It's talking to you?"

With an absent nod, Ryder watches the snaking figure move in and out of shape. "It wants us to get Olessia out of here. Something is coming." Her voice sounds distant and dreamy to her own ears.

"What is coming?"

"I don't know," Ryder stares into the shifting silhouette. Whatever the Cyne are, they are mesmerising. If she could gaze at it all day it wouldn't be long enough.

They come. They come. You and the Laudess must leave here. Tell her. She will trust you.

Then, without warning, the silhouette collapses. It doesn't rise again. The light is snuffed out as surely as a candle being extinguished. The pang that comes is sharp and deep inside Ryder's chest. "No." They've left her. Again. The loneliness sets her shivering.

Sophie tugs at Ryder's jacket sleeve. "What is it saying?"

"I think it's gone." Ryder cups her hands round her mouth and shouts into the fog. "Hello? Are you still there?"

"Ry, what's going on?"

"Shhh…" But they are alone. The disconnect hollows out her chest.

"So," Sophie whispers. "What do we do?"

Ryder stares at the empty space. The apparition, Padellah, needed her help. Warned her. And the urgency was unmistakable. "We're going to get Olessia out of here."

CHAPTER 23

DECISION MADE AND ADRENALINE pumping, Ryder turns, ready to make a beeline back to the power station. Problem is, she has no idea which way to go.

"Which direction did you come from, Soph?" she says.

"Pretty sure it was that way." Sophie holds her hand above her eyes, like that will somehow make it easier to spot the station.

"Are you sure you didn't come from over there?" Ryder gestures in the opposite direction. "I could have sworn you came that way."

Sophie groans. "I can't see a thing. We are the worst rescue mission ever."

Then a voice calls out through the gloom. "Ryder, are you there?" Olessia's lilting accent gives her away.

"Okay, now I can hear that," Sophie says. "And it sounds a lot like-"

"It's Olessia."

Hunched shapes approach from off to Ryder's right, silhouetted by a soft blue glow.

"And I can see that," Sophie says. "I am two for two."

The figures draw closer. "Can I just say that they are coming from the direction I pointed out?" Ryder says.

"No, you cannot." Sophie digs a gentle elbow into Ryder's side.

A moment later Olessia and Sebastien reach them. Sebastien has one arm wrapped around Olessia, and she stumbles along beside him. The elthar around his torso illuminates her face, turning her pallor a sickly ashen blue. Ryder meets Sebastien's gaze. It's probably just the light, or her exhaustion, but she could swear he appears relieved. The wind is strengthening and it takes hold of loose strands around his face. Sebastien ducks his head, fixing the locks behind his ears. When he casts his gaze up again his usual scowl is in place.

"Ryder, what happened?" Olessia says. "I couldn't sense you for a moment. Are you all right?"

"Sense me?" Ryder lifts her fingers to her temples. "You're still in my head?"

Olessia shrugs off Sebastien's support, her eyes bright with curiosity. "I'm not reading your thoughts if that's what concerns you. I was merely…" She tilts her head, studying Ryder. "I was keeping an eye on you. You seemed very distraught when you left. But then you were just…gone…Sophie was alone out here. I thought it best we check on you."

"And I did not." Sebastien puts his arm back around Olessia. "You can see the girl is quite well, we should go back inside before I am being lectured again by that imbecile."

Ryder's shoulders tighten with indignation. The *girl* has some information he might just want to consider.

"No." The word jumps from her lips, loud and forceful. "You can't go back in there."

Sebastien peers down his nose at her. "And why not?"

The guy could strip paint off a wall with those stone chips he calls eyes, but Ryder holds his gaze. He has to listen to her; the girl who saved his butt not so long ago.

"We need to go. We need to get away from here." Not exactly a speech that will go down in history. And Sebastien will never just nod and say, of course Ryder, whatever you want. But he has to listen. She's never been more certain.

"Why do you say that?" Olessia watches her. "Why do we need to go?"

"Because...I think we should just..." Ryder hesitates. Surely the Cyne could have gone directly to Olessia to warn her? Or Aresh perhaps. But they came to her. Kind of odd, considering. "I've got a bad feeling...Sebastien, you need to get her on the Aventar, take her away from here."

Sebastien makes a dismissive sound. "Because you have a bad feeling? Don't be ridiculous."

The mist curls and twists under the touch of a strengthening breeze. Sebastien and Olessia's coats shift and sway.

"It's not ridiculous," Sophie matches his indignant tone. "You should listen to her."

To Ryder's surprise, Olessia seems to be doing just that. She brushes off Sebastien's attempts to move her, focused on the two cold, damp humans in front of her.

"Please." Ryder flutters her hands, searching for the magic word. One that could possibly convince a preternatural, kick-ass, life-sucking princess to just simply turn tail and run.

"All right." Olessia turns up the collar on her coat. "Sebastien, we will do as she says."

He and Ryder ask the same question at the same time. "What?" Wiping condensation from her cheek, Ryder exchanges a shocked half-smile with Sophie. The flappy ears on her friend's fox beanie wiggle back and forth with the brush of the wind. The gusty change hasn't shifted the fog though. Walls of it continue to press in on them. Olessia opens her mouth to speak when a spot of bright light suddenly appears on one of the devices on Sebastien's utility belt. Two sharp beeps ring out. He wrenches the device, the size and shape of a compact mirror, free from his belt.

He stares hard at Ryder. "How could you possibly know-"

It hits her for the first time that she has no clue *what* they are running from. Only that they need to. Now, seeing the strain on Sebastien's face, icy fingers trace their way down her arms.

"Sebastien, what is it?" Olessia says.

"She was right, we need to get to the Aventar," He gives her no option this time, grabbing her arm and pulling her roughly past Ryder and Sophie. "We've been compromised."

Olessia struggles to pull away. "Sebastien, what about the others?"

"Aresh and her Claven friends are more than capable of defending themselves," he says. "You are my assigned priority."

Ryder's chest tightens. Whatever it is, it's here now. Close. Padellah has barely given them any time at all. "But Jack and Christian are back there," she says. "You have to tell them."

"If you wish to go back, then do so. But make your choice now. I won't wait for you." Sebastien holds Olessia against his side, her feet barely reaching the ground as he takes her weight. By the time he finishes speaking they are barely visible in the gloom.

"We can't leave Chris and Jack back there." Sophie clutches at her beanie.

"Nope. We're going back." Ryder spins round. She remembers exactly which direction Sebastien and Olessia came from. And there is no way, no matter how many lies, she isn't going back there now. Ryder and Sophie race across the field, matching stride for stride. They only cover a few metres though before a blast of wind slams against them.

"Oh, whoa." Sophie stumbles, and Ryder steadies her before they both start off again. But they might as well be walking through the wall of a tornado. Flecks of debris whip up from the ground. Ryder covers her eyes, her jacket billowing out behind her. A single step is difficult; making it across the whole field will be exhausting.

"This isn't going to work," Sophie shouts over the hiss of the wind.

"No. It isn't." Ryder spits out a piece of something gritty in her mouth. She has a sudden idea. Stopping, she turns around, waving at Sophie to follow suit. The moment they both face in the opposite direction the wall of wind drops to nothing more than the very lightest of breezes. Despite the turbulence, the fog still hangs like curtains around them. Testing her theory, Ryder swings back towards the station and is rewarded with a blast of icy air.

"I guess somebody doesn't want us to go the other way." Sophie plucks a grass stalk from her fringe.

"No. Doesn't look like they do." Ryder searches for signs of Padellah, scanning the darkness for the tell-tale ball of light. They are alone. "I guess we go to the Aventar."

Every step she takes away from the power station weighs heavy. Anger spills through her. This hardly seems a great reward for playing messenger. Olessia might be safe but what about everyone else? If anything were to happen to Christian and Jack, Ryder will find a way to contact the Presider herself and get Olessia the hell off this planet.

"We've lost them." Her words are sharp with frustration. "I can't see Olessia."

"There, look, over there. That's them." Sophie says.

A haze emits from a light in the scrap yard, where Olessia and Sebastien stand either side of the gap in the fence. Olessia is leaning against one of the car bodies. Sebastien catches sight of them as he crouches to follow her through, and he waves them forward. "Quickly, why are you moving so slowly? Get through, now."

Sophie follows orders first. Her jeans catch on a bit of barb wire, tearing a hole in the red fabric over her knee. She untangles herself before pushing on. Ryder bends to follow, conscious of Sebastien's glare.

"When we are on board," he says. "Perhaps you'd like to tell me how you knew about this."

A terrible screech tears across the field behind them; a hoarse cry and scream twisted together. It isn't a sound easily forgotten.

"Oh my god." Ryder's hand goes to the laceration on her shoulder. "That's one of those things, the Placer, isn't it?"

"Just move," Sebastien snaps.

Ryder scrambles through the wiring, falling onto her knees

on the other side. The impact makes her hiss through her teeth, bruises from the earlier run in with the Placer still tender. Behind her a fresh sound rents through the air. Some new kind of nightmare. This creature growls, a deep and guttural sound, contrasting starkly with the ear-shattering pitch of the Placers. Panic spears Ryder's lungs and she struggles to catch her breath. Christian and Jack are back there. She's left them both behind. The awfulness of it threatens to paralyse her. The others are already leaving. Sophie supporting Olessia and hurrying her deeper into the yard. Sebastien follows.

Bellowing roars and cries echo from every direction, bouncing off the mist. There isn't a scrap of skin on Ryder's body not covered in goosebumps. She races after them.

"What is that?"

She can't make out Sebastien's grunted reply. Whatever it is out there, it isn't from Earth. Sophie and Olessia stumble, and Olessia goes down on one knee. In one smooth movement Sebastien scoops her up in his arms. The effort seems to be nothing for him, his stride barely altering.

"Sebastien, how many are there?" Olessia struggles for breath, like she's been winded.

"Too many for us to handle with you in this state." Sebastien's pace quickens, and Ryder has to break into a jog to stay close.

"How did they get so near?" Olessia stares over Sebastien's shoulder, beyond Ryder and Sophie who follow right behind. The narrow path between piles of crushed cars is full of overgrown grass and weeds that brush against Ryder's jeans. "Why was there no warning?"

Ryder keeps her eyes on the path, sensing Sophie's gaze. She did warn them. Padellah failed to mention she had all of five minutes to do it. The spirit has lurked in Ryder's peripheral vision for what might be years, now, when it finally makes contact, everything is desperate and urgent.

"I have no idea," Sebastien says. "They evaded the Aventar's surveillance somehow. I don't-"

"Wait, stop," Olessia cries out. "Christian is out there."

"We have no time for this, Olessia. The boy is with Aresh, she'll protect him."

Olessia has found some renewed energy, and shakes her head vigorously. Sebastien curses, struggling to hold her. "No, no. He's not with her. He's out there."

Ryder darts in front of them, bringing Sebastien to a sudden stop. He gives up trying to hold onto Olessia, and lets her feet touch the ground.

"What are you saying, Olessia?" Ryder says. "Christian is out in that field?"

A deep, guttural roar rings out again, somewhere off to their right, followed by the harsh return cry of a Placer. The rawness of it digs into Ryder's skull.

"Yes." Olessia's voice cracks. "He's out there."

"With those things?"

"If he is out there then he's more of a fool than I thought," Sebastien says. "There is nothing I can do for him right now. My priority is you, Olessia."

He grabs her shoulders, attempting to force her forward.

"They'll find him, they'll kill him." Olessia twists in his grasp, trying to break free.

"And it will kill you if you extend yourself again so soon." Sebastien easily dodges a kick she levels at him. "You're too weak."

Olessia's violet eyes are churning funnels of colour. Another gut-wrenching cry bursts through the air.

Flinching at the sound, Sophie turns to Ryder. "What do we do?"

Ryder knows what she's going to do, but she's not about to let Sophie join in. "Stay here. Stay with them, Soph."

She doesn't wait to see if Sophie listens. She sprints back the way they came. Sophie hollers at her to stop, and then she's shouting at Sebastien to let her go. Ryder says a silent thanks for the unexpected save. Then the wind returns. Ignoring the push of it, she dashes along the overgrown pathway through the metal jungle, dodging rusty panels being lifted by the gusts. If Padellah doesn't want her to find Christian, it is too bad. She stops to grab a piece of piping and then races through the narrow opening in the fence. She might have torn another hole in her jacket, she doesn't know or care. Ryder's breath is roaring in her ears, her throat aches with the effort of breathing the chilled air.

The field is a vast, swirling mass of white. She has no sense of direction, no idea where to even begin searching for Christian. But he is somewhere out there, in amongst the shrieks and bellows and hellish shadows. She's done what Padellah asked, Olessia is safe, she can't let Christian pay for it. Her skin burns where her fingers wrap around the cold metal pipe, but at least it stops them shaking.

"Christian," she bellows.

Adrenaline carried her here, but she has no clue what to do next. "Christian," she calls again. "Can you hear me?"

Screams propel out of the fog nearby, a sound like a fox caught in a trap. Ryder cringes. It is close. Horrifyingly close. She shifts her grip on the pipe, her jaw clenched. Every instinct shouts at her to turn and run. Head back to the Aventar. Back to safety. Olessia is exhausted, so maybe she's made a mistake. Maybe Christian is safe back at the power station. She lifts the pipe with shaking arms. He's not. She knew it the minute she saw Olessia's face. There's no mistake.

"Christian, are you out here?" She swings the pipe, slashing it through the air. It feels too light to rely on. "Christian! Over this way."

She edges further out into the field. A light drizzle starts to fall. The Placers' nails-on-chalkboard cries fracture the damp air. With each shrill they draw closer.

"Damn it, Chris, where are you?"

"Ryder! Is that you?"

Christian's voice, strained and heavy with terror, comes from somewhere nearby.

She bolts towards the sound. "Here, over here."

He hurtles out of the mist, and Ryder has to dodge to avoid a full on collision.

"Oh, thank god." He flings his arms around her. She can feel his chest heaving, and he is shaking even harder than she is.

She pulls away. "We need to get out of here."

"Those Placer things are back."

"Yep, kind of figured that. What the hell are you doing running out here?"

"I came to find you guys." He puffs. "You'd been gone ages."

Grabbing his hand, she heads back towards the hole in the fence. A moment later a shuddering boom fills the air.

"Oh man, it's the power station," Christian cries. "Look."

Ryder's chest hollows at the sight. The heavy wall of fog has softened enough that they can see a cascade of bright orange sparks raining down from one of the high towers. Below it the whole complex is aglow, a searing blaze that flickers and dances. The power station is on fire.

"Jack," Ryder says.

"No." Christian blocks her way. "What are you doing? You can't go back. Those things are everywhere out there, not just Placers either. Ryder, where is Olessia?"

She considers pushing him aside, ignoring the logic of what he is saying, and bolting back to the station. Jack is there. She left him there. A needling sensation moves across the still-healing wound on her shoulder. Then out of the darkness, something tall and fast-moving lunges towards them.

"Move." She shoves Christian out of the way.

The Placer lashes down with a black-taloned claw. Ryder braces her feet and throws all her weight behind a desperate swing of the pipe.

CHAPTER 24

THE WEIGHT OF THE METAL throws Ryder off balance. She gasps, certain she's missed entirely, but the metal hits the Placer's talons with a sharp crack. The creature pulls back before re-centring and lunging again. This Placer is taller than the one from the carpark, but it's equally grotesque. And the stench is even worse; fish in the sun, garbage in a heatwave, everything foul. Orbs of solid white fix on her, and it breathes hard and wet through the cluster of holes that serve as nostrils.

"Ryder, just run." Christian is somewhere nearby.

Aiming another swing, Ryder clenches her teeth at the cramp that radiates across her shoulder. The Placer dodges, surprisingly quick for its height, then swipes again. Ryder feints to the left drawing the Placer with her. With his right side now open and vulnerable, she slams the end of the pipe into the creature's chest. Its scream set her eardrums ringing. But as it lifts its bony arms to grab at the pipe, she notices something.

In the flesh beneath its armpits, halfway down the protruding ribcage, there are slits, like the gills on a fish. Intent on the discovery, Ryder is slow to move when it lunges at her again. This time the talons make contact, ripping through the shoulder of her jacket, just near the laceration. Throwing herself backwards, she hits out with the pipe and is rewarded with a solid thump against the creature's right arm. It screams at her, opening a wide mouth full of broken teeth and no sign of a tongue. This thing has really just stepped right out of a horror novel. Ryder's ears hum, and the pipe is an unwieldy lump in her right hand. She struggles to catch her breath. Every limb jellied, her legs barely holding her.

"For god's sake, Ryder, get out of there." Christian's voice cracks with panic.

The Placer turns its skeletal head towards him, attention moving from Ryder to a new target. With the creature's long limbs, and whip-like speed, there's little chance Christian can make it to the fence line before the Placer reaches him. It crouches low, bony limbs taunt, preparing to launch itself. Ignoring the pain in her arms, Ryder raises the pipe once more. Wiping her head clear of all reasonable thoughts, the ones that bellow at her to race in the opposite direction, Ryder hurls herself towards the Placer, a strained war cry falling from her lips. She levels the pipe ahead of her like a rider in a jousting match, and aims for the gills under its arm. The gray skin tears and the pipe pierces through, slicing into the Placer's chest. It arches its back, mouth stretched wide in a silent scream. Ryder pushes the pipe deeper. She closes her eyes, dry-retching. Something cold runs over her hands. The pipe sinks deeper still, and she is right up close to the creature now. Her fingers make contact with the Placer's side. The skin is rough and cold.

Images explode in her head, popping in and out so fast she can barely make sense of them. They slow, and she sees Olessia, crouching beside a woman who lies deathly still. There are other bodies around them, and Olessia gestures to them as she shouts at a wiry man who stands over her. Ryder can't hear anything being said, the vision is completely silent. There is a yellow sky, with twin streaks of orange light, like comets blazing, and a fast-moving river that runs forest green. The image blurs and fades. Ryder opens her eyes.

The Placer sways on its giraffe-like legs, before its knobby knees buckle. It happens too fast for Ryder to move out of the way. The creature comes down on top of her, but the pipe stops the body from crushing her. Ryder huddles in the small space left between dying beast and cold wet ground. The pipe and Ryder's hands are covered in the Placer's dark, oily blood. The stench of it, like the smell of scorched meat, makes her dry-retch. Ryder knows she should let go, but she can't loosen her fingers. The Placer's weight and odour bear down on her. Dizzy from both, Ryder closes her eyes again.

She is in a cave. A great cavern, with stalactites dripping from the high curved roof. Two Placers lurk in the shadows off to the left, and in the centre of the cavern stands a man flanked by three other creatures Ryder doesn't recognise. They are dog-like in shape, easily double the size of a Great Dane, their paws almost as wide as their heads. Scruffy, with black-red speckled coats of knotted fur and bony, crooked wings protruding from their shoulders. The creatures' heads droop, orange eyes watchful. The man himself has long stringy dreadlocks that cascade almost to his middle, intermingling strands of black and dirty white. He wears a brown military-style uniform but it is his ears that capture Ryder's attention. Or rather, lack of ears. There's nothing there, where the lobe and curve of an ear should be, just the barest of indents and a slight mound of flesh around the canal opening.

All at once the image shatters into a thousand specks of light, and the bulk of the Placer above her draws into focus. The stench of foul, rotten things makes her gag. Someone is tugging on her arms, threatening to pull them from their sockets.

"Ryder, you're going to have to help me a little." Christian grunts. "Are you all right? What were you thinking?"

Ryder grasps his arms, using the momentum to edge free. He helps her to her feet, the Placer's tar coloured blood smeared all over his white hoodie.

"I'm okay. How about you?" Ryder catches sight of her hands. They're black with blood, her jacket sleeves soaked almost to the elbows. Her legs wobble, but Christian catches her before she falls.

"I've got you, I've got you." He holds her, pressing his forehead against hers. "That was officially the most ridiculous thing I've ever seen you do. It was amazing."

Swallowing hard, Ryder manages a weak, "Yeah."

A low, rumbling moves through the air around them. Small pieces of debris scatter in every direction.

Christian jerks his thumb towards the sound. "Here comes the cavalry."

The dark shape of the Aventar manoeuvres to the ground, a short distance from where they stand. The door opens and Sebastien's athletic build is silhouetted by the interior lights.

"Get in," he says.

It's easier said than done with the craft's rotating blade stirring up dirt and dust. Ryder turns her head, shielding her eyes. The blaze at the power station resembles a brilliant setting sun on the far side of the field.

"Take his hand." Christian pushes her forward.

The base of the Aventar's entrance is just above head height. Sebastien leans down, waiting. Ryder's movements are heavy, everything in slow motion. She's trying hard not to think about the sticky blood covering her hands. Sebastien grabs her wrists, his grip strong and sure, hauling her up. Backing them away from the entrance, he cradles an arm around her waist. Her head only reaches mid chest, so he leans down to speak to her.

"You could have gotten yourself killed." The warmth of his breath caresses her forehead. Sebastien's hand presses against the small of her back. She expects him to let her go, leave her lurching unsteadily on her feet, but he shifts his arm, wrapping it around her shoulders. A good thing, Ryder doubts she would stay upright for long. She can't stop staring at her blood-soaked arms. The creature's blood. The one she killed.

Sophie and Christian hug it out. Sophie demanding Christian twirls round to prove he has no injuries. The door slides shut with a breathy hiss and the Aventar lifts off. The subtle jerk of the aircraft pushes Ryder against Sebastien, and she can't summon the energy to shift away. He adjusts his hold but says nothing. The unfamiliar pattern of his heartbeat is clear against her ear. Two deep beats, followed by three lighter, faster beats. Over and over. Irregular but reassuring. He is very much alive. Ryder flexes her stained fingers.

"I thought that…" In truth, she has no idea what she was thinking when she stormed out into the field. And now she's killed something. It should feel horrendous. Her body should shake and her guts should churn. Instead, there's just numbness. The world around her moving in a weird, sluggish way. "We need to go back. Jack…he is there…with those things. We need to go back."

Sebastien releases her but he doesn't step away. His stone gray gaze takes in every inch of her face.

"I had brief communications with Aresh. They have fled. Your elder is unharmed." Sebastien takes one of her hands in his. "Is any of that blood yours?"

"I don't think so." His fingers run over her bloodied skin, his thumb tracing the palm of her hand, moving in wide circles, just barely kissing the skin. "I don't understand you at all." Through the haze engulfing her, the softness of his words reaches her.

Ryder shrugs, her hands still oddly steady. "That makes two of us."

"You're sure you aren't hurt?"

She nods. Then shakes her head. Her gaze drifts, runs itself along his arms. There are scars, fine veins of pink, running along the inside of his bare right arm, and snaking out over his shoulder. Lifting her gaze, Ryder meets his. The hard stone gray has melted into smoky concern. Ryder flinches, and her hands start to tremble. He can't stare at her like that, and the gentle words have to stop. Shout at her, tell her she's an idiot, but he can't stare at her like he's frightened she will break. Tugging her hands from his grasp, Ryder steps back, wiping her hands against her jeans.

Olessia calls out to them, haughty and frustrated. "When you are done, Sebastien, some co-ordinates would be useful."

Sebastien's glower returns. He pulls a dull yellow cloth from a pocket and thrusts it at Ryder.

"You reek," he says. "Clean up."

Ryder entwines her fingers to hide the tremor that grips them. The stupor is fading, the sounds and smells inside the cabin pushing in. Sophie berates Christian for running around in the dark on his own, the barest whiff of the Placer's putrid scent clings to Ryder's nostrils. Deep inhales are slowly loosening the knot above her diaphragm. Sebastien strides towards the pilot's seat, not giving her so much as a backward glance. He flicks his fingers towards Olessia who sits in the pilot seat. "I'll take it from here."

Olessia steps aside to let him take a seat. They speak rapidly in their own language, and Ryder watches Olessia's face. There is concern in the tilt of her eyebrows, but a determination too. No hint of the anguish that burrowed deep in every curve in the Placer's vision. Olessia turns her attention to Christian and smiles, the curve of her lips illuminating her face. There are shadows under her eyes, but there is a bounce in her step as she goes to him. She pushes up on tip-toes to wrap her arms around him, not seeming to care about the still-wet blood on his clothing.

"Whoa, okay." Christian laughs, olive skin deepening with a blush. He doesn't edge away though.

Olessia lets him go but remains close enough that their arms brush. "That was truly impressive, I must say Ryder. I didn't know you had quite that much warrior within you."

"No, neither did I." Sophie scowls from beneath the beady eyes of her fox beanie. "We need to have words, my friend."

CHAPTER 25

SEBASTIEN MANOEUVRES THE Aventar away from the power station in a rough swinging turn. Ryder settles in her seat, activates her harness, and tries to avoid Sophie's gaze. She is all alone with Sophie's rare temper, an unfamiliar and uncomfortable place to be. Olessia sits on Christian's far side, the two of them speaking in hushed tones.

Ryder attempts a lop-sided smile, trying to dowse the fire from Sophie's glare. "Look, I know you're mad-"

It's a failed attempt, the flames bloom, reddening Sophie's cheeks. She leans in, voice low and tight. "Well, congratulations, Einstein. The ghost told you to warn them, not fight off the bad guys single-handedly. That was the dumbest thing I've ever seen you do, and you do some stupid things."

Sophie's not big on insults, not with her anyway. Ryder can count on one hand the number of times she's seen her friend this mad. And this time is probably justified. Ryder winces. It was stupid. The whole thing. Padellah shouldn't have come to her with such a last minute warning. If the entity was that concerned, it should have gone straight to Aresh, or Sebastien. Christian was nearly killed. And Ryder can't seem to shift the Placer's blood from her skin. The yellow cloth Sebastien threw at her is next to useless. There's still a faint tinge of pink on her palm. She rubs the silk thin material hard, her skin tingling with the friction.

"Next time you decide to play hero." Sophie isn't done. "Give me a chance to say goodbye."

Ryder stops, the cloth clenched between her fingers. "What's that supposed to mean?"

"It means you could have gotten yourself killed and that you were an idiot." Christian leans in to the conversation as Olessia makes her way to the front of the Aventar. "Don't get me wrong, I owe you, but what were you thinking, Ry?"

Thinking hadn't come into it; that was the whole problem. She stares at the back of Sebastien's head. His hair has almost loosened from its binding. He had intended to leave Christian out there in the field. Olessia is his priority, he made that crystal clear. Ryder's teeth dig into the softness of her bottom lip. Next time he needs help with the senlier, he's on his own. And Padellah too. The entity has haunted her, made her believe she's going mad, and then, the first time it chooses to communicate, all hell breaks loose.

"Okey dokey, enough Ryder." Sophie grabs the cloth. "You're going to draw blood."

Blinking, Ryder stares down at her hands. Her skin burns. All the black blood is gone, the cloth no longer yellow but a blue-gray. Her jacket sleeves are damp and dark though. Releasing the harness, Ryder tugs the jacket from her shoulders, pulling both arms down at once, faltering when the left sleeve catches at her wrist. She makes a little sound, somewhere between a cry and a hiss, struggling to free herself. The elthar bracelet has snagged against the button on the cuff.

"Hey, slow down, let me help you." Sophie's temper is short-lived. Her level tone smooth with reassurance. She edges the thin bracelet over the button, and the jacket slides free. Sophie dumps it at their feet, nudging it with her foot till the blood soaked sleeves are hidden. Ryder flashes her friend a grateful smile, and it's returned with gentle concern.

"Oh wow." Christian's eyes widen. "Check that out." He points to the window, beyond where Sophie sits at the end of the short row.

201

Sebastien has banked the Aventar in a wide left hand turn and the glow of the burning power station is visible in the distance.

"Jack." Ryder rushes to join Olessia where she stands at the great curve of glass that makes up the entire front section of the Aventar.

"I told you he's not down there," Sebastien says. "None of them are."

"Then where is he?" Ryder presses her fingertips against the window. "We need to find him."

A thin line of flashing lights snake their way towards the station. Emergency response or C-21? Both? Ryder's thoughts shift to Lucas, and the angst that comes is a punch to the guts. She braces herself against the glass, forcing wild thoughts away. *Your friend is still free.* That's what Padellah told her back in the quarry. It has to be true. Lucas owes her. It's not fair if she doesn't get a chance to tell him what a giant jerk he is for all this. He has to be okay.

"Can't you contact Aresh again?" Ryder says.

"Not until I am summoned to do so." A holographic display appears in the air before Sebastien. Dials and panels all with symbols like the ones on the Tyius. "The Laudine will initiate next contact. She has enough to concern her for the moment, Verran sustained burns in the attack which require immediate attention. We stay silent until the-"

"Was anyone else injured?" Olessia regards him in a cool imperious way. "Aresh is declining my attempts to contact her."

His reply is equally icy. "And I've told you multiple times to desist with all mindreach communications at this time, Olessia. You must remain undetectable. The Laudine and the human elder are uninjured. Dashel is unaccounted for at time of last mindreach."

Sophie breathes an audible sigh. "Jack's okay, Ry."

Sebastien shifts his shoulders, like he's trying to dislodge an irritating bug. "I had already imparted that information."

Olessia curls her fingers into fists, pressing them against the glass. "Dashel is unaccounted for?"

"Gone to procure supplies for Verran's wounds, I believe, and has gone mindreach silent."

"Do you have any idea who is behind this?" Olessia holds herself rigid, eyes fixed on the fading glow of the station.

"You have a variety of enemies to choose from, Olessia." Sebastien's reply is flat. "But, considering the tech required to conceal the approach of Arlion creatures from our detection, perhaps Verran is right about the Zentai knowing of your presence here. And if that is indeed the case, we will require your father's escort back through the Paldrian River."

"No," Olessia snaps.

He tilts his head, regarding her with the same haughty disdain she levelled at him earlier. "Do you think so little of this world, Olessia, that you would bring war here?" He focuses back on the holographic panel, tapping at a rhombus shape there. "Your inability to accept your position continues to endanger others unless you-"

"My refusal to accept my position is what will keep others protected." Olessia paces across the onyx floor towards him, fists still clenched. "Vale Leven is what happened when I was forced to take my *position*. He sees me as a weapon, and I will not bend to his will."

"And the Beckoning will not bend to yours without the proper guidance," Sebastien says. "The Presider pushed you too far, too early. Vale Leven was an unfortunate error, but you must learn control it if you truly wish no harm. That you do not desire to be Laudess, does not simply make it so."

"Vale Leven was an error?" Her words are wrung high with incredulity. "People died, Sebastien. My people." Olessia returns to stand near Ryder. She leans against the glass, forehead pressed against it. The cabin is pin-drop silent. Ryder lifts her hand, hesitating. Vale Leven is in her head, too. The horror of it etched into her memory. She blinks, seeing again the utter desolation filling Olessia's expression. It makes the hairs on Ryder's arms stand to think of it. She could reach out, offer a reassuring touch on Olessia's shoulder or a gentle squeeze of her hand. But the memory is so personal, so intimate in its pain, that Ryder decides against it. She's an intruder, just as the Placer was when it watched Olessia on the banks of that emerald river. Ryder gazes at the speckling of lights below. The death of one Placer, as disgusting as the thing was, has carved a hollowness inside her. It's impossible to imagine what consolation she could offer Olessia that might make the slightest bit of difference.

The Aventar drifts higher, rising like a hot air balloon up into the night sky. Beneath them, the dots of light scattered across the ground grow smaller, and the burning station vanishes from sight altogether. She sighs and turns back to the interior of the cabin. Sebastien is watching her, gray eyes thoughtful. Then, those gray eyes widen.

"Hold on, everyone," he shouts.

The Aventar tilts, sweeping hard to the right. Sophie cries out and Ryder is thrown off her feet, thumping down onto the smooth floor. The momentum slides her across the cabin, Olessia at her side. They hit the opposite wall, bodies slamming against the glass. Sebastien shouts commands at the craft and is answered with a series of negating tones.

"What's happening?" Olessia presses her arms against the glass, trying to brace herself. Ryder does the same, but there is nothing to hold on to, everything so smooth and polished. Christian reaches for them from his seat, but his fingertips don't even come close to Olessia's outstretched hand.

"We are being pursued," Sebastien says. "Stay down."

The Aventar swerves sharply. Ryder presses against the glass, heels gaining no grip on the ice-like floor. Outside, a dark mass hurtles through the sky towards them. It draws closer, and Ryder's breath sticks at the back of her throat. A huge dog-like thing with a shaggy red-black speckled coat and gleaming orange eyes. And wings. Bony appendages sprouting out between its shoulder blades. The same beast she saw in the Placer's memory, huddled around the man with the dreadlocks and gross, missing ears.

The wings on this creature are fully extended, spanning double the length of it's body. It's surprisingly fast, keeping pace with each manoeuvre Sebastien makes. His frustration flows in long, foreign curses.

"Sebastien, there's another one here-" Ryder's words dissolve into a shriek as a second creature slams into the craft. A line of dark ooze runs down the glass, but the flying beast seems unperturbed, swinging around and readying for another assault. The creature has a long snaking tail, and at its tip is something like a great chunk of broken concrete.

"What's wrong with the Aventar's shields?" Olessia says, measured and clinical now, no trace of panic.

"Clearly, they aren't working. Neither are the interior stabilisers." Sebastien's fingers fly over the controls. "Get to your seats if you don't want to break bones."

Panels in the armrests of the bench seat open, revealing grooves that Sebastien slides his lower arms into. He steers the Aventar in hard turns, zig-zagging them through the air, the muscles in his shoulders flexing as he shifts his body. Olessia pushes herself to her feet. She grabs Ryder's hand and guides her back to the chairs. A jolt of the Aventar throws Ryder against hers, her hip cracking hard against the solid metal. With unexpected strength, Olessia steadies her, before giving Ryder a shove that lands her in her seat. The harness whips into place. Olessia braces to run the short distance to her seat. The Aventar levels out.

"Come on, go now." Christian urges, arms raised towards her.

She launches herself at him, clutching his outstretched arm. Just in time too. Sebastien banks the Aventar and drops altitude.

"What are those things?" Christian says.

"They are Celtren," Olessia replies. "The Arlion produces some truly horrendous things. This is what was stalking you in the field."

Christian's gaze darts to Ryder. And she gives him a grim smile. Sebastien throws the Aventar around like a pilot trying to

205

shake off heat-seeking missiles. It's making Ryder's head spin, and she presses her lips tight. But whatever the Celtren actually are, they are fast and far more agile than their bulk suggests. Another hurls itself against the front left window panel. It's weighted tail shuddering against the glass. Although it doesn't crack, the impact vibrates through the cabin.

"Sebastien what are you doing?" Olessia says. "The Aventar should be able to out run a Celtren."

"Yes, I'm aware," Sebastien says, tightly. "But we have lost acceleration."

A loud thump comes from the back of the craft as another Celtren hits target. The creatures seem intent on bringing the craft down.

Sophie points beyond Olessia, who sits closest to the window. "There's more coming."

Sure enough, two murky spots hurtle through the air towards them, their wings sweeping shadows in the night sky.

"Surely you've got guns or something? Weapons?" Christian says.

Another Celtren approaches the Aventar head on, its orange eyes like two beaming headlights. Ryder can't tear her eyes from what seems a certain collision.

"Don't you think I'd be using them if they worked?" Sebastien snaps back. "Nothing is working. We've lost shielding, surveillance, and weapons. I'm going to try something different. Hold on."

Sebastien levels them out, aiming straight at the encroaching Celtren. Ryder presses her body against the chair. The beast is less than a couple of metres away when Sebastien dips the nose of the craft and they drop. The harness pushes the breath out of Ryder's lungs. But the creature isn't quick enough to alter its flight path, and it lets out a guttural roar as the Aventar's blade slices through its wings, sending it plummeting to the ground below.

Sophie claps wildly. "Amazing."

Something heavy thuds against the floor beneath them.

"How many of these things are there?" Christian cries. "This is completely out of control."

"Olessia, get up here." Sebastien stands, fingertips still on the arm grooves. "You're going to have to pilot the Aventar. I need to get into the circuitry and try and find the problem."

She races from her seat before he finishes his sentence.

"Just hold a steady path," he says. "I just need some time. Can you do that?"

"I can do more than that Sebastien, I know I can-"

"Olessia, just fly. That's all I'm asking."

"Fine." She slides her hands into the deep grooves in the armrests, and the lighting in the craft dims before reigniting, brighter than before.

"Is it supposed to do that?" Sophie's face is pale. Ryder shrugs, hugging her arms tight around her waist.

"Yes. Change of pilot, change of assimilation." Sebastien crouches behind the pilot seat. A panel in the floor opens at his touch, and a glow of pearly light illuminates his face.

"Brace," Olessia shouts, but her instruction comes too late for Sebastien. The impact throws him hard against the back of the pilot seat. The crack of his head against the metal panel is cringe-worthy, likely so too are the hissed words that follow.

Ryder. She jumps at the sound of Olessia's voice in her head, the now familiar pressure in her skull coming on quick and strong. Telepathy is, she decides, incredibly annoying. *Protect him like you did before, if anything goes wrong. I know you can protect them all. Just stay close to them.*

Ryder stares at Olessia's back, hoping Sophie and Christian mistake her shocked expression for simple fear. Her friends are freaked out enough already.

Olessia? Can you hear me? What are you going to do?

Olessia's reply rings back loud and clear. *We don't have time for Sebastien to play with wiring. I can bring these things down. We can do this.*

The sense of being underwater, the pressure bearing down

on Ryder's sinuses and eardrums, is much stronger now than it was on the train. She cringes. *We? Do what?* But she can already guess at the answer, and it does nothing to steady her trembling hands. *Where is that little crown thingy? Don't we need that?*

Ryder massages her temples, trying to ease the tension.

The senlier impedes the Beckoning and disperses the excess energy created, but it didn't protect you. It didn't stop the Beckoning draining Sebastien's energy. I believe you did that. So stay close to them, Ryder. Do not leave their side. Are you ready?

One of the Celtren lands on the bulge of the front window panels. Its claws drag across the glass, the sound like the roof of a tin shack being ripped open by the wind. Sophie and Christian both sit with eyes squeezed shut, hands pressed to their ears.

No, I'm not ready. What are you talking about? Ryder shouts in her head. *I don't know what to do.*

Then all at once, the Aventar drops from the sky.

CHAPTER 26

THE SUDDEN LOSS OF ALTITUDE throws Sebastien into the air. His arms flail, searching for something to hold. Ryder gasps, expecting him to slam up against the curved glass ceiling, but he stops just shy of it, hanging in the air like an astronaut in zero gravity.

"Olessia, don't do this." He presses his hands against the ceiling, trying to shove away from it. But he barely moves. "Put me down."

Olessia doesn't answer. She keeps the Aventar in free fall, engines idling. They are a giant onyx paperweight. Ryder's stomach presses up into her throat, she hates roller coasters with a passion, and this isn't fixing the phobia one little bit. Just when Ryder's eyes feel like they are going to pop, the Aventar slows. It's a controlled and steady descent, like a lift approaching the ground floor. Beside her, Sophie's knuckles are white from clenching the armrests. Ryder gives her hand a reassuring squeeze, her own heart sledgehammering the inside of her ribs, and sweat beading on her top lip.

"Olessia, do not land. I can fix this," Sebastien says.

Still Olessia ignores him. The Aventar's speed diminishes further as they approach the ground. There is dense bushland out to their left, but on the other side the land is flat and dark. Whether Sebastien wants it or not, Olessia is landing. Ryder presses her hand to her chest. Her face is flushed with heat, and no matter how deep she breathes she can't get quite enough oxygen into her lungs. There's a gentle thump as the Aventar touches down. Olessia jumps from the seat and moves to stand in front of Ryder. The violet in her irises bleeds into the whites; thin lines of lavender staining her pupils.

"No, no." Ryder shakes her head. The humidity, the sudden stifling heat, this is what happened to her back at the carpark.

"I know you can do this." Olessia leans down, her words for Ryder only. "I know I can do this with you here."

She presses something into Ryder's hands. The senlier. But it's hard to fixate on anything except Olessia's eyes. The Beckoning, whatever it truly is, writhes there in the violet. Invisible tentacles of energy brush at the edge of Ryder's senses, stifling the air. Olessia runs her fingers over the release for Ryder's harness and the straps pull back into the chair.

"Olessia, don't be ridiculous." Sebastien still floats above them. "Release me."

She ignores him and activates the cabin door. It slides open with a low hiss. Cold air rushes in, soothing against Ryder's hot cheeks, but pungent with the smell of dank water. They have settled on the edge of what appears to be a near-dry lake bed. It stretches out into the distance, its far end swallowed by bushland. Beyond that, resting like a dark blob on the horizon, is the recognisable bulk of Mount Wellington, the mountain standing over the city of Hobart. But there's little time for further orientation. The Celtren rain down on the Aventar. One of them lands up near the nose of the craft - its eyes two points of light in the darkness.

"Not good, not good." Sophie kneels on her seat. "They are completely surrounding us."

"Olessia, what are you doing?" Christian hasn't left his seat.

"It will be okay." Olessia smiles back at them. Her eyes are terrifyingly beautiful. Both now solid pools of violet that shine as though some internal light illuminates them.

Sebastien bangs his fist against the glass ceiling. "Olessia, stop now. Stop."

She steps out onto the ramp angled down to the muddy ground. The cabin door closes behind her, but it does little to deaden the sounds of the Celtren, their hoarse, grating cries cluttering the air. Ryder runs to the window, Christian and Sophie barely a pace behind. Sebastien is still pinned near the ceiling, his face a dark, angry mask. "That stupid girl."

"What is she doing?" Sophie says.

Ryder doesn't answer, it's hard enough just breathing. The moment Olessia stepped out of the Aventar, the tightness in Ryder's chest increased two-fold, as though someone slowly tightened a strap there. The air is unbearably dense, and sweat runs down the side of her face. If this is the effect of the Beckoning, how does Olessia stand being right at its heart? The weight of it is crushing Ryder where she stands.

Olessia walks further out onto the lake bed. Her feet sink ankle deep into the mud, and her pace is slow and laboured. The Celtren, five in total, circle around her. Five monstrous hunters stalking a lone prey.

"Why is she walking in the mud?" Christian's words fog up the glass in front of him. "She can fly."

A rush of dizziness swamps Ryder before she can answer. She closes her eyes, the world spinning even behind her eyelids. Her skin tingles, like a sunburn kisses it. Eyes still closed, Ryder lets her fingers trail over her skin. It's cool to the touch.

"Sebastien." Sophie yells. "You have to do something."

"What exactly would you have me do?" He fairly spits the reply.

Ryder opens her eyes. The world has changed. At least, the colours have. She stares at the Celtren who pace around Olessia. Auras of powder blue lift off them, like steam off a hot body in cold air. It's starting. She surveys her friends, and her body flushes with panic. A faint shimmer of rose plays around Christian's hand where it rests on the glass. Ryder grabs the back of his shirt. "Move back, Chris."

"Why? Ryder, what are you doing?"

211

Sophie takes one look at Ryder's face before grabbing his arm and helping her pull him away. "Chris, come on. Let's just do what she says okay." Her aura, a similar dusty rose colour to Chris's, halos her face. Ryder wishes there was some way she could show her how incredibly beautiful it makes her. Vibrant and strong.

"What's going to happen, Ry?" Sophie says.

"I'm not sure, which is why I think we should all just move back. Stick together."

The pressure bares down on her, and it's hard to think straight. Never mind the fact she has no idea what is going to happen, let alone what she's supposed to do when it does. Olessia put a lot of faith in a clueless person. A loud thump, and a strangled cry, makes them all turn. Sebastien is on the floor, knees bent like he's just nailed a super-hero landing. A narrow edging of light silhouettes his body, his aura strong and defined. Whatever hold Olessia had on him, she's released it. His bitter mutterings making it clear he's unimpressed with the unceremonious dumping.

"Sebastien, are you all right?" Sophie hurries to his side and Ryder braces for a snide reply or some dismissive wave of his hand. Neither come. He gives her a fleeting glance, then nods. Everyone jumps when the Celtren suddenly let out a chorus of hoarse, rough cries.

Keep them close. Olessia's thoughts are calm. *Here we go.*

Sebastien takes a determined step towards the door. Ryder races forward and grabs him, her fingers finding the solid curve of the muscles in his upper arm. The white band of his aura shimmers over her own skin. He is warm—and softer than she expected.

"Stay, you need to stay." She knows it as surely as she knows her own name.

He stares at her hand on his arm, his expression oddly unreadable. She lets him go. But he remains in the cabin, stepping to one side so he can watch Olessia.

Ryder inhales, opens her mouth to try and fill her lungs. No one else is sweating, no one else is gasping like a fish on dry land. The others don't seem to notice the thinness of the air. They are all focused on the stand-off outside. Olessia is so small and alone in the mud. The most visible thing about her is the bright pink t-shirt she wears, the hand-me-down from Sophie. The cries of the Celtren grow higher, more frantic, and draw out into ear-ringing screams. They circle Olessia in the mud, but make no move to creep closer. Ryder knows why. She can see it. Their auras, faint sky blue, stream out from their bodies, trailing towards Olessia in long ribbons across the darkened ground.

Sebastien shifts, clearly rethinking his decision to wait here.

"Stay." Ryder breathes out the word. If he decides to ignore her, she's not sure she could stop him, too faint to do much more than lean against the highbacked seat in front of her.

"They are strong, and she is still weak," Sebastien says. "Will you at least give me the senlier, let me do that much?"

He's asking her. As if things weren't weird enough, the guy wants her permission to help his precious, number one priority. All Ryder can do is shake her head. She keeps her focus on breathing, staying upright and conscious. If she doesn't, the Beckoning threatens to suck her down like an ocean undercurrent. Her eyes dart from Sebastien, to Sophie, to Christian. Over and over. Watching their auras. Searching for any sign that the Beckoning has reached too far.

"Why is she letting them get so close?" Christian stands half hidden behind one of the seats. "We should do something; surely you've got some kind of hand held weapons? What about that thing you did, with the knuckledusters?"

Sebastien makes a dismissive sound, an ugly laugh or a grunt, it's hard to tell. "Olessia believes she already has the perfect weapon."

"Maybe she does," Ryder counters.

Each of the Celtren extend their bony wings, several rear up on their back legs, sweeping their wings forward, like they're trying to wrench themselves free from Olessia's unseen hold.

She stands perfectly still, arms at her side. They're too far away to read her expression but her poise is relaxed, and serene. Perhaps Olessia is right. She can do this. Ryder studies the people around her. Their auras cling to their contours without a hint of lifting away, each is strong and vibrant. All except hers, and Olessia. They have nothing surrounding them. Ryder pushes the bubbling question down deep. Time for wondering later.

"Well, why isn't she doing something?" Christian presses his hands to either side of his face, like he's considering covering his eyes so he doesn't need to watch anymore.

Sophie wraps an arm around his waist. "She is doing something…I think they're dying."

For a moment Ryder thinks perhaps Sophie can see it too, the growing, spreading waves of colour spilling from the Celtren and pooling around Olessia. But then she spies the lifeless body of one of the Celtren on Olessia's far side. The outline of its body is dull. No trace of any aura. The rest of the Celtren continue to buck against the pull of the Beckoning. One of the creatures lets out a baying cry before its legs buckle beneath it. Long mournful howls fill the air. Three of the creatures stretch their thin-skinned wings and try to reach for the sky. But they have nothing left to lift them. They fall back to the ground with sickening thuds, their bodies imprinting deep in the mud. The last remaining Celtren doesn't try to fly away. It tries to run instead, the very last few tendrils of its aura trailing from its wings.

"I know they're the bad guys," Sophie whispers. "But this is horrible."

The panicked creature runs straight at the Aventar. Despite knowing these beasts tried to slam them out of the sky, it's difficult not to wince at the fear on the creature's dog face. Orange eyes are panic-stricken wide, revealing a thin rim of white at the outer edges. Ryder finds herself willing it to run faster. All at once, Sophie dashes across the cabin.

"I can't watch this," she cries, hitting the door release. "Stop, Olessia, stop."

The cabin door slides open, and Sophie dashes down the ramp, waving her arms.

"No." Ryder stays Christian with a glare and Sebastien with a raised hand. "Stay here. Do not come out."

Bolting after Sophie, Ryder staggers when she hits the bottom of the ramp. The closed cabin of the Aventar must have offered some shielding from the Beckoning, because out here in the open, it's weight is tremendous, a full suit of armour thrust upon her.

"Sophie, stop. What the hell are you doing?" Ryder pants, the world spinning around her.

The Celtren is dangerously close, but the Beckoning is almost done with it. Barely a wisp of the creature's aura is visible now. It stumbles, down on one knee, its jaw finding the mud. Olessia cries out. But she's not facing the Celtren. Her eyes are on Sophie. A narrow ribbon of Sophie's aura trails away from her feet, slithering along the ground towards Olessia. Ryder lunges, willing her overburdened body not to fail her now. She grabs a hold of Sophie's puffer jacket and wrenches her back. They land in a heavy heap on the angled surface of the ramp, and Sophie cries out. Ryder wraps her arms around her friend, no idea what to do next. She presses her hand over Sophie's, watching the ribbon of pure energy thread through her own fingers. Sophie groans, her head rolling side to side. Ryder hugs her friend in tighter.

"No, Sophie. Please. Stop, just stop." Ryder pleads. With the Beckoning. With her friend to hang on. The tendrils of dusty-rose falter. Sweat drips from Ryder's chin, landing on her hands tinged with the rosy glow of Sophie's aura. The solitary ribbon of light meandering towards Olessia flickers, like a flame touched by a light breeze. Then begins to retract. The Celtren collapses no more than a metre from where Ryder holds Sophie. The very tip of its left wing actually touches the side of the ramp. It gives a great laboured sigh and then is still.

"I'm sorry, Ry." Sophie coughs, leaning to one side, trying to sit up. "Did I hurt you?"

Ryder gulps in a breath. Then another, sucking at the air like

215

a swimmer underwater way too long. "No, but you could have been killed. Didn't you just give me this same speech?"

"It must hurt her, Ry, killing all those things." Sophie waves her hand toward the Celtren nearest them. Its eyes are wide open, long gray tongue lolling from its slack jaw. "I know she doesn't want to do it, I just wanted her to stop."

Ryder sputters, still trying to catch her breath. "They were going to kill us, Sophie, in case you missed it. Olessia had to do something, but she can't always control it. Don't you get that?" She's snapping every word. Glaring at Sophie in a way that's making her friend wince, but losing Sophie is unthinkable. Ryder has to make sure she's listening. "She's still learning to control the power she has. And you cannot get in the way like that. Promise me, you'll never do that again?"

Sophie wavers close to tears, but she nods. "Promise."

Olessia still stands out in the mud. And Ryder sees straight away why she isn't making her way back towards the Aventar. The Celtrens' stolen auras billow around Olessia's slight frame, a pulsing cloud of powder blue that curls out in long, reaching tendrils around her. "I need to go and help her. Sophie get back inside, make sure the others stay there too."

Sebastien strides down the ramp towards them, a face like thunder. Ryder steels herself for a fight.

"Sophie, inside." He extends his hand. Sophie takes it after a moment's hesitation and walks quickly up the ramp to where Christian waits for her. Sebastien's thundercloud eyes rest on Ryder. "Do what you have to do." No contempt, no impatience, nothing snide in his tone. He retreats back up the ramp.

Ryder pulls the senlier from where she tucked it into the waist of her jeans. It's left an indent against her skin. She gets to her feet, and steps out into the mud. The sodden ground makes the trek to Olessia's side slower than she'd like.

"Hang on, Olessia." Ryder brandishes the senlier, mud sucking at her Dr Martens. It's impossible to tell what colour they are now. "I'm coming. Just stay calm."

She nearly drops the senlier when she sees Olessia smiling at her. Eyes clear, irises two small rings of violet. "I'm all right, just give me a moment. Don't come any closer." The snaking tendrils of the auras retract in towards her. The haze around her pulls in closer to the contours of her body, sucking in until it is a barely visible line edging her silhouette. The icy wash of the night breeze caress's Ryder's cheeks, cooling the beads of sweat. She lifts her shoulders, finally free of the tremendous weight of the Beckoning. Olessia's eyelids flutter open. "Senlier, please," she says. "Just to be sure."

Ryder steps forward and places the narrow band of gold on Olessia's head. It's like being part of some weird crowning ceremony. And Olessia is the queen of control. The senlier brightens, the metal glowing a deeper orange, like it's being held in a fire. Ryder steps back, remembering what happened in the carpark. But everything about this seems different. The glow reaches a blinding pitch, and Ryder shades her eyes. Perhaps she was wrong, maybe it's best to move back a bit.

"You are safe." Olessia touches her arm, and Ryder uncovers her eyes. "It is done."

They stand staring at one another, and Olessia doesn't take her hand from where it lies on Ryder's forearm. The right words just won't come, anything Ryder mulls over in her head sounds lame - gee that was fun, thanks for not killing my friend, how did I get to be a Beckoning safety switch - so she says nothing. The silence stretches out until Sebastien pounds his way down the ramp. He moves to the nearest Celtren and places something on the hunched back of the creature. Olessia glances at him.

"What's he doing?" Ryder's words scratch their way into the air.

"Initiating a complete biological deconstruction. It will… dissolve." Olessia really does resemble a queen now with the circlet glinting against the short black strands of her hair.

"Oh, right. Okay." Ryder watches Sebastien a moment longer. He moves with purpose, from beast to beast. Her belly does an odd little flip and she turns away. "So you did it. You controlled it."

Whatever it was. The Beckoning. How did an ability like that develop? Sucking the life out of people and then balling up their energy like little nuclear bombs. Ryder baulks at her own thoughts. How did *she* get to be immune to it?

Olessia regards her, a smile playing on her lips. "I controlled it, yes. But I was not alone, you were here. Perhaps that is why the Beckoning feels easier to command." Her smile falls away. "Ryder, I didn't wish to kill them, but their minds were not their own. The creatures of the Arlion don't hunt through the realms like that. Someone manipulated them. They might have killed you all. Sophie will understand, won't she?" She nods towards the craft. Sophie paces back and forth across the open doorway. Christian leans against the frame and when he sees them staring, he raises his hand. Olessia lets go of Ryder, her eyes fixed on Christian. "They'll both understand, won't they? I tried to reason with the Celtren, I wanted another way, but there was nothing left to reason with."

Olessia just saved their lives. She had to kill to do it. And Ryder hates the fact she knows exactly how it feels. "Of course. They'll understand."

"Good. Now, we should go."

They step through the mud, side by side, matching one another's pace. And though Ryder darts glances at the swathe of disintegrating bodies around them, Olessia stares straight ahead.

CHAPTER 27

SEBASTIEN SKIMS THE AVENTAR LOW over the trees. With the engine locked in gear, the pace is glacier slow but it gives Ryder a moment figure out where they are. Below them is national parkland, the north-west side of Mount Wellington. For the past thirty minutes, the beat of Sebastien's impatient fingertips against his armrests, has been pretty much the only sound in the cabin. Interrupted only by the occasional whisperings of Olessia and Christian. Ryder's uncertain if Olessia's whispering because she doesn't want anyone to hear, or if she is just too exhausted to raise her voice. She sits slumped low in her chair, the harness the only thing stopping her from sliding onto the floor. At one point Christian laughs, loud enough to make Sophie jump. It's odd to see him so comfortable with Olessia, despite everything that's gone on. At school he's the one getting grief for being so quiet, for hanging out with two girls all the time. Ryder rests her head against her seat, watching Olessia lean across the gap between seats, getting closer to her friend. A niggle of worry eats at her. This fling isn't going where Olessia seems to want it to.

Ryder rubs at her eyes. The Aventar banks slowly to the right. She presses the release on her harness, turning to a dozing Sophie. "So where exactly are we going? I'm guessing we can't just take this thing into the nearest repair shop."

Sophie flutters one eye open, but Sebastien replies first. "Are you incapable of remembering what this *thing* is actually called?" The baleful glare he throws over his shoulder targets Ryder.

"Aventar." Sophie stands up, yawning and stretching her arms over her head. The run in with the Beckoning doesn't seem to have affected her in any particular way. She is tired but then, so is everyone. "It's called an Aventar and it's very lovely, Sebastien."

She gives Ryder a gentle nudge as she passes. It's the second time in less than twelve hours that Sophie has told her to play nice with Sebastien, and Ryder has to concede she has a point. They're stuck together for now, in a confined space, with a bunch of monsters out of a horror movie trying to kill them. Sebastien hasn't said a word since they lifted off from the muddy lake bed. Not even to Olessia. Especially not to Olessia. They have spent the last half hour ignoring another, neither willing to speak first and break the stalemate.

Sebastien stands and paces past them. Ryder rotates her seat to follow him, loving any excuse to activate the mechanics which move the chair, relishing the chance to act like a judge on one of those singing shows. Sebastien waves his hand towards the back wall, and the screens embedded there spring to life.

"So you seem like a man with a plan." Sophie approaches him, keeping a cautionary distance. "Care to share?"

Sebastien taps at a keyboard interface set between two of the screens. At least this part of the Aventar seems to be working fine. The interface is filled with more of the symbols Ryder recognises from the Tyius. Thinking about the GPS, means thinking about Lucas. Both Jack and Lucas are never far from mind, but Jack, at least, she knows is okay. No one has heard from Lucas since he propelled her out of the car.

The screen to Sebastien's right comes to life. Aerial footage of the Derwent River. The river starts up in the Tasmanian central highlands, meandering through Hobart, then travelling fifty kilometres down to Storm Bay and out into the Tasman Sea. It's hard to make out what part of the river they're looking at, even with night vision giving the image near-perfect clarity. Tiny red circles appear on the screen, then disappear to spring up elsewhere on the map. Each time they encircle a point it is magnified, highlighting the space; a huge shed, some heavily forested ground, an abandoned barn. Ryder glances outside. There is no sign of the river below them, still just the blot of bushland.

"Is that camera on the Aventar?" Ryder frowns as one of the red circles brings the Brennan Shot Tower into view; a turn of the century stone tower used to manufacture lead shots. It's nowhere near where they are now. The tower is about an hour out of town, on the south side.

"No, it's-" Olessia's explanation doesn't see the light of day.

"It is an unmanned aerial vehicle." Sebastien stands right up close to the screens.

The scanning map doesn't appear interested in the shot tower, highlighting it only once before moving on. Ryder smiles at the daggers Olessia sends Sebastien's way. But she might as well be invisible. Apparently he's not a fan of being pinned like a biology specimen to a ceiling. Olessia mutters under her breath and swings her chair, putting the highback between them.

Christian moves to stand beside Sophie. "A drone, that's pretty cool."

"Ry, we need one of these for ghost hunting, Oh, wait we're never going to do again 'cause we are currently in a spaceship, and ghosts just seem lame." Sophie smirks at Ryder's eye-roll. But the mention of ghosts brings Padellah to mind. Like the entity was ever really out of mind. For the millionth time Ryder tosses up whether to say anything to Olessia about the Cyne. And for the millionth time she can't decide.

"So what is it looking for?" Sophie says.

The drone drifts across the river and runs close to the shoreline, low enough that they can make out the yachts and other boats moored beside it. A melodic jingle emits from the screen, not unlike the sound Ryder's washing machine makes when it's done, and a stationary image appears in the top right of the screen. "This is where we are going." Sebastien folds his arms, nods towards the screen. "Do you know of this place?"

Sophie steps closer, squinting, but Christian jabs a finger into the air. "Yes. That's Sleighter Dam," he says. "It's not far from our school, on the opposite side of the river."

"It's near your favourite phone tower." The words slip before she can bite them back, and Ryder's rewarded with one of Sebastien's death stares.

"So why do you want to go there?" Christian shrugs. "It's just pine plantations around that area, the department of forestry controls it all."

But Ryder sees the link. "Hydroelectricity. You're hiding us there while you check out the Aventar." Sebastien's smile is uneven, as though he's fighting to keep it from existing at all, and the curve melts the hard contours of his face. Smiles really, really suit him.

"Correct." The smile vanishes, and robo-guardian is back. Locked tight and in control. "The energy levels will distort traces of us and the Aventar. I need time to find the problem. Obviously we can't enter the River in this state."

Ryder realises she's still staring at him and snaps her mouth closed. Sebastien though hasn't noticed. He is focused on the screen. Sebastien lifts his hand, touches fingertips to the screen and then steps back. The entire view expands out into the cabin, in a 3-D image, like those old pop-up books Ryder used to read.

Sophie steps backward to avoid ending up in the middle of Blackmans Bay, just south of where their high school perches on the banks of the river. The image floats at hip height, and covers most of the empty space in the back of the cabin. Ryder stares down at the dark ribbon of the Derwent River. It's so tangible. If she reaches out her hand she might touch the water itself. Car headlights trace the paths of vehicles driving along the roads. Their school, Taroona Bay High, creeps into view as the footage moves further north. They skim past it. The pool building, the newest of all the school buildings, is bright with security lighting.

"I swear I'm never going to put so much as a toe in that pool." Sophie touches a hand to her brilliant red hair. "Imagine what it would do to this, all that chlorine." She shudders.

On the 3-D map one of the red circles blinks brighter than all the rest. Sleighter Dam. The great, towering slab of concrete that makes up the dam wall is clearly visible. At its top, a gaping expanse of darkness marks the water held back by the man-made barrier. The drone moves on, reaching Blackrhine Hill. And the phone tower. The top of the spire is in the same condition as on the news report, hanging by just a few wires, the top metre or so of the spire dangling against the lower structure. Beside the tower is a huge crane, ready to start repairs. There is nothing to suggest this is anything but bare, boring hill top. The gateway to another world completely hidden.

"Oh dear." Sophie taps her index finger against her chin, frowning. "There's quite a bit of damage to the tower, isn't there."

Sebastien says nothing but his hand pauses over the interface. A second of stillness before he resumes.

"Pity the damage is only to the tower." Olessia kneels on her chair, chin resting on the seat back.

All at once, the 3-D images disappears. Sophie lets out an audible sigh. And Ryder almost joins her. The cabin seems oddly hollow without it.

"Leave well enough alone here, Olessia," Sebastien says. "We are going home. It is the best thing you can do for them. For yourself."

Olessia narrows her eyes. "We both know that is not true. But justify it as best you can. At least you will regain some lost reputation. You will return with your prize, and all those who doubt you will be quieted for a little longer. Perhaps you'll convince them yet, that you are not your brother."

She claps her hands, in slow, laboured applause. Full of antagonism. Sebastien rubs the heel of his hands against his eyes and takes a deep breath. "This is pointless and I don't have the strength for it right now, Olessia. Nor do you. I'm going to start running what diagnostics I can, I suggest everyone else get some rest. It will be another hour before we reach the location. I've decreased velocity to keep engine output minimal. Though it will take longer, we won't be generating any output that might be detected."

Olessia says nothing, though the sheepish lowering of her eyes hints that she knows she went too far. She slides back into her seat, shifting her chair so she is hidden from view. Sebastien stares at the back of her chair, exhaustion etched into his face. Ryder had been so caught up in his smile, she missed what lurked behind it. He turns and walks towards her.

"How are you feeling?" he says.

"Fine." The word tumbles out too fast, but that's because he's too close. "It doesn't hurt anymore. I'm fine." Stronger and steadier, Ryder congratulates herself. Speaking isn't so hard after all.

Then he's gone, long, heavy strides taking him back to the pilot seat where he lowers himself slowly like an old man settling into a rocking chair. He doesn't touch the controls. Just sits there, staring out ahead, watching the dark shadows of the national park beneath them. Olessia's venom must have hit home. Whatever his brother did, he's still struggling with it. Sophie nudges her. If she notices Ryder jump like she's been busted, she doesn't show it.

"Are you sleepy? I'm not. Maybe we can play charades?" Sophie ventures. "It always lightens the mood."

Ryder lets out a long, slow breath. "Soph, let's just get some rest okay. Everyone is wiped." Christian is already settling into his seat, arms folded and eyes closed. Olessia tucks herself up into a ball on the contoured chair, leaning against the curved wing of the headrest. It is comfortably warm in the cabin. Ryder shifts a couple of times, getting settled, and the silence makes it easy to drift off.

Ryder's caught in a dream before she realises her eyes are closed. It has to be a dream because Lucas is with her. Right there. He's talking to her but his words are garbled and incoherent, in that weird way dreams have of making you think you understand at first, then you realise the words make no sense at all. Lucas is asking her something. Ryder tries to speak back to him, tell him where they are. But she can't seem to get her dream-tongue around the name of the place. Sleighter comes out more like hater. Lucas takes long even steps that move him away from her faster than they should, like he's on a travelator. Ryder tries to reach for him. Calling him to come back. He stops, and whirls to face her. Lucas smiles, dimples on full display, green eyes shining with happiness. He moves towards her, calling her name.

Someone drops a saucepan right beside her. Ryder's eyes fly open.

"Lucas?"

Ryder sits up, and the harness digs hard into her shoulders, reminding her very abruptly where she is. There are no saucepans. There is only Sebastien. They've landed. Pine trees surround the craft, rows of evenly-spaced sentinels. The scent of them fills the cabin.

"You were dreaming." Sebastien has a silver smudge across his left cheek, below the black marking there, and most of his hair has come loose from its binding. It hangs in untidy strands around his face. "You were agitated. I had to wake you."

He lifts his hands, showing her what he is holding. In one hand something that resembles a tent peg, in the other, a piece of metal, shaped like a kidney bean and about the size of a mobile phone.

"So you woke me by banging on metal? Seriously?" There is sweat on the back of her hands and dampness beneath her armpits. It's been a long while since a shower or deodorant. She presses her arms tight against her ribcage, praying that Sebastien can't tell just how long.

"It seemed the most appropriate way to wake you," he says in the distracted, nonchalant way she is getting used to.

The v-neck vest he's wearing leaves his arms bare. The scarring there is in full view. Ryder spots a very precise scar running the length of the inside of his right arm, a surgical mark rather than an injury. There is another, smaller one, on the inside of his left shoulder too. If this is all from protecting Olessia, then Ryder's beginning to understand his antagonism a little better.

"You slept through landing, and you slept despite this." He gestures to the pilot seat. The panels that make up the base of the bench seat have been removed, revealing an interior mess of wires and moving parts. Some sections are strewn on the floor. The level of disassembly suggests he's been at work for a while, which makes her conscious of the fact she's known to drool in her sleep, especially when she's super tired. Ryder presses her fingers to the edges of her mouth, a blush heating her cheeks.

"You know what? There are nicer ways to do it than scare the hell out of me." Ryder stands up. Her left foot is asleep, full of pins and needles but she isn't going to show him how much it hurts. "If that's how you wake Olessia up, I'm not surprised she doesn't like you much."

She bites down on her bottom lip, wishing she could wipe those words out of the air. The dream's strangeness flustered her, and she's groggy with the memory of it. Sebastien regards her with an irritatingly blank expression, his eyes the shade of clouds after dusk.

"Loud noises are the least of the things that scare you, I'm sure." He returns to whatever it is he's doing, kneeling beside the machine parts.

"That's not...why would you say that?" Ryder needs some air. It is too warm inside the cabin despite the door being wide open. A light breeze sways through the pines.

Sebastien peers down at a flat transparent square, woven with multi-coloured wires, fitting snugly against his palm. "Because I am not blind. The things you are capable of are beyond your kind. And you understand that. I believe what frightens you the most, is yourself."

Ryder breathes into a stab of panic. "Do you people have any idea how not cool it is to poke around in other people's heads?"

Sophie's laughter drifts into the cabin, that high giggle that usually makes Ryder smile. She is alone in here with Sebastien, the others chatter somewhere out in the fresh air. They must be nearby, their words are clear, but the gap between where Ryder stands and the world outside, yawns deep as an abyss.

"I read people. I do not read their minds." Sebastien presses his fingertips to a random spot on the floor and a panel opens, revealing the belly of the Aventar. It's bathed in an emerald green glow which radiates up onto his face. "I can see for myself that you are not what you seem. Your bravery might be human, but your ability to withstand a Placer's toxin and, more importantly the Beckoning itself, is most definitely not. The force behind the Beckoning enables the Presider and his bloodline to rule our world. It is a preternatural energy mastered by so very few. You not only walked through it without consequence, you appear to enable Olessia to keep her control. Those abilities are extraordinary and incredibly dangerous. I am aware I owe you a great deal. Not only my life, but what you've done for Olessia. You are pulling her out of a darkness I thought I would lose her to." He stops, staring down into the light. She can't decipher his expression. Maybe he is as surprised at his little speech as she is. Outside, Christian and Sophie try to outdo each other in convincing Olessia that pizza will change her life. So long as she never puts pineapple on it. Ryder's fingers drift to where the Placer pierced her shoulder, tracing the roughness of the healing wound through the material of her shirt. She loves pineapple. Olessia definitely needs to try it on pizza. What Ryder wouldn't do for a good old, cheesy, benign pizza right now.

Still, Sebastien needs to keep talking. She doesn't want him to stop.

"What happened?" Ryder kneels on the floor, just the other side of the open panel. She moves slowly, not wanting to spook his prickly mood back into place. "At Vale Leven, I mean."

Sebastien lifts his head, and the steely guardian vanishes, the young man reappearing. But it's not a smile bringing him out this time. A haunted shadow darkens Sebastien's face. "A lot of people lost their lives," he says, "her father pushed her too far, too soon. The Presider sees the power she has, stronger even than his, and he doesn't care that she can barely contain it. He only seeks to know if it will win him his war. If she can be his greatest weapon."

The vision Ryder saw through the Placer, flares in her mind. Olessia kneeling beside a woman's body on the river bank, surrounded by others.

He frowns. "Olessia told you of Vale Leven?"

"No...I just...for some reason the name stuck in my head. She talked about it back in the carpark...before she...before she lost it." Ryder keeps quiet about the Placer's memories. About the death she saw. It chills her to realise the man standing over Olessia in the memory was the Presider. He doesn't sound like the sort of dad who'll win any awards too soon. Ryder's thoughts move to her own father. For the first time, in a very long time, she truly misses him.

"That is what she is running from." Sebastien's jaw tightens with his words.

"I can see why she's running."

"But I have to take her home." He closes his eyes, tilting his head forward so that his dark hair hangs over his face. "I have no choice. Neither does she."

For whatever reason, Sebastien's walls are down. The blunt talking, brusque guy has disappeared and in his place is someone drowning in hopelessness. Tough-as-nails Sebastien is annoying, irritating and distracting. And she's beginning to think that's the whole idea. He has to keep Olessia together, holding on, fired up and too distracted by their animosity to have a moment to feel sorry for herself. When Ryder was dragged onto the Aventar, soaked in blood and so numb she could barely breathe, the concern on Sebastien's face almost tipped her over the edge. Sophie keeps telling her to play nice with Sebastien. But Ryder sees now that he can't do the same.

"What are you doing with all this?" She wants to touch him, but she reaches for one of the metal parts instead. "Do you want some help fixing this thing?"

Calling the Aventar a thing again should get a response, get him fired up. She needs to see the smugness on his face again. But Sebastien just shrugs. "I can't fix anything until I find where the issue is, and according to the diagnostics the error points keep changing. I'm going to fragment the search. Do an independent run through, section by section, with external equipment."

Ryder tries a different tack. "Sounds complicated and time consuming, how do I help?"

He shakes his head, and she holds up her hand. "I can do this," she says. "I'm doing a cert four course at school, interactive media design. I'm nailing it. I know my way around a computer, and this is basically a giant computer right? All the modern aircraft on Earth are, so are our cars."

His scowl chases back the fragility. She's a bug in his sandwich again. Good. "It is a little more complicated than that."

"I'm sure it is. I just need to bring it down to a level my little human brain can understand."

He turns his head, tries to cover his smile but Ryder catches it. He hands her a device that is something like a small artist's palette, minus the blobs of paint. It even has a hole for the thumb. But that's where the resemblance ends. This palette is made of a clear plastic that softens with the warmth of her hand and moulds itself into her palm. Ryder congratulates herself on not dropping the thing the moment it starts to change shape. Her skin is visible through the material, which is laced with threads of gold wire.

"Bring your little human mind and we will get started."

Sebastien hangs his feet into the belly cavity of the Aventar before dropping down into it. Ryder follows. She may as well have dropped into another world. There is a solid metal platform running the distance of the underbelly, a work platform she assumes, that enables them to stand in amongst a vast array of illuminated wiring which covers every available space around her. It lines the walls and hangs from the low ceiling, like super intricate spider webs. She sucks in her breath. This is the workings of an alien aircraft, and she has never seen anything quite so beautiful. Kind of crazy to think her pathetic thermal camera led her here. Wherever *here* actually is. She crouches down, taking in the intricacy of the tiny veins of light covering the innards of the Aventar. Some of them pulse like they have a heartbeat.

"This is...incredible..."

"Don't come in direct contact with the system matrix. I need to keep it live to assess. Be careful." Sebastien crouches down and makes his way towards the nose of the craft.

Ryder tilts her shoulder away from some string lighting hanging unsettlingly close. "Okay." she holds up the device. "So what am I supposed to do with this thing?"

The cavity beneath the Aventar's floor isn't deep, and if they stand up their heads will poke out of the openings. They'd look like over-sized meerkats. Sebastien glances over his shoulder, the bright lighting chasing all shadows from his face. He is almost doubled over in the small space.

"The relke will pick up anomalies." He gestures to the device she holds. "You've worked out how to handle it. Now just hold it over the matrix, it will do the rest. I suspect the interference is actually external. The relke should find it, if I'm right."

Ryder lifts the device, the relke. She has no idea how far away from the wiring she should hold it, whether she needs to press any buttons or whisper any magic words, but the less aggressive Sebastien is kind of nice to have around, so risking a dumb question is out. She picks a spot and kneels down, holding the device close to the wires until it emits a steady ticking noise, much like the K-2 meter they use for ghost hunting. The same meter that's probably a melted piece of junk now back at the power station.

CHAPTER 28

T HEY WORK IN SILENCE, AN oddly comfortable silence. The devices on Sebastien's belt clink together as he shifts back and forth. Once or twice he hits his head, his tall frame not negotiating the space quite as easily as hers. The monotonous bleep of the relke is hypnotic. Ryder relaxes into the simplicity of the sound, even if the task itself isn't so relaxing. The platform digs into her knees and she has to shift position every few minutes to keep her feet from going to sleep.

Sitting down, she stretches her legs, wiggling them to get blood flowing. "So how are you guys and Aresh planning to get back together? Or are you doing this alone?"

"Aresh has blocked all communications. I know she survived the attack. So I have to assume she will be in contact again when it's safe." He sits back on his haunches. "If I hear nothing, then yes. I am doing this alone."

He returns to his wires, and Ryder does the same. Up and down, up and down, sweeping the relke over the mass of illuminated workings. Christian comes in to ask what's happening and then leaves to tell the others, giving Ryder a weird smile before he goes. After fifteen minutes, Ryder's neck aches from craning her head to peer at the webbing above her. Sebastien's chattiness died as abruptly as it began, he doesn't answer her when she asks how he learned to speak English so well. She's lost in her own thoughts when the relke erupts with sound, buzzing like an electric toothbrush on steroids.

"I think I've found something." She tightens her hold on the device.

Sebastien doesn't even glance up from his section. "No, you haven't. You've done that section before, that's all."

"Right. Good to know," Ryder says. "Want to give me a hint what this thing will do when-"

The relke sounds off with a stream of unrecognisable words, in a mechanised voice that nearly startles the device out of Ryder's hand. Symbols gleam over the clear surface. She turns to tell Sebastien, but he is already on his way, crawling along the five meters or so that separates them, his knees and boots making heavy contact with the metal platform.

"Hand it to me, quickly."

He all but snatches the device from her hand and waves it over the lattice work of wiring until it sets off once again. He tilts the device, peering at the flashing symbols. Sebastien shoves the relke back at her, a distant expression on his face.

"What is it? Is it bad?" she says.

Reaching into one of the external pockets on his cargo pants, he pulls out a pair of gloves. If they had been made on earth she would have said they were black leather.

"It is setting off alarms. It's hardly going to be fortuitous." He pulls on the gloves and leans towards the area of wiring that set off the device. With a slow careful pace he pushes his hand further into the intricate structure, leaning his slim body in to the workings. A frown of concentration wrinkles his face. Ryder grimaces in sympathy, holding her breath.

"We have decided that food is becoming vitally important. I would like to order some pizza." Olessia's voice booms into the confined space, startling them both. Sebastien's arm jerks and there is a crackle like a burst of static electricity. He hisses, barely stifling a curse.

"Olessia, be quiet. All of you." Sebastien's body shakes with the effort of holding the odd angle it takes to reach into the networking. Whatever he is aiming for is way back near the outer wall. Ryder edges closer, trying to see.

"Is everything okay?" Sophie's head appears alongside Olessia above them.

"I don't know." Olessia sniffs. "I've been told to shut up so I can't ask any questions."

Sebastien's lips press white with the effort of trying to reach whatever it is the relke found. His right shoulder brushes against one of the strands and the contact sparks and sizzles against his skin. He winces but holds steady. She loops her arm through his and leans back, giving him something to weight himself against as he reaches in the opposite direction. His arm is tense, solid muscle. He nods at her, an unspoken thanks. There is another snap of energy, this one more intense than the static pops of earlier.

"Pull." Sebastien demands, his weight shifting back towards her. Ryder strains to haul him free of the wiring, and they shove up against one another. Sebastien quickly moves away. "Olessia, shut down the core and initiate a restart."

"What have you found?" Olessia hangs her head and shoulders over the edge of the cavity, peering down at them.

"Now Olessia."

She is on her feet a second later, the thud of her boots marking her path across the cabin floor. A moment later a subtle tremor goes through the Aventar. The brilliant emerald glow in the underbelly shuts off, and the hum of the ship's systems ceases. The silence makes Ryder's ears ring. She peers at what Sebastien holds in his hand. "Is everything-"

"Go, back up into the cabin," he says, his expression hard and cold. The guardian is well and truly back.

Ryder scrambles to her feet, reaching for the edge of the opening. She makes an ungraceful exit, with Christian and Sophie helping to pull her back up on deck.

"What's happening?" Sophie whispers.

Ryder shakes her head. "He's found something."

Motorised sounds come from below them; a mix between a drill and a muffled leaf blower. A moment later Sebastien hauls himself up into the cabin, the muscles in his arm flexing with the movement. There are fresh pink marks on his skin where the wiring burnt him. The cabin is heavy with silence, the same flatness that hangs in the air during a power blackout.

"Sebastien?" Olessia says. "What is it?"

He doesn't answer. Instead he crouches down on the ground, reaching for something on his belt. A flick of his wrist and the tiny oval shaped item expands, like a balloon being blown. It could double as a sunglasses case, Ryder decides, cylindrical and matte black in colour. Sebastien opens it and places what he found inside, then snaps the container closed again. Ryder caught a glimpse of something white and delicate. Kind of like a doily, the type Sophie's mum loves to crochet. Ryder's guessing it's not that type of doily. The cylindrical case illuminates. Symbols stream along the surface, mostly triangular in shape, with embellished curls surrounding them. Olessia and Sebastien stare down at the case. If they are reading what they see there, the glower on Sebastien faces says he's not impressed. Olessia's fingers travel to the base of her throat.

"Sebastien," she says. "How is that possible?"

"I don't know."

The steel in his voice makes Ryder nervous. He reminds her of a jack-in-the-box, all coiled and ready to pop. He opens the casing again. In reality, the item is more snowflake than doily, and it seems such a delicate and insignificant thing to be causing such a stir. Sebastien scowls down at it like he hopes to burn it out of existence with his thoughts alone.

"That's what's causing the problems?" Ryder says.

"What is it?" Sophie shrugs.

"It's a modified disabler." Olessia is mesmerised by the little snowflake. "The Siros military developed them to-"

"Olessia, stop. Enough. Do you have no sense at all?" Sebastien shoots the words at her, hard and fast. Violet bolts are thrown right back at him.

"If you are suggesting they had anything to do with this then you are truly the fool," Olessia says. "This is Siros military tech with a Zentai modification blaze. Do you think Ryder or Sophie or Christian are making these in that school they attend?"

Sebastien's chest lifts with the deepness of his breath. He is clearly trying to keep a grip and Ryder's not so sure he's succeeding. "I'm fairly certain, Olessia, that I don't know half of what there is to know about any of these people. And it is beginning to irritate me beyond acceptable levels."

"The way I eat irritates you beyond your acceptable levels, Sebastien." Olessia leans forward to punctuate her words. "They are not our enemy."

Sebastien grips the cylinder so hard it seems impossible it won't crack. "Our enemy has managed to disable this craft, Olessia," he says. "Do you understand what this means? This is Zentai modified tech. They have been in this ship. There is no doubt now that they are behind the attack at the power station. The enemy are here."

As if the moment needed any more drama, the Aventar's systems whir back online. First the hum of the engines vibrates through the floor, and then the lights in the cabin blink. Sebastien glances towards where Ryder stands off to one side with Christian and Sophie. Ryder holds his gaze, seeing through the sheen of anger and frustration there. He is confused, uncertain. And it's contagious. A creeping chill traces its way along Ryder's arms. Did the Cyne try to help or hinder? Perhaps what Padellah wanted was to isolate Olessia. When Ryder dragged her away from the safety of the power station, and the protection of Aresh and the men with her, maybe she'd done exactly what was intended all along; she'd made Olessia vulnerable, put her on a ship no better than a floating taxi.

"We didn't have anything to do with this, you know that Sebastien." Ryder speaks quickly, drowning out her own doubts. It didn't make sense. If the Cyne were working with the Zentai, then why were they all still safe? "What do those Zentai people even look like, I mean, do we look like them?" Because they certainly didn't look like anyone from Siros. There was nothing ethereal, or otherworldly about Ryder, or Chris or Sophie.

Sebastien's gaze doesn't leave her face, and his scrutiny burrows deep. Ryder shifts under the weight of it. Telling him anything about Padellah right now seems fraught with problems. He's not going to be a fan of secrets.

"You would be surprised how close a resemblance there is," he says. "And the reconstruction of ears is a straightforward procedure."

The chill running up Ryder's skin bristles into hard goosebumps. She forgot what Aresh told her, that the Zentai are genetically similar to humans. The whole reason Ryder nearly died when she was a kid. She pinches her nose. It's a stressful day when something like that slips your mind.

Olessia flicks her hand, like she's throwing the whole crazy notion into an invisible rubbish bin. "Enough. Sebastien doesn't believe for a moment that you had anything to do with this. If he did, I would be stopping him from immobilising you with Holgraft cuffs right now."

Sophie clears her throat with a small, delicate sound. "I'm very grateful you are not trying to do that Sebastien. It sounds unpleasant."

Christian frowns. "But hang on, if they are here, these Zentai people, then why not come for Olessia themselves? I mean why send those freaky monsters to do their work? And why not shut down this thing altogether, why just disable parts of it?"

He sweeps his arm, taking in the cabin around them. Ryder braces for Sebastien's indignant reply, but it doesn't come. Instead, his brows lower. "Because," Sebastien says, slow and thoughtful, "they don't want it destroyed."

"They need it." Olessia's violet eyes shine in the low lighting.

"They need it," Sebastien repeats and nods. He paces to the pilot seat, rubbing at the back of his neck. "The disabler would normally shut down and destroy all of the Aventar systems. It's used in combat when the craft is potentially going to fall into enemy hands. Disabling the craft means its systems and weapons are not compromised. But the modification blaze on this one has been reprogrammed to target very specific systems. They want the Aventar operational."

"It was a precaution then." Ryder catches the drift of where they are going. "Maybe no one was supposed to get to the Aventar when the Celtren attacked?"

They were all supposed to be inside the electricity station, huddled in one confined space. If Ryder hadn't had her little freak out and the Cyne had been able to reach her in the field outside, maybe they'd still be there now. Perhaps that's why Padellah's warning went to Ryder and not Aresh. The electricity did its job too well. The ethereal being couldn't get a message through.

Only, they hadn't *all* been in the power station. "Hang on, I ran into someone, when I-" Tried to make a run for it. "When I went out to get some air. It was one of those guys with Aresh-"

"The bald one." Sophie snaps her fingers. "I saw him come back in while I was looking for your jacket. Not very chatty."

"Yeah him," Ryder says. "He was coming in from somewhere out in the field."

Sebastien cradles the cylinder against his chest. "Travel through the slipstreams can induce severe nausea. Dashel asked for some of the elixir I had on board to ease the discomfort. I told him to get it himself." His gaze drifts, his thoughts taking him beyond the cabin.

Olessia eyes him with disdain. "Sebastien, you are being paranoid. Dashel is Claven. Don't you dare suggest that-"

"What is the Claven exactly?" Ryder asks. "I mean you keep talking about them like they're the Knights Templar."

"I have no idea who the Knights are, but the Claven come from loyal families. They exist entirely to protect and guide Siros and its rulers," Olessia replies, but her focus is on Sebastien. "The very first Presider came from their ranks. Their loyalty to the Presidership is without question."

"No loyalty is without question," Sebastien says. "You know full well I can assure you of that."

All at once, a holographic screen flickers open beside the pilot seat. It's joined by the low monotonous chime of an alarm. Sebastien mutters something harsh under his breath. Olessia must see the confusion on Ryder's face because she says, "It's a perimeter alarm. It's detected someone who is getting too close."

The screen shows footage of the area outside the Aventar, rows and rows of towering pines. The drone lifts and the slick body of the Aventar, nestled in the clearing, draws into the shot. The camera angle tilts away from the craft and coasts through a row of pines. The image switches from night vision to thermal vision. Ryder recognises the bloom of paler colours emanating from the living trees and the cooler blues and greens coming from the dense, dead undergrowth. She clasps her hands tight together. As beautiful as it is, these images are nothing compared to true auras. Then a flash of red and yellow fills the screen. It is the unmistakable red and yellow silhouette of a body. Someone walking through the pine forest. And something about the stride is familiar. The drone speeds towards the heated image and the footage slips back to night vision. There is no mistaking who it is.

"Oh my god, it's Lucas." Christian's voice pitches with excitement.

"He's okay, he's really okay." Sophie launches herself at Ryder and they cling to each other. Lucas is here. He's all right.

Sebastien's glare brings the celebrations to a halt. "You contacted him? Do you have any idea what danger that puts us in?"

Heart still knocking out a crazy rhythm, Ryder shakes her head. "When have you seen me making any phone calls on my non-existent phone, since we arrived?" She raises her hands, exasperated. "Our phones were destroyed. It wasn't me."

"Then how does he know we are here?"

"I have no idea." She laughs. "I dreamed about him and here he is. It's a modern day miracle." She lays on the sarcasm, thick and clear, but Olessia and Sebastien exchange a glance.

"Dreamed about him *when*, Ryder?" Olessia says.

"Before," she hesitates. "When we landed here, he was talking to me…in my dream…" Had he actually been trying to talk to her? Telepathy is one thing, but this was different.

"What did he say?" Olessia is too calm, pronouncing her words too carefully.

Ryder steps back, needing the support of her chair. "I couldn't understand what he was saying. It was a dream, dreams are weird."

"Is something wrong?" Christian says. "Is Lucas okay?"

"Oh, he is fine." Sebastien watches the screen with hawk-like intensity. "Not only is he capable of a far-reach, but it seems he can make his way through the pitch dark without assistance too. The definitive traits of a particular race."

Olessia presses her hands to her head. "That doesn't make any sense. Sebastien, we must be missing something. Aresh knows Lucas, she vouched for him. Let him come, I will see if I can-"

"If you can what?" Ryder stares hard at Olessia, not liking the weighty glances going back and forth between her and Sebastien. Ryder edges closer to the door.

"No, we are leaving," Sebastien says. "Take your seats." He reaches towards the panel. Ryder assumes he means to close the door. So does Christian apparently. He lunges forward and shoves Sebastien away from the panel. The shocked cry that comes from Olessia's moody guardian is almost cute.

"Ryder, go," Christian shouts, dodging out of Sebastien's reach.

She doesn't need to be told twice, one foot already on the ramp before Sebastien regains his balance. Running is getting to be a theme of this weekend. Her boots hit the spongy ground. Olessia calls out to her. But she's not warning Ryder to stop. "Be careful, Ryder. Lucas isn't who you think he is." She doesn't try to follow.

Pine needles crunch underfoot as Ryder races from Olessia's words. The moment Lucas appeared at the carpark, he stopped being who she thought he was. Till now she'd kept her focus on him being okay, and drilled a deep hole in her thoughts, shoving everything else down there till she could deal with it. It's hard to ignore the black hole now. Ryder stumbles, grabbing at the nearest tree to right herself. The coarse bark scratches at her skin. Her lungs heave, a stitch nestles in her side. She forces herself into an unsteady jog, determined to reach him.

The guy out there, somewhere in the pine-scented darkness, is still the same one who dressed up as Dumbledore at her tenth birthday party because she asked him to. He's the one she goes to first with exam results, the one she's spent countless afternoons alongside watching terrible reality TV. He is her brother. She's not leaving that guy behind.

CHAPTER 29

T HE WIND LIFTS AND DANCES the strands loosened from Ryder's braid in the air around her. A shiver brushes her skin. The murmur of the hydroelectricity turbines rumbles like thunder in the distance. So far away from any city lights, it is much darker out here than Ryder expected, and it's impossible to keep up a fast pace.

"Lucas, Lucas," Ryder shouts.

Her unplanned plan is full of holes. She's not sure what direction he was coming from. Ryder peers into the gloom. The drone swept off to the right hand side of the Aventar so she knows by doing the same she's vaguely headed the right way. There's no crackle of feet on the undergrowth behind her, no one has followed. Perhaps Sebastien left without her, it's something he'd do. Or they're all standing around watching her blunder in the dark via the drone. Ryder tilts her head, scanning the air above her, but she can't make out anything. It's impossibly dark. Ryder stumbles over a lumpy mass in the soil beneath her.

"Lucas are you there?"

The breeze moves through the pine needles, making them whisper. Her toes catch on an exposed root and for the third time in about a minute she nearly crashes to the ground. Is she even walking in a straight line? The trees all have the same gnarly silhouettes, low branches bobbing up and down like string puppets.

"Ryder?"

The sound of Lucas's voice is tossed about by the wind. Ryder freezes, trying to work out what direction it is coming from.

"Lucas, I'm here. Where are you?"

"Right here."

He appears out of the darkness, closer than she expects, and the shock of it wrenches a broken cry from her lips. She hurls herself at him, throwing her arms around him. Ryder holds on tight. Everything about Lucas is perfectly familiar: the smell of his shampoo, the easy sound of his laughter, even the black *Tour de France* sweater he's wearing. Her dad bought it for him on the same trip he bought Ryder's jacket. It's little wonder she couldn't spot him though, Lucas could be a ninja with all the dark clothing.

"Seriously, how can you see where you're going out here?" Ryder pulls herself out of the hug. Even this close his features are hard to make out.

"Oh, I have a few tricks up my sleeve." He clears his throat. "Let me look at you. How are you holding up? Aresh told me some crazy stuff went down, are you all okay?"

"You've seen her?" Ryder's thoughts jump to Jack. "Did you see Jack too?"

Lucas hasn't let go of her hand. "No...sorry...I didn't *see* her that way."

"Oh." Disappointment washes over the excitement.

"But she told me he's okay. He's fine, kind of freaked about you guys though."

A pitched whine joins the low growl of the hydro turbines, a plane high in the sky somewhere. Or maybe the drone, with its little audience of spies watching both of them.

"Yeah well, he's not the only one losing it. How did you find us, Lucas?" she blurts out. "Sebastien thinks you are stalking my dreams. He called it something..." The word escapes her.

"A far-reach. Yeah, I kind of have a few talents you don't know about."

242

He's not the only one. Ryder kicks at the dank bed of needles beneath them, digging the toe of her boot into the soft ground. "Well, aside from me just saying for the record that it's incredibly creepy to know you can hop into my dreams." She holds up a hand to silence his protest. "I'm not sure you're safe right now. Sebastien and Olessia think someone has messed with the Aventar, and Sebastien seems pretty sure he doesn't like you." She can't make out his expression in the dark, but she hears the crack of the undergrowth as he shifts his feet. "Then they saw you walking around in the dark, like you knew where you were going, and they..." A niggle of doubt gives her pause. The pine plantations around the dam are enormous, spreading for acres. And judging by what she saw from the drone footage, the Aventar is nestled nice and deep. Yet, Lucas found them. No flashlight. No sign of the Tyius guiding him.

Lucas blows out a deep breath, and passes his hands over the crown of his head. It's his go-to move when he's stressed.

"Lucas, something you want to tell me?" Ryder digs her hands into her jean pockets. One of the elthar bracelets snags on the material, pinching her skin, like it's trying to answer her question too.

"No, and yes." Lucas doesn't laugh. She isn't even sure he's looking her in the eye. He takes too long to continue, and Ryder jumps in.

"You're not human." The breeze caresses the back of her neck, raising the hairs there.

"I'm not human." Lucas groans and shakes his head. "Wow, that sounds even more bizarre than I thought it would."

This time last week, she would have agreed. Likely would have told him off for being an idiot and talking rubbish.

"Bizarre is pretty much the theme of this weekend." Ryder interlaces her fingers and a few knuckles pop under the strain. What would he think of her day so far if she told him about it? "But I don't get it. You look nothing like the others."

"Now see that's the part that might not go down too well." Lucas scratches at the auburn stubble around his jaw. "I was kind of hoping Aresh might let Olessia know but I guess-"

"What part, Lucas."

"Have they mentioned a place called Zentai?"

Ryder winces, glancing up, hoping Sebastien isn't anywhere close with his surveillance toy. The sky is pitch dark, it's like staring into a black hole. "That is not a good place to be from right now. You need to go, Lucas."

"It's all right, Ry." Lucas's voice deepens with a more serious edge. "I'm not their enemy. Aresh knows that, she brought me here, a long time ago. She saved my life-"

All at once the darkness is chased away by the sheen of blue light directed at them. Ryder doesn't need to turn around to know who is approaching. Lucas straightens, squinting into the glare but not shading his eyes. The determined set of his chin says he's unafraid, but the way his fingers clench and unclench betrays him.

"Hey." Lucas lifts one of those nervous hands, and waves. "Sebastien, we meet again. I just found out Aresh hasn't had a chance to tell you about me."

Ryder turns. Sebastien doesn't blink as he watches Lucas, he's as still as a cobra before it strikes. "It would seem Aresh has neglected to tell me a lot of things."

All trace of the guy she'd thought she'd seen, the one who ached over having to force Olessia's return to her father, is well and truly buried now. Ryder resists the urge to move away from him. Right now, Sebastien is a soldier with one, singular mission; protect the Laudess of Bax Un Tey. If Ryder steps aside, Lucas will be even more vulnerable than he already is.

"You have to believe me, I am not your enemy. I've been here since I was a baby." Lucas is holding it together well, considering Sebastien's rage is sucking the oxygen out of the air. "I don't even know this Zentai place. Or Siros. Okay?"

Sebastien shakes his head in a measured, dangerous back and forth. "Why would the Laudine bring you here?"

"Because of my dad." Lucas stops, runs his hand through

the short spikes of his auburn hair. He glances at Ryder before he continues. "No doubt you know your Siros history. So you know about the First Treaty signing? The one held on Zentai... that was supposed to stop the war? Aresh was the Presider's representative, you know all this. It was a long time ago, about nineteen years ago actually." He points to himself. Lucas is a few months shy of his twenty-first birthday. "I was a baby. So I'm just going by what I've been told."

Sebastien is still watching Lucas like a hawk on a mouse. "There was an assassination attempt on Aresh, one that the Zentai Crown was accused of orchestrating to keep the war going. Are you going to tell me your father was the assassin, and this is Aresh's misguided empathy leading her astray again? Go on, give me another reason to hurt you."

Lucas drags in a breath through his nose, and when he speaks again it's not to Sebastien. His eyes are fixed on Ryder. "My father was the one who died saving her. He found out what was planned, and he tried to get her out of there before it could go ahead. He and my mother were killed. Aresh was saved, and the war didn't escalate."

Ryder's hands flutter to her mouth, but no sound comes.

"You are the Reigner's son?" The acid fades from Sebastien's tone.

Still reeling, Ryder steps out from between them, giving herself some space, some room to catch her breath. Her life is a muddled lump she doesn't recognise at all.

"I am." Lucas nods. "Whatever that really means. Like I said, that's not my world. I only know what I've been told."

Sebastien raps his fingers against one of the devices on his utility belt, a distracted, impatient rhythm. "How much more does Aresh expect of me?"

There's no answer to give him, even if the question had been meant for her. Ryder stands in the glow of the elthar, trying to process the words that just came out of Lucas's mouth. A jolt of laughter threatens to spill out, manic and bewildered.

"What the hell is a Reigner?" Ryder swallows. "Please tell me you're not like some extra-terrestrial prince or something."

Lucas screws up his face. "Hell, no. I think he was more like a chief of staff or something. Right hand man to the queen, type of thing."

"You're not supposed to be real." Sebastien has his back to them, but at least he's done with the death stares. Maybe Lucas will survive this after all. "You're just a story the Laudine's supporters like to tell, to show how much more benevolent a ruler she would make."

The disc-shaped device at Sebastien's waist makes a shrill sound, like a cicada stuck on high speed. A glance at it and a moment later he's ushering them back towards the Aventar.

"What now? Please tell me it's not more Celtren." Ryder winces as a low branch catches in her hair. "I really couldn't deal with that right now." If there are awards for understatement, that just won her the gold.

"Not Celtren. Humans." Sebastien says. "Too many aircraft in the area. I need to ensure their attention isn't drawn this way."

Aircraft in the middle of the night over Hobart doesn't sound like a typical Sunday night. Ryder trains her eyes on the ground, watching every step. Actually, she has no clue what time of night it is. Or even what night for that matter. The long weekend has stretched into something impossible. They break into a clearing. A wide space that could easily accommodate the Aventar. Some younger saplings lie horizontal to the ground, broken in half.

"Hello!" Sophie appears in the middle of the clearing, floating a couple of feet off the ground. At least that's how it appears when Ryder first glances at her. The Aventar is in camouflage mode, which has to be a good sign that the ships systems are up and running. Ryder can just make out a sliver of the cabin through the doorway. It's only open wide enough to allow a single person to pass through, and right now Sophie is the only person visible. "Lucas, I am so glad Sebastien didn't kill you. He said he was going to. Come on, I'll guide you up the ramp. It's just here."

Sophie gestures up and down, like she's guiding in planes on the tarmac. She's not going to be thrilled when she learns how close Sebastien was to keeping his word about Lucas.

"Lead the way, Ry." Lucas waves her forward. "I'll follow. You have some idea of what the ramp looks like."

It's logical, but she can't shake the feeling it's also a great excuse for Lucas to put a safer distance between himself and Sebastien.

CHAPTER 30

S EBASTIEN MOVES STRAIGHT TO THE pilot seat
where the holographic screen awaits his input. He swipes
at a few symbols, and voices fill the cabin. Static distorts
most of the words being spoken, but Ryder catches a few snippets;
it's English, which makes a nice change. Radio transmissions,
judging by the tango-tango-foxtrots thrown into the succinct, terse
conversations. Lucas is the last to enter the cabin. He steps inside,
and then does something rather odd. He bows. Bending his body so
far forward his torso is almost horizontal to the ground. He presses
his left fist against his chest, high up near the base of his throat.

"Laudess," he says. "It is my honour."

Seeing him act like a butler in a Victorian mansion, it's
hard not to burst out laughing. And Ryder's not the only one
struggling. Christian stands alongside Olessia who reclines in
her chair. His mouth twists with the strain of keeping a straight
face. Sophie's not faring much better, eyebrows raised so
high they've disappeared beneath her fringe. The only person
unsmiling is Olessia. She regards him with a wistful gaze.

"Aresh taught you the acknowledgement, I see," Olessia
says. "How sentimental of her."

Ryder's amusement evaporates. "Did you know about
Lucas?"

The garbled chatter Sebastien is listening to falls silent. He
wears ear buds now, frowning in concentration.

Olessia gets to her feet with Christian's help. Funny, she didn't seem so tired and needy when she was chatting outside earlier. "I knew of Lucas, but not about him. Aresh told me we could trust him and that was sufficient at the time. Sebastien however, has just informed me of what else there is to know about Lucas. Now I understand Aresh's reluctance to request my father's assistance."

She studies Lucas carefully, but with none of the rancour Sebastien directed at him. Lucas straightens, but seems reluctant to meet Olessia's gaze. This is a version of her friend Ryder hasn't seen before. He's never been one to shirk from anything. Sophie rescues him now. Launching herself at him for another hug, even though she did the same moments earlier when he got to the top of the ramp. He embraces her, lifting her feet off the ground.

"God, I'm so glad you guys are all okay." He sets her down, ruffling his hand over her hair, making a mess of the shock of red strands. But Sophie is nonplussed, not even trying to slap him away as she normally would.

"And I am so glad you are here. We all are," she says. "Lucas, we're in a spaceship. Can you believe this? Oh wait, of course you can. You're one of them. What's with keeping that secret? Bad call, my friend. Really bad call." She gasps. "Oh, tell me you have one of these ships somewhere? Please say you have one 'cause this is totally-"

"Sophie, geez," Ryder cries. "Stop talking."

It's Chris's turn to come to the rescue. He steps forward from where he's been waiting, wringing his hands, for the past couple of minutes. "It's good to see you, Lucas."

"Good to see you, man." Lucas and Christian embrace, pounding each other's backs in that way guys do. "Sorry about the rain check on that ride."

Christian laughs into Lucas's shoulder. "Just glad you're here." They cling together for a long moment, and Ryder glances at Olessia. Her expression is marble smooth and distant, but her eyes are calm rings of lavender. Christian pulls away first. His olive skin dark with a blush. He doesn't seem to know what to do with his hands now, tucking them into his jean pockets, changing his mind a second later and folding his arms instead. Ryder doesn't see Olessia move until she is alongside Lucas. It catches him off-guard too, and he jerks away from her.

He grimaces. "My apologies, Laudess."

"Please stop calling me that," Olessia says after a weighted silence. "I have never been this close to one of your kind. How long have you known who you are?"

There's only a heads difference in height between them, but Lucas's athletic frame accentuates Olessia's slightness.

"I haven't always known the details, but I've always known enough," he says, eyes shifting towards Ryder.

She glances away from the sting of his words; years of lies. But it doesn't shake her concern for him. She shifts, moving so she can catch a glimpse of Olessia's eyes. Whoever said the eyes are the windows to the soul, must have met these aliens. The shimmer of vibrant amethyst swirls in a lazy rotation around Olessia's pupils. Ryder relaxes, uncurling her fists. Amethyst is good, Olessia's in control. Intrigued and fascinated too, if the way she's peering at Lucas is anything to go by. Every sharp angle of Olessia's face is pronounced alongside Lucas's rounder features. There's no mistaking Olessia's differences, but the only thing that stands out about Lucas is the auburn tinge of his hair. Aresh wasn't kidding when she said the Zentai were genetically similar to humans.

Olessia reaches and traces her fingers along the curve of Lucas's ears. He isn't quick enough to conceal a startled jerk.

"Sorry, Laudess."

She sighs. "Again, stop calling me that." Her snow white fingertip follows the curve of his ear down to the lobe. "When was this done?"

The bewilderment contorting Christian's face is mirrored on Sophie's. Ryder shrugs at their unspoken question. She has no idea what the sudden ear fascination is. Sebastien mentioned something about Zentai and ears too.

"When I was a baby, I believe," Lucas says, head bowed as he addresses Olessia. "A plastic surgeon in Melbourne who's silence was well-"

Sudden recall grips Ryder and thumps the air out of her lungs. Zentai and their ears. "They don't have ears. The Zentai. Am I right?" Ryder's body twitches, she bounces like a game show contestant with the winning answer. "No lobes or anything."

"That's right," Olessia finally moves away from Lucas. She steps back, searching for something to lean on and finds Christian. "The Zentai have no external evidence of an ear. Lucas has prosthetics to ensure he blends in. I have to say, it's extraordinary what lengths Aresh has gone to here. At least the journey home will be interesting. She has so much to tell me." Her gaze lands squarely on Ryder as she speaks. "So many secrets for one person to maintain."

"What are we missing here?" Sophie says, hands on hips. "Why does Lucas have no ears? Where are you from exactly?"

"Zentai. He is from Zentai." Ryder says, conscious of how easily the words roll off her tongue. And how unimportant the information is compared to what she wants to say next. "I've seen one, without the prosthetics. When that Placer attacked Chris and I in the field, when I...stabbed it...the blood, it did something. I saw its memories. There was this tall Zentai guy, with dreadlocks and no ears, in this cave. No idea where. But there were Placers and Celtren with him."

Lucas stares at her like she's just spoken in tongues. "You stabbed a Placer?"

She waves off the question. He'll have to deal with it later. She waits for Olessia to reply. It takes longer than expected, and Olessia's expression grows guarded. The snap of one of the clips on her utility belt is the only sound filling the cabin. Sebastien moves to join them, pulling the earbuds from his ears. He watches Olessia but stays silent.

Finally Ryder raises her hands and shrugs. "Nothing? You know who the guy might have been?" Or better yet, does she have any clue why Ryder could see any of that through the creature's blood?

Olessia frowns. "There is little doubt the Zentai are involved in this. But I do not understand why they themselves are nowhere to be seen." She turns to Sebastien. "What are they waiting for? This is hardly their usual tactic; I've never known them to use creatures of the Arlion this way."

"Whatever their intention, it continues. Listen to this." Sebastien traces his finger in the air, and the cabin fills with the hiss of voices and static. It's unclear if what they are listening to is recorded or live, but the transmission is much clearer than what they heard earlier.

"We have visual on the anomalies, Sir," a woman says. "They appear to be biological."

Another voice, deeper and sterner, clips in. "Estimate on numbers, Simmons. We're having trouble with the video feed at this end. Seems to be interference."

"Three sighted so far, sir. I can't confirm exactly what I'm seeing but they are substantial in size." The pilot breathes hard into the comms. "One I'm seeing I estimate to be the size of a brown bear-" A high screech wipes out the rest of the pilot's words.

"Agent Cooper advises to maintain distance. Do not engage until further instructions."

Lucas runs his hand over his face. "Not good."

"What?" Ryder says. "What is it?"

"Cooper." He stares up at the domed ceiling. "Benjamin Cooper. That must be C-21 we're listening to. He's the head guy."

Sophie edges in closer to where Ryder stands, her hands flutter with nerves. "But where are they? I mean where are they seeing these bear things exactly?"

Sebastien gestures to the back of the cabin. "Where we need

to be. They're at the entrance to the Paldrian River." The central screen blooms with an image that's too blurry to make out. "There's interference of some kind, I'm having difficulty getting clarity with the BD."

Ryder assumes he's talking about the drone. She squints, trying to make out the shadowy feedback. The comms between aircraft and ground control continue. "Continue to maintain watch only," says a grim-voiced man with a faint English accent. "We are instigating quarantine protocol for the area."

"That's him," Lucas mutters. "Cooper. Would know that lovely pommy accent anywhere. Unbelievable, all that time I spent trying to throw them off, and now there's some kind of Arlion party happening right under their noses."

Benjamin Cooper doesn't sound so scary. In fact he sounds a bit like Ryder's science teacher, with a monotone voice that lulls everyone off to sleep halfway through class. She blinks as the footage draws into focus. It's Blackrhine Hill, the damaged phone tower tilts like a giant art sculpture.

The pilot radios back a shaky reply, confirming Cooper's last instruction. The view sweeps along the bank of the Derwent, the BD running low to the open paddocks which pock-mark the surrounding area. The drone frightens a couple of dozing cows, and they trot away across the paddocks. Rain drizzles down on the landscape, and in the distance the sky sparks with lightening.

"Sir, we are requesting further airborne assistance. We believe some of the anomalies may have flight capabilities. They have wings, sir." The pilot's words come just as the BD draws in close to the slopes of Blackrhine Hill. Dark shapes form an untidy circle around the base of the structure, before the BD draws in close enough to see them clearly; the bulky silhouettes of the Celtren, and the towering haggard frames of Placers.

"Oh man," Christian says in a hushed tone. "So many of them."

Olessia sits on the very edge of her chair. Eyes dark as plums and the swirl of her irises moving so fast it's almost a solid colour.

"But not that many," she says. "Not so many that I couldn't deal with it. I think I understand why we haven't seen the Zentai yet." She glances at Lucas. "The ones that are a problem I mean. I think you are right, Lucas."

The volume of the radio transmissions lowers to a murmur.

"Laudess?" Lucas says, forgetting for the third time her instructions not to use her title. "I'm not sure I'm following."

But Ryder, still watching the meandering cluster of beasts, thinks she might be. "A party, right at the River entrance. Someone isn't worried about getting attention, because it's exactly what they want." Olessia nods and Ryder rushes on. "Maybe they're not here, the Zentai, and they're using those walking nightmares to draw attention to the entrance."

"Hinder us when we try to enter the River," Olessia adds.

But Ryder shakes her head, another thought taking shape. "Or stop you completely. Lucas, you said yourself that Cooper has Siros tech. That they reverse engineered it to find us, right?" She pauses long enough for him to nod. Sebastien's eyes haven't left her, his cool stare unblinking. "What if they've developed something that could stop the Aventar, and whoever is behind this knows that?"

She splays her arms, like she's just nailed the million dollar question in a quiz show. Sophie gives her a thumbs up. Ryder seeks out Sebastien. She's not expecting a thumbs up, but astonishment or even bemusement would be nice. Her enthusiasm wanes when she finds only a scowl and dark eyes. A few of those words she doesn't understand leave his lips and she lets her arms drop to her sides. She hadn't stopped to consider what being right actually meant. Olessia is silent, eyes closed.

"What tech did they get hold of Lucas, is it something they could make a weapon out of?" Christian sits on the arm of Olessia's chair, one foot tapping out a nervous rhythm against the metal.

Lucas lets out a sigh, pressing his hands against his scalp. "Maybe. Basically, they have parts of a ship, like this." He spreads his arms, indicating the Aventar.

"You're kidding me," Ryder says.

"No. Sadly I am not." He hesitates, glancing at Olessia. Her eyes are wide open.

She inclines her head. "By all means, go ahead. What else am I not privy to?"

"Aresh is going to hate me for telling you." Lucas winces. "She's still horrified it happened, but, well, she kind of lost one of the Aventars once. On one of her trips here. Didn't put it in camouflage mode, and some people bushwalking up near Evandale found it. She couldn't do a full self-destruct 'cause there were too many people around by the time she realised. Some Claven guy came and got her eventually, but they had to leave the remnants here."

Ryder is surprised to see a smirk on Olessia's face. "Well, I have to say I'm beginning to like this Aresh so much more than the one I know."

Sebastien bangs his fist against the wall, making everyone jump. "Which Claven guy?"

Lucas shrugs, shoulders staying up high, as he struggles to recall. "It was a long time ago, started with B I think. Bushell or something? I always remember thinking his name sounded like the tea. She talked about him quite a bit, seemed to be the only one of them she liked."

"Dashel." Sebastien chews the name like it's a piece of gristle. Olessia leans forward putting her face in her hands.

"What is it?" Lucas frowns, searching back and forth between Olessia, Sebastien and Ryder. When the others stay silent, Ryder steps in.

"Your Bushell tea buddy, is here," she says. "Dashel. He's here now. And he's looking even more dodgy by the second. Sebastien thinks he may have sabotaged the Aventar. A bunch of Celtren nearly brought us down because half the systems were disabled. Like someone wants this thing to fly, but not defend itself."

Lucas whistles, glancing at Sebastien. "No wonder you weren't happy to see me." There is no reply. Sebastien doesn't need to say a word, the whirlpool swirl of thundercloud gray in his eyes is enough. But Lucas continues. "I'll do what I can to help you, but I need to get these guys out of here, this is all way too much now. Take them across the river, drop them off somewhere safer, like the school. This spot is too isolated to leave them here."

"That is hardly my concern."

Ryder's mouth drops, ready to tell Sebastien what she thinks of his concerns. The guy is a certified mercurial, arrogant jerk.

"Yeah, well maybe not." Lucas reaches underneath his hoodie and pulls out a flip-top mobile phone. "But Aresh is, and I know that she's on full blackout for mindreaches right now. So, if you want to reach her, you're going to need this phone."

CHAPTER 31

THE AVENTAR LIFTS OUT OF its pine tree hideaway and coasts towards the river. Ryder stands beside one of the great panes of glass, staring down at the passing terrain. The rain is steady but not heavy, leaving winding streaks down the window. She presses the phone hard against her ear, and her heart beats in time with the ringtone. Sebastien is piloting, but the others are all huddled at the back of the craft, talking in hushed tones. The phone clicks and Jack's voice fills her ear.

"Lucas, have you seen her? Are they okay?" He speaks quickly, panic edging his words.

"Hi Jack, it's me." Ryder's reply is flat and hard in comparison. It takes an effort to keep the anger at bay, despite everything. Actually, because of everything. If he'd told her something sooner, then perhaps, this wouldn't be happening.

Jack makes a choked sound. "Ryder. Oh, you have no idea how good it is to hear your voice."

She wants to be able to tell him she feels the same way, but the words stick, not fully formed. "We're okay." Sebastien watches her from the pilot seat, chin propped on his raised fist. "I'm going to ask you a question but I need to know if anyone is around you. Are those guys with you?"

Thankfully, Jack doesn't bombard her with questions. "Aresh is with me. And Verran, he's hurt but he's doing okay. But we lost track of Dashel after the attack. Is he with you?"

The narrowing of Sebastien's eyes tells her he heard the reply. She almost pities Dashel if Sebastien ever catches up with him. "No, he's not."

A flash of lightening bursts in the sky over the city centre.

"Where are you, Ryder? Let me come and get you, please. This has just gotten all way out of hand."

"Yeah, you could say that." Ryder rubs at a fleck of dried blood on the hem of her t-shirt. She'd kill for a hot shower right about now. "Look, Jack there are some issues that Aresh really needs to know about. I know she's trying to stay low, but she really needs to speak with Sebastien. Can you put her on for me?" He agrees but then tries to ask her more questions about whether she is hurt at all. If she is really okay. "We'll have plenty of time to talk. We're going to meet you at the school. But I'm going to put Sebastien on now, just get Aresh for me, please?"

"Sure, sure. Will do that now. I'll see you real soon, luv."

His tone is laced with pain. Little wonder, Ryder's never been so short, or so hostile with him in her life. Handing the phone to Sebastien, Ryder joins the others at the back of the cabin. Sophie takes one look at her and sidles in for a hug. Lucas gives her a lop-sided smile. It's meant to be reassuring, but only reminds her Jack's not the only liar in her family. If her dad is in on this, she'll be packing her bags for good. Ryder leans into Sophie's hug.

"Does Jack know about you?" Ryder asks, though she's not sure what difference Lucas's answer will make.

"No." Lucas is getting well practised at appearing sheepish. "Aresh always thought it would be best not to. For him and me. Though over the years I tried to convince her he should know."

"Aresh makes a lot of decisions for people, doesn't she?" Ryder doesn't meet his apologetic gaze.

Sebastien's voice rises. He's speaking in whatever the Siros language is, but it's clear he's unhappy with where the conversation is going. Ironic, that despite all the mind reading, armour that makes you fly, and oh-so-advanced spaceships, he's using a years old mobile phone to communicate. Olessia watches him too, listening in. She winces at parts of it, bites on her lip at others. Finally Sebastien hangs up the call, slams the phone down on the seat beside him, just as thunder rolls through the sky.

"I think she understands his feelings on the situation quite clearly," Olessia says, not without a trace of a smile.

"They will meet us at the school within the hour," says Sebastien.

And that's it. Not a word more. He slumps back into the seat, one foot up on the seat, his chin resting on his knee. An alarm shrills through the cabin, like the squawk of a very angry bird. Sebastien mutters something to himself, dropping his foot to the floor and settling into the seat. The Aventar dips hard towards the left bank and slows, hugging the water's edge. Ryder holds her breath as they skirt over some boats moored in close to the shore. The Aventar comes to a stop beside a rocking tin dinghy. The silver boat is dwarfed by the aircraft that hovers alongside it.

"What's the problem?" Olessia sits straight in her seat, peering outside.

Sebastien just points. Dark, sleek patrol boats slide up the river towards them. Two of them, racing almost parallel, their sharp bows piercing the inky water. They sit low to the water, and the illumination of the searchlights they carry dances off an array of radar and sonar equipment that juts from the roof of each cabin.

"Water police," says Christian. "Everyone is coming to this party."

Sebastien holds the Aventar steady above the water. They are in a shallow cove, alarmingly close to the rocky shoreline.

"They won't be able to see us right?" Ryder stands and moves behind the pilot seat.

"Not us," Sebastien says. "But they may detect the disturbance of the water surface. I need to stay low, so I'm just going to let them pass."

At least he answered her question and didn't tell her it was none of her concern. Ryder tugs at her shirt, picking at a non-existent stain, annoyed at the curl of warmth in her chest. Give it five minutes and she'll be wishing him gone again.

On the opposite bank, a few hundred metres north, the glow of the school's pool house is visible. The patrol boats shoot by it and continue on down river, reaching the section where the Aventar hovers like an enormous bat over the water. Sebastien waits until their lights are pinpricks further down river, before he guides the Aventar over towards the school.

The upper levels of Taroona High's three main buildings come into view, peeking over the line of trees planted close to the water's edge to serve as a windbreak against the cold river breezes. Not that the windbreak actually works. The school is always cold. The winds manage to work their way down the halls and into the corners of the classrooms no matter how many doors are closed. The school is laid out in an H shape, and Ryder guides Sebastien towards the dark blot that is the sport oval on the far side of the buildings.

"There's more than enough room to land there," she says.

He doesn't reply but follows her instruction. They touch down with a shudder. The rain streams down in light, glittering strands.

Lucas drapes an arm across one of Ryder's shoulders, something he's always done, trying to exaggerate the small difference in their height. "Bet you never thought you'd be arriving at school quite like this, huh?" His eyes twinkle in the dim cabin lighting. He is trying to make her smile, but Ryder shrugs him away. It's going to take some time to get her head around everything he's told her. He nods, as though he understands without her saying a word.

"So, this is it huh?" Sophie wrings her hands. "This is goodbye."

"It is." Sebastien stands, his back arching as he stretches. He hands Ryder the mobile phone and their fingers brush as she takes it. "Now let's do this quickly. All right, everyone out." His long legs carry him quickly across the cabin floor. The door is already open halfway.

The phone's clock tells her it's four thirty-five in the morning, a couple of hours before dawn, and the air sweeping into the cabin brings the touch of ice with it. Tomorrow is Tuesday and the long weekend will be over. The school grounds will be full of students chatting about what they did on the weekend.

"Feels so weird being back here, doesn't it?" Sophie whispers.

Ryder nods, watching Sebastien at the open doorway, the way he flexes his fingers when he moves, the tilt of his head when he speaks. Her eyes drift to Olessia who has joined him. He's telling her in a not so gentle way to get back in her seat, using every inch of his height to glare down at her. In return she's unflinching, not tilting her head to stare up at him, and ordering him out of the way. Ryder's body hollows out, like there is air where her bones should be, and dizziness washes over her. Hunger. It's got to be. She hasn't eaten in what feels like an eternity.

"Stay inside, Olessia," Sebastien says. "As soon as Aresh and Verran are on board, we'll leave."

Olessia opens her mouth, but her reply is stopped short when Christian takes her hand. A few gentle words see him leading her back to her seat. He glances at Lucas who is busy tying up a lace on his once-aquamarine, now dirty brown, trainers. When he catches Ryder watching him, he ducks his head and leans in closer to Olessia.

"Is that them?" Sophie taps Ryder's arm, pointing out through the gap in the doorway.

Shadowy figures approach the craft. When Sebastien doesn't even raise an eyebrow, Ryder assumes it must be Jack and the others.

"Jack?" She calls out. One of the figures begins to jog towards them. She runs down the ramp, hitting the rain-drenched ground, her sneakers sucking at the sodden grass. Clear of the brightness of the Aventar cabin, her eyes adjust, and she can make out the familiar shape of Jack's bulky figure. He sweeps her up in an all enveloping bear hug. Her anger melts, trickling away with the rain.

He holds her tight. "Oh thank god, thank god."

"Jack." Ryder coughs. "Can't breathe."

"Sorry." He laughs softly, easing the embrace but still keeping her in his arms. "How are you doing?"

"Just peachy." She presses her cheek against his shoulder. "I'm okay really."

"No thanks to me, I'm afraid. I'm so sorry I didn't tell you all this sooner, luv."

The slap of feet in puddles announces Sophie's arrival. And she's in for an equally enthusiastic hug from Jack. Ryder hunches her shoulders against the rain and catches sight of Aresh. She stands a short distance away, still dressed in the flowing green gown, the scarred side of her face hidden by snow-white locks of hair that don't move despite the breeze. She draws closer, a beaming smile on her face.

"Hi." Ryder gives her a self-conscious wave. The last chat they had didn't end so well. And the memory of Aresh pinning Verran to a wall comes to mind.

"Are you not cold, Ryder?" Aresh says.

Till that moment the answer would have been no. But when Ryder glances down and sees that she's only wearing her t-shirt, her skin bristles with goosebumps. Mad at him or not, she'd forgotten all else when she saw Jack coming towards the Aventar. Now she's freezing to death, and she's clenching her jaw to stop her teeth chattering. As though he read her mind, which is entirely possible, Sebastien appears at her side, jacket in hand.

"Oh, hey," Ryder says, fervently wishing she hadn't just jumped like a startled cat. "Thank you."

"Welcome." Sebastien clears his throat. "Good luck then."

"Same to you." The awkwardness of the moment is truly horrifying. Ryder begs her brain to think of something remotely amazing to say but it's too slow. He marches away, asking Aresh where Verran is. She directs him to the carpark. Verran is holed up in Jack's car there. The old beat up station wagon is the only car in the lot. Sebastien alters course and heads towards it. When she pulls her gaze away and turns back, Lucas has joined them. Aresh embraces him, her hand cupped to the back of his head. Lucas nods at something she says to him, a rueful smile crossing his lips. Then, before she has a chance to avoid it, Ryder finds herself face to face with Aresh again.

"You are a remarkably strong young woman, Ryder Carlsson." Aresh lifts a hand, like she wants to touch her, but stops short. "I'm sorry that so much has been kept from you."

"So am I." Ryder is trying very hard to stay angry. She failed miserably with Jack, crumbling as soon as she saw him. And her resolve is weakening here too. Aresh is practically beaming at her. Ryder's dad doesn't even look at her like this; like the sun is shining out of her proverbial. All at once, Aresh steps up way too close.

"When this is all said and done," she whispers, her hand on Ryder's arm, stopping her from backing away, "when Olessia is safe and when you are safe. We will talk. I promise you."

Ryder doesn't move when Aresh presses her hands gently against her shoulders. "You and Lucas, look after each other. As you've always done. And don't be too hard on your grandfather. He loves you so. We both do."

A quick press of lips to Ryder's forehead and then Aresh is gone. Sweeping away in a flurry of flowing skirts to join Sebastien and help him carry the limping Verran up the ramp into the Aventar. The sullen man doesn't seem so intimidating now. There is bandaging over his left shoulder, and he grunts in pain as they help him. The rain starts to patter down again. Olessia and Christian stand off to one side of the ramp. Ryder should go to them, go to Olessia. It's time to say goodbye. That knot tying itself into every part of Ryder's belly, winds its way up into her ribcage. Her tongue sticks to the roof of her mouth. Then it's too late. Olessia hurries up the ramp, no backward glance, and disappears into the cabin. Ryder blinks, flicking droplets off her eyelashes. That can't be it.

"Come on." Jack herds them back. "Let's get to the car."

"But I haven't…"

Whatever Ryder hasn't done, doesn't matter. The smooth rectangular door of the Aventar slides closed. Jack puts his hands on her shoulders and soldiers her towards the carpark. The faintest rumble shudders through the ground as the engines engage. The single blade winds in a lazy rotation. The Aventar flickers into camouflage mode and out of sight.

CHAPTER 32

RYDER SETTLES INTO THE FRONT passenger seat and pulls the car door shut. Jack has the engine running, and the heater whines in a desperate attempt to warm them.

"Oh wow, our bags." Sophie exclaims from the back seat. "I didn't think we'd see them again."

Their bags are heaped in the back of the station wagon. Ryder sighs, catching sight of her red duffel bag. There are dry clothes in there, including a pair of gray jeans that won't be lead weight like the ones clinging to her legs. They suck against her body, trying to meld with it, and a patch of skin at her waist is near raw from the rub of the material. Sophie leans over the back seat, unzipping her bag. "I can't quite get to your bag. You want to wear this for now, Ry?" She hands her one of her own jumpers, a black crocheted stunner with multi coloured, miniature pom-poms all over it. It's hideous and Ryder knows it will be a size too small, but it's dry, and it doesn't have blood on it. She takes it from Sophie and shrugs off her denim jacket, no small feat in the cramped confines of the car.

Jack smiles at Sophie in the rear vision mirror. "I had just loaded them into my car before everything went pear shaped. A lucky move as it turns out. Now, where do we head to? Ryder, I'm guessing your place is the best bet?"

"Yeah, well my place is empty. As per usual." Jack frowns. He doesn't get along with his son, but she knows it pains him to see the cracks in her relationship with her dad. "Well, it's true. Hang on a second, where is Lucas?"

The car radio suddenly seems to need all of Jack's attention. "Lucas is, ah, well he's…" He coughs, rubbing at his beard beneath his chin. "He's gone to borrow a car."

Ryder stares at him. The radio in his car hasn't worked properly for years. "There's plenty of room in this one."

It isn't entirely true, he would be squashed in the middle of the back seat, but Ryder doesn't think Sophie or Christian would mind. Jack gives up on the radio dial.

"Ryder, he'll be fine." If he really believed that, then she wouldn't be able to see so many lines bunching around his eyes or the nervous way his fingers toy with the dial.

"He's gone to Blackrhine Hill." She presses herself back in her seat, her empty belly churning.

"Why would he do that?" Sophie leans forward but her seatbelt jerks her back. "It's full of people with guns—and animals with fangs. Really humongous fangs-"

"He's not going to go near either. Lucas just wants to have a little look around, see what he can find out. Turns out that boy is as stubborn as the rest of you." Jack flicks on the headlights, adjusts his seat, and avoids Ryder's glare. "Aresh thought it was a good idea, having some eyes on the ground up there. Any extra information they can get a hold of, is a good thing. She has my mobile, we're keeping it simple. He will ring her with anything that might help."

"Aresh doesn't seem capable of keeping things simple." Ryder gives up trying to eyeball him. The rain is hammering down, bouncing off the tired paintwork. The car is in desperate need of a new coat of paint, with a rust mark the shape of Africa spread across the bonnet.

"Ryder, he won't do anything foolish. I promise you."

"Pretty sure he already has, again. He didn't have a car in his back pocket last time I looked." The windscreen wipers squeal across the glass. If C-21 need a legitimate way to hold Lucas, if they catch him on the hill, then grand theft auto will be perfect.

"Exactly how many cars is he intending to steal before this is over?"

Her voice is raised too loud, and her eyes burn like sand's been thrown in them. She's seen the movies. Clandestine government agencies are never a good thing. It never ends well for the aliens.

"As many as it takes," Jack says. "He knows the risks, and he's willing to take them." He grips the steering wheel, his gaze set on the road ahead of them, doing it with so much fervour, he gives away what he's trying to hide. This isn't just about Olessia. It is about her.

"We're in trouble, aren't we?" she says. She, is in trouble.

Jack crunches the car into reverse. "It will be all right. They just need to get the Laudess out of here." He fights to get the car back into first once he's out of the parking space. "She can't be here. It's too dangerous. For everyone."

Sophie lays gentle hands on Ryder's shoulders. "Breathe, Ry." Ryder takes a breath she didn't realise she was holding. "It is going to be okay. You've got this."

But Ryder doesn't *get* anything at all. She is just plain scared. And her thoughts are not helping. She is thinking about Dashel. About how much the guy might know about her, and about Lucas. Is he passing on the information to the Zentai at this very moment, while she sits in a car that could barely protect them against bugs splatting on the windscreen, let alone powerful extra-terrestrials. Hey overlords, Dashel might say, I know this earth girl who seems to be immune to the most powerful force in our universe. Want to know who she is?

No matter how Ryder holds her hands, clenched in fists or pressed into her lap, she can't stop shaking.

"This is a mess." She whispers, not to anyone in particular but Jack hears her. She wishes she could find the light in his eyes that says this is all going to be all right. She can't.

"Maybe, but I'm going to keep you out of this one." Jack declares. "I swear to you."

Ryder bites her lip, stopping herself from asking why he didn't do that ten years ago. Partly because it's mean, partly because she thinks she might cry.

Christian speaks up for the first time since they piled into the car. "Olessia told me a lot about her dad, man, he's not a nice guy. Not by a long shot. I told her that if it was me, I'd keep running." He laughs a small fragile sound. "I told her my dad's family has this little cabin just on the edge of the Tarkine..." Breathe, Ryder reminds herself, only half listening to Christian's meandering story. Breathe. "Anyway, it was a dumb idea."

"Is there a point to this story, Chris?" Sophie says.

"Yes, Sophie. There is a point." Ryder can practically feel him roll his eyes. "When I told her to keep running, she said she didn't need to anymore. That she was ready to go back. I just wanted Ry to know that she helped. That it's not all a mess. Olessia isn't afraid anymore. That's what she said."

Now it's Ryder's turn to avoid Jack. She can't handle the deep furrows of concern a second longer. He knows. It's there in the downturn of his mouth and the melancholy stirring behind his eyes. He knows things have changed. She's not the same girl he greeted at the station on Friday. Ryder focuses on the little pom-poms on the jumper, plucking at the little fuzzy balls. They are halfway around the school buildings, Jack driving them along the road between the buildings and the river. A long line of willow trees form the first line of defence against the winds coming in off the water. Rubbish, ripped from a poorly closed bin somewhere, flutters across the road in front of them. Every whine and clunk from the engine is audible as they sit in silence. Despite the warm air coming from the vents, Ryder shivers, the cold sinking down into her bones. Her thoughts drift to Padellah. The entity has been skirting at the edges of Ryder's life for so long. Was it all for this? Ryder jabs her thumb against her bottom lip, pushing till it hurts. Olessia thinks Ryder helped her, when she might have just delivered her to her enemies.

Sophie drums her fingers against the window. "It is killing me not knowing what's going on out there."

"We'll be home soon enough, hot showers all round." Jack is trying too hard to be jolly. "Too early for pizza orders, but I'm sure we can find something in the kitchen to whip up."

They pass the pool house, the car moving through the glow of security lighting that spills out onto the road. It's an impressive building, the principal's pride and joy. It's about two years old, with one whole wall constructed entirely of glass panelling that can be swung open in the summer. It's Olympic size too, which is impressive apparently, but Ryder's never stepped foot inside the complex.

"Wait, stop." She runs her hand through the condensation on the window. "I can see the hill from here."

It's just a sliver of a view, through a spot where one of the willows had to be taken down because it had some worm infection. But it's enough. The base of the hill is aglow with lights, with smaller spots, searchlights presumably, darting around higher up the slope.

"Ryder we need to keep moving," Jack says, as the car rolls forward. "I'm really sorry love but-"

"Stop," Sophie cries.

The station wagon's brakes are the only thing in great working order. They shunt everyone forward with a savage jerk. On the road ahead, at the far reach of the headlights a huge fallen Melaleuca tree blocks the road.

"Okay, well we're not moving that thing," Jack says. "Can anyone see a space to turn around? Back window's all fogged up, I can't see a thing."

But Ryder keeps her gaze fixed on the blocked road ahead. Something just moved; up near the bushy head of the fallen tree, in the shadows beyond the headlights. The car rocks as a gust of wind blindsides them. "There's someone out there."

"Where?" Sophie asks.

But there is no need to answer. Someone steps clear of the branches and stands in the full glare of the lights. Ryder can't even cry out, her breath stuck somewhere between lungs and mouth.

"Dashel?" Jack leans forward over the steering wheel. "What the hell?"

"This is bad," Christian says. "Really bad."

"We need to go, now." Sophie cries. "Please, Jack. Drive."

A gust of wind whips Dashel's coat around him. He stands perfectly still, his bald head glistening in the rain. It might be a trick of the light, but Ryder could swear his eyes are on her.

She shouts, "Jack, go." It does the trick. Jack crunches the car into reverse so hard it sounds like he's broken the gearbox. They lurch backwards as a violent shudder runs through the car. The windows rattle in their frame, and the pine tree air freshener hanging off the rear vision mirror swings like it's trying to do a loop-de-loop. The car jerks, the engine sputters and then dies. Jack turns the ignition key, foot pumping the gas. But the car is as dead as the proverbial dodo. He swears, the first time she's heard a curse cross his lips.

"What do we do? Do we run?" Sophie's voice pitches high.

The car shakes, moves with a jolt from one side to another. Someone's head hits the window, judging by Christian's hiss it was him. Then the car lifts, drifting up from the surface of the road. But Ryder doesn't dare take her eyes off Dashel. Her gaze fixes on him as the car rises higher. He stands there. Arms at his side, relaxed, like he's just out for a stroll in the rain. The car tilts forward. Luggage thumps against the back seat.

When I say so, you will leave the vehicle.

Ryder cries out with relief as Padellah's strange multi-voice fills her head. If she could kiss a ghost, Ryder would do it now.

"Ryder?" Jack says. "Hang on, love. Just hang on."

She shakes her head. "When I say so we're going to get out."

"What?"Jack says. "Ryder, no-"

The car rocks hard to one side, the force of it slamming Ryder against the door.

"Loving seat belts right now." Sophie squeals.

Dashel has a lazy smile on his face, seemingly oblivious to the rain and the wind around him. He flicks his fingers towards them, and a huge crack appears in the windscreen. He gestures again and the back window shatters, glass and rain sprays through the car. Sophie and Christian cry out, covering their heads.

"He's crazy," Christian shouts.

And they are completely vulnerable. Ryder presses her feet against the dashboard, trying to keep some of the strain off her seatbelt. This car is old, there's no telling how much the straps can handle.

Prepare to leave the vehicle. The moment will be brief.

It takes an effort to pull her hands away from where they brace against the roof. Her weight bears down on the seatbelt, and the almost-healed wound on her shoulder niggles. Ryder grips the door handle.

"Get ready to open your doors. Follow my lead. We're getting out."

Jack shakes his head, a wild swing back and forth. His knuckles are white, wrapped tight around the steering wheel. "Don't be-"

"Jack, with all due respect," Sophie says, panic pitching her voice. "We need to listen to her."

After Padellah, Sophie is getting a kiss too.

"What's the grand plan, Ry?" Christian grunts, his knees jammed up against the back of Jack's seat.

It's a very good question but she doesn't have the answer. Not yet. Padellah has vanished again. They just need to be ready to get out. That's all Ryder knows. All at once, the fallen tree behind Dashel shakes, leaves splaying into the air. The massive tree lifts and then rotates, the root end of the trunk slams against Dashel's back. He goes flying, landing flat on his face into the mud on the side of the road. It happens so quickly he doesn't make a sound. The car drops like a stone to ground, and the impact shudders up Ryder's spine. If she doesn't need a physio after this, she'll be lucky.

Padellah's command is sharp against her senses. *Go now.*

"Get out, get out now." Ryder swings open her door. The others follow suit.

"Is he dead?" Sophie cries, clambering out of the car.

"Not going to check, go." Ryder races towards the shelter of the nearest building. "Follow me, run, just run."

She has no idea where, nowhere seems safe right now. The wind and rain are relentless, buffeting her from every direction. Ryder calls out to Padellah. Nothing but her own panic echoes through her senses.

"This way." Christian waves them to the left, his long legs taking him ahead. He leads them towards an arched passageway in the building block, a few metres down the road. It will lead them into the central courtyard of the school yard. Everyone streams into the narrow, dim passageway. Ryder hesitates, glancing back at Dashel. He lies motionless in the middle of the road.

"Ryder, come on," Sophie calls out, her words echo down the enclosed passageway.

"We need to split up." Ryder runs to join them. It's a relief to be out of the biting rain, the droplets like shards of ice bearing down on them. "We can't all stay together, it's just too easy."

"No way I'm letting you kids run around here by yourselves with that maniac out there. We stick together, safety in numbers." Jack's breath comes in short, sharp bursts. The panic and the pace aren't easy on him. It's a short passageway and it's not long before they're back out in the elements. Ryder's jeans are soaked through to her underwear, and her boots heavy with mud.

"Which way?" Jack hesitates. "We need to get round to the front of the school. Try and get out onto the main road."

There is an archway directly across the courtyard, and another to their right.

"This way." Christian waves them towards the right.

The courtyard has a rose garden at its centre, usually meticulous, but now it's a mess of broken stems and cowed plants. Rose petals cover the soil and rubbish has snagged on many of the thorns. The storm that passed through here, the night Sebastien nearly downed the tower, has turned the place into a disaster zone. Ryder is the last to head across the courtyard.

She glances back one more time down the dark passageway. Checking for Dashel. And hoping she might see hint of the light that tells her Padellah hasn't abandoned her.

"Ryder, look out." It is not Padellah, but Sophie who shouts the warning.

She spins round and is confronted by a fresh horror. Ryder's scream lodges behind her tongue, and her feet skid on the muddy ground as she backpeddles. A Celtren stands barely a metre away, cutting her off from the others who've reached the far side of the courtyard. Its huge dog-like head tilts to one side, orange eyes fixed on her, bony wings folded back against its red-black body. The grotesque creature is huge, at least a grizzly bear if not more, and the stench rising from its wet fur makes her gag. The Celtren crouches low, its huge paws sinking deep into the drenched ground and it hisses, like the world's loudest cobra. Dipping its head low, it unfurls its wings and cuts off Ryder's line of sight to the others. They shout at her to get out of there. But she's equally exhausted and terrified, and her legs don't respond.

The Celtren lunges. Its wings spread wide, the tip of one smacking against the flag pole in the middle of the courtyard. That might be what throws it off balance. Something makes it stumble, down onto bulbous knee joints. It bares its teeth and a waft of stale breath makes Ryder dry retch. But her legs find their go button. One in front of the other, unsteady but upright. She races away from the monster. Because it is all she can do. Whatever else she might be, she is not Olessia.

CHAPTER 33

THE PASSAGEWAY IS TOO NARROW for the Celtren to press its bulk into, which makes the corridor the most beautiful place on earth. Ryder hurls herself into the passageway, and presses herself against the brickwork, chest heaving. The beast prowls just beyond the archway, but it's not looking her way. It's only when it lumbers off to one side that Ryder sees why.

"Run, Ryder, go girl." Jack shouts.

He stands in the courtyard, waving his arms like a madman. He hurls a tin can and then something more solid which hits the Celtren square in the snout, making its head jerk. It roars, wings extending to full stretch and beating down. It sends a great gust of air down the passageway, and Ryder backs further away when the club-like tail swings towards her. A chunk of stonework shatters and sprays out into the courtyard. If there was ever a time to do as she's told, it would be now, but Ryder can't take her eyes off her grandad.

"Jack, are you crazy?"

The Celtren seems to think they're both crazy. It swings its broad head back and forth, coal fire eyes shifting between Ryder and Jack. Monster or not, it's not stupid. The only way it could get to Ryder would be to tear down the brickwork. It chooses an easier option. The Celtren sinks down on its haunches and shifts to face Jack before it launches itself at him with an air-renting roar, hind legs throwing up a squall of mud and grass. Jack spins round, but has little chance of getting beyond the creature's far-reaching wingspan. The Celtren uses the tip of its wings to swipe at his legs, knocking them from under him. Jack's head smacks against the stones edging the rose garden. The crack of it reaches her.

"Jack, no." Ryder's scream fills the passageway, magnifying the sound. Her face fills with heat, the fire pumping through every vein and burning away the damp chill that's reached her bones. Jack lies in a crumpled, lifeless pile in front of the Celtren's massive paws. The blood roars in Ryder's ears, muffling the sound of the world around her. Her joints ache, consumed by the fire rushing through her. Ryder hurtles towards the archway, fingers curled into claws, her eyes fixed on the Celtren. She reaches the threshold and the air hardens, knocking her back. Ryder stumbles, the impact knocking a shocked cry from her lips. She tries again, shouldering her way forwards. But the air in front of her may as well be a pane of glass. She balls her fists and slams them against the invisible barrier.

You are not ready.

"Padellah?" Ryder whirls around, squinting into the gloom. "Is that you? Let me out. Right now."

You are not ready.

The Celtren leans over Jack, raising a paw easily the size of Jack's head. Ryder claws at the air, and kicks out at the barrier.

"Padellah, let me out." She is ready. To do whatever it takes to get that thing away from Jack. The heat pulsing through every cell of her body could melt her bones. Only the bracelets clasped around her wrists remain cool, two narrow bands of chilled metal.

"Let me out, Padellah. I swear if you don't-"

A shadow darts down from the rooftops. For a moment Ryder thinks the entity itself is intervening, but this is no shifting, weaving apparition.

Lucas, face lit by the burnish of elthar's sky-blue light. He's wearing a plain black t-shirt and the armour reaches down his arms from beneath the short sleeves. He touches one foot to the ground then launches himself up and over the Celtren swaying above Jack. Lucas raises his arms, holding aloft a small blade. With one forceful blow, he drives it into the back of the Celtren, right between its shoulder blades, where its skeletal wings jut from matted dark fur. Ryder covers her ears against the terrible screech pouring from the creature's widened muzzle. Its wings thrash about, whipping back and slamming against Lucas. He holds steady, then pulls the blade free. A somersault later and he is on the ground in front of the Celtren. The blade comes down again. This time the blow strikes deep.

The creature staggers back, head lolling, blade embedded in the softness beneath its jaw. Orange eyes widen into giant orbs before it crashes to the ground, letting out a choked breath before falling still. Ryder hurls herself at the barrier and then scrambles to right herself as she tumbles headlong into the courtyard and driving rain. Padellah has removed the unseen barricade. Heart slamming, Ryder stumbles towards Jack and Lucas. The thrumming heat has left ice in its wake. Her body shakes with the chill, her teeth chattering as she throws herself onto the soggy grass beside Jack. Lucas presses his fingers to the side of Jack's neck. Blood flows from deep gashes on the back of her grandad's legs, staining the ground.

"Lucas, is he alive? Please, tell me he's alive."

Water clings to his pale eyelashes and the elthar light transforms the droplets into glistening sapphires.

"He's alive, Ry. We need to get him inside, out of this damn rain."

Ryder doesn't register Sophie and Christian are there until Sophie shakes her. "Hey, Ryder, you hear me? Let's focus on getting him inside. Those cuts look worse than they are okay. I promise you."

Ryder manages to nod, but all the bravado from earlier has evaporated along with the burning rage. Christian asks Lucas if he is okay and tells him how incredible he was. Ryder listens from a distant place, her entire body trembling. All she could do was run. That monstrous thing almost killed her grandad, and all she could do was run.

"They aren't poisonous too are they?" Christian says.

"Chris." Sophie hisses.

"Sorry, I just…okay just tell me what to do all right?"

"Help Ryder onto her feet."

Christian puts his hand under her elbow, offering leverage to get her to her feet. Ryder leans against him, clawing her way up his arm till she is upright. The world tilts and blurs. "Dashel." She breathes out the name. "Dashel is here, Lucas."

And he did this to Jack. The thought clears away the cobwebs, bringing the world back into crystal focus. Lucas lifts Jack, cradling the older and much stockier man with the ease he would a child.

Sophie cups her hands over Jack's face to try to shield him from the rain. "He just showed up and tried to turn the car into a pancake. But how did you know, Lucas? Were you tracking him?"

Lucas stares hard at Ryder. "I got a heads up you guys were in trouble." He says, raising one eyebrow, and giving her the *we really need to talk* face. "Then I used the bracelets to find you."

Ryder touches the elthar round her wrists absently. Had Padellah called him here? But her focus shifts quickly. All that matters is Jack.

"We need to get him to a hospital." Lucas shifts Jack's weight in his arms. "Is the car still good?"

Ryder can't take her eyes off her grandad's face. Off the blood staining his gray hair, just above his right temple. "I don't know, but we can't go back. Dashel is there, somewhere and we don't know if he's…" The word is a sharp barb that digs into her tongue. Now that her blood no longer bubbles and spits with fire, it's unsettling to think they may have just seen someone die.

"It's all right." Lucas inclines his head, green eyes gentle. "We'll go the opposite way, till we work things out." Lucas heads across the courtyard, towards one of the double doors into the building. When he reaches it, the doors swing wide open. An ear-piercing alarm fills the corridor ahead of them.

"Quick, Soph. The code is 4598," Lucas says. "Same as the stadium. Their security is kind of pathetic, been telling them since I started coaching."

He strides down the hallway with Christian at his side. Sophie pauses to disable the alarm, punching in the code. Silence drops on them, curtain heavy.

"You doing okay?" Sophie waits till Ryder nods before she jogs after the others. "Come on, let's get out of here."

Only the emergency exit sign throws any light down the windowless corridor. Lucas is cracking a quick pace, despite Jack's weight. Sophie gives instructions on where to go, a room that has a first aid station. It will have to do for now until Lucas secures a car to transport Jack out of here. Ryder holds back, making sure the double doors close behind her, and the others turn a corner and disappear from view. It takes her a minute to work out how to re-lock the doors. Not that re-locking a door like this will stop any of the things that might follow. Ryder stares out at the corpse of the beast in the courtyard. She's not sure she will ever stop shaking. She is about to turn away when she catches a glimpse of a reflection in the door's glass panel. The soft glimmer of a human-like figure drifts in the hallway behind her. Ryder spins round.

"Padellah." Her breath hits the air in a soft cloud of white.
Ryder.

The whispered voices drift inside her head. An orb of light, just a fist-size of bright air, floats in the hallway. It ebbs and flows, building into a human shape then falling into a cloud of soft light, over and over. Just as it did in the field. There are no discernible features, no definitive lines that denote fingers at the ends of the elongated arms, or feet at the base of the wispy ribbons that might be legs. It's a suggestion of something human, definitely not the real thing. But the fluid beauty of it lulls Ryder

278

into a deep calm. The hypnotic sway of Padellah's ever-shifting form is peaceful, as far from frightening as anything she's known. Ryder sighs, a weight lifting from a place she hadn't realised it was being held.

"Thank you," she says. "You brought Lucas here didn't you?"

We did. You were not ready.

The 'not ready' thing, again. Ryder chews down on her lip. "Want to tell me what I'm not ready for?"

You need to know your truth to begin with.

A new shiver crawls beneath her wet hair. From somewhere far down the corridor she can still hear the others talking.

"My truth?"

Padellah's light-form shifts, losing shape like a sandcastle being eaten by a wave. Then it rises up again, spilling out into a shape most definitely human. Features begin to appear; a subtle twist of light forms a rounded nose, eyes take shape beneath a shadowed brow. Narrow shoulders, arms and long, fine fingers. Long hair spills down to just above a barely-there waist. Ryder's own reflection gazes back at her.

Know your truth so you know your worth. The Laudine's blood saved your body, but it did not revive your soul.

Padellah speaks quicker than before, the multi-voiced words tumble out in a stream that Ryder struggles to understand.

"Her blood? Aresh's blood…that's how she saved me?"

She called on us when she knew she alone could not save you. But we refused her. The Cyne judge her for her brother's wrongdoings and fail to see the goodness and fairness in the Laudine. One day, I believe my brethren will see the value of the alliance I made on their behalf that day. I headed her call.

Ryder grips the door, knuckles whitening. "I don't understand, heeded her call?"

You have felt our presence since that day, Ryder. Heard us when others could not. Seen us when others could not. You thrived in the Rising, your soul growing in strength as I held you there.

279

The jumble of voices, whispering echoes that make up Padellah's voice, dissolve into a sigh. The apparition seems to fight to hold shape.

"Padellah?" Ryder's voice is small, a plea. She's spent years parched for information; this is dangling water in front of a desperate, dry mouth. "Please, don't leave me now. I need to know what you mean."

A pulse of light, and the silhouette bulges, widening like a balloon. For one terrible minute Ryder fears it might burst from existence completely. But Padellah holds it together, the shape shrinking back into a humanesque form.

You are not expected, Ryder.

"Expected to do what?"

Live. Ryder. You are not expected. When your soul returned from the Rising, when your body healed, the Laudine did not have to bind you. Something beyond all realms holds you in your world. Child of three realms. I protect you as I can, and the Laudine does the same. But we cannot be with you at all times. That is why you must escape, Ryder. He must not know your truth.

The silhouette convulses, losing all definition.

Go now, Ryder. He wakes.

"Do you mean Jack? Wait…hang on, no, no. You can't leave now, no way." Ryder clenches her fists. "Child of three realms, what the hell is that supposed to mean?"

But Padellah has either lost control or lost patience with the conversation. The light form pulses before it explodes into a brilliant ball of light. Ryder throws up her arms, shielding her face. But nothing more than a cold breeze hits her. She blinks away the spots in her vision. And catches sight of a figure striding into the courtyard. Padellah wasn't talking about Jack waking up. She meant Dashel. He is alive and, if not well, very much conscious.

Ryder curses under her breath. She should scream out a warning, but she can't move. If she releases the door she's not sure she won't fall. She's shaking so hard she's probably going to fracture something if this keeps up. The wind in the enclosed yard whips into a frenzy around Dashel, a mini-tornado centring on him. The debris driven into the air strikes against him; paper, chip packets, rose petals that dance like flung snow, all finding their target. But Dashel walks on, not bothering to even shield his eyes. He reaches the centre of the courtyard. The ropes dangling from the flagpole rise, pulled high by unseen hands, and serpentining towards him. His expression shifts, moving from hardened focus to seething confusion as the ropes lash around his ankles. Dashel's hands illuminate with the brightness of the elthar encasing them, and he swings at the attacking ropes.

Go little one.

Padellah's whispers strain with urgency. The entity is protecting her. And Ryder is standing here like a stupefied zombie. Dashel brushes his knuckles against the ropes and they drop away from him, limp and lifeless in the mud. Ryder whirls, finds her footing and races for the end of the corridor. Left or right? She hesitates then turns left. A short distance down the hall Sophie steps out of a doorway,

"Ry, where have you been? I was about to come looking-"

"It was here...Padellah...I saw her...him...it...again." Ryder says. "Where is Lucas?"

Grim faced, Sophie points towards the back of the carpeted drama classroom. One of her favourite in the school; with bean bags instead of desks and chairs, and old movie posters clutter the walls. *Poltergeist* among them. A faded red couch rests at the back of the room and Jack is lying there, eyes closed. Christian adjusts a pillow beneath Jack's head. Lucas stands over them, a Jarran stone between his fingers. He turns when Ryder bursts into the room.

"Dashel," she says "He's alive and he's headed this way."

Lucas presses the stones into Christian's hands, giving quick instructions on where to place them, before hurrying to Ryder's side. "Which way?"

"In the courtyard now," she says. "Heading for the door we came through. How did he even find us here?"

Lucas's elthar slides from beneath the sleeves of his shirt, moving easily down his arms. It is a deeper metal-gray than Sebastien's, but it follows every curve and rounding of muscle in the same precise way.

"Does it matter right now?" Lucas says. "Tracking device on Jack, or in the car I'm guessing. He had time to plant it at the power station. I'll give the guy credit. Dashel's resourceful if this is unplanned. I'm going to try and lead him away from here, and when it's safe I want you guys to run, find a phone, call Petra. She'll know what to do. And get as far-"

Ryder shakes her head. "But Jack-"

"You can't carry him, Ry. He will stay here, while you go and get help." Lucas is curt, giving her no time to reply before he turns to Christian. "You told me you know a way to get to the basement of this building-"

"Yeah it's-"

"No," Lucas cuts him off. "Don't tell me, I don't want it in my head. Just get them there, okay buddy?"

Christian's olive skin is washed out to a pale white, his eyes wide with panic, but he nods.

A loud bang reverberates down the hallway. Lucas presses a finger to his lips, and then gestures to the far end of the room where a connecting door links the classroom to the next. Ryder wraps her arm around Sophie and follows directions, keeping her gaze locked on Lucas. He nods, concentration tightening the edges of his mouth, and his shoulders rise with a deep breath.

Lucas steps into the hallway, closing the door behind him. A moment later, the world ruptures.

CHAPTER 34

T HE DOOR TEARS FROM ITS hinges, wood splintering and the glass in the central panel spraying into the room. Ryder drops, pulling Sophie down with her. Blinding orange light fills the air. It is sudden and brilliant and gone a moment later. Ryder lifts her hands from her face, taking a cautious peek. The door lies propped against one of the bean bags. Christian crouches just inside the next room, sheer terror contorting his face.

"Lucas," Sophie says, "We've got to do something."

Lucas is on his knees in the hallway, definitely in one piece but blood runs from cuts on his face. He uses the wall as support to push to his feet, azure energy eddying around his clenched fists. He lunges forward and Ryder loses sight of him. A ferocious crackle, the snap and pop of a bush fire, erupts down the corridor. A brilliant light flares, like the sun decided to set inside the building, and an enormous vibration shakes the walls. The emergency sprinkler system kicks into gear, and Ryder grimaces. She tugs away from Sophie, scrambling on her hands and knees towards the door.

"Ryder, no." Sophie grabs the hem of Ryder's jeans.

"Are you crazy?" Christian cries. "He told us to go."

"I need to see what's going on." Ryder kicks her leg free, careful not to thrust a careless heel too close to Sophie's frightened face. She means well, only trying to keep Ryder safe, but what's going on out in the corridor is thunderous and terrifying. And Lucas is right in the middle of it. Ryder sends out wild cries for help in her head, pleading with Padellah to so something. The entity can't just dump all that stuff on her about being special, about being some kind of freak of nature, and then just leave them all here. Leave Lucas to die. But silence is the only reply. Ryder kneels beside the door and peers into the hall. It is empty. But the walls are scorched black, and large patches of the linoleum has melted, the wood beneath it buckled. Whatever happened turned the area into a Salvador Dali painting, and it's not only empty, but silent. The mist of water cascading from the overhead sprinklers tinkles against the destruction, the only sound Ryder can hear, save for Sophie's strangled breaths as she joins Ryder. The alarms haven't gone off.

"Don't go out there, Ry." Sophie pleads, her hair pressed to her head like a strange swimmer's cap. "We need to head down to the basement."

That's what Lucas told them to do. And it is what Ryder should do. But leaving Jack so vulnerable, and Lucas with Dashel, just isn't an option. Not when there's a chance Ryder could help them. She uses the door frame to haul herself to her feet. Waving aside Sophie's frantic protests, Ryder jogs down the hallway, hugging close to the wall. It's not like she could blend into it suddenly if Dashel appeared, but there is comfort in the solidity of the plasterboard beneath her fingertips. Reaching the corner, Ryder angles her head and peers with one eye down the corridor towards the external doors. Empty, but with plenty of signs Dashel and Lucas have been this way. Melted lino and scorched ceiling are a giveaway, so are the missing double entrance doors. Edging closer, she spots one of them lying at a slant on the steps. But the courtyard is not empty. Ryder gulps back a cry and presses her back against the wall. Lucas and Dashel face one another across the carcass of the fallen Celtren. Lucas's armour sparks with energy, fireflies of azure dancing around his hands. It doesn't seem as complete as Sebastien's, no hint of it beneath his t-shirt. Dashel watches him the same way Sebastien did back at Sleighter Dam. Hawk on mouse.

The padding of feet on the floor behind her makes Ryder start. Sophie hurries up the corridor, doubled over, one shoulder scraping against the wall. Trying to be stealthy, but resembling someone on a bowling alley run-up. She sinks to her knees beside Ryder, her breathing shallow and fast. "You don't get to play crazy risk taker all on your own, you know," she says. "What's happening?" She shakes harder than Ryder, her fringe a wet flat mop against her forehead. Her hazel eyes couldn't open any wider if she tried. She's terrified, but she's here. Ryder couldn't love her more. But there's no chance to answer questions. Dashel raises his hands. He thrusts them towards Lucas, pure, dazzling white light shooting from his fingertips. Short, pulsing bursts, like luminescent arrows. Lucas lifts high and fast. Dashel's light arrows slam into the brickwork, sending red chunks flying. Lucas drifts back to the ground, throwing a dimpled grin Dashel's way. Ryder knows that smug look too well, usually after he's beaten a boss she's been trying to take out for days in *Dark Souls.* So self-satisfied. But she hopes she's never looked at him the way Dashel does now; like he wants to peel the skin off Lucas's face.

"Guys." Christian's whisper may as well be a shout down the corridor. "Come on. We need to go get help." He waves at them from the turn in the corridor.

He's right of course. But neither she nor Sophie move. Water drips off Ryder's chin and goosebumps prickle her skin, but she can't do anything but watch. Lucas sweeps his hands in a wide arc, drawing a shimmering blue circle in the air. He takes a hold of the shape, grasping it like it's something solid, and then hurls it towards Dashel. When it draws close to the man, small darting pieces of light, like a flock of sunshine sparrows, pour out of the ring. He jerks back, covering his face against the jabbing onslaught. They continue to rain down on him, and Dashel is forced to his knees, his curses flood the air but the phosphorescent army continues its attack in total silence.

285

"She has kept you well hidden." He grunts, sweeping an arm through the torrent. Some pin points extinguish, but more replace them. "Who are you, boy?"

Lucas steps towards Dashel, the grin wide on his face and a certain cockiness in the way he folds his arms. "Wouldn't you like to know?"

In reply, Dashel raises his head, a contemptuous scowl darkens his features. The smile on Lucas's face drops, and he tries to lurch back. But the man is fast. With one grand, sweeping gesture he spreads his arms, and the light scatters away from him like he's swiping away flies. The balls of light flash wildly before vanishing. Dashel rises to his feet, menace in the slow way he moves. White curls of energy snake around his fingertips.

"Lucas, get out of there," Ryder whispers. Beside her, Sophie presses her hands to her mouth, trying to stifle her cry.

Lucas crouches, preparing to catapult himself into the air, but Dashel hurls the energy from his fingertips, this time it trails out in long ribbons of light that snap around Lucas's legs. His cry of pain fills the corridor. Dashel shouts something at him. Ryder can't make it out, but Dashel's fury doesn't need translating. He wrenches his arms back, and the ribbons coil higher around Lucas's body, choking another anguished yell out of him. The sound hits Ryder's ears and ignites a rush of heat to her face. The sensation crawls down deeper, moving into her joints, and seeping into her bones. It's happening again. Ryder presses a sweaty palm against the wet floor.

Ryder doesn't realise Christian has joined them until his hand rests on her shoulder. His touch is gentle, but she flinches nonetheless. Her skin feels sunburn raw. "He's going to kill him. We have to do something." Christian's body is restless with tension, his voice tight with anguish. "I can distract him-"

Sophie and Ryder grab him in unison when he moves towards the courtyard. They pull him back so hard he ends up on his backside and growls his disapproval at the sudden stop.

"Don't be stupid." Ryder's eye burn as though she has a

fever. "You can't do anything Chris. Take Sophie and get out of here. Get help." It's so damn hot, she can't tell if it's water or sweat streaming down her face.

Dashel's bindings have knocked Lucas off his feet and onto his back. The way Dashel stares down at him sends pin pricks up Ryder's spine. He is so still, a snake readying himself to strike. He leans in close to Lucas, who eyes him with a baleful glare. Dashel's confusion about Lucas might just be the saving grace.

The ache in Ryder's joints creeps into the muscles, her blood blazes with scorching heat. Ready for this or not, she might be Lucas's only option. The alarms haven't gone off. The shrill ring could normally wake the dead. But now it's quiet. No alarms, no fire brigade. And the school is nestled on acreage. Isolated. With a thunderstorm approaching over the city. The battle between Dashel and Lucas could well go unnoticed.

"Ry, you're hurting me." Christian tries to tug his wrist from her grasp. "Ryder."

She blinks and releases him. Her palm stings where it touched Christian's skin, the joints in her hand flaring with pain. It occurs to her that maybe this is how Olessia feels, when the Beckoning takes over, inching into every pore and cell, pushing her into a cramped corner of her own body.

"Ryder, the Cyne...can they help us again?" Sophie's eyes are bright.

The sprinkler water warms when it touches against Ryder's skin. She shakes her head, a bitter smile on her lips. The entity comes and goes as it pleases, so it seems. Spouting about keeping herself hidden and safe. Expecting her to stay away when the people she loved were being hurt. Not going to happen. If Ryder is really some preternatural bargaining chip, then she's going to play her hand.

Christian jumps to his feet. "Guys, Lucas is...he's...we need to...guys, they're gone." He's beside himself with panic, muddling every word. But he's right. The courtyard is empty save for the dark pile of fur and stench of the Celtren. They bolt the length of the corridor, stopping at the top of the stairs. Despite the obviousness emptiness, Ryder keeps scanning the open space. "Which way did they go?"

"I didn't see, I didn't see. I mean they were there and then, they just weren't." Christian pushes his fingers into the tangled damp mess of his hair. "Ry-"

She raises her hand. "This is what we are going to do. Chris, you are going to find a phone, and you are going to call Petra like Lucas told us too. If you can't get hold of her, call the police, the fire brigade, anyone. Just get people here." Christian and Sophie listen without interruption. She has their undivided attention. Her little army of two. "Sophie, go to Jack, please. I need to know you're with him."

Sophie doesn't ask why, she doesn't ask where Ryder is going and she doesn't insist on going with her. A good thing, considering Ryder isn't sure herself, but her nerves are lit up like a Christmas tree. She must be a walking, preternatural bullseye right now. Dashel has to notice her, and he has to let Lucas go.

CHAPTER 35

R YDER LEANS AGAINST THE BRICK wall at the end of the passageway. The cold stone barely penetrates the heat enveloping her. Beyond the cover of the enclosed corridor, the trees sway under the wind, dancing like multi-armed puppets on the roadside. Thunder beats a rolling distant rhythm across the sky. Little wonder no one has come. With the storm and everything happening at Blackrhine Hill, no one's focus is directed this way.

Edging out, she catches sight of Jack's station wagon. Dashel's ensured they won't be leaving that way. The car is on its roof, one half of the body flattened, like it made it halfway through a compactor. The tyres are messes of slashed rubber, and copper coloured oil oozes from one of the axles. Too late, she remembers Lucas's mobile phone. The one Sebastien handed to her and she slipped into her jacket pocket. The very same jacket that is in the pile of twisted metal.

"Where are you, Lucas?" she whispers, her breath white in the cold air.

The answer comes in a flash of light from over by the pool house. It's not lightning, too subtle and low to the ground for that. Ryder moves from the relative safety of the passageway and onto the muddy road. Now that she's on her own, the fire eating at her wavers. Her body still aches but it's duller, the murmur of recovering muscles, instead of the pinch of freshly used ones. Ryder hurries across the road, aiming for the cover of the trees that line the river bank. There's a good mix of thick trunked eucalypts and finer willows, with enough low dense shrubbery to keep her hidden. A wayward branch catches her in the face and Ryder recoils. A muscle in her neck protests with a grumbling twinge. The sunburn sting has left her skin, and she's starting to feel, well, kind of normal. Tired, but normal. All too human. And stupid. This walking target idea, is a bad one. Her jumper catches on a twig, and a fluoro pink pom-pom drops to the ground. At least the rain has let up.

Out to Ryder's left the river is a wide slick of black. On the far bank, up toward Blackrhine Hill, searchlights bob and skip across the water. Probably the patrol boats they'd seen earlier. Up in the sky more search lights sway back and forth, beaming from the aircraft flying low over the hill. She's too far away to make out anything on the hill but tries to imagine what C-21 plan to do with the beasts lurking there. How does the protocol on that work? Seek and destroy or capture and study?

Ryder shoves aside the branch of a Banksia tree, and the spiky leaves catch on the sleeve of her jumper. A black thread comes away and Ryder has to tug herself free. For some bizarre reason, Ryder thinks of the bright yellow cardigan that Sophie gave to Olessia, and the expression on Olessia's face when she pulled it on. Gift-giving must not be a big thing on Siros, because Olessia was floored. Ryder turns away from Blackrhine Hill and the memories it stirs. She picks up her pace, shouldering her way through the bush, ignoring the foliage that snatches at her hair. Why is Dashel here, toying with them? Olessia is the prize everyone is after. An uneasy flutter runs through Ryder's belly. That ugly yellow jumper is her answer. It's barely been a few days, but in the chaos, Olessia has become a friend. And friends make people vulnerable. Anyone who's seen a superhero movie or read a comic knows that. Dashel came here for them, but he found something more interesting.

The pool building marks the end of the wilderness. It is an

impressive structure, and the night lights illuminate it into an even grander thing. The roof is domed, made of gray, Colorbond steel, which crowns three red brick walls and a fourth made entirely of glass. The lawn around it is mowed to within an inch of its life, the school wanting everyone to see exactly where their money went. Ryder dashes across the open space, the wind chilling her to the bone. Its icy fingers trace a path along her arms, and across her shoulders. All sense of the crazy fever has evaporated. She punches a fist against her thigh. Maybe she's actually caught some alien disease, and her superhero mindset is just delirium. Ryder slumps beside one of the ventilation grates at the base of the wall. Despite the breeze, the waft of chlorine is strong.

"Right, now what? Come on genius, what now?" Ryder leans against the wall, and the rough texture snags her jumper. There will be nothing left of Sophie's hideous jumper by the time this is over; at least one good thing will come from this weekend.

An agonised cry erupts from inside the building; a throaty sound caught between a scream and a groan.

"Lucas." Ryder drops to her knees, ignoring the squelch of mud, and peers in through the gaps in the grating.

Dashel stands at the edge of the pool, in front of empty rows of tiered seating. The pool is massive; six-lanes and fifty-metres in length, and all its underwater lights are on. Dashel stares out over the water, gray-trimmed jaw set hard. Ryder presses her hands to her mouth. Lucas floats on his back, about a metre above the surface of the water, hanging as though suspended on invisible strings. His head hangs limp, eyes closed. There is no trace of his elthar armour, his black t-shirt and his well-worn jeans offering little protection. To her horror, Ryder notices the surface of the water is stained dark with blood dripping from Lucas's back.

"Come now boy, stop playing so human. Wake up. Talk to me." Dashel's voice bounces off the concrete surroundings. He laughs, the snap of a hammer on a nail. "This is serendipity at its finest. There I was thinking the humans might be valuable somehow. But Olessia's weakness is far less interesting now I've discovered you. I must say, there really is no limit to what the Laudine Aresh thinks she can get away with, is there? Now boy, this is not interesting if you say nothing. Did I dig too deep? Wake up."

He raises his hand. Ryder cringes, bracing for what he might do. There's no sparks of light this time, it's something far more corporeal he brandishes. A short coil of what appears to be rope, strands of a material interwoven in a tight braid, hanging in his left hand. He casts it towards Lucas, with the wide arching throw of a fisherman, and the line uncoils. It strikes Lucas's hip, the crack echoing through the cavernous building, and he cries out. His body jerks and shudders, arms stiffening at his sides. The weapon is more Taser than rope, more whip than fishing line.

"You really should talk to me, you know. The others might not be so lenient on you." Another flick of Dashel's hand and the line slithers out again, this time slicing across Lucas's arm. Lucas shouts, sounding more infuriated than anguished. Blood streams from the wound, and the crimson cloud beneath him spreads. "They will be most interested in a Zentai traitor. Especially one who is so close to the Laudine of Bax Un Tey."

"The Laudine," Lucas struggles to speak, "has nothing to do with me."

Dashel swings the line in lazy sweeps in front of him. "Lies. Aresh tries so hard, I will give her that. She is far less preposterous than the wretch we call our Presider, and she does what she can to stabilise the Presidership, true. But she fails to see, it will never counter the flaws of her brother. Perhaps you are nothing more than a toy she likes to play with. Perhaps you are far more, but either way you are undoubtedly a link. My colleagues will find the truth. They are your brethren after all."

Dashel whips the line a third time. He does it so easily, not a brush of emotion on his hard face. The line slaps across Lucas's forehead, and this time his yell is all pain. The sound reverberates off the high ceiling. Ryder presses against the wall. She can't watch a single minute more. A small cry dies against her palms. Her thoughts are a mess, her heart a racing, crazy thing in her chest. But she is cold, and shaking so hard her insides ache. Dashel isn't done with Lucas. Ryder closes her eyes, shoving her hands to her ears. The elthar bracelets press against her cheeks. Lucas's elthar. And in her hands they are utterly useless, no more powerful than the jewellery they imitate.

Ryder whimpers, knocks her head against the bricks behind her. There's no heat, no rush of rage, no mind-bending sense of her own strength. Child of three realms? There's only a pathetic, delusional child here. One who thinks a ghost watches over her. Her mind has cracked with the weight of this weekend. Ryder sobs, and the tears burn their way out, refusing to stay where she buried them. They wrack her chest, trying to crack ribs with their ferocity.

"Shhh, stop." The speaker's breath is warm against her ear. "He'll hear you. You have to stop."

Ryder blinks through the sting of acid tears. But she doesn't need to see to know who is with her.

"He's killing him, Sophie. I can't do anything." The helplessness drags at her, sinking her deeper into the mud.

"And you'll stop him." Sophie intertwines their fingers and tilts Ryder's face so they are eye to eye. "Do you hear me? There is always a way. Like that poster with the cat hanging off the tree branch, you know. Hang in there, kitty."

Ryder snorts. Not a great idea with a runny nose. She wipes at her face and straightens. Sophie gives her a thumbs up, and waits for Ryder to respond.

"I'm good." She nods, taking a shuddering breath. And it's the truth. The tears flushed out the crushing panic. Gave her breathing space again in her own head. Keeping a check on a meltdown drained her more than she realised. But now her breathing finds its pace, a steady flow instead of frantic gulps. Together, Sophie and Ryder shift to peer through the grate, pressed shoulder to shoulder. Ryder is lighter somehow, despite the drenched clothes and the ringing of Lucas's cries. But there's still no sign of the body burn, no aching joints or fever-touched skin. And she needs it. Whatever *it* is. Whether Padellah thinks so or not, Ryder has to be ready.

Dashel shouts something in the Siros tongue, before thrashing Lucas again. The double-doors at the far end of the building fling open and two people enter. They're dressed in matching dark brown uniforms, military-style jacket and pants. The shorter of the two is androgynous, the short bob-cut and slight sway of hips hints female, but the figure is boyish and thin. They are considerably shorter than their companion, a lean man with long, stringy dreadlocks that reach to the base of his back. White strands mixed with black.

Dreadlocks. "I know him," Ryder gasps. Sophie gives her a warning glance. *Keep quiet*, she mouths.

As the couple draw closer to Dashel, Ryder catches sight of their ears. Or lack of. Around where an ear canal should be there are no external lobes, just a slight rise in the flesh. There is no mistaking it. This is the man Ryder saw. The Zentai. The man standing in the cave with the Celtren and Placers. Giving orders? Co-ordinating this whole thing?

"Where is the Commandant?" Dashel says. "I told her this was important."

"The Commandant decides what is important." The shorter Zentai's voice is raised enough for Ryder to decide she might be a woman. "And right now her priority is ensuring the Laudess does not enter the gateway. Is it evident to everyone but yourself, Dashel, that she merely sent you on a fool's mission to keep you out of the way?"

The acoustics in the pool house bounce every word up to the grating. Dashel laughs off the slight but there is an edge to his voice. "Perhaps then, Seah, the Commandant has sent you and Banon here for the same reason." Dashel gestures to the man who gazes at him with cool disregard. "It was not I who failed to secure the Laudess when they had ample warning and opportunity. I advised you of our location, I placed the disabler on board the Aventar as instructed. Yet, the Laudess eluded you. We are all fools, it would seem."

He leans back on his heels, clearly impressed with himself. Ryder grinds her fingertips into the brickwork, barely feeling the pinch of the coarse material against her skin. They are trading insults while Lucas bleeds. He hangs so still in the air, not so much as a tilt of his head to suggest he is still conscious.

"We were not the ones in the Laudess's company for hours," Seah says. "At the very least you could have terminated her guardian, struck down the other Claven. Don't talk to me of inadequacies, Dashel."

"Enough." The dreadlocked man, Banon, finally speaks. He gestures to Lucas. "Why do you bring us here for this human boy? Is the Laudess attached to him?" His voice sends a shiver up Ryder's arms. Each heavily accented syllable slithers off his tongue.

"No, not this one. But this one is even better than the boy child Olessia fawns over." Dashel laughs, real mirth there now. He is talking about Christian, and it sends the steel creeping higher into Ryder's chest. "This is far better than any Earth child."

Ryder rocks back on her heels. Lightheaded. The rumble of the storm is distant, and the wind has dipped. The world is quiet as Dashel pauses.

"Get on with it, Dashel, we are wasting time here," Seah says.

He lifts his arm over his head and sends the line out towards Lucas in a wide curving arc. It sweeps round Lucas's torso, lashing tight against his body. Dashel wrenches his arm back and Lucas skims across the surface of the water before landing with a heavy thump on the concrete at Dashel's feet. Ryder clenches her teeth but steely resolve keeps her eyes lock on her friend. Her muscles are rocks of solid tension beneath her skin.

"Take closer inspection," Dashel declares. "Do you not recognise your own kind, Seah? This boy is Zentai."

Seah presses a foot against Lucas's shoulder, rolling him onto his back. His arm slaps against the concrete. Lucas's eyes are closed, his mouth parted. But his chest rises and falls. He is alive. Sophie clutches Ryder's arm.

"Zentai?" Seah crouches beside Lucas, pressing fingertips against his cheek, tilting his head back and forth.

"He has been enhanced to fit in with the humans of course, but the construction of the ears is something even they are capable of. They cannot, however, change his core." Dashel's words drip with self-satisfaction. "I felt it when I fought him earlier. I believe he has been here for some time, but his skill with the elthar armour leads me to believe that he has long been in contact with someone from Siros. I believe that someone is the Laudine."

The woman rises to her feet, one foot resting on Lucas's shoulder. Sophie's grip on Ryder's arm is near unbearable, her face white with shock. There hadn't been time to fill her in on Lucas, and this is a horrible way to find out.

"He has been in mindreaches with Aresh?" Banon says, gravelly voice sending unpleasant shivers up Ryder's spine.

"Undoubtedly," Dashel says. "I knew there was someone here she was contacting but she refused to disclose who. She was quite clandestine about it. The Laudine is nothing if not secretive. I think you'll find there is a nicely established telepathic pathway between this Zentai and the Laudine herself. A connection I believe the Commandant will be very eager to exploit. This boy is quite the find, don't you think?"

Lucas's chest heaves in an uneven rise and fall. The crimson stain blooming on the concrete around him creeps further outward. Ryder stares at the blood, focusing so hard her vision blurs. Her fingertips tingle, and the joints in her hands stiffen. She cracks her knuckle, and with the snap of release, understanding floods her. It's happening. Different to before, it's not a sharp, angry rage burning her up, it's stealthier. Creeping through her, not blasting a path through her synapses. Steel in her veins, instead of flame. Ryder doesn't dare breathe, she's not certain she should even blink, for fear of losing it again.

"Get him on his feet," Seah snaps. "I want to confirm this before we go any further."

Banon lifts Lucas, who hangs like a rag doll in his arms. His head lolls forward. Banon is clearly the only thing keeping Lucas on his feet. Seah steps up to them. She is about Lucas's height, so she places her hands easily on either side of his head. Lucas screams, and it is a sound that will echo forever. It is the sound Ryder will hear when she lies in bed at night and the house is deathly silent. The one true ghost that haunts her.

It snaps then. That steel holding her together. It cracks wide open and spills through her in a rampaging fever, reaching out into every vein, every fibre of muscle. Lucas's agonised howl fills her ears and tears at her insides. She closes her eyes against the unrelenting build of the fever. It isn't kind or gentle, it is sharp and it burns and it tears its way into her. Pouring in, sinking deeper, moving into her blood and her bones. Gasping for breath, Ryder grips the metal of the grating so hard either her fingers or the steel itself will break. Everything shifts in and out of focus, the world around her losing shape. Every pulse in her body pounds in unison as the relentless energy breaks through her. She isn't sure who is screaming now; her or Lucas. The pain melts her.

Ryder forces her eyes open, too afraid to be in the dark anymore. And all at once, it is gone. The pain vanished as if it never existed at all. The world slips back into focus. And it's brighter than she remembers. The sounds are different too, hollow somehow, like they're coming from the bottom of a well.

She isn't where she expects. Where she should be. She isn't crouched in the mud alongside Sophie. She isn't soaked to the bone, terrified, watching them torture Lucas. Ryder stares at the figures in front of her. She blinks. Everything is fuzzy, as though a wall of water runs between her and the people around her. Ryder is less than an arm's length from Dashel, but he doesn't even glance her way. None of them do. Seah and Banon are focused on Lucas. Dashel wears a smirk as he watches Seah tear into Lucas's mind. Blood runs from Lucas's nose, and his skin holds a deathly gray tinge. She wants them to stop. Stop hurting him. Her mouth opens but she can't force a word out. Not even a gasp. And they ignore her. They don't see her at all.

CHAPTER 36

LUCAS IS DESPERATELY CLOSE, AND yet she still can't help him. Ryder opens her mouth wide with a scream but not a sound escapes her. Her vocal chords are useless, paralysed instruments. A noise, like the hollow snap of ice against warm air, comes from behind. Ryder turns to follow it. Her movement is drawn out, laborious, like moving through molasses, and a shimmering haze surrounds her. When she lifts her hands, there is little more than a shadowy blur where her arms should be. Her hands, her arms, her body are all little more than shading, a hint of form but nothing substantial, as though someone started to draw her but got as far as the outline and gave up.

"I don't like the look of this," Dashel says, frowning. His gaze passes right through Ryder, to a space just beyond her. "We need to get him out of here. Something is wrong."

Her slow rotation finally brings her full circle and it is clear what he's referring to. The something wrong is one of the panes in the glass wall. There is an elaborate spiderweb of cracks, tracing their way across one of the central panels. It hasn't shattered but it's come as close as it can get, and it is, Ryder realises, the source of the snap she heard.

Seah drops her hands from Lucas's face. "You wish to run from a pane of cracked glass? Does betrayal not agree with you, Dashel? You sound most paranoid."

"I do this for the betterment of all Bax Un Tey, not for its fall. I betray only a warmonger," Dashel says. "And your arrogance will get the better of you, Seah. We will leave now."

Ryder gazes down at the water. The dappled surface shimmers with diamond points of light. Crisp and clear, when everything else in sight is smudged and blurry. Then it strikes her. The water. She is standing over it. No. Not standing, floating above it. At some point she has drifted here, halfway across the pool. Ryder's lower body is even less defined than the rest of her, like her imaginary illustrator tried to rub out her legs. The artist has managed to remove her reflection in the process too. She stares into the crystalline water. There's no sign of her own image; the roof and its lights above, but not her.

Oh god. I'm dead. I've died. Ryder's thoughts bounce around inside her head, echoing back and forth. Distorted and pitched at a level she doesn't recognise. Ryder strains again to lift her arms. Fighting to find some calm spot in her thoughts. Not death. She must be unconscious, dreaming crazy dreams about morphing into an ethereal being. And Sophie is with her, right now, trying to wake her up. Putting on her no-nonsense voice, telling Ryder this isn't funny anymore. That much at least, is true. It's not funny at all. Ryder wades through her molasses world, fighting to edge closer to Lucas. There is a sense of her limbs being here, the sense her body is in all the right places, but the bleary eyed focus won't shift. She is undefined. Death might feel like this. Being, but not being. Yourself, but not. Barely existing.

If she were substantial, flesh and blood and a mess of nerves, Ryder would clasp her hands to her head and she'd yell until she was hoarse. Instead, she's nothing but her thoughts; chittering, whispering voices that dart at her from the edges of her insubstantial world. Voices she recognises. And they are not her own. They agitate the haze, quivering around her like a spectral flock of birds. Just as they have always done on the edge of her dreams.

And Ryder needs them to stop. She screams at them to stop.

The glass in the panelling shatters, exploding inward, sending shards spraying out over the pool. Some of them pierce the brilliant sheen of the water beneath her, spearing through her as they fall.

"Am I paranoid now?" Dashel says.

Ryder finds herself staring at him before she's even thought about moving. Dashel is in sharp focus, more defined than the others around him. Perhaps because of the pearlescent energy sparking from his fingertips.

"Banon, get him out of here," Seah shouts. She has pulled a weapon from somewhere, it's difficult to make out exactly in this smudged world, but appears shaped like an odd cross between a hand gun and a ping-pong paddle.

"Is the Zentai doing this?" Banon lets Lucas fall to his knees before shaking his shoulders roughly. "Are you doing this, boy?"

Lucas opens his eyes. Ryder wants to call to him, tell him she is right here. A world away perhaps, but somehow with him. Her words still won't come. But Lucas is awake. Better yet, he is telling Banon exactly what he thinks of the man's question. His words slur, but the venom in them is tangible. Hearing Lucas's voice is pure bliss. Ryder wants to be closer. Dashel steps in, the energy in his hands racing up the length of the whip he struck Lucas with earlier. He lashes it around Lucas's upper body, pinning his arms to his side. Though he bites off his cry, Lucas's pain is loud and clear. The choir of voices rises, morphing into a unified hiss. Or is that sound coming from her? A crawling, smoldering anger moves through Ryder's gossamer self, the most tangible thing about her.

"If you think these theatrics will help you, boy," Dashel says. "Think again. On your feet."

Dashel hauls Lucas towards the doorway, walking him like a half-conscious dog on a leash. With Dashel's energy illuminating Lucas's body, Ryder makes out something on the back of Lucas's neck, three small protrusions in his skin just below the sharp edge of his hair. Each wound weeps blood. Ryder wants to reach for him but a strange feeling settles over her. She's not sure how to lift her arms. Her memory of movement, how to make her limbs work, is as distant and blurry as the rest of her. The flock of insistent voices has grown faint. Something is slipping from her. She's been here too long. But she can't leave. Not yet.

Banon and Seah follow after Dashel. Ryder pours all her focus into watching them. They are dark shadows, and she can't make out their features anymore. They walk backwards, arms raised and sweeping back and forth as they retreat. She guesses they are holding those weird ping-pong bat weapons but their hands are just dark blobs. All she knows for sure is they're taking Lucas away from her. She is losing him. Ryder hangs there, a puppeteer who can't make her own strings work, embers of dying rage sputtering inside her. Trapped in a cloudy cocoon. Lucas stumbles, and Dashel kicks him before dragging him back to his feet with a cruel tug on the cable. Banon steps in, speaking to Dashel, but Ryder is having trouble hearing properly. It's garbled, like they are talking under water. Dashel releases the cable from Lucas's midriff. Banon lifts Lucas up and throws him over his shoulder. The group has almost reached the main doors at the far end of the building.

They can't leave. She won't let them. Ryder fights to control some part of herself. Whatever this is, she needs to take it over. Whatever *she* is, dead or alive, delusional or dreaming, she needs to use it. Now. Think, Ryder. Use that little shadow brain and think. If this is Padellah's world, if Ryder has stumbled into the world of the Cyne, then the entity has abandoned her. Padellah's voice doesn't rise out of the cacophony, nor does she answer Ryder's call.

Seah opens the double doors, brandishing her weapon back and forth before gesturing for the others to head out.

No. You're not leaving. Ryder thinks, with a calm and clarity that settles out of nowhere. Her little flock resonates her words around her. Murmuring their many-voiced agreement.

The doors sweep back towards Seah, tearing from their

hinges and slinging through the air like enormous out-of-control Frisbees. One glances against Dashel, knocking him onto his back. The other slams into Seah. She rag-dolls through the air and crashes to the ground near the starting blocks. Seah's face is a blur, but Ryder hears the crack of her head on the concrete clearly enough. An echo of the sound Jack's made when the Celtren attacked. Ryder flutters her watercolour hands, for a fleeting moment the memory of movement returns. Maybe it is the shock of what she's just seen. What she's just done. Dashel and Banon jump up from where they cower on the ground. Lucas is between them, he rolls onto his side, attempting to prop himself up on one elbow.

"Move, take him." Banon's figure is an obscure haze, running to Seah's side. He darts his weapon around, searching for a target. But he'll find nothing.

Dashel wrenches Lucas to his feet. Though Lucas finds some strength to fight back, he's too weak to do much more than irritate a shaken Dashel. The older man ends the one-sided battle by laying a solid punch into Lucas's belly. It gives Ryder all she needs to take control again. She spots the lane rope storage reels, two wheels as tall as she is and three times as wide. Each has white and red lane ropes coiled around them. The haze around her is thickening, pulling everything more and more out of focus. She is running out of time. Ryder settles her concentration on the wheel, pictures it rolling across the concrete and slamming into Dashel. Just as she'd imagined the doors flying open. The equipment jerks, shudders, and rolls the tiniest bit. The drag of effort is heavier than it was with the doors. Her choir murmurs gently, filling her with calm. Ryder lets the sound wash away everything but the thought of moving the ropes. Of saving Lucas.

One of the wheels rolls forward and then stops.

Come on! She shouts into the brightness. *Move, you stupid damn thing.*

Ryder? What are you doing here?

Padellah. The entity's voices come from everywhere and

nowhere in particular, all at once. Ryder can't see the apparition. Her own world is barely comprehensible now. All becoming one giant smudge, closing in on her.

Help me. Stop them.

She can't make out Dashel and Lucas anymore. Ryder knows she should turn away from them, but the way how escapes her, like a forgotten word on the tip of your tongue, or the answer to a question sitting at the back of your mind, refusing to come out.

You must go back. You must leave the Rising. Go back now. Help me. Don't let them take Lucas.

They will do something to him. Something bad. Ryder can't remember what. Or why. She can't recall who *they* are. Only that she has to stop them. The storage wheel shoots forward, racing towards Banon. He stands up, lifting his arm to aim the weapon but he is far too slow. The impact sends Banon toppling backwards. His gun discharges. A thin red beam of light tears a gash through the metal roof, sending a spray of sparks like fireworks raining down around them all. Lifting her head to gaze at the damage seems way too complicated. Instead she focuses on the darkness of Banon's shadowy form as he struggles to his feet. Before he can find his footing, she directs one of the ropes towards him. It whips out from the wheel, hitting him square in the chest. His body slams into one of the starting blocks and then jerks over the edge and into the water. He floats there, a still mass of black. Ryder sags into her cocoon, completely drained of all the rage now.

Is he dead? She wants to look away but that would involve remembering how to tilt her head. She doesn't recall. It is so much easier to exist like this. A presence, rather than a solid, fragile mass of skin and bone. *Did I kill him?*

Padellah doesn't answer. Ryder struggles to focus in her increasingly bright world. Someone needs to turn off the sun. Turn down the blaze. Something shifts in the air around her. And Padellah finally responds.

You must go. You lose yourself.

The voices are a baseball bat slammed against Ryder's senses. The world turns supernova, an impossibly luminous thing that she can't stare into. Ryder closes her eyes. Squeezes them shut. But the fireball has got her. There is nothing here but light.

"This way, Ryder, come on. Listen to me."

Sophie is still here. She's out there somewhere in the auroral glow. Distant, a minuscule voice in a vast space. Ryder wants to take a breath but the air won't pass her lips. Her eyes won't open. She doesn't know which way is up. If there is even an up or down at all. Small, darting cramps play with her muscles. Random and painful.

"She said you would come back to me Ryder, she said it, so you have to do it. Are you listening? I'm right here, don't leave me hanging," Sophie is closer this time. Choked up, struggling to get the words out. "Please, Ry…come on…I'm right here."

Ryder strains to open her eyes, wanting to go where Sophie is. Her body jerks under the hard unrelenting spasm that seems to take a hold of every muscle. The agony bolts through her. Her mouth opens wide with a cry. Then it's over. Sophie is leaning over her, her red hair a stringy, soaked mess beneath the ridiculous fox beanie. A deliriously happy grin so wide, her gums show.

"Never, never, never, do that again," Sophie says. She cradles Ryder's head on her lap, her legs trembling. Ryder blinks against the fall of rain touching her face. It is wet and icy and glorious. She is back. Ryder presses her hands into the mud, feels it squelch through her fingers and decides it the most beautiful feeling in the world. Ryder leans forward to sit up, but Sophie holds her down with a gentle hand to her shoulder.

"Just take it easy," she whispers. "Padellah said you'll be pretty bleary after that. I saw…well, I'm going to say she's a girl, but I really don't know what Padellah is. But I saw her. She told me to guide you back, to wait for you. That she would send you back. I finally saw something, Ry. And it was beautiful, the most perfect thing I've ever seen. But I don't want to see it again. Not if it means you leave me like that."

"Leave you?" Ryder croaks. A glass of water would be heaven.

"You were gone, Ry. Really gone. No pulse. No breath." Sophie pauses. "I didn't think I was getting you back."

"I wasn't sure I was coming back." Fresh shudders course through her. Ryder's exhausted brain tries to remember what Padellah said to her, inside that luminescent, ethereal world. The Rising. The name breaks through her thoughts, like the name of that song you've spent all day trying to remember.

"Lucas? Did they take him? Did I…" Ryder lets the question hang. When Sophie smiles Ryder closes her eyes. The Rising; the place where Aresh sent her soul while she healed Ryder's body. Whatever that strange world was, whatever it has done to Ryder, it also just saved Lucas's life. A solitary tear slides free, running warm down her cheek, chasing back the goosebumps.

"He's safe, Ryder." Sophie cradles her closer. "Dashel is gone. He left the others and hightailed it out of here. Sebastien has gone in to help Lucas."

Halfway through wiping her nose, Ryder freezes. "Sebastien? What is he doing here?"

A perfectly surly voice answers her. "Cleaning up your mess."

CHAPTER 37

RYDER SITS UP, FAST ENOUGH to make her head spin. Sebastien towers over them, staring at her in his customary down-the-nose way. But Ryder only has eyes for the guy leaning against him.

"Lucas, oh my god. Are you okay?" Ryder scrambles to her feet, ignoring Sophie's pleas to take it slowly.

"I've been better." Lucas braces his free hand against the brick wall, the other presses against Sebastien's shoulder in a white-knuckled grip. "Is everyone okay? Where's Christian?"

The lacerations from Dashel's brutal assault have cut deep. The gash on Lucas's arm will need stitches for sure. His right eye is swollen closed with a black bruise, and he is far too pale. Ryder throws her arms around his neck, realising too late it's a bad idea. He whimpers and the metal impaled in his neck grazes her skin as he rocks back.

"I'm so sorry," she gasps. "Chris is...he's fine." So far as they know. It's too much to think about. Ryder leans in to steady Lucas. Sebastien reaches at the same moment, to do the same thing, but ends up embracing her instead of his intended target. He glowers, shifting away like he's just touched a hotplate. Any other time Ryder might scowl right back and tell him to get over it, but her attention is all on Lucas. She shifts in behind him, staring at the three jagged objects that protrude from the base of his neck and down the right side of his upper vertebrae. They are like three jagged shards of black quartz, no bigger than one of the few remaining pom-poms on Ryder's sweater, embedded in his flesh. The skin around them is red and angry. And it takes a monumental effort not to cry out at the sight of them.

Sophie sucks in her breath. "What are those?"

"How do we get them off him?" Ryder glares at Sebastien, daring him not to have an answer.

"I am not certain. The sooner we get him somewhere sheltered and dry, the better. I can examine them then." A muscle clenches in Sebastien's jaw but his expression remains its usual guarded self. The markings under his eyes are gone and his hair is untied from its usual severe pull-back style, the rain putting a kink into the dark strands. With his war paint gone and hair loose, he is surprisingly boyish. Still other-worldly, with his sharp features and storm eyes, but he could almost blend in. Almost.

Lucas winces as Sebastien shifts, trying to gain greater purchase and take more of his weight.

"Is Aresh coming too?" Ryder says. "She could help him couldn't she?"

Aresh has a knack for healing, if nothing else. That much is certain.

"No." Sebastien's tone is sharp. "The Laudine cannot help him, she sent me in her stead. She must protect Olessia now. I have some Jarran stones, they will help for now, until we work out what to do about all this."

His gaze rests on Ryder. The scowl is long gone. She stares back, unblinking. He knows something is up with her, but then, he's always known. It catches her off-guard, what a relief it is to see him. A light misty rain falls, and she uses the excuse of wiping the condensation off her face to glance away.

"All right." She pushes a strand of hair behind her ear, wondering what state the braid is in. It feels like a saturated birds nest on the back of her head. "So what do we do now?"

Sebastien snaps a small compact device from his belt and studies it. "There is a boat at the water's edge," he says. "I secured it to reach you. We will go to it now."

"Chris and Jack," Ryder says. "They're back in the -"

"No." Sebastien holds up the device, like she'll understand what the symbols flashing on it mean. "Leave them here. That group, the one you call C-21, have been alerted to this area and they're headed this way. They will take care of the man and the boy, and they will be distracted by the dead Zentai."

His words rock her back on her feet, and Ryder presses a trembling hand against the wall. Dead. Not a beast, not a witless monster she can make herself believe the world was better off without. This time it was a breathing, thinking, almost-human man. Her bones are leaden, too heavy to imagine ever being able to move again.

"Ryder," Lucas's pained voice reaches into her reverie, and washes the weight away. "Benjamin Cooper can't find-." His eyes flutter and his legs buckle. Sebastien grunts, taking his weight. He bends to lift Lucas into his arms. But Lucas is still conscious and he shakes his head, a weak and laborious movement. "Help the girls," he says.

"They can help themselves. They can stand." Sebastien's elthar ignites with a subdued blue gleam around his hands. He lifts Lucas with ease, and this time there is no protest. Lucas slumps against Sebastien, eyes rolling back in his head as he loses consciousness. "Head to the water line, follow my direction."

It's not just Sebastien's markings that are gone. So is his militaristic garb. Ryder notices for the first time he's wearing clothing definitely made on Earth; a pair of distressed denim jeans, loose fit, with a high-necked, light gray puffer jacket stamped with a familiar wolf print logo. It suits him. Really suits him. Without the severity of the facial markings and the harsh cut of his uniform, Sebastien could pass for a high school senior. Oblivious to her thoughts, he nods to them, before lifting into the air, cradling Lucas. Barely a metre above the ground, he drifts out over the wide expanse of lawn that separates the pool house from the row of trees marking the windbreak.

"Can you walk?" Sophie takes her hand.

"Yeah, I'm good."

Ryder kneels beside the grating. Her back twinges with the effort of bending but she needs to see. It's a war zone. One of the doors that was blown off its hinges landed on the spectator seating, the other is an oversized surfboard floating on the water. The lane ropes lie like giant snakes, haphazard and intertwined at the far end of the pool. Glass twinkles where it lies on the white tiles at the bottom of the pool, shimmering beneath Banon's body. The water around him is pale pink. His dreadlocks float upwards, weaving back and forth around his face. Ryder can't look away. Her breath is sandpaper in her lungs. It's a small, confusing consolation that there is no sign of Seah.

"Come on Ry, I'm losing sight of them." Sophie leads her away, gentle but determined.

They trudge across the lawn. Lightening shivers overhead, brightening the well-lit area even more. Sophie starts to jog. It's possibly the only time Ryder has ever seen her do that.

"Do we know where we are going?" Ryder's sore muscles pull her thoughts away from Banon. Everything aches, but she welcomes the distraction. Her calf muscles cramp hard, in short-lived but brutal spasms.

"He went in there."

Sophie points towards one of the majestic willow trees along the windbreak. They have spent many a lunch break under these trees. On hot summer days it's a little oasis beneath the cascading branches that capture the cooler breezes. Ryder is pretty sure they sat under one the day she first told Sophie about seeing the shadows. Hearing the whispers. It's a long way from that day to this one. Sophie reaches the tree first and disappears into the thick cover. Water flicks off the leaves as Ryder follows her in. She almost collides with Sophie who stopped just inside the green walls.

"Soph." Ryder dodges to avoid her, nearly losing her footing in a puddle of mud. "What are you doing?"

"Oh my god he's not...he's not..." Sophie's voice shakes.

It is light beneath the canopy. A familiar blue shimmer brightens the enclosed space. Sebastien kneels beside Lucas who lies on his side. The back of his shirt is soaked with blood, more still trickling from the punctures.

"He's alive," Sebastien says, tugging Lucas's shirt down from the metal protrusions in his neck. "But doesn't want me to take him any further."

Ryder stares at him. "What are you talking about? We're getting him to a doctor, or a hospital or something. He told me he has this friend, one who could help. He was going to take me to him after the Placer tried to rip my head off." Ryder steps over Lucas's legs and kneels in front of him. "What's his name, Lucas? Tell me where we need to go."

"Ry, I'm not going with you," Lucas says, his voice barely above a whisper. "You need to keep going."

"Not without you." Ryder leans closer. "We're not leaving you here."

He manages a smile, not wide enough to set off his dimples. "Well, I'm not going with you."

"Lucas hang in there, the blood loss is making you feel really weak," Sophie says, steel in her voice. "But you can do this."

Lucas reaches for Ryder, the effort pulling at the edges of his eyes, and pressing his lips into a tight, white grimace. She takes his outstretched hand, feeling him tremble. "Listen to me," he says. "Sophie's right about one thing, I'm weak. But I can't do this. I can't out pace anyone right now. I'm still losing blood and there's nothing you guys can do. But Benjamin Cooper can."

Ryder's fingers curl tight around his. "What are you talking about? You want them to find you?"

"I need a doctor, Ry, a Band-Aid and some *Dettol* isn't going to fix this." Lucas attempts another smile, a weak effort that barely lifts a corner of his mouth. "Believe me, C-21 are not going to let me die. This is their moment. Two aliens in one day. One of them still breathing. They are going to want to keep it that way."

He coughs and to her horror, flecks of blood land on her hand.

"There's got to be someone else, Lucas." Sophie crouches beside Ryder.

"Anyone else is someone else who could get hurt." Lucas takes a laboured breath. "We don't know what these things on my neck are, if they are some kind of tracking device. I can't risk that. C-21, Benjamin's guys, can defend themselves."

"This is your call, Zentai." Sebastien stands over them, the compact open in his palm. "Your plan is not without merit, but I will carry you to the transport if that's what you choose. Just choose quickly. They are almost here."

"Go." Lucas can't seem to keep his eyes open. "Sebastien. Take them and go."

"No." Ryder grabs Lucas's shoulder, not caring in that second whether or not it hurts him. "This is crazy. Get up, try, please."

"Ryder, this isn't just about me. I need you to be safe. Go with Sebastien."

"I've already left Jack behind, and Christian. I'm not leaving you." She touches his arm, planning to wrap it round her shoulder and drag him to his feet. His skin is icy and damp. Lucas hisses through clenched teeth. "Ry, stop it. Sophie, please, you understand don't you? I need you to get her out of here."

It's always been something Ryder loves about Sophie. Her ability to size up a situation and react to it. But right now, she hates her friend for what her doleful expression says she's about to do. "No, Sophie. No, I am not going."

Sophie places a hand on her arm. "Yes, you are. We need to go."

"We cannot linger here," Sebastien says. "The goodbyes need to conclude."

Ryder slumps back onto her heels. Soaked to the bone, more tired than she's been in her entire life, muscles aching like she's run ten obstacle courses. She doesn't have the strength to argue.

"Hey, come on." Lucas doesn't let go of her hand as she straightens. "You're making this sound like it's the last time you'll see me."

She sits back, shifting out of reach. "Promise it's not."

"Promise," he says. "Things are going to be okay. You're doing great, Ry. With all you're dealing with. And I knew you would. I told her you would. They wanted you to have an ordinary life, Jack and Aresh. I kept telling Aresh, you were never ordinary to begin with."

Sebastien barks at them to hurry up. That they aren't going to be alone much longer. She can hear the drone of helicopters in the air. But Ryder isn't hurrying up this moment for anyone. She takes Lucas's hand in hers and leans forward so only he can hear her. "I will get you out of there, when the time comes. I'm promising *you* that. You have no idea what I can do."

His eyes are half closed, his skin gray under the light of Sebastien's elthar, but his smile finally curves dimples into his cheeks. "Don't think you can get rid of me that easily, my little misfit sister. Keep those bracelets on, and we'll always find each other. Do me a favour. Make sure Chris knows it's going to be okay." Green eyes watch her, closing when she nods.

Ryder stands up, tears threatening. "We're going, big jerk brother, we're gone." She cups her hand around the bracelet on her wrist, squeezing it, reassured by the unyielding firmness of the metal.

Sophie is slower to rise. Despite her bravado she hasn't held it together quite so well. Tears stream down her face. Now it's Ryder's turn to reassure her friend. She squeezes Sophie's hand. "Not goodbye. Just, see you later."

"No goodbyes," Sophie swipes her nose with her sleeve. "They are totally overrated."

Sebastien hands something to Lucas. "This is set to activate in ten minutes. Believe me, they will notice it."

Lucas whispers something to him that Ryder doesn't catch. Sebastien grips Lucas's shoulder and nods, but says nothing in reply. Then he ushers them all out. Out of the confines of the willow and back into the cold onslaught of a fresh downpour. The dark river ahead might as well be a vast canyon. One dividing their old life from this new, strange world. Sophie stumbles in the shadows and Ryder catches her before she loses her footing. When they near the water's edge, Sebastien slows, picking his way carefully as the bank slopes away from them. The boat isn't much, certainly no Aventar. It is someone's holiday speedboat, a four-seater, painted an unappealing shade of green which has peeled away in chunks. Judging by its upkeep the owners don't holiday often.

"I don't understand," Ryder says, as Sebastien brings the boat in closer to the shore. He's doing it the old fashioned way, hauling at the rope that anchors it to the bank. "Shouldn't you be with Olessia?"

She points to Blackrhine Hill. The sound of gunfire, faint and very distant, reaches them. Twin lights of the approaching helicopters shine down onto the murky waters, a few hundred metres upriver.

"Aresh decided it was too dangerous to take the Laudess through the Paldrian River some time ago. We have waited to see the true enemy and there is no doubt now that Dashel no longer sides with us. Verran will take the Aventar through the River, proceeding as though he carries the Laudess. He will lure them to Bax Un Tey. None of this was shared with you for your own safety, the information best not kept in your heads. Prudent, in light of what happened with Dashel."

The bow touches the bank, the water pattering against the fibreglass hull. Ryder stares at it, feeling the weight of Sebastien's gaze on her. She still hasn't convinced herself not to turn around and go back to Lucas. And she is sure he knows.

"But if the Aventar is in the River, isn't Olessia vulnerable?" Sophie asks, rubbing the arms of her sopping purple jacket, trying in vain to warm herself.

"She is with Aresh. And she is not as vulnerable as she once was." There is a smile in his voice. Pride, even.

Sophie smiles. "Yes, it turns out we humans aren't quite so useless after all, huh? Two in particular."

"Two?" Sebastien frowns.

"Well, Christian makes her smile and,"- Sophie nods to Ryder - "Ryder makes her strong. Olessia's dad should be careful. Never underestimate the power of a happy, strong, all-powerful daughter. He might find his crown missing one day."

It's stupid and corny, and Ryder wouldn't expect any less from Sophie. Condensing something as overwhelming as this whole weekend, into a summary that could sit on the back cover of a book. The thud of the helicopters pounds out of sync with her breathing.

"You are a strange girl." Sebastien leaps onto the bow of the boat, the elthar carrying him. He moves like a dancer, limbs stretched, controlled and strong. "But you are right about one of them at least." He doesn't elaborate, but Ryder sees the glance he darts at her. One of Aresh's secrets is a secret no more.

Sophie doesn't hesitate when Sebastien extends his hand to help her onto the boat, but her boarding is far less graceful. She falls against him, and then drops onto hands and knees and scrambles towards the cabin. Ryder pulls the rope from the rock it is looped around. She throws it towards Sebastien, who catches it easily. The boat drifts out. She needs to jump now or the gap will be dangerously wide, and she's soaked enough without a dunking.

"Ry, come on." Sophie waves her on. "What are you doing?"

Ryder knows her friend will never leave her side, but what if she were to give Sophie no choice? Let the boat drift further out and walk away. Sophie will be safe with Sebastien, but would she remain safe if Ryder was with them?

"Ryder?" Sebastien could start the engine. He could move the boat back towards her but he is waiting. Letting her make the choice. She supposes he's met someone like her before. Someone frightened by what she might become, by what she has already done. Someone who thinks running is her best solution. A sudden blaze of light illuminates the trees behind her. "It's the signal I gave to Lucas," Sebastien calls out. "To allow them to find him. It is done. He made his choice, now it's your turn. Which way are you going, Ryder?"

"With me." Sophie braces herself against the low railing trimming the boat's bow. "Come on, Ry. It's not the right thing to do if you have to do it without me. I might not be super woman like you, but I still have a power. I'm damn persistent. I will find you if you leave me now."

The chill leaves Ryder, the shaking stops, and despite everything, she laughs. "Never write greeting cards, Soph. Promise me."

Olessia fled her world on her own, and her attempt to run away brought chaos in its wake. Ryder traces her fingers over the elthar bracelets. She is a part of that chaos. Whether she likes it or not. Running away won't change that. It won't keep Christian and Sophie safe. Leaving will only make them more vulnerable.

"Promise me you will get on this boat and it's a deal," Sophie calls out. "I'll turn down Hallmark immediately."

Ryder backs up, gives herself space to work up some speed. The gap between shore and vessel is almost too wide to contemplate. Almost. Ryder runs straight at the murky water, her Dr Martens pounding out a determined beat on the undergrowth. Warmth blooms against her wrists, and the slumbering elthar bracelets spring to life. It encases her forearms, the glow an unfamiliar, but dazzling ocean green. She leaps and flies out over the water. Ryder spreads her arms and soars upward. Lifting so high the blinking lights of Blackrhine Hill and the searching beams of the helicopters are visible at the same time. She hovers between them, an indistinguishable speck of light in the gloom.

Ghost hunting is over. It's time for a new hunt to begin.

COMING IN 2017

EXTRA|LIMITAL

Acknowledgements

Big thanks go to my writing buddies, the Metalunatics, for keeping my hopes up about Ryder and her gang. To the amazing people on Scribophile.com who did likewise, especially Doreen and Matt. A shout out to @madeleine_deste and @AderynWood who inspired me to jump on in and do this thing. To my editor Rebecca at www.katejfoster.com, who polished it up, and helped me cross off a few more items on my 'Things to Learn' list.

My sis, Monique whose encouragement and enthusiasm never falters. And of course, my hubby Mike. Quite simply, it wouldn't be happening without you.

....And thank you to these incredible locations for actually existing in real life.

nationaltrust.org.au/places/clarendon
discovertasmania.com.au
wellingtonpark.org.au
mona.net.au

ABOUT THE AUTHOR

Danielle K Girl is an Aussie who recently moved from Melbourne, Australia to Lititz, Pennsylvania - a town she's convinced is actually Gilmore Girls' Stars Hollow. She chose Girl as her pen name because she got tired of reading about female authors having to hide their gender. She adores animals, loves peanut butter pie and wishes her car was actually a Transformer.

This is her debut novel.

Made in the USA
Charleston, SC
02 January 2017